Praise for

THE GUARDIANS OF TIME

An International Reading Association Young Adult Choice
(*The Named* and *The Dark*)

"Swashbuckling time-travel plus soap-opera relationships
make for a page-turning start to a promised trilogy. . . . An
ongoing guilty pleasure." —*Kirkus Reviews* on *The Named*

"Readers will likely be swept up by the ever-growing
complications and want to return for the series' next
installments." —*Publishers Weekly* on *The Named*

"Curley's special effects, whether magical or a product of
super science, are successfully realized." —*VOYA* on *The Dark*

"Lively, believable characters. . . . [An] imaginative,
suspenseful novel." —*Booklist* on *The Dark*

"Curley is enormously imaginative." —*VOYA* on *The Key*

THE GUARDIANS OF TIME

The Named

The Dark

The Key

THE GUARDIANS OF TIME

the
Key

MARIANNE
CURLEY

BLOOMSBURY

NEW YORK BERLIN LONDON

Originally published in Great Britain by Bloomsbury Publishing Plc in 2005
First published in the United States of America in June 2005
by Bloomsbury Books for Young Readers
This edition published in April 2011
www.bloomsburyteens.com

For information about permission to reproduce selections from this book, write to
Permissions, Bloomsbury BFYR, 175 Fifth Avenue, New York, New York 10010

The Library of Congress has cataloged the hardcover edition as follows:
Curley, Marianne.
The key / by Marianne Curley. — 1st U.S. ed.
p.   cm.—(The guardians of time trilogy ; 3)
Summary: Australian teenagers Matt and Rochelle overcome their misgivings to help the
other Named confront the forces of evil and chaos.
ISBN-13: 978-1-58234-953-4 • ISBN-10: 1-58234-953-3 (hardcover)
[1. Space and time—Fiction. 2. Fantasy.] I. Title.
PZ7.C9295Ke 2005   [Fic]—dc22   2004062364

ISBN: 978-1-59990-545-7 (paperback)

Typeset by Dorchester Typesetting Group Ltd.
Printed in the U.S.A. by Worldcolor Fairfield, Pennsylvania
1 3 5 7 9 10 8 6 4 2

All papers used by Bloomsbury Publishing, Inc., are natural, recyclable products
made from wood grown in well-managed forests. The manufacturing processes
conform to the environmental regulations of the country of origin.

For my sister Therese,
with love and admiration

Before the world can be free
A bloom of murdered innocence shall be seen
In the woods above the ancient city of Veridian
Where nine identities shall be revealed

It will come to pass that a king shall rule
But not before a leader pure of heart awakens
And an ageless warrior with an ancient soul
Shall guide with grace and providence

Beware, nine shall see a traitor come and go
From whence a long and bitter war will follow
And the Named shall join in unity
Yet suspicion will cause disharmony

A jester shall protect, a doubter cast a shadow
And a brave young warrior will lose his heart to death
Yet none shall be victorious until a lost warrior returns
And the fearless one emerges from a journey led by light and strength

Take heed, two last warriors shall cause grief as much as good
From the midst of suspicion one shall come forth
The other seeded of evil
Yet one shall be victorious while the other victorious in death

Prologue

They agree to meet in an abandoned monastery at the top of an ancient monolith of rock and cliff in Athos. Lathenia, known as the Goddess of Chaos since her quest for domination began, is first to arrive. She is accompanied by her loyal soldier Marduke and trusted magician Keziah. The rules are simple: bring no arms and only two allies. Instigated by Lorian, this meeting is for peace, for brother and sister to come to an agreement and stop the prophesied final battle from destroying life as it is known on the earth.

The night is black. A blizzard roars through the gorges. Lorian appears at the foot of the monolith, trailed by Tribunal members Lord Penbarin and Lady Arabella, and a third figure.

Swathed in thick warm cloaks the Immortal and his party trudge up the two hundred and seventy-two slippery steps of icy rock, one after another.

Lord Penbarin steps hurriedly but carefully to catch up with Lorian. 'I can't help but suspect, my liege, that there is more to this meeting with your sister than you have allowed us to believe.' His eyes shift purposefully to the third member of their party.

Lorian halts. All three behind him stop and look up.

'And you, Lord Penbarin, are far too cynical as usual.'

Lord Penbarin scoffs, though gently, for he knows Lorian speaks the truth.

As the wind drives the shifting snow even harder, Lorian's eyes momentarily drift past Lord Penbarin's shoulder to the third member of his party. He gives an acknowledging nod and a wry smile.

'Will the meeting take long, my lord?' Lady Arabella asks.

Lorian's gaze shifts sideways to the lady, and even while her face remains almost completely concealed beneath the shadow of her deep hood, the Immortal finds it difficult to drag his eyes from her. She lifts her head to meet his gaze and Lorian wonders for the millionth time in a thousand years how he has the strength to maintain his determination to remain genderless. He is tiring of the task; he has made many sacrifices for the sake of unbiased and unprejudiced rule.

Finally they stand before the monastery door. Made of cypress wood, centuries of neglect have seen it reduce to a few dark and rotting boards. It creaks open. A flurry of servants, hired especially for the occasion, usher the esteemed party within. Once inside, warm air washes over them. Only Lorian, unaffected by either cold or heat, seems indifferent to the change.

To their left a sweeping staircase of stone bricks raises their eyes to the upper level. It is there Lathenia stands watching. Lorian nods in her direction. Their minds meet and clash, and a rough greeting of sorts follows. She descends, her white gown trailing on the steps behind her, the purple sash at her waist defining her narrow figure, while long fingers slide elegantly down the banister railing.

Behind her Marduke and Keziah keep a suitable distance. Their Mistress is the focus, the reason for this meeting. They are, after all, only her humble servants, as she is apt to remind them.

'Brother,' she says as she comes and stands before Lorian. 'Or … being neither male nor female, is there another term by which I should call you?' With these words she glances briefly at Lady Arabella, but the action is so swift and fleeting none in the room perceives it.

Sounding irritated and slightly bored, Lorian lifts a hand in a brief dismissive gesture. 'As you so obviously have difficulty grasping the concept of impartiality due to gender, you may refer to me in the masculine as I have allowed others to do for their own comfort.'

'What a pity,' she sniggers. 'I could have enjoyed calling you … It.'

Lorian stares deeply into her eyes. Lathenia is first to glance away, her gaze coming to rest first on Lord Penbarin and then briefly on Lady Arabella. Although it's impossible not to notice her brother has brought a third party, she ignores the uninvited guest's presence – for now. 'It has been a while, my lord and lady.'

'How unfortunate that we have to meet at all,' Lord Penbarin says in a mocking tone.

Lathenia's shoulders lift, the only indication that the insult penetrated. Her face remains a stoic mask of indifference. She allows her gaze purposefully to single out her brother's third supporter. As if commanded, the cloaked figure steps forward. Piercing blue eyes are the first things she notices. A shiver begins at the tip of her spine and slithers along every vertebrae as she inhales a sense of the importance of the man standing before her. A Tribunal member for sure. But not one she recognises. She pins her cold gaze on her brother, trying hard to conceal her surprise and interest, but fails.

'We agreed on only two allies! Who is this *intruder*?'

Lorian acknowledges his sister's reaction, keeping his sense of gratification well hidden. It is exactly as he hoped. He motions the cloaked figure forward. 'Allow me to introduce the former King Richard II of England.' Lorian waits while his sister absorbs this much first. Then, 'He is now the new King Richard ... of *Veridian*.'

She moves backwards. 'Veridian has a *king*?' A slender hand lifts to hover above her breastbone.

Lorian doesn't say a word. He doesn't need to. All those present understand that now Veridian has its King, the Tribunal will be complete, and the power of the Guard will be stronger than ever before.

'My lady.' King Richard bows deeply before the stricken goddess. 'I am ... *intrigued* to meet you. I look forward to further acquaintance.'

Their eyes hold for indefinable seconds while Lathenia takes a moment to regather her thoughts. King Richard has affected her on many levels. Lorian gloats inwardly, while Marduke, fully aware of his Mistress's sudden interest in this stranger, makes a snorting, grunting sound through nostrils that resemble a pig's snout. Physically altered from his earlier experience in the middle realm, Marduke has fallen out of favour with Lathenia.

The sound of Marduke's displeasure is enough to jolt Lathenia's senses, though it is with an effort that she drags her emotions away from sudden public scrutiny. She sighs, appearing disinterested. 'We shall see, my lord.' Abruptly she lifts her gaze and stalks off towards an open doorway, leaving behind a tense, suffocating atmosphere.

The servants show the Tribunal members to a large room of stone bricks lit with hundreds of glowing candles. In the centre stands a table made entirely of crystal with seven matching stools brought here from Lathenia's own palace especially for the occasion.

Lorian notices the seven stools but says nothing. Surely she couldn't have known about King Richard! But then nothing his sister does should surprise him now.

All seven sit around the table, Lathenia and Lorian opposite each other. For a long moment there is silence and King Richard, being a recent addition to the Tribunal, wonders whether they are communicating without his knowledge, something he understands to be quite possible. He rather hopes they aren't. It would be enormously arrogant on their part. After all, what else are the rest of them doing here if not bearing witness to these proceedings?

Lorian glares in his direction. Instantly King Richard regrets his outspoken thoughts. But Lorian's stare soon softens and he gives an almost imperceptible nod. 'You are quite right, my lord.'

King Richard grunts a soft acknowledgement, vowing to keep his thoughts under a tighter rein from now on. He still has much to learn.

'What I was thinking,' Lorian continues to address King Richard, 'is what my parents would say if they were alive today.'

'Bah!' Lathenia waves a hand into the air. 'While I was thinking how my brother has grown so melancholy lately. A sign of weakness I find amusing.'

'The fact is, Lathenia, an immortal can only be killed by another immortal.'

Lathenia's silver eyes flash the colour of obsidian while her long fingers slam down on the table top. 'Are you threatening me, brother?'

Lorian appears amused at the dramatic leap his sister makes. Their parents loved and fought so fiercely that they ended by killing each other in a moment of inflamed passion. 'You think I find the deaths of our parents amusing?'

Lathenia remains silent, but something in her silence alerts Lorian's senses. 'What more do you know about our parents' death than I?'

'Nothing. You were there.'

'Yes. I saw each holding a blade at the other's throat. But while I walked in after the deed, you were there before me.'

'I walked in only a second before you.'

'A lot can happen in a second of immortal time,' he says accusingly.

Lathenia takes the defensive and quickly changes the subject. 'Listen to *you*. When it is *I* who should be asking questions. Questions about our brother. You are more devious than you would have your supporters think.' She stares at each of the Tribunal members in turn. 'You don't really know him. He's not the honourable Lorian you trust. He murdered our own brother!' She turns her gaze to Lorian. 'Dartemis was no threat to you. *I* was the threat! So why did you destroy an innocent child?'

Lorian recalls how Dartemis was never an 'innocent child', but the youngest and most powerful of the three siblings. He'd had to take his brother to another world for the boy's own safety. A world where he remains very much alive today. A world where even his greedy sister cannot detect life. And it is there he will remain, continuing to harness his powers – a lord, a magician and much more.

Lorian remembers the day he saw his brother working magic – such powerful and unusual magic. He knew then that with Dartemis's talents at her fingertips, Lathenia would become too strong.

But for now there are other matters more pressing – the resolution of this conflict, without war.

Allowing this last thought to penetrate all minds in the room, everyone's attention is quickly refocused. Lathenia scoffs at the thought. 'What is happening to you? You are more melancholy than I thought. If I didn't know better, I'd say you have allowed yourself to fall in love.'

Her words anger him. 'I am not so foolish as to allow the very notion of love to interfere with my judgement!'

A quiet descends, where Lathenia finds she has to struggle with the urge to look upon Lady Arabella's face.

Stirring emotions circle the room. Lady Arabella dares not lift her eyes and takes to scrutinising the ice-blue veins that reveal themselves beneath the pale skin of her hands, while Lord Penbarin stares across the table as if seeing his fellow Tribunal member for the first time.

It is Marduke's rough, guttural voice that penetrates and dispels the atmosphere. 'This meeting is a waste of time. Nothing will be resolved here. Nothing is ever resolved without war. It is the way of the universe.'

Lorian asks, 'Does Marduke speak the truth, sister? Is there no hope for peace between us?'

Lathenia stares pointedly at her brother. 'There can

only be peace when there is justice, for you rule by default.'

'Need I remind you that of the three of us, I was born first.'

'So you claim,' Lathenia argues. 'But it should have been me!'

With eyes as fiery as coals Lathenia leaps from her stool, her body upright and rigid with rage. 'Marduke is right. This meeting is pointless. Only force will give me justice. Control of all the realms should be mine, and I will have it!'

Calmly, Lorian replies, 'Sister, neither of us controls the realms. The humans govern themselves. They have free will and choose their own destiny. For as long as they are mortal we are only their caretakers.'

'That will change.'

Lorian's shoulders stiffen and he too rises. Around the room all eyes move from one angry god to the other.

'You cannot change what must be,' Lorian hisses. 'Marduke speaks of the way of the universe, but I speak of the way of life.'

'It is my ambition to combine the realms,' Lathenia explains. 'And I will succeed.'

'But that would be disastrous.' Lorian is aghast. 'The humans would … alter. Their very existence would be in danger of domination from the soulless. The inconceivable will become reality, and over time the line between mortality and death will blur.'

It is in her silence that Lorian understands the depth of his sister's determination. And for the first time in his long life the makings of real fear flutter within. It quickly turns to anger. In a whisper-soft voice that has the hairs prickle on the back of Lord Penbarin's neck, Lorian says, 'You cannot do this.'

'Don't lecture me, Lorian.' Lathenia raises her hand, pointing one long finger directly at the narrow opening in the ceiling. 'This is what I think of your peacemaking.'

The ceiling begins to peel away. Great chunks of rock and brick jettison into the sky. With another wave of her hand the ceiling completely disappears into the raging blizzard.

'What are you doing?' Lorian asks, his violet eyes flashing with concern.

Lathenia doesn't answer. Instead she angles her face up towards the blizzard. In a flash of lightning and resounding thunder, the thick clouds swirl and begin to scatter. In seconds the blizzard blows away, revealing a night sky sparkling with clarity and millions of stars.

But Lathenia is hardly finished, and Lorian knows it. His eyes remain riveted to the brilliant night sky. An explosion of light, followed by a hiss, quickly grows into an ear-piercing whistle. It has the mortals diving to the floor a second before the descending chunk of rock explodes above their heads.

Lady Arabella screams and joins King Richard further beneath the table.

Lorian doesn't move, but the power radiating from him is tangible in what's left of the exposed room at the top of the cliff. His eyes shift upwards, centring on a blue star vivid in the distant sky.

'Uh-oh,' Lord Penbarin remarks. 'Keep down and out of the way. This could get interes—'

Before he finishes, a blazing light starts hurtling towards them, accompanied by a high-pitched whining sound that near deafens the Tribunal members. The star shatters in the atmosphere, showering the room in heat and light and burning debris.

Servants pour out of the monastery, covering their ears and whimpering about the heavens falling. Like ants they run from the cliff as fast and as far away as possible.

Within minutes the earth is showered with the most brilliant meteor display ever witnessed by human eyes. One explodes so close that the entire monolith shakes and the walls of the monastery crumble on one side. Lorian stares at his sister in disgust. 'Do you respect no life but your own?'

She shrugs.

Another meteor careers almost horizontally across the sky to crash into some far distant land.

'That was Angel Falls!' Lorian glares at his sister.

'Really? Are you scared of losing a few soldiers?'

'Have you no thought for your own soldiers who live there?'

'I can risk a few to see the death of your elite.'

Lorian stares at her in silence for a moment. Disgusted. 'You go too far.'

'Know this, brother, I will always go one further than you.'

He pauses, and all those cowering beneath the table emerge just enough to see what he plans next. Without moving, Lorian closes his eyes. Lady Arabella peers across the table to Lord Penbarin. She has never seen her liege look so focused, or so angry. Lord Penbarin gives a light shrug, then watches as his Lord and Master begins to glow from the inside out, then slowly starts to shake.

Lathenia's eyes shift to Keziah, her aged but trusted Magician. Even Keziah, who has lived a long time, has never seen anything like this before. He shakes his head. 'I know not, Your Highness.'

'Brother?' she says. 'What are you up to?'

Finally the light from Lorian's body begins to dull, his shaking slows and he sags. It becomes obvious that whatever he was doing, is over. Some look to the sky, but Lord Penbarin keeps his eyes firmly on his Lord. Slowly Lorian becomes aware of where he is. He opens his eyes and finds those of Lord Penbarin. Through his mind he shows him what he has done and Lord Penbarin lunges for breath. He wonders fleetingly what it has cost his liege, but it is done now – there are only the consequences to follow.

Lady Arabella looks to Lord Penbarin for answers. In fear the Goddess will hear him, he sends her only a single thread of thought … *The Named.*

Chapter One

Rochelle

School is different now. There are security guards at the front gate. We don't wear uniforms any more. And the grounds are filthy with litter. It's as if no one cares. About the grounds, the classrooms, or even themselves. And I know this because I hear their thoughts. Before I learned how to control them, I heard them all. I nearly went insane. Suddenly there were non-stop voices in my head. One day I was really tired and couldn't handle it. We were gathered together in the auditorium at school. I was right in the middle of the room and had to run for the door. I didn't stop running until I had stumbled halfway into the bordering forest. But what I'd wanted to do was scream and tell them all to shut the hell up. Even now, the things I overhear sometimes shock me. People can think such horrible thoughts even about their best friends.

The bus pulls up to the school gates, but I wait, looking out the window until the other kids pile out. With music pumping in my ears, I don't realise when the bus is empty. I become aware of the bus driver staring at me through his rear vision mirror. When he sees me looking he raises an eyebrow. He's in a hurry. His run is probably finished and he can't wait to get to the pub. Sure, it's only eight-thirty in the morning, but life is different now. There aren't as many rules.

'Hey, you getten out, girlie?'

I pull the plugs out of my ears and pack up my CD player. While shoving it in my backpack I allow his thoughts to penetrate my mind. *Hmm, ain't that the Thallimar girl? Her father's doing time for murder. Better not tick her off ... Then again, she sure has got a nice –*

'You need a life.' I interrupt his thoughts and get off the bus quickly.

The others have arrived at school already. Ethan, Matt and Isabel. Ever since they got back from the underworld they've been a really close group. It's like whatever they experienced there has created a bond between them. A strong bond. And now that I'm not with Matt any more, and my friend Dillon has disappeared, I've got no one to hang around with. Even that new girl, Neriah, spends most of her time with them now.

I walk down the steps and wait for one of the two security guards to check my backpack. He makes me empty the pockets of my jeans. As I do this Matt looks in my direction. Turbulent emotions hurtle towards me. Surely he's not still angry at what I did to him? He loved me, while I had to pretend to love him as part of Marduke's vengeful plans. If I could say sorry a thousand times and know that it would make a difference, I would.

Ethan notices where Matt's looking and sees me. For a second our eyes connect and an overwhelming feeling makes me lose concentration, something that tends to happen often when I'm near Ethan. His thoughts rush into my head. He's remembering that moment we first met, before I started going out with Matt, and we'd felt an amazing connection. A connection I'd had to sever. At least now that I'm with the Guard, I don't have to do things like that. The hardest thing I have to do is to earn everyone's trust. I know what they're all thinking – how does one trust a traitor? Only Arkarian believes in me. I've never known anyone as gentle or understanding. Isabel is so lucky.

For a second I think about going over and sitting with them. I mean, how can they learn to trust me when they only know the worst of me? I tell myself it's simple: just walk.

But something makes me stop. Did I see relief in their eyes? Maybe I should listen to their thoughts. No! That's intrusive and I won't do it – not on purpose. But really, it's not as if I don't know these people. Matt and I used to go out. So why do I have to think twice about making a single move? All I need is courage. I glance briefly around. No one's looking, not even Isabel, whose head is buried in a notebook, pointing something out to Ethan. I take a step towards them. OK, that wasn't too hard. I take another, then another. Look natural, I tell myself as I get close enough to hear them talking among themselves.

'Hey.' Isabel looks up with a greeting.

'Hi,' I reply.

Matt notices, but glances away.

I swallow deeply as words dry up in my throat.

Ethan gets up and comes over, leading me off to the side. My heart does this funny little leap, like it's trying to clamber up my throat on awkward feet.

'You know,' he says, 'it probably isn't a good idea you coming over here.'

'What?'

'All of us hanging around together could look suspicious.'

'Oh? Oh yeah. I wasn't going to sit here. I … I was looking for Dillon.'

Ethan goes still. A strange reaction. Instinctively I open my mind to his thoughts. He picks up what I'm doing and his eyes narrow and go cold and hard. Oh great! I could kick myself. How can anyone learn to trust me if they think I'm reading their heads whenever I want information?

'Sorry, Ethan, I didn't mean –'

'To read my thoughts? Or be so obvious doing it?'

'That's not fair.'

'Isn't it?' His head shakes and he turns slightly away.

I try to explain. 'You know how hard it is sometimes to switch off your powers.'

Slowly he turns back. 'Look, I don't know how long Dillon's going to be away. He defected to the Guard, like you. He's going through a debriefing right now. But I heard he's making really good progress. So I'm sure you'll have someone else to get your claws into soon.'

What is he talking about? As if I would be interested in Dillon! He has no idea. All the same, Ethan's news is interesting. I had my suspicions about Dillon being a member of the Order, but all the time that I served Marduke, our identities were kept secret from each other.

Mr Carter turns up and says something, but his words float away, lost in the air.

Ethan misses them too. 'Did you say something, sir?'

Mr Carter smirks, and if I'm not mistaken, his smirk is directed at me. Ethan used to think Mr Carter hated him, but Ethan doesn't really know what it's like to have

Mr Carter's hate thoughts sent straight into your brain. Mr Carter doesn't even try to appear friendly to me, and he doesn't seem to care who knows. I worked for the enemy, and as far as Mr Carter is concerned, that means I can't be trusted. Not ever.

'What did I tell you people only this morning? Wasn't anyone listening?'

I stare at him blankly and he says, 'No, not you, Miss Thallimar. You weren't here, were you?' Neriah comes over and sits next to Isabel. When he sees her, Mr Carter's eyes practically melt. 'Why don't I repeat myself for the benefit of those who just joined us. For the purposes of … discretion, don't make it obvious the five of you are a defined group. If one of you should give your identity away, it would be too easy for the *other side*,' he pauses and looks directly at me, 'to pick you off one by one.' Still staring at me he pointedly says, 'Am I clear?'

'Perfectly,' I snap back at him. Adjusting my backpack I start to move off, more pleased by Mr Carter's words than he could imagine. Ethan's earlier comment had not been an insult, but the same warning Mr Carter had just given us.

But I don't get far before a hissing sound has everyone look up to the sky. The morning buzzer sounds, but no one takes any notice as the hissing sound turns into a shrill and eerie whistle. Ethan grabs my arm and shoves me over. 'Take cover!'

From out of nowhere a flaming ball of fire comes sweeping into view, careering and spinning wildly. Everyone – and I mean every single person in the entire school grounds – starts screaming and running in all directions. The fireball – or meteorite – or whatever the hell it is, suddenly explodes. Burning rock-like debris

24

shatters over the top of the school. Some fragments hit the ground, burning holes, while others hit and roll, leaving a trail of fire behind.

Ethan falls on top of me as a piece of burning debris crashes so close that the heat from it scalds my skin and singes my hair. Before I realise what's happening, my hair catches fire. Ethan tries to put it out with his bare hands. I grab his wrists to stop him, but he's strong and doesn't stop until the fire is completely out. We sit up and I take his hands to look at them, but he pulls them away. He's badly burnt and I can smell his burning flesh mingling with the smell of my burnt hair.

'Are you guys all right?' Isabel comes running over with Matt.

'Ethan's hands are burnt,' I tell her.

She takes his hands and turns them over. She's going to heal them right now in front of everybody! As always, Isabel's heart rules over her head. Some call it courage. It will get her into trouble.

'Don't be so obvious,' I tell her.

She snaps at me. 'Would you rather I leave him in pain?' She looks at my hair, singed right up one side. 'He did this for you, obviously.'

If only I wasn't so conscious of Ethan's eyes on me. I don't dare wonder what he's thinking. My mind switches to auto sometimes and I can't help what I overhear. But right now I don't want to know. He probably thinks I'm cold and heartless, happy to see him suffer.

Within seconds of Isabel's touch, Ethan's red and blistering skin starts to heal and smooth out. He gives his hands a little shake and thanks her, which reminds me I haven't thanked *him* yet for putting the fire out in my hair, or for knocking me out of the direct path of that fragment of burning cosmic debris.

Strangely, it's as if *he* can read my thoughts for a minute. When I look up from studying my toes, he says, 'It's all right. You just happened to be the closest to me at the time. I would have done it for Carter if he'd been standing in your place.'

Deflated, I take a look around. The school yard is a mess, with little fires dotted all over the place, but amazingly, only one classroom appears damaged, down in D Block. People are still screaming though. The two security guards and a half-dozen teachers are running from one person to another checking to see if anyone has been seriously hurt. There are sirens in the distance, drawing nearer, so someone in the office must have already phoned for help.

'Look at that,' Isabel says in a stunned tone.

The whole sky from one end of the horizon to the other is lit with flashing streaks of falling stars. It's a meteor shower, dazzling even in the bright morning sunlight. The sight is simply amazing. Everyone stares, mesmerised.

Then one comes careering in our direction, and we start running for cover again. It explodes high enough in the atmosphere to burn up before hitting the ground, but creates a brilliant flash of light right over the top of us.

The teachers have started organising students to go home. Some line up at the office to call their parents. Others pull out mobile phones. The first siren has arrived and it's a fire truck. It's then I realise that part of D Block is now burning away to the ground!

Another flash and hiss overhead has everyone screaming. This is soon followed by a series of explosive bursts of hot gas. Mr Carter runs over to us, grabbing our arms and pushing us together. 'Get to the mountain. Tell Arkarian what's happened. He might have some answers.'

'I have to stay,' Isabel says. 'I can help if anyone is seriously injured.'

'No!' Mr Carter yells. 'You can't risk exposing your powers, Isabel. It's against the rules. I shouldn't have to remind you about that. Besides, medical help is on its way. There are ambulances and rescue vehicles headed here right now.'

'Mr Carter, I can't turn my back on someone who is injured if it's in my power to help. The Tribunal will understand. I promise I'll be careful not to reveal my identity.'

Mr Carter looks at Matt, then Ethan. 'Whatever you have to do, get Isabel out of here, even if you have to drag her screaming with her hands tied behind her back.'

Ethan and Matt share a brief look of amusement.

'What about Neriah?' Matt asks. 'How much does she know? Should we take her with us?'

Mr Carter frowns. 'She needs to get home. By the time I call her guards to come back and collect her ...'

'I'll take care of her,' I volunteer. 'I'll make sure she gets home all right.'

Mr Carter stares at me for a second too long. I don't even try to read his thoughts. He's projecting his hostility for clear viewing anyway. 'All right,' he agrees reluctantly.

With that decided we move off, when another hissing sound draws our attention back to the sky.

'Look!' Matt calls out. This time a meteor hurtles

wildly across the sky, leaving a trail of fire where it passes. 'It's headed for us!'

Mr Carter screams in our ears, 'Get out of here! Everybody run!'

The meteor takes no more than a few seconds to descend thousands of metres. It seems impossibly close when it explodes, shattering right over our heads. Burning pieces of rock hit like cannonballs, wiping out anything in their path. Trees tumble, fences come down. Several cars in the carpark are annihilated. I look around for a safe space when I hear someone nearby scream out in agonising pain. I spin around and see Mr Carter, half buried in the ground, his legs crushed beneath a slab of misshapen and steaming rock.

I run over to see what I can do. The rock isn't on fire, but the heat radiating from it keeps me at a distance. Matt and Ethan run over and are also stopped by the pulsing heat. Both look shocked. Mr Carter is in big trouble.

Ethan and Matt peel off their jackets. Together, with their clothes covering their hands, they attempt to shove the boulder off with their hands and feet. But the boulder is too heavy and the heat is still intense. How can Mr Carter stand it?

'We need a crane here!' Ethan calls out.

I can't help thinking that by the time that sort of equipment arrives, it will be too late.

Isabel and Neriah come running over, looking stunned.

'I'll get the firemen,' Neriah suggests. 'They'll know what to do.'

Even though Mr Carter is so badly hurt, he tries to wave Ethan and Matt away. He's dying, and he must know it.

'We're not leaving you!' Isabel gets down near his head. She's going to try and heal him, but how can she when that boulder is still there, crushing his legs? She exchanges a look with Ethan. 'Get this thing off him! Hurry!'

Mr Carter grips her arm and struggles to whisper, 'Forget it, Isabel.' He tries to stifle a moan. 'Forget what you see here. I want you to go. Just get out of here!' He turns his head towards Matt and Ethan, pleading with his eyes. 'Take Isabel and go!'

Neriah returns with two firemen. They quickly assess the situation and one runs back to the truck for some equipment. The other talks into a radio attached to his collar, requesting urgent backup and heavy wrenching gear. He then tells everyone to stand back, including another teacher, a very distressed-looking Ms Burgess.

'You'll be all right, Marcus,' she calls out.

Isabel doesn't move. The fireman insists and Ethan and Matt drag her away. Mr Carter is treated by two paramedics, but they share a look filled with silent hope-lessness.

At last the machinery arrives and the rescue team work quickly to set it up. Before long the boulder is secured and ready to be mechanically lifted. The crane takes the strain, but nothing moves. The boulder is too heavy.

Isabel attempts to run over but Mr Carter, weak from blood loss, shock and severe burns, pierces her with warning eyes, and Ethan drags her back. Matt urges her to hold on.

'But Matt, he's still alive! As soon as that boulder is lifted, I can heal him,' she hisses. 'But I have to be close enough to touch him.'

And as if this day hasn't freaked us all out already, suddenly a golden light appears in the sky. It swells and shimmers and starts to pour down towards us. We gasp, but have no time to move. Within seconds it goes through me, warming and tingling as it passes through every cell in my body. I shake with it, unable to speak, and wonder what on earth is going on. What could this possibly be?

'What's happening over there?' Ms Burgess calls out as she sees the light surround us.

The shaking continues for several seconds, until suddenly the light disappears and I drop to the ground on all fours. Out of breath, I try to regain some balance and realise I was somehow hovering in the air.

As I start to get up I can't help becoming aware of the grass beneath my fingers. It's my hands that are my special skill. My sense of touch is analytic. I can tell the structure of things like chemical substances, rocks, metals and soils. But right now my hands are feeling much more. I'm aware, and can somehow 'see' the structure of the earth for a depth of several kilometres. It's like my mind is on auto-focus, zooming through the layers of earth with a video camera.

And then I hear the voices. They sound like hundreds! I look around the school grounds, but there's no more than twenty people in the immediate surrounding area. I try to shut them out, but nothing works. A girl is screaming in her thoughts. Her leg is burnt and the pain from it is making her think she's about to die. I cover my ears with both my hands, but the voices won't go away. I can even hear the thoughts of the firemen still trying to put out the fire in the classroom down the other end of the school.

I sit back on my heels and wonder what's happening to me. It's as if my powers have been magnified. How am I going to handle this? I try to focus, to slow my own thoughts down enough to control the voices.

It's then I see Isabel. She's experiencing something strange too. The glow over her body is only now dissipating. Untouched by the light, the rescue workers and Ms Burgess stare as if we have each grown three heads.

'Are you all right over there? The five of you were sucked into the air,' one of the firemen calls out. He shakes his head. 'This is turning into one hell of a day.'

Ethan nods to reassure them, though he still looks dazed. But it's Isabel who looks the strangest; her stare is odd and vacant. I try to single out her thoughts from the others bombarding my brain. For a moment I can, but there's way too much power in her head right now. I get a strange buzz like an electric shock and pull away.

Suddenly the boulder crushing Mr Carter's legs lifts. And as the medical team moves in to shift Mr Carter to a stretcher, I understand what's going on. The gasps of awe from the medical crew are the first signs. They're saying now how the earth beneath Mr Carter's legs must have collapsed with the impact, creating some sort of cushioning effect. Another medic says it's just a miracle and that he should be dead, or even paralysed. But Mr Carter is neither dead nor paralysed. He's not even burned, even though his pants are ashen shreds. He's just shaken up. And if it didn't attract too much attention I'm sure he would simply stand up and walk, but he knows better than that. Isabel has healed him. Whatever that golden light did to me, it also had an effect on her, and by the looks of Ethan, on him too. Even Neriah looks strange, kind of vague.

Ms Burgess runs to Mr Carter's side. Just before she gets to him, he nods once at Isabel, and his look is filled with awe and gratitude.

She smiles at him with glassy eyes. 'You'll be OK,' she mouths.

Isabel healed Mr Carter without so much as laying one finger on him. She healed him from a distance! A short distance, but a distance all the same.

Ethan comes over and takes my hands, turning them over gently. I look down and see them for the first time. They make me gasp.

'Do they hurt?' he asks.

I'm lost for words. I can't stop staring at my hands. Streaks of vivid colours are running across them like little electric currents. 'They tingle. What happened to them? Do you think it's permanent?'

He shrugs. 'One thing's for sure, they're going to attract attention.'

He's right. I pull them away and shove them into my coat pockets. 'What's happening to us?'

'I have no idea.'

'How have you changed?'

Softly Ethan says, 'Those rescue workers didn't have a hope of lifting that boulder even with all their equipment. Whatever it's composed of, it's heavier than any rock or mineral found on this earth.'

'*You* lifted it?'

He nods. 'When that light came down on us I got a sense of ... I don't know, it felt like a thrust of power surged through me. I felt stronger. So I tried to use my skill of animating objects, and it worked.'

'Luckily for Mr Carter.'

Matt hears us talking, and his mouth hangs open.

'Anything happen with you?' Ethan asks him hopefully. Everyone knows how desperate Matt is to gain his powers. According to the Prophecy, Matt is supposed to lead the Named into the Final Battle against Lathenia and her Order of Chaos. *It will come to pass that a king shall rule, but not before a leader pure of heart awakens.* But so far Matt can't even lead himself. And his doubts are destroying his confidence.

Matt's eyes flick to the sky, where the meteorite shower has slowed to a trickle of shooting stars in the distance, then jerks his shoulders.

'Nothing, of course.'

Chapter Two

Matt

The Prophecy is wrong. I'm not the one who's supposed to lead the Named. I doubt I was ever *named* in the first place. The Tribunal, or whoever it is who decides these things, are wrong.

We're on our way to Arkarian's chambers now. He should have some answers, at least answers to what happened back there at school. Ethan says Arkarian knows everything. But Arkarian thinks I'm one of them. So Ethan's theory can't be true.

Mr Carter is on his way to the hospital, but they won't find anything wrong with him. Somehow he'll avoid unwanted attention. There's enough turmoil with that bizarre meteorite shower for him to slide into obscurity soon enough.

Rochelle is taking care of Neriah. If I didn't feel so strongly about seeing Arkarian, I would have volunteered. There's just something about that new girl that invokes a strange protective impulse inside me. It's not like how I feel about protecting my sister Isabel. That's a responsibility I wouldn't have any other way. But with Neriah it's as if she's made of everything that is soft and beautiful and … strangely real. But why I feel this way, or how this can be, I have no idea. I'm not looking for a relationship, and, well, Neriah is Marduke's daughter. And he's the opposite of anything good.

Beside me Ethan and Isabel are quiet, and my thoughts drift back to Neriah. I start to wonder what it would be like to be together in a girlfriend–boyfriend kind of way. But who am I kidding? This will never happen. No girl is going to have free access to my heart ever again.

We arrive at the secret entrance to Arkarian's chambers, halfway up the mountainside. He knows we're here; an opening the size of a small doorway forms before us. Ethan and Isabel hurry inside, but now that I'm here, I'm not in such a rush. Maybe the answers to my questions are not what I want to hear. If there has been a mistake, and I'm not really *named*, do I want it confirmed? I've been involved in the Guard for over a year now. I've seen things, some of them stranger than life itself, especially when I was in the underworld. And while I haven't been allowed to go on any real missions yet, the thought that it might never happen fills me with dread.

I take a deep breath and go through the opening. Instantly the rock wall reforms behind me and I'm swamped with that uncomfortable feeling again. The same one I always get when I'm in Arkarian's chambers. I'm not quite sure why. I'm not claustrophobic or anything. Maybe it's because this otherworldly stuff suddenly becomes real and I have to face it. The technology Arkarian uses to monitor the past is just one example.

Isabel comes back down the candle-lit hallway towards me. 'Are you OK? I turned around and you weren't there. This morning didn't freak you out too much, did it?'

'Yes, it did,' I reply honestly, but with a small smile.

She yanks on my sleeve. 'Come on.'

She's in a hurry. A hurry to see Arkarian, of course. He's there waiting for us in his octagonal chambers, surrounded by soundless hi-tech machinery. The 3-D holographic sphere illuminates the room from its centre, humming with the rhythm of a softly-beating heart.

Arkarian is talking to Ethan, but looks preoccupied, and keeps glancing towards the hallway. When he sees Isabel his whole face breaks into a wide grin, his violet eyes softening and creasing at the corners.

Isabel runs over and jumps into his arms. The power of her embrace propels them backwards. They stumble and look for some privacy behind a silver screen. It's hardly enough. Arkarian's vivid blue hair affords more of a screen as it falls across Isabel's face. They kiss, and well, keep kissing. Ethan glances at me, grins and shakes his head. I can't help but groan and look away. My sister's relationship with Arkarian makes me uncomfortable. Their relationship has developed in intensity just a little too quickly for my liking. Everyone knows they're soul-mates. They have the rest of their lives to be together. So what's the rush?

Finally they pull apart and have the manners to look embarrassed. But it doesn't take long for the seriousness of this morning's events to bring us back to reality quickly.

Arkarian greets me by clasping my forearm. Picking up on the tension I'm feeling towards him, he lets go slowly. After a lingering look, he motions for us all to sit on wooden stools he provides.

'What happened out there?' Ethan is first to ask.

'There was a meeting,' Arkarian explains, 'between the immortals. It didn't go well. While my reports are so far incomplete, it appears that both of them lost their temper.'

Ethan makes a scoffing sound. 'So what did they do? Play ping-pong with the universe?'

Arkarian attempts to give a small smile. 'Something like that.'

'What about Angel Falls?' Isabel asks. 'The school took a beating this morning. Did you see? Mr Carter had to be taken to hospital.'

'Yes, but thanks to you two,' Arkarian indicates Ethan as well with a brief look, 'Marcus is going to be fine. There have been reports of damage as far east as the coast and west to the border of South Australia, but you're right about the school, Isabel – the heaviest impacts occurred directly over Angel Falls.'

It doesn't take a genius to figure out what this means. 'Lathenia tried to kill us! She almost eliminated Mr Carter!'

Isabel frowns. 'What about her own people that live here?'

Ethan has the answer. 'She was willing to sacrifice the lives of her own soldiers for a chance to kill off some of us.'

'I'm sure Lathenia would love to see you all eliminated,' Arkarian explains. 'But she's a very clever adversary. She lost her temper in the way that siblings are prone to occasionally …'

My mind drifts off with this thought. It's something I can relate to. Isabel and I get into fights sometimes, mostly about how I'm overprotecting her, or 'smothering' her as she likes to say. But lately she's been really quiet. She won't even take a bite. There's something on her mind that she's not ready to talk about, or is scared to. Although the idea of Isabel being scared is a strange concept. All I know is that something happened to her when we were in the underworld and she hasn't been the same with me ever since.

Arkarian is staring at me intensely. He's heard my thoughts about Isabel and looks worried. He realises Isabel is watching us both and pulls himself together, pretending nothing happened. He turns his attention back to Ethan. 'Lathenia has worked long and hard on her plans to achieve her ultimate goals. She's not stupid enough to let her temper get in the way. What happened in Athos is a one-off.'

'Something else happened during that cosmic shower,' Isabel says softly.

Arkarian clasps her hand in his. 'Yes, I know.'

'You too?' she asks.

'All of us. All nine of the Named have had our powers magnified.'

'I knew it!' Ethan exclaims, starting to get excited.

I can't help but scoff at the idea. I don't feel any different, which only confirms my doubts more. Nothing 'magnified' is still nothing.

Arkarian turns to me. 'I have news for you.'

I brace myself for what can only be a dismissal, or an acknowledgement that I've been right all along and the Tribunal has made a mistake.

His head starts shaking and now there's a smile. 'Such little faith! Now listen to me. You're not Ethan's Apprentice any more.'

I see the others; they look as confused as I feel. 'But … how will I come into any powers without a mentor?'

'Oh, you will have one.'

'Is it going to be you, Arkarian?' Isabel asks.

'No. And I can't tell you any more about Matt's new Trainer. There's something else he has to know first.'

Ethan interrupts. 'I failed,' he says. 'I couldn't train Matt and now the Tribunal is disappointed in me. I'll never get another Apprentice.'

'Don't even think it!' Arkarian replies. 'You're a fine Trainer, Ethan. Just look at what you did with Isabel, and in only those few short weeks you had with her.'

'Yeah, but she was already skilled.'

'There are other things that need learning besides the physical arts.'

'But that's all I was able to do for Matt. And now the Tribunal's dumping me for someone else.'

'Matt's new Trainer will teach him things that you couldn't in your whole lifetime.' Arkarian holds a hand up. 'Things that no one can. No one from *this* world.'

Arkarian's explanation doesn't lessen my confusion, although Isabel and Ethan are more content to accept it.

Arkarian turns to me. 'There are other things beside managing your powers that you have yet to learn. It is your destiny, Matt. And your new Trainer is a Master, a master above all others. He has been waiting his whole life for this chance.'

'He has been waiting his whole life to train *me*?'

'So I am told. Now we'll speak again on this when the time for your training draws nearer and I am given more information.'

'But Arkarian –'

He cuts me off. 'Enough for now. While we can assume to be safe in these chambers, we can't forget that a traitor walks among us. I've told you all I can.' He turns to Ethan. 'As for you, Ethan, you will be getting a *new* Apprentice.'

Isabel's head bobs as if she knows already. 'It's Neriah, isn't it?'

'Really?' Ethan can't keep the smile off his face.

'Yes, but Neriah is classified as high-risk. Her life is in danger from Marduke. She is under the protection of the Guard. So the two of you must never train alone. You will be allocated an assistant. Someone who will stand watch at all times.'

'Do you want me to do it?' Isabel asks.

'I'm assigning Rochelle.'

'Rochelle!' Ethan's enthusiasm takes a nose dive. 'But Arkarian, do you think that's wise?'

Arkarian studies us all in turn. Not one of us holds eye contact for more than a brief second. 'Haven't you learned to trust Rochelle yet? She is Named, just like the rest of you. That means she is trusted by those who are above you. Where is your faith?'

When he puts it like that, it makes sense to let our guard down where Rochelle is concerned. But my distrust isn't simply because Rochelle was once Marduke's spy, it's because of all the things she did for him.

'Rochelle will be your assistant, Ethan,' Arkarian confirms. 'Her Truthseeing skills – now magnified – mean she can pick up the thoughts of others outside normal hearing distance. She can even hear the thoughts of people coming from behind a barrier such as a brick wall or thick glass.'

Ethan nods and says nothing, but it's clear he's still unhappy about working with Rochelle. He's better off keeping away from any emotional entanglement, anyway.

'There's one final thing I have to tell you.' Arkarian gets our attention quickly with these words. 'An unusual mission is planned.'

'Yes!' Ethan says.

'Where are we going?' Isabel asks, then adds hopefully, 'Are you coming too?'

Arkarian takes his time answering. 'I will be going, Isabel, but this mission is not what you think.'

She's picked up on Arkarian's serious tone and has already started to worry. I know my sister – she can't hide her emotions from me, or from her face right now as she stares up at Arkarian, waiting with anxious worry lines around her eyes.

He explains, 'We have to go back to the underworld.'

Isabel screams out, 'No way! Why would they send us there again?'

Arkarian touches her arm. 'They're not. At least they're not sending *you* there, Isabel.' His eyes shift to Ethan. 'Nor you, Ethan.'

His head moves in my direction and this time his eyes are *not* saying no. 'But they are sending you, Matt. You, me and Rochelle.'

'What!' Ethan calls out.

Isabel jumps to her feet and stares Arkarian down with her hands on her hips. 'If you and Matt are going, then so am I!'

Arkarian reaches up to touch her arm as he tries to explain. I tune out as he says something about Rochelle's touch and how she can now visualise the different compounds or layers of the earth beneath her hands, and how *he* is needed to open the rift between worlds.

All I can think is that the Tribunal chose me. *Me!* 'But I have no powers.'

Everyone goes quiet and Arkarian says, 'Without your presence, Matt, our mission would be pointless. Even without your powers, you are the only one who can touch the key to the treasury of weapons with your own hands and not die as a result. You did it once before, when we escaped from the temple. You thought it was a dial that opened the secret passageway between our worlds. In a way it was, but it has a much more valuable purpose. So now we have to go back to the temple and find that key in the rubble of what's left after Lathenia and Marduke destroyed it. And we have to hurry. We have to secure that key before Lathenia gets there. Movement has been detected at the rift. That's why we have to go straightaway.'

Isabel is still standing with her hands on her hips, her face drawn tight and hard. I've seen her fired up before, but right now she looks as if she's about to explode. 'Now wait a minute!'

Arkarian looks up at her and for a second I feel a moment of empathy for him. A small smile breaks out on my face and I pretend to cough into my hand. When my sister sets her mind to something, heaven help anyone who gets in her way.

Getting up, Arkarian reaches out and touches her face with an open palm. He holds it there as if through it he is passing a wave of calmness and reassurance. 'We'll be all right without you. Trust me as I trust you.'

She inhales deeply, then relaxes her head against his chest. His arms weave around her and they stand holding each other. Glancing over the top of Isabel's head, Arkarian looks at Ethan. 'When I'm gone I want you and Isabel to monitor the sphere.'

Ethan sits forward on his stool, his eyes widening.

'What are we watching for and which time periods?'

'There are two under suspicion. But so far no portal has opened. When it does, we'll have to act fast. We can't let the portal close without getting a team in there.'

Isabel turns her head up to peer into Arkarian's face. 'What is the Goddess up to this time?'

'From what I have been able to ascertain, Lathenia has set her sights on the explorers.'

Ethan nearly jumps out of his seat. 'Yeah? Who?'

Arkarian pauses for a moment before he speaks. 'Cook. Or Columbus.'

Chapter Three

Rochelle

I can't believe I'm going to the underworld. It's because of my power that Arkarian chose me, but I don't care really. I'm just glad he did! It will be another opportunity to prove my loyalty to the Guard.

Matt and Arkarian are coming too. And this is not going to be like any other mission. It's not the past we're headed to, it's another world. That means we'll be using our own bodies, with no disguises.

We meet in one of the front rooms of Arkarian's chambers. Matt is already there, his hands thrust deep into his trouser pockets. He sees me and his eyes stay on me for a long moment before silently sliding away. His thoughts come thundering into my head, and as hard as I try to stop them, they just keep coming. He's still angry! I wish I had never been given this Truthseeing skill. Since my powers increased, I've lost control over what I hear and what I can shut out. I shake my head to rid myself of his thoughts. 'Enough is enough!'

Matt looks at me with a frown. 'What's wrong with you?'

I tug my hair behind my ears, something I've always done out of habit, but my hair falls short. So much of it was singed, I had to have it cut. It's all in layers now, short around my face. 'Nothing is wrong!' I find myself snapping out of sheer frustration. Great. I'm really going to make friends yelling at people! 'I'm fine. OK?'

I try to distract myself and start looking around. But there's not much in this room to amuse me, just a couple of stools and an old wooden desk. 'I wonder where Arkarian is?'

Matt shrugs and rocks back on his heels, his hands still in his pockets. 'Probably giving some last-minute instructions to Ethan and Isabel.'

Even though it's obvious he'd rather be anywhere else in the world than standing in a room alone with me, his thoughts are also letting me know he's excited, like a little boy in a toy shop with cash in his pockets. Lots of it.

Arkarian suddenly appears before us. Matt jerks back with a start. He's unfamiliar with Arkarian's ability to materialise at will. Ethan can do this too. I wish I was able but I have to earn my wings first, just like they did. When I was with Marduke, he didn't want me to have them. They would have lessened his power over me.

Without wasting any time, Arkarian transports the three of us to a room in the Citadel that I've never seen before. It's huge and could easily fit a thousand people shoulder to shoulder. I look up and can't draw my eyes away from the ceiling. There are eight panels and so many colours! Glass, or maybe crystal, I think, etched in myriad intricate designs. Instinctively I lift my hands into the air. I want to touch it, feel its texture, see its depth. But the panels are too high, the single point at the centre disappearing into oblivion.

Arkarian grins at me. 'Wondrous, isn't it?'

I nod, and he says, 'This ceiling is identical to the one in the temple we're about to visit in the underworld. Although now it is nothing more than dust and debris. It's just as well you're coming with us, Rochelle. Your hands will be worth their weight in gold.'

It's such a sweet thing to say, my mood lifts for the first time in months. He glances down and notices my hands. They've still got electric currents running through them. He takes one and turns it over. 'Can you feel the energy?'

'They sting. When will it stop?'

'The stinging?'

'Yeah, and the electric charges, or whatever they are.'

He remains quiet for a moment, just looking at me with those all-knowing eyes. It's as if he's wondering how well I cope with bad news. Even though my powers have increased I still can't hear any of *his* thoughts. I wouldn't dream of trying either. He's an expert at shutting out his thoughts from Truthseers. I've never heard any unless he's wanted me to.

But he doesn't have to say, or think anything out loud – it's there in his eyes.

'They're not going away, are they? This is it. My hands for ever.'

'It would be a good idea if you wore gloves. I'll have some made that imitate skin, so no one will suspect anything is different about you.'

I shake my head. Unbelievable. When I was with Marduke I had to wear a mask to conceal my eyes, my one easily identifiable feature. Now it's my hands.

'There is something you should know.'

Arkarian's words send a chill through me. 'What is it?'

Matt comes close enough to listen, but stays quiet.

'There's more power in your hands now than you realise.'

'More than the touching and visualising thing I do?'

'Be careful, Rochelle, until you learn what your capabilities are and how to control the power. You could probably injure a small animal with these.'

I yank my hands from his. 'Injure an animal?'

'Or a child.'

'What are you saying, Arkarian? I don't want to hurt an animal, or a child!'

A soft whoosh from behind has me spinning around. My nerves are suddenly on a razor edge.

'I assure you my dear, you won't be hurting anyone.' It's Lady Arabella, cloaked in a golden cape and looking very regal, even with her delicate skin and frosted eyelashes.

I first met this woman in a safe room here in the Citadel. Along with Arkarian, she debriefed me and helped with my transition into the Guard.

She smiles and her ice-encrusted eyes appear softer. 'Don't fret, Rochelle. I'll teach you how to control your new-found power so that your hands will be completely safe.' Her words are a relief. I thank her and she glances past me to Arkarian. Her eyebrows lift. 'Unfortunately we are still picking up the pieces after that disastrous meeting.'

'How is my father?' asks Arkarian.

'Tired. He asks about you. He warns you to take care and stay out of sight. He says to tell you that there has been some suspicious movement on the borders of the realms of late. And he gives you these.' From within her cloak she hands Arkarian what appear to be three small crystals. 'They will give you light.'

Arkarian takes the crystals and stashes them in his trouser pocket, while Lady Arabella's eyes drift to Matt. She greets him by smiling and bowing her head. Bowing! What is going on? She's acting like a gushing schoolgirl.

Finally she pulls herself together and starts explaining how we're to stand within the inner octagon frame. I look around, but can't see it until Arkarian points to the ground, where an octagon is displayed through a series of patterned floor tiles.

'Your exit from this world will be smooth, but your delivery into the remains of the temple will be anyone's guess.' From nowhere Lady Arabella produces three thick long cloaks. 'Put these on now and keep them wrapped tightly around you. They will cushion your fall and protect you from injury. Remember you don't have Isabel to heal you on this journey, and even with her newly-enhanced powers of being able to heal without touching, she is still limited by distance and barriers. And of course she can't heal unless she knows what the injury is.'

After a few more instructions to Arkarian on how he will return us, Lady Arabella guides the three of us to stand within the inner octagon. Content that we are in the right position, she steps back. Almost instantly a humming sound draws our attention to the high centre point above us. The ceiling panels begin to move. They move slowly at first, and it's quite a sight as the panels are just so big. As their movement increases the colours and patterns intertwine and soon become one colourful blur. It becomes hard on my eyes and I lift an arm to shield them. Suddenly the highest point in the ceiling opens and fills with a light so bright it's as if the sun is falling.

Surrounded by this light my body lifts and spins, leaving me disoriented. The light changes, loses its brightness, and darkness rushes in. Arkarian calls out, letting me know he's not far. But I can't see either him or Matt any more. There's a strong wind now, pulling my limbs in different directions. It strengthens until it becomes too much to handle and I wonder if I will survive the experience, when the wind suddenly disappears and I begin to fall. Remembering Lady Arabella's warning, I pull the cloak around my body as tightly as I can.

It's just as well I do, for moments later I hit the ground. Hard. The impact knocks the wind out of me. For a second I think I must be out cold, but it's just the dark here – total and completely consuming. Suddenly I can think of nothing else. I put a hand out in front of me, but can't even make out an outline of my fingers. Is this how it was for Matt and Ethan and Isabel when they came here? How did they handle it?

'Are you OK?' It's Arkarian.

Leaning on his arm I climb to my feet. 'Everything feels fine.'

'Good,' he says. Running his hand down my arm he puts something small and cold in my hand. It's one of the crystals Lady Arabella gave him.

'How does it work?'

'Like this.' Suddenly the crystal in his hand glows with a gentle light that encompasses his face. He makes it increase until he's happy with the rounded glow.

'How did you do that?'

He smiles. 'I just asked it.'

'Yeah?' I look at the crystal in my own hand, unconsciously bringing it up closer to my mouth. 'Turn on!'

It turns on all right. Instantly. But the light coming

49

from it is so bright it almost blinds us both and sends beams radiating into the black atmosphere above. We've landed inside the temple, but the walls are in tatters and the ceiling non-existent.

'Turn it down, quickly,' Arkarian whispers, one hand shielding his eyes. 'We don't want to alert anyone or anything to our presence.'

I lift it up again and ask it this time to turn down. The light reduces to a softer glow.

'We sure could have used one of those when we were here looking for you, Arkarian,' Matt says, coming over from wherever he landed.

Arkarian passes him the last one of the crystals. As soon as it hits Matt's palm it begins to glow gently. 'Excellent.'

'Isn't it?' I can't help my voice filling with relief, remembering the feeling of that absolute darkness only moments before. 'I hate the dark!' I mutter nervously. It reminds me of when my father used to beat my mother and I would hide in the little cupboard beside the front door, with my mother's overcoat on top of me. I would stay there until the screaming stopped, wishing that I were invisible.

Arkarian sends me a sympathetic look. He's heard my thoughts, but thankfully doesn't refer to them in any way. 'We should hurry,' he says. 'Lady Arabella didn't say how long these crystals will maintain light.'

The three of us begin our search of the floor, systematically dividing what's left of the temple into sectors. Arkarian gives me the centre section, warning me against touching the key with my bare hands. I am, apparently, to use my skill of touch to 'see' what's beneath my fingers. Arkarian produces a rake and uses it

50

to wade through the rubble. I have to be careful to skim the surface only. That's all I need to 'see' below it, anyway.

I get down on my hands and knees and start searching. Instantly, layer upon layer of scalded fragments of timber, glass, rock and other elements become clear in my head. After a while my hands start to go numb with cold. I stick them inside my cloak occasionally to bring some life back into them.

After another hour of fruitless searching I sit back on my heels as a troubling thought occurs: what if this 'key' disintegrated along with the rest of the temple? I grab a handful of sand-like dust and let it dribble through my fingers.

'The key is made from the hardest element in the universe,' Arkarian explains. 'It is indestructible. There is no way it could reduce to dust.'

We keep looking, and once we've worked through our own section, we begin working on each other's until every square centimetre has been searched three times. When I'm done I get up and walk outside. Arkarian glances up, but he doesn't say anything, only sends me the thought that there's a lake nearby and I'm not to touch the water, for it's not what it seems. I nod to let him know I understand and he goes back to sifting through the rubble.

As I near the lake I find a boulder to sit on and wonder at the consequences of this journey. The key is nowhere to be found, not in that demolished temple, that's for sure. Lathenia must have got here before us. Her magician, Keziah, probably used one of his tricks to locate it without so much as bending one of his ancient knees.

Suddenly there's a voice in my head. I remain still until I realise it's only Matt. I look around but can't see him. His crystal light is off, but as mine is still glowing softly, he would be able to see me. He's obviously comfortable with the darkness, sitting out here alone. Maybe he even likes it. Some people are like that, not bothered by nightmares, content with their own company, unafraid of the dark.

His thoughts penetrate and I realise with a start that he's thinking of me. He's noticing my new haircut. He thinks it suits me, adds a warmth to my face that wasn't there before. He notices how the dark strands are shining with the rays of the light upon them, and how my hands lie one over the other as delicate as flower petals. I suck in a hard, deep breath as his thoughts shift to shared memories. He recalls the touch of my hand on his face, and how we used to lay together for hours and not speak. And how in those quiet times he had felt his soul was one with mine.

I try to shut out the rest of his thoughts, but they're filled with so much passion that I find it impossible to do so. And then he is standing beside me.

'Rochelle …'

My hands have started shaking. I clasp them together and turn slowly towards him. He sees me and takes a step backwards, his own thoughts suddenly thrown into turmoil. 'Why are you crying?' he asks.

It's difficult to find the words, but I know I have to try. 'I'm crying because I hurt you and keep doing it just by being near you.'

He makes a scoffing sound. 'Don't get any ideas that I want you back!'

'I know that. I just want you to know that I'm sorry. I

never loved you the way you deserved.'

He looks over the top of my head, then exhales a long breath. 'It was a cruel thing you did – pretending to love me.'

I grip the crystal so tightly my hand begins to ache. 'You need time to get over it.'

He swings a hand dismissively into the air. 'Time? Did you say *time*? Yeah, that's what I need all right. Time will heal everything. Isn't that how the saying goes?'

His tone is so cynical it's hard to listen to. 'Matt, please don't do this –'

'Do what, Rochelle? Pour my heart out to you? Don't worry, I won't embarrass you like that.'

'Don't say that!'

'I was such an idiot. You took me for a ride.'

'We were both taken for a ride.'

'But you knew all along our relationship was a lie. You listened when I told you that I loved –' He gives a horrible sarcastic laugh and shakes his head. 'You say I need time. Well, let me tell you what I really need. I need to go *back* in time.'

'What?'

'It's what we do, isn't it?'

'I don't understand.'

'I want Arkarian to send me back in time so I can choose not to have ever met you!'

He turns to leave and I go to run after him, but Arkarian suddenly appears. His eyes are full of compassion and I understand he's heard it all. He puts a staying hand on Matt's arm.

'Easy, Matt. Slow down.'

Matt quietly calms, and I'm grateful for Arkarian's soothing touch.

Reassuring himself that Matt is all right, Arkarian turns to us both. 'The key is gone. There's no point in looking any more. Turn off your light, Rochelle. We have to get out of here. There's movement on the other side of the lake.'

His words are like icy water trickling slowly down my spine. Without wasting any more time, we make our way back to the remains of the temple. As we climb higher, a reddish glow in the distance appears in our vision. Getting down on our haunches, Arkarian leads us over to a pile of boulders for a closer look.

'What is it? Can anyone see?' I ask.

Arkarian holds a finger to his lips and now the thoughts of another penetrate my brain. It has me frozen to the spot. The memory of Marduke's hold over me is still too vivid.

Matt reaches up to peer over the boulder. For a moment he is completely silent, but his eyes have opened wide. 'What are they doing down there?'

I reach up to see what has Matt in such a state of shock. But even Matt's reaction isn't enough of a warning. On the other side of the lake hundreds of torches are burning around an area so vast it must spread backwards for kilometres. There, within the frame of these torches, are thousands of strange creatures with human limbs, pig-like heads and awkward-looking wings. But it's not the look of these creatures that has the hairs on the back of my neck suddenly electrified. It's the way they're standing at attention, row after row of them, all in strict formation.

Finally I find my voice. It's merely a whisper. 'What are they?'

'They're called wren,' Matt says. 'They answer to your

old Master. Just like you did.'

I try to ignore his cheap shot of sarcasm. 'What are they doing, Arkarian?'

It takes Arkarian a moment to draw his eyes from them. Finally he turns to me.

'They're preparing for war.'

Chapter Four

Matt

As soon as we get back to the Citadel Arkarian instructs us not to tell anyone what we've seen. 'Not until I've briefed the Tribunal. Decisions will have to be made. Plans brought forward. New ones set into place.'

'Does "anyone" include Isabel?'

Arkarian hesitates, and for a moment I wonder if he is in the habit of keeping things from my sister. Just how much control does he have over her, now that the two of them are so close? And with Lathenia advancing her cause, will their relationship affect his judgement? I would kill Arkarian if he hurt Isabel as a result of putting his duties to the Guard first.

His eyes swing to mine, and it feels as if they are scorching right through flesh, blood and spirit. Mine. 'Know this, Matt: I would put a knife through my own heart before hurting Isabel.'

I nod. It is all I am capable of. My tongue feels like glue in my mouth.

'But,' he goes on, 'don't expect me to restrict her activities to "safe" duties.'

These words break the tension and I laugh. 'You'd have a hell of a job trying.'

'I would never insult her that way. The Guard is her life. It's in her blood. And her powers are vital to the cause. But you will have to trust me, because sometimes things are not what they seem. It's a strange double life we lead. But if it's any assurance, all of the Named will know of what we saw before noon tomorrow. Everyone will have to be prepared, especially those of us who have seen these creatures in the flesh and who will be able to identify them as soon as they start appearing in our world.'

'Just how dangerous are they, Arkarian?' Rochelle asks.

'Their mere presence in our world would be a great threat.'

'What do you mean?'

'The balance of good and evil would be disrupted.'

'What could happen?'

'The same thing that happened to the underworld. Waves of darkness will sweep across our lands, and the world will grow darker and darker. Eventually the moon, and then the sun, will be completely obliterated. No crops will grow. Oceans and rivers will have no tides and confusion will reign. Ultimately, all that is natural will die and evil will win.'

It's hard to believe *anyone* would want this to happen. 'How can Lathenia want this?'

'She is the Goddess of Chaos. Cold and darkness, fear, greed, and all that is evil, are the very things that make her stronger, the things that bring her contentment.'

We're quiet for a moment, absorbing Arkarian's disturbing words, when Rochelle asks, 'How soon before they attack?'

Arkarian breathes in deeply. 'By the looks of those troops, I would have to say *very* soon.'

Quietly Arkarian shifts the three of us back to the

mountain, delivering us directly into his main chamber. When we appear, Isabel and Ethan can't conceal their relief.

'What's happened?' Arkarian is quick to ask.

Ethan points to the sphere. 'A portal has opened.'

Arkarian stares into the sphere, adjusts its magnification several times, studying the past. 'It's Plymouth on the 24th of August, 1768.' He looks up. 'The night before Captain James Cook sailed the *Endeavour* in search of a great southern continent.'

'Is that Cook down there among that rabble?' I can't help asking.

'Yes,' Arkarian confirms. 'A complement of ninety-four are preparing for the adventure of their lifetime. A journey that will last just under three years.'

'Where is the danger going to come from, Arkarian?' Isabel asks.

He glances at her, and as usual when their eyes meet, his soften. 'I need more time to study this, but by the looks of this narrow portal, it's not going to be open for long. This means the Order are planning a quick and decisive mission. My guess is that there will be two of them: one to distract us, while the other attempts to assassinate Cook.'

'What are we waiting for?' Isabel asks.

Arkarian pulls back from the sphere and looks at each of us in turn. 'I would send Jimmy, but his skills are needed on another mission tonight.'

'Arkarian,' Isabel says in a tone devised to get his attention. 'I will go.'

Without answering her directly, Arkarian looks at Ethan, then at me. 'It will be Ethan and Matt.'

A wave of excitement and relief washes through me. The relief is that Isabel isn't going. Unlike Arkarian, I don't care about insulting her. The excitement is at the prospect of my first mission into the past. And I haven't even got my powers yet! Suddenly that wave of excitement turns to slop in my stomach as nerves kick in.

Beside me, Isabel fidgets restlessly, then pulls on Arkarian's arm, tugging him to the side. 'What are you doing?'

'Just my job, Isabel. What I'm trained to do. Assessing the situation and making judgements based on those assessments.'

'But why are you sending Matt?'

'Hey!'

She glares at me. 'Shut up, Matt. I just need to know why.'

Obviously these two are still finding their way. Working together and being together would have to strain anyone's relationship. I glance briefly at Rochelle. Well, at least I don't have to worry about that.

'Isabel,' Arkarian says patiently while pointing to the sphere. 'There are ninety-four *men* down there.'

She starts to get it. 'Oh.'

'If I sent you, or any female for that matter, you would attract a lot of attention. Look at those men.' His head tilts towards the sphere. 'I don't need to tell you how that would put the entire mission in jeopardy.'

Ethan can't help himself. He bursts out laughing.

Isabel whacks him hard. He rubs his arm.

'I didn't realise they would all be men,' she mutters. 'I just don't want you overprotecting me, that's all.' She glances at me. 'I get enough of that from my brother, thank you very much.'

Arkarian folds Isabel into his arms, and holds her there as he asks Rochelle to go and inform Mr Carter,

Jimmy, and Ethan's father Shaun that there will be a meeting here first thing in the morning, when everyone has returned from their missions. 'And don't use a phone. Their signals are too easy to overhear.'

Rochelle leaves and Arkarian turns to Ethan and me. 'You two had better go home and get some rest. I'll meet you in the Citadel before you leap, and give you final instructions. And remember, Matt, you will be transported through your sleep. So just relax and go to bed as usual. When you arrive at the Citadel your soul and your eyes will be housed in bodies that resemble your own until you are given secret identities. Do you understand?'

I nod. 'Ethan has explained the details of transportation to me in our training sessions. Except, that room we were in today looked different to how Ethan described the rooms of the Citadel.'

'That's because we were in a different part of the Citadel today. The Citadel is split into two distinct sections. Transportation takes place in the labyrinth, where the rooms and staircases are always changing to suit the requirements of the travellers and to keep their identities intact. Where we were today serves a thousand other purposes, but mostly it houses the living and working quarters. The labyrinth wouldn't work without the machinery and the co-ordinating that originates from this other half. Anything else?'

I can't think of anything off-hand.

'Good, now go. It's nearly evening already out there. Your mother will be wondering what's keeping you so long.'

Ethan tugs on my arm and I make to leave, but notice Isabel is still glued within Arkarian's embrace. 'Are you coming?' I ask her.

She lifts her head to Arkarian and they hold eye contact for a moment, then Arkarian says, 'Soon. You two go ahead.'

Ethan nudges me again. I follow him at a slower pace, giving my sister a lingering look on the way out. I wish I could get used to seeing those two together.

Outside, the evening air is chilly and I shrug deeper into my jacket.

Ethan says, 'You just can't stop worrying, can you?'

'Huh?'

'About Isabel.'

'I promised our dad I would look after her. That's all I'm trying to do.'

'Isabel's my best friend. Trust me, I wouldn't walk away from her if I thought she was in any harm.' He thumps my shoulder. 'Now come on. You have to concentrate on tonight's mission. You don't want to blow it, do you?'

'Of course not!'

Ethan starts to explain about the Citadel. It's stuff he's gone over before, but since my earlier question to Arkarian, he must think it needs repeating. 'It's where we learn the language, accents and other details we need to know so that we don't stick out …'

Listening carefully, I start walking with him down the mountain. We don't get far when a voice calls out from behind. 'Hey, wait up!'

It's Isabel. I can't help but grin when I see her. She reads my look of intense relief. 'You jerk. When are you going to realise I don't need looking after any more? We just wanted a few minutes alone. There's nothing wrong with that!'

Unable to keep doubt from my voice, I bite back

words and simply mutter, 'Hmm.'

With a few more instructions, Ethan leaves us at my front door. All I can think is that I want to take a quick shower and jump straight into bed. But Mum is waiting on the other side of the door.

'Where have you two been?'

Her voice is tight and anxious. I guess after what happened at school this morning, she would be. I called her earlier to see if she was all right and to let her know Isabel and I were unharmed; and then, since school was cancelled for rest of the day, I had told her we were going up to the national park for a hike.

'Are you sure you're both all right? Why do you insist on taking off like that? Just as well Jimmy said he bumped into you and assured me you were safe. You know I don't like you hiking in the park any more. It's dangerous. Do you want to get lost again?'

Of course she would be worried. 'Sorry, Mum. I didn't mean to upset you. I'd forgotten about … getting lost that time. We didn't go far. I promise.'

Jimmy's in the kitchen; I can hear him singing from here. He's a member of the Guard too, also one of the Named. And he's Mum's boyfriend. I often wonder whether his feelings for Mum are true, or if he's only here in our house pretending to care for her so that he can be in a position to watch over Isabel and me. It's an uncomfortable thought, and not totally without reason. After all, Rochelle pretended to love me as part of her job.

Jimmy comes out wearing an apron around his waist, wiping his hands on it. 'Told you darl they were all right.' He looks at Isabel and me and smiles. 'You two got time for showers if you want. But don't be long, dinner's on soon.'

'I don't want any –'

I don't get to finish my sentence before Isabel kicks me in the shin. 'Thanks, Jimmy. I'm starving. And Matt was just saying how that hike today has given him a huge appetite.'

She gives Mum a reassuring hug and runs upstairs. I get her message. Ethan was clear on this point. I've got to act normally so Mum doesn't worry that I might be sick or coming down with something and want to come and check on me through the night. While my body will be sleeping in my bed, if she tries to wake me, I will look as if I'm in a coma and scare the life out of her. And apparently it's worse for the person who's travelling through time. They get sick and can even die.

I shower and go down for dinner. It's chicken, crumbed and baked with potato wedges and sour cream. One of my favourite meals. But tonight it tastes like cardboard. I force down every bite with a smile to assure Mum I'm fine. Jimmy appears amused, but he's the type of person who can laugh at someone else's discomfort. Isabel would totally disagree with me over that, but then Isabel disagrees with me over everything.

As if his intention is to torture me, after dinner Jimmy suggests that he and I do the washing-up together. 'We'll give the girls a night off, eh?'

His humour is irritating me more than usual. But there's no point in arguing. I don't want to prolong the evening when all I want to do is go to bed, go to sleep, and go on my mission.

In the kitchen Jimmy hands me a tea towel. 'I'll wash,' he says. And when Mum disappears with Isabel, he takes the towel from my hand. 'I just wanted a chance to say good luck tonight without your mother overhearing us.'

The joking manner is gone. Even his eyes seem, I don't know, more serious.

'OK.'

'I also wanted to say, be careful. Everything we do now has a rushed feel. And this forces us into making decisions sometimes on the spur of the moment, or with our backs up against a wall.' He's obviously talking from experience. And while he usually annoys me so much I purposefully try *not* listening to a word he says, this time he has my full attention. 'It's hard to judge in a split second what's the best choice.'

I nod, understanding.

'Now I know you haven't got your powers yet, but you're well trained. Ethan's made a good job of that. And, well, the best advice I can give you is to trust your instincts. If a situation doesn't feel right, look into it. If your gut says get the hell out of there, then run, as fast as you can. OK?'

'OK.'

'Now you better get to bed.' He glances at the sink full of dishes and winces. 'I'll look after these. It's generally hard to get to sleep the first time.'

Upstairs in my room I drop on my bed and take a deep breath. Everyone's warnings are running around in my head. I try to block them out, but they're jumping around in there, vying for attention. I start to wonder what the time-shift is going to feel like. Will there be a sign? Or a sensation that will let me know it's about to happen? What if I wake during the transportation process?

In the end I force my eyes shut. When the adventure begins, I'm sure I'll know it.

Chapter Five

Rochelle

After leaving Arkarian's chambers I head back to school. I have to find Mr Carter to pass on Arkarian's message about the meeting tomorow morning. He's probably still in hospital, but I should check at the school first. It could save me a trip into town. I should have asked Arkarian before I left, but, well, I didn't think of it at the time.

The school is still a mess, and because of the damage to D Block, temporary classrooms are being set up on the sporting ovals. Apparently these rooms will be used until D Block is rebuilt. I overhear this last bit of information as one of the office staff, Mrs Walters, tells someone on the other end of her phone.

It turns out the office is the only place in the school that isn't cordoned off. 'They're everywhere,' Mrs Walters waffles on. 'Government scientists have been flying in to our little town all day! And the press –'

I tap my fingers on the bench top to get her attention. She flicks me a slightly annoyed look, then covers the mouthpiece of her phone. 'School's out for the rest of the week. It's going to take that long to assure the safety of the buildings.'

'But I don't –'

'An announcement will be made on the local news, dear.' She waves me away and goes back to her phone conversation.

I call out in a loud voice, 'I just want to know if Mr Carter's been released from the hospital yet?'

At last she realises I'm not here to find out when classes are returning. As if I would be that keen!

'Oh,' she mutters. 'Well, why didn't you say? I believe they're keeping him in the hospital for observation.'

Just great. 'How long?'

'I'm sorry, dear? Did you say something?' She looks around as if seeing me for the first time, then stares at the phone in her hand with a frown. Suddenly she hangs up, without even saying goodbye. 'They wanted us to leave the office, you know. The engineers. But students needed to call their parents. The phones haven't stopped ringing. Reporters are pouring in from all over the country. They're calling it a remarkable phenomenon.'

I speak slowly, enunciating each word separately, so the woman can focus on my question. 'How long is Mr Carter going to be in hospital?'

'Oh dear. A couple of days, I think. They want to run tests. He insists there's nothing wrong with him, but you know what they're like.'

My head shakes. 'Who?'

'Doctors. Nurses. Scientists. They're saying it's a miracle he's alive. He doesn't even have a scratch on him. The gods were shining on that man.'

Hmm. Well, not quite. And lucky for him Isabel and Ethan were nearby. A news reporter comes in with his microphone pointing at me. I duck out of his way and make a quick exit. But the media is everywhere and it proves a battle just getting to the front gate.

66

I catch a bus to the hospital just as it starts getting dark. I still have to tell Shaun and Jimmy about the meeting. The way this is going, it's going to take all night.

About twenty minutes later I get off the bus in the centre of town and take the short walk to the hospital. At reception I quickly find out that Mr Carter is being kept on the third floor, and when I get there, he's telling a doctor off for keeping him in so long.

I knock, halting their conversation.

The doctor sees me and attempts to smile, but doesn't quite make it. Mr Carter is being difficult, testing the doctor's patience. But his survival is a miracle and certainly worth investigating.

The doctor waves me inside. 'I'll be back to continue this conversation when your visitor leaves.' He passes me on his way out, mumbling, 'Good luck.'

When he's gone, Mr Carter motions for me to close the door. Suddenly we're alone and I don't know where to look. We're not exactly the best of friends. In fact we're not friends at all.

I move in closer and see all the wires and tubes attached to him. 'What have they done to you?' A heart machine is beating steadily in the background, while other machines have little wavy or zigzag lines running across a green screen. I point to the equipment. 'Is this necessary?'

'Of course not! But try telling them that.' His head shakes, and after peering at the closed door, he starts pulling stickers and tubes from his head, chest, arms and legs.

'What are you doing?'

'Getting out of here.'

67

'But Mr Carter, don't you think they'll notice? I mean, we're always being told not to draw attention to ourselves.'

'I'm drawing attention to myself just by being here. They're asking questions already about my miraculous recovery. If I'm not here, they can't run any more tests. Actually, your timing is perfect, Rochelle. I need a lift.'

'I came by bus.'

He pauses for a second, then yanks off the last tube with one swift tug. 'Aren't you old enough to drive?'

I smirk at him. 'In case you haven't noticed, I haven't exactly been around lately, and who has time for driving lessons anyway? You wouldn't believe where I've been today.'

He raises an eyebrow but I don't elaborate. Getting the hint, he starts pulling clothes out of a draw beside him and motions for me to turn around. I do so gladly. When Mr Carter finishes dressing he taps me on the shoulder. 'Let's get out of here.'

'How are you going to escape? The nursing staff is bound to notice those machines aren't bleating any second now.'

It turns out one of Mr Carter's powers is extrasensory hearing. Well, that figures! All those times in the classroom when he knew exactly what people were whispering right down to the back corner. No wonder Ethan had such a hard time in his class.

'There's a stairwell two doors to the right. I've been hearing footsteps going up and down all day – forty-seven down to the ground floor.'

Peering into the hallway to make sure no one is looking directly this way, we walk out and turn right. But the nurses' station is almost directly opposite the stairwell and there's an alarm going off. Probably Mr Carter's inactive machinery. Nurses look panicked.

One spots us and recognises Mr Carter. 'Hey! Where do you think you're going? Come back here!'

We walk faster, diving into the stairwell.

'Quick!'

Following Mr Carter's lead I run down the three flights of winding stairs, then another set into the basement car park. 'There'll be security waiting at the front doors,' he says by way of explanation.

Minutes later we're in the open air, but we don't stop running until we've cleared a whole block.

Finally we stop. I put my hands on my waist. 'Well, thanks for the exercise, but I only wanted to tell you there's a meeting scheduled in Arkarian's chambers tomorrow morning. Be there.'

I look around for the nearest bus stop, turning my back on him. He comes up beside me. 'What's happened?'

Still looking for a bus, I give a light shrug. 'I'm sure you'll be fully briefed tomorrow.'

A bus approaches, and I put my hand up, but I'm not standing at a bus stop and it sails on by. 'Shoot.'

Mr Carter puts his hand up, and a yellow cab going in the opposite direction swings around, almost causing a traffic accident. He opens the back-seat door and motions me in. 'The next bus won't be for half an hour,' he says.

I get in the cab and explain, 'I have to tell Shaun and Jimmy.'

'I'm going to see Jimmy tonight,' Mr Carter says. 'We have a mission together. I'll tell him then.'

Mr Carter gives the directions to Ethan's house, but

asks the driver to swing by Angel Falls High School first. When we arrive there, Mr Carter gets out. 'This is where I left my car.' He turns to me and says, 'Here.' He holds out his hand, and when I pull mine out of my pocket, he shoves a few notes in my fist. His fingers touch mine, and I get a strange sense of something familiar. I don't get a chance to think about it though, because Mr Carter's reaction is so dramatic. He jumps back with a squeal. My hands have hurt him, given him a sting or a burn. That's when he notices the little currents flashing. Quickly I put my hand back in my pocket, where it's been for most of the afternoon. He doesn't say anything, but his eyes study me in a curious way for a long moment. Finally he looks at the driver. 'Take her anywhere she wants to go.'

We drive off towards the national park and the driver waits while I run in and tell Shaun about the meeting. Thankfully he's home. I say a quick hello to Mrs Roberts, who's looking better these days than ever before.

I get back in the cab and give the driver the directions to my home. Part way there I ask him to turn around and head back towards the national park. 'There's an old gravel road that used to be a fire trail,' I tell him.

He peers at me through his rear vision mirror. 'You want to go there!'

'Yes,' I mumble, wondering what the hell I'm doing. Arkarian didn't tell me to go and see Neriah, but something inside is telling me to do just that. While she's one of the Named, the last to be identified, she doesn't know it yet. As her Trainer, it will be Ethan's job to tell her all about it. About us. So I'm not quite sure why I'm doing this. I just feel it's right.

It's completely dark now, and when the cab turns up

the narrow gravel path, a shiver passes through me. Occasionally the driver looks back at me. He's wondering when I'm going to tell him to stop.

'Keep going.'

At last we get to the end and he pulls up in front of a set of high iron gates.

'Wait for me, I'll only be a minute.'

'Fix me up first,' he insists.

He's going to bolt. It's in his thoughts. I try to convince him that I won't be long.

'You pay me first, then I'll wait.' He's lying, but I don't have much choice.

I pay him and plead with him to wait.

I get out of the cab and the second the door closes the cab takes off, spinning gravel and dust in my face. Great. How am I going to get home now? I watch as his tail lights disappear into the darkness beyond. I hang on to the look of those lights for a few more seconds; the dark is not my favourite time of day.

Eventually I lose sight of the cab altogether and become aware of other lights beyond the gates. Dull lights. I walk up to the iron bars and peer into the yard, but from here it looks as if I'm peering through glass or perspex. It's some sort of barrier.

A sudden voice pierces the quiet night. It asks my identity and has me jumping almost clear out of my skin. I look to where the voice bellowed out of a small white box. 'My name is Rochelle Thallimar and I want to see Neriah. I was here earlier today, when I brought her home.'

It takes a minute, but eventually the gates make a clicking sound, then slide open to about the width of my body. But the gates are only a decoy for the barrier behind them. A hole appears before me, enlarging to an opening about the size of my body. It's strange how it happens, like the glass – or whatever the barrier is constructed of – becomes malleable. I reach up to touch the edge of the hole when that voice returns. 'Go through now!'

It makes me jump again. I walk through the opening and the barrier folds down behind me, the hole completely disappearing with a sucking sound. I look up, and even though it's dark, the barrier can be seen high above the trees, distorting the view of the night sky. The whole yard is shrouded beneath this protective dome. And now that I think about it, Neriah is chauffeur-driven to school and back in a black Mercedes, her two white dogs along for the ride. I guess she needs the security to protect her from Marduke.

I start walking along a paved, sweeping driveway when lights ahead illuminate Neriah's house. For a second I stop and simply stare. 'Wow,' I say to nothing but cold air. The house is like a palace, with little jutting windows on the upper level and overhanging balconies adorned with pretty flower beds beneath a series of thatched rooftops. 'Someone sure is looking after you.'

As I say this, the thoughts of someone in the yard flit through my head. It's a brief encounter. Did I imagine it? The hairs on the back of my neck freeze at the roots, making my spine tingle. I look around, but it's dark beyond the few garden lights outlining the driveway.

I have to force myself to take another step because my legs have decided to stay put. That flash of thought could have come from anywhere. Now more than ever, I can hear thoughts from quite a distance away. Maybe there's someone in the forest, camping illegally. People do that around here all the time.

Then it happens again, just as a twig falls from a branch that hangs almost directly over my head. I look up. But with no moon out yet, and that protective barrier overhead blurring the night sky, it's too dark to see anything except the rough shapes of branches in shadow.

OK, I try to reassure myself, just keep walking. It could be nothing. I could be hearing things. I look ahead, but the house is still a good distance away. Too far for my comfort. Why did I take it upon myself to visit Neriah? And why did I choose to do it at night?

A sound to my right stops me dead. Slowly I turn my head. This time I see something – two glowing lights, oval-shaped and small enough to resemble a pair of eyes. And this time I hear a distinctive snarl. There's an animal in the yard!

It moves and I see a shadow bolt across the lawn beyond the trees. My mouth goes dry. *Move!* I scream this word as loud as I can inside my head. *Just move!*

I get to the house and Neriah opens a door for me. Beside her are two white dogs looking restless, whining and jumping about. 'Hey, Rochelle,' she says while telling her dogs to heel. 'Come in.' She glances down at the dogs, who still look uneasy. 'I don't know what's got into these two.'

'There's something in your yard.'

Her eyes come up to meet mine. 'Are you sure? What did you see?'

'Some sort of animal.' I'm reluctant to tell her this 'animal' had thoughts like a human. At least, human enough for me to detect them briefly. I can't hear the thoughts of animals. That's not my skill.

73

A woman comes up behind Neriah. I wonder if it's her mother. They have the same wide, oval-shaped eyes, flawless skin and silky dark hair. 'Let the dogs go,' she says.

Neriah raises her arm and points to the open doorway. The dogs give a short bark each, then leap. They leap high and long, and, to my amazement, as they do so, they change shape. They turn into leopards! Snow leopards with thick, whitish fur, sprinkled with black rosetta spots. I stare after them, my jaw hanging open.

Neriah's mother closes the door. 'I'm Aneliese. Welcome to our home, Rochelle.'

'This is nice,' Neriah says. 'I don't often get visitors.'

'Well …' I don't finish the thought out loud. The girl lives deep in a forest, at the end of an old fire trail, in a house that looks like something out of a fairy tale, surrounded by two-metre-high brick walls, a thick barrier right over the top, with two dogs that change into leopards, and a strange animal roaming the yard. Is it any wonder? 'You're a little out of the way.'

Aneliese remarks softly, 'Security is tight here, but it's necessary.'

I'm still trying to get my heart to slow down after that encounter with the creature in the yard, then seeing dogs turning into leopards, so words are a little hard to form.

Neriah notices I'm trembling. 'You've had a fright. Here, come into the living room and sit by the fire.'

I follow her into a large room furnished with antique buffets, tables and drawers, the walls covered in classic paintings. They look authentic. Aneliese leaves us alone, but soon returns with two mugs of hot chocolate.

We talk for a minute about how Neriah is fitting in at

school, and I notice how Aneliese chooses her questions carefully. And then it hits me what else is strange around here. It's the silence. I mean, the silence in my head. Like Arkarian, Neriah and her mother know how to shut their thoughts off. They've both been trained. And that gives me the creeps.

'Do you two live here alone?' I shiver at the thought.

Aneliese replies, 'We have a small staff of five.'

Hmm, then why can't I hear *their* thoughts? 'Ah, the voice from the box.'

'Yes, that's William. I'm afraid he can sound abrupt at times. I hope he didn't frighten you.'

Did she see my reaction? 'He was fine. I just wasn't expecting it.'

Aneliese gets up. 'It was nice to meet you, Rochelle. When you wish to leave, our chauffeur will drive you home.'

That's a relief. I don't want to walk through that yard again. 'Thanks, that will be great.'

'Don't hurry.' And to Neriah she says, 'I'll inform William about Rochelle's encounter and get him to check on the dogs. Nothing is coming up on the monitors.'

She leaves and Neriah closes the door behind her. As she does this my eyes skim around the room. The furniture is not just antique, it's ancient. Every piece in this room must pre-date the colonisation of this country! A gold-coloured metal clock on the mantel gets my attention. I go and run my hand over it – late Renaissance period, 1600, Augsburg. But there's something else my touch reveals – it makes my chest tighten as if something is crushing it. Neriah goes to lift the clock when her fingers brush mine. And there it is again, that strange familiar feeling. She pulls her hand away and stares at me with a frown. Don't tell me I've hurt her too?

'Are you OK?' I ask, ready to apologise.

'I'm fine. Your touch tingled and took me by surprise. What happened to your hands?'

I'm not sure how much she knows. 'Just an accident,' I reply lightly, and focus back on the clock.

'It was my father's,' she says.

Her words surprise me. From what I understand, she has lived in isolation and in hiding from her father since she was a small child. 'So you know him, then. Your father, I mean?'

'Of course,' she says, looking straight at me. 'He is the most evil man in all the realms.'

She knows more than any of us realise. I wonder what else she's aware of. 'Are you a Truthseer?'

'No. But you are. I can tell by your wariness. I think Truthseers know too much. The hearts and minds of people must be an uncomfortable burden at times.'

She's not wrong there! Especially lately, now I'm having trouble shutting them out.

'I've been trained to screen my thoughts from a young age,' she continues. 'It was necessary because my father is a Truthseer, and we never knew when he might find us, or be near enough to hear our thoughts and discover our identities.'

I decide to be honest, as she is being with me. 'I was under the impression that you didn't know anything about us.'

'Do you mean the Guard?'

I nod.

'If it wasn't for the Guard, and the protection they

offer us, I would be under my father's control right now, and my mother would be dead. But I have lived in hiding and now I have to take my place among the Named and fulfil my duties to the Prophecy. I'm the last,' she adds, and pauses. 'When I'm Initiated, the Named will be complete.' A shiver passes through her, and her whole body shakes with it.

'Are you afraid?'

'No. I'm looking forward to being a Guard. To being part of a team. It's been ... lonely, growing up on my own. It's just, I believe that my joining and completing of the Named will act as a trigger, a catalyst, you might say, that will bring forward the deciding battle.'

What a horrid thought! She's probably right, though. I try to think of something to say to lighten the atmosphere. 'Do you know that Ethan is going to be your Trainer?'

It works. She smiles. It makes her look very young. 'That's great! He seems nice.'

I can only nod at her words. 'Nice' is an understatement. He's everything I could ever want.

'But I wish ...' Her dreamy look snares my curiosity.

'You wish what? Or should I say *who*?' I prod when she stops.

She glances down to the floor and doesn't tell me. When she lifts her head her eyes meet mine and I'm overwhelmed by a sense of loyalty, courage and calm emanating from her. Neriah is more than she appears. Much more.

'Whoever he is, he would be lucky to have you,' I say.

She giggles and we talk for a while about the boys she's met since starting at the school, and I tell her what I think of them. We talk about a lot of things, and she tells me of her concerns that her father will find them and exact revenge on her mother, as he has sworn to do. 'He wants to punish her for taking me away from him.'

'Arkarian won't let that happen,' I try to reassure her.

The door opens and Neriah's dogs come bounding in ahead of her mother. Neriah introduces them. 'This one with the droopy ear is Aysher.' She tugs his ear playfully, then nudges her face against his. The other dog clambers half on top of her, trying to get his mistress's attention. She laughs at his playful, attention-seeking antics. 'And this is Silos, not known for his patience.'

'They're beautiful. Are they really dogs? I mean, they changed into leopards earlier.'

After patting them both, she tells them to sit and they do so immediately, keeping their intelligent eyes on her every move. 'It's something they do when they sense danger.' She looks up at her mother. 'Did they find anything lurking in the yard?'

'Nothing.' Aneliese turns her attention to me. 'Do you think you were mistaken, Rochelle? That yard can be rather intimidating at night.'

She's not wrong there.

'Other than Aysher and Silos,' she continues to explain, 'there are no other animals here. There's a protective barrier that covers the entire property like a dome. Nothing can get in, not even a bird, unless we allow it.'

'Is there another way into this place besides the front gates?'

Aneliese and Neriah exchange a worrying look at my question. 'There are the escape tunnels,' Aneliese explains. 'But the doors are secured and are checked regularly. I carry the keys with me at all times.' Her hand flutters over her chest while her voice rises, revealing her concern. 'There's been no breach or it would have been reported.'

'Look, I don't want to alarm you, but I know what I saw. Something has broken through your barriers. Something *unusual*.'

Chapter Six

Matt

I drop straight on to my butt, into a Citadel room that is more like a florist shop, but with rainbows streaking across the ceiling. I can't help but stare, and then sneeze as the scent of the flowers irritates my nose.

A hand reaches down and I grab it. It's Ethan, looking apologetic as he helps me up. 'I thought I taught you how to land.'

'Well, I don't remember getting any instructions.'

'Oh. Sorry.'

'Forget it. I've got a tough hide.'

'You're more generous than your sister was. She used to yell and hit me when she missed her landings.'

I shake my head. 'That would be right. Isabel is obsessed with proving her ability to stand on her own two feet.'

Arkarian materialises before us and notices the fragrant air and shifting rainbows above. 'I haven't seen the Citadel this happy since my return from the underworld.'

'You say that as if the Citadel has emotions. Isn't this place just a building?'

'It's far more than a building, Matt. It was designed by

one Immortal, restructured and perfected by another. And when I speak of it having emotions, I'm referring to the beings that live there and are as much a part of it as the bricks and mortar that make its walls. But let's not get distracted from what you two are about to do.'

He runs his hand along the back of a white leather high-back chair, one of three in the room, then decides to sit in it, motioning for Ethan and me to follow. 'You will be assuming the identities of scientists,' he explains. 'Ethan will be the botanist Henry Robins, and Matt, you will be the astronomer Edward Cowers. These people do not really exist, but we have been able to establish your reputations. The *Endeavour*'s official astronomer, Charles Green, is especially looking forward to meeting you, Matt. His particular talent is finding the longitude at sea purely from observing the moon and stars. Not many scientists of his time can do this. He is keen to discuss navigational instruments with you.'

'But how will I sound convincing? I don't know anything about navigating.'

Arkarian glances at Ethan, sparking my memory of the knowledge dust. I wave my hand in the air to let him know I remember Ethan's explanation, but he's probably reading my thoughts anyway. After all this time training, I still don't know how to screen my thoughts from Truthseers. I just don't get it.

Arkarian continues with his instructions. 'The two of you will be given a guided tour and introduced to several prominent members of the crew. You are not expected to sail with the ship. Learn what you can about recent activities. In the short time the *Endeavour* has been docked at Plymouth eighteen men have deserted the ship. The Captain has taken aboard marines and

81

volunteers to make up the full complement. Joseph Banks, the scientist and adventurer, will be arriving just ahead of you, along with his friend, a Swedish doctor by the name of Daniel Solander. Apart from these two gentlemen, no other crew members should change in this last twenty-four hours. Do you understand so far?'

He waits for us to both nod before he continues. 'The most important thing you have to remember is to make sure you are off the ship before it pulls out of the harbour. I can return you from anywhere, even from out to sea, but if you are seen by the crew when it departs, you will have to stay on board until they reach land. You can't afford to let this happen. That ship will go for months without docking.'

'OK,' Ethan says. 'We get that. Do the job and get out.'

Arkarian leaves us and Ethan takes me up a series of staircases that disappear beneath every one of my steps. 'Why does it do that?' I can't help asking.

'For protection,' Ethan explains. 'It leaves no trail or scent of where you arrived or departed.'

We end up in a room with clothes lining every wall. As we walk past them, our own clothes change, and when I look in one of the many mirrors I can't believe how different I look now. I'm wearing white stockings that go all the way to my knees! My shoes are black and fastened with big silver buckles. I turn sideways and shake my head. My shoes have high heels! Looking up I notice the shirt, white and frilly with baggy sleeves. This is tucked securely inside tight black knee-length pants that have buttons running all the way up the outside of my legs. Over the top of all this is a brown vest and rust-coloured coat.

I look ridiculous.

'Do they really expect us to wear this get-up?' I glance at Ethan. His outfit is similar, but he doesn't look uneasy at all. 'Are these costumes close enough to the real thing that we won't be seen as frauds?'

'They're authentic,' Ethan explains, tugging his vest down at the front. 'These coats were the peak of fashion in 1768. Didn't you study this period in history with Mr Carter?'

'I didn't take history.'

'Everybody had to do history in the lower years.'

'Well, I don't remember learning about it.'

'Never mind,' Ethan says, pulling me into the centre of the room. 'You might need an extra dose of knowledge dust.'

A fine layer of dust settles over the top of us from the ceiling; instantly I feel comfortable in the outfit, but, stranger still, I'm aware of having a vast knowledge of the universe, the positions of stars and constellations. An image of a sextant comes to mind and somehow I just know that this instrument has recently replaced the quadrant because it can measure altitudes and angles with a higher degree of accuracy.

Brushing away some of the extra dust on my head and shoulders, Ethan urges me on to another room on a lower level. The colours of the rainbow are back again, but in softer, pastel tones, the scent of flowers more subtle. I get the feeling the Citadel is not only happy, but is being gentle with me.

A doorway opens in the opposite wall where Ethan instructs me on how to take the fall and land on my feet. I glance out and see the pier where the *Endeavour* is docked. There sure is a lot of activity going on down there. It's daytime, but the sky is cloudy and dark.

'What can you see?' Ethan asks.

My shoulders lift in a light shrug. 'Everything. The ship, the crew, sacks, instruments, casks, barrels of all shapes and sizes being taken on board. They're rowdy down there, and there's music coming from one of the pubs.'

He peers at me, frowning.

'Is something wrong?'

'No. Not at all. It's just that most first-timers don't see so clearly.' Still staring at me, he motions for me to leap. 'You go first. I'll be right behind you.'

I take a deep breath and try not to think about what's ahead while I jump.

I land on my two feet in a quiet back-street alley. A thump behind me and I spin around to see Ethan. He pats my back. 'That was great. Let's go, then.'

We walk into a cobbled street, moving out of a sailor's way. He's carrying a hammock on his back. 'Excuse me, gentlemen,' he says. 'Are you heading to the *Endeavour*?' Ethan nods and the sailor rushes on, 'We've been waiting for the wind to pick up.' He holds up the hammock. 'I got myself a bed today. The Captain likes a neat ship.'

Ethan tips his cap at him. 'We shall see you on board.'

Suddenly it hits me – where I am. I'm about to meet Captain James Cook, the explorer who discovered the east coast of Australia. That much I do know. I also know a little about his present occupation – a young captain of His Royal Highness's Navy. 'What was so important about Cook's travels?'

Ethan is only too keen to explain what he knows. 'His journeys to find the great south land paved the way for Australia's colonisation.'

'Yeah, I know that.'

'Well, his journeys contributed to the world's knowledge of seamanship, navigation, even geography. His surveys and maps were so accurate they were used for over a hundred years. His men didn't die of scurvy because the diet that Cook insisted they eat included fruit and vegetables, and he was the first captain to calculate his longitudinal position with mathematical accuracy. He completely charted the north and south island of New Zealand, as well as the east coast of Australia.'

We draw near the ship and I stop and just look. She's larger than I imagined. She creaks as she sways and rubs against the dock. She seems so … real. Ethan taps my shoulder, pointing up ahead. A man dressed similarly to us, but with a bright red coat, comes towards us.

'You must be Robins and Cowers. Welcome to the *Endeavour*.'

Ethan introduces us and the man shakes our hands. 'Zachariah Hicks. First Lieutenant. Please come on board. The Captain is expecting you.'

Hicks takes us on board and shows us around. Sailors make way for us as we pass. On the main deck he rattles off statistics. 'She measures one hundred and six feet from stern to bowsprit and twenty-nine feet and three inches across the beam.' He then explains what some of the ropes and rigging are used for. 'You're fortunate we're still here. If this wind continues to pick up, we'll be sailing soon.'

Hicks shows us all twenty-two of the *Endeavour's* guns, then takes us down into the well-stocked hold. He explains how they'll be sailing with eight tons of ballast, several tons of coal, spare timber, barrels of tar and pitch, tools, canvas for repairs to the sails, hemp for the ropes and rigging, and a stash of other supplies like food.

'Twelve hundred gallons of beer, sixteen hundred gallons of spirits, four thousand pieces of salted pork ...' As he rattles off the rest of their impressive supplies, he takes us through to the quarterdeck where six small cabins have only recently been built for the Captain, Charles Green, Joseph Banks and some of Mr Banks's party.

The next part of our tour is the lower deck, where most of the men will live, eat and sleep for their three-year voyage. It looks crowded as the men continue to find their places, hang their sleeping hammocks and stash their gear. There are so many men, I wonder how we're going to identify which two are the ones we're looking for. Ethan must be thinking the same thing. His eyes run over the men's faces more than the ship's quarters. 'Will you be sailing with a full ship's complement?' he asks Mr Hicks.

'We lost two men only this morning,' he says, then looks at the two of us. 'There's room for you two, if you're willing. I'm sure the Captain would be pleased to have two scientists of your calibre aboard.'

Ethan has to be thinking about those two seamen who jumped ship only this morning. Didn't Arkarian say the ship's crew should not have changed at all in the previous twenty-four hours? But Hicks is apparently serious about his offer for us to sail with the *Endeavour*. I motion towards Ethan. 'Unfortunately we don't have sea legs,' he says, plastering a huge smile across his face.

Hicks continues with the tour, and we eventually make our way to a room tucked away in the ship's stern. Lanterns hang from the ceiling, giving extra light, even though it is still daytime and the sky is starting to clear.

It's in this room that we meet both Captain Cook and

86

Joseph Banks. The Captain greets us by clasping his hands around ours, then introduces us to the other scientists he wants us to meet. Joseph Banks quickly engages Ethan in conversation, while the astronomer, Charles Green, seems extremely keen to pass his knowledge on to me.

We're served a light meal, but there's an atmosphere of adventure in the air as the wind continues to increase in intensity. Ethan works his way over towards me. 'I'm going to take a look around and see what I can come up with. Keep your eye firmly on the Captain.'

But the Captain has decided to set sail. He explains he has things to put in order above deck, but kindly suggests his colleague, Mr Green, show me his mathematical equipment before I leave. I can't very well chase the Captain, so I accompany Mr Green to a room called the Great Cabin. It's a small room with timber desks and chairs, and will be shared by the Captain as well as the other scientists and artists. I wonder what it would feel like in here after almost three years, and, if Captain Cook knew how long his journey would take, whether it would make any difference to his enthusiasm. I doubt it. He appears calm and totally at home.

After Charles Green has showed me his instruments, I go in search of Captain Cook. I find him above deck, issuing orders to a couple of sailors scrambling up the ratlines and working their way along the yards to unfurl the mainsails. Hicks spots me. 'Are you still here, my good man?'

'Ah, just giving the ship a final look over before I leave.'

'Better be careful or you'll end up sailing with us.' He winks and tips his cap.

As Hicks walks off, Ethan comes running towards me. 'This is bad.'

'What is? I haven't seen anything strange.'

'Those two deserters.'

'Yeah, so what do you think that means?'

'It means the Order has done its job already.'

'But …' My eyes drift to where Captain Cook is standing at the wheel, his head tilted right back as he watches two sailors up at the crosstrees setting the topgallants to the wind. 'He looks safe enough.'

'Exactly.'

'I don't get it.'

'They're going to blow it up, Matt.'

I stare at Ethan. 'The ship?'

'Yeah. With everything and everyone on it. The maximum amount of damage. Don't you see? Not only does Lathenia annihilate Captain Cook, but if she destroys the *Endeavour* as well, the voyage will be cancelled.'

Geez, he's right! 'The *Endeavour* is about to set sail!'

Ethan looks up as deck hands work the ropes and hawsers. 'I noticed.'

'So what do we do? A bomb could be anywhere.'

'We sure could do with Rochelle's hands right now. She would only have to run them over the timber and find it for us.'

'Well, we don't. Got any other ideas?' I don't mean to sound so abrupt. 'Sorry.'

'Don't worry about it. Let's just try to figure this out.'

But where would those 'sailors' plant an explosive? 'They would have come on board and gone straight –'

'To their allocated area in the lower deck!' He hits my chest with the back of his hand. 'You're a genius!'

Trying to look inconspicuous, we make our way

down. There's still a lot of activity, but amazingly most of the men's gear has been stored away neatly. Ethan spots a sailor that he was chatting with earlier. 'Those two seamen who jumped ship this morning, I don't suppose you saw where they stored their baggage?'

The sailor points to the far stern and chuckles. 'Up there in that corner. Nice and cosy, like.' He grins. As we take off he calls out, 'Oi, the ship's about to leave, y'know.'

Ignoring him, we rummage around, feeling for cavities, searching through boxes and other paraphernalia. A rumble overhead sounds like wind filling the sails. This is quickly followed by a creaking of timbers. Suddenly the ship lurches.

Ethan looks at me with widening eyes. 'We have to hurry!'

We start searching frantically, throwing gear around in our rush, making a mess. 'It's not here!'

'It has to be!'

We keep looking but don't find anything. 'Maybe you're wrong about the explosives. Maybe Arkarian's wrong too and nothing's going to happen.'

'Shhh,' Ethan warns. 'Don't say his name until we're ready to leave. Now think, and believe me, we're not wrong.'

A sinking feeling hits my gut as the ship begins to pull away from the dock with the shrill cries of seagulls taking flight. 'There's a cabin.'

'Huh?' Ethan asks.

I start to move with an idea forming in my head. 'If they wanted to create the most damage, and make sure they annihilated Captain Cook and his most precious belongings, then it makes sense that they would plant

89

the explosives directly under his Great Cabin. The place where all the scientific equipment is stored.'

'I don't remember seeing that room.'

But I do. Somewhere amidships. Somewhere in the middle. Ethan joins me in the cabin, and within seconds he has his hands on a suspiciously loose board. Jimmying the panel open, the explosives are soon revealed – six thick rods bound together with string. 'It's dynamite,' he mutters. 'Trust the Order to play to their own rules every time.'

'What are you talking about?'

He glances up for a second. 'Dynamite hasn't been invented yet.' He notices an old-fashioned timepiece at the centre. 'Look at that. It's set to go off in three minutes!'

'We have to get rid of it.'

'Yeah.' He gives it a tug, but it doesn't move. 'First things first.'

'Right.'

Working carefully Ethan holds the bomb as I attempt to cut the straps holding it in place. It seems to take for ever with the clock ticking loudly in my ears. When it finally comes loose too much time has passed. We only have fifteen seconds left!

'Just enough time to get this baby into the water,' Ethan says with amazing calm, considering he's holding a pile of explosives in his hands.

But it just isn't turning out to be our day. Hicks makes an appearance, with two other sailors close behind. 'Hey! What are you two doing here? You're up to no good, aren't you? Good grief, what's that you're holding?'

Ethan looks at me and shakes his head. 'No time to explain, sir,' he calls out. 'Just let us through!'

No one moves out of the way. 'Here, you're not going anywhere. Not with that! I thought there was something funny about you two.' Hicks calls over his shoulder, 'Lock 'em up!'

I glance at the timepiece in the centre of the bomb, my heart sinking. Five seconds. 'What are we going to do?'

'We'll take it back with us.'

Four ...

'What? The bomb? But it's going to explode! And those three over there will see us disappear.'

Three ...

'We can't worry about that now. It's a risk we have to take,' Ethan explains.

Two ...

He adds quickly, 'If we don't, this bomb is going to kill everyone on the *Endeavour* and the two of us will die in the past. We can't risk that.'

One ...

Without conscious thought I snatch the bomb out of Ethan's hands and call, '*Arkarian!*'

Chapter Seven

Matt

Arkarian transports us back to the Citadel, but in the split second after transit begins, the bomb explodes. Heat, light and fire catapults the two of us into a rapidly darkening oblivion.

My eyes open and I find myself on a hard floor in a room with black, crumbling walls, the remnants of the explosion littered all over me.

Arkarian grabs my shoulders. 'Are you all right?'

'Huh?' I glance down at my chest, patting it a couple of times quickly. 'Yeah, I think so.'

'Are you sure?'

I nod and he spins and looks around. I follow his eyes. 'Oh no,' he mutters, running across the room.

Ethan is lying in a massive pool of blood. I crawl across the floor to him, dread growing deeper with every movement.

Arkarian picks Ethan up and starts carrying him to the door. I get up quickly and run after them. 'Where are you taking him?'

We run through one corridor after another. 'To a healing chamber.'

Up ahead Lady Arabella is standing holding a door

open. 'Quickly, in here.'

Arkarian lays Ethan's body down on a narrow crystal table. Lord Penbarin appears, doing up his bright red gown. 'Let me see the boy!'

All three examine Ethan, then Lady Arabella whispers to Arkarian, 'We need Isabel.'

Arkarian turns around and looks straight at me. 'This is what we're going to do.'

But my thoughts are only with Ethan. 'Is he all right? Is he …?'

Arkarian grabs my shoulders with both of his hands. 'Matt, listen to me.'

'But –'

'Listen!'

The urgency in Arkarian's voice breaks through and I focus on his face, on his deep violet eyes. 'I'm listening.'

'All right. Firstly, I'm going to transport you back to your own body in your own bed and wake you up. OK?'

I nod, understanding.

'Then I want you to get Isabel, go up to my chambers, and call my name. Loudly. Just like you did on the *Endeavour* when you grabbed that bomb out of Ethan's hands. OK?'

'Yes.'

'Then I will transport you here, and Isabel can work on healing Ethan. It's his only chance to pull through this. Be quick.' Arkarian's hand comes up over the top of my face. 'Now go.'

A second later I wake in my bed, my heart thundering against my ribs. And for a mad second I think I'm dreaming, a horrible nightmare. Isabel comes running into my room, the door banging behind her. Still caught in the thought that I'm moving within a freaky dream, my mind trips out and I see her as an angel or a spirit. Her hair is out, flying around her face, and she's wearing a long white nightgown.

But her words soon bring my thoughts crashing back to reality. 'What happened? I felt something. Are you all right? Is Ethan all right?'

'No. He's not.' I get out of bed and start running for the door. 'Ethan needs you. Come quickly. We have to go now!'

In the hallway, the door to Mum's bedroom opens. Jimmy is there and he throws me something. They're keys. 'Take my jeep. You'll get there faster.'

Long minutes later we're halfway up the mountain and climbing out of the jeep. It occurs to me that Arkarian is not inside his chambers. 'How is the secret door going to open when Arkarian is at the Citadel?'

'Arkarian can open it from anywhere. Come on!'

As she speaks the doorway opens. As soon as we're both inside she calls his name. Instantly we're transported. We end up standing outside the healing chamber door where Arkarian is waiting. Isabel rushes towards it as if she can walk straight through both Arkarian and the closed door. Arkarian pulls her back and makes her focus. 'Isabel, take a deep breath.'

'Arkarian, let me go to him. Precious seconds –'

'– are important for you to get your thoughts together. You have a lot of work to do in there and you need to be able to concentrate. Clear your head now, Isabel. I need you to prepare yourself … before you see him.'

'How badly is he injured, Arkarian?'

'You will need to use your powers like never before. Not only do you have to heal him, but for Ethan to survive, you're going to have to … *restructure* his vital organs.'

Chapter Eight

Rochelle

I'm the first to arrive for the scheduled meeting. Not even Arkarian is here, though I have no problem getting into his chambers. I walk around trying different doors, looking for one that is set up for our conference. The rooms are mostly bare, although some have gym equipment inside with mats and bars. The central chamber, distinctive by its octagonal shape, is completely dark. The sphere is motionless.

Something has happened. Something terrible. Stirrings of fear start surging inside me. I try to recall everything I know about last night's events. There was a lot of activity. Jimmy and Mr Carter had a mission, while Ethan and Matt were going to rescue Captain Cook. As for Isabel and Shaun, I have no idea if they were doing anything. I was with Neriah, and she seemed all right, despite the intruder.

A noise in the hallway has me spinning around. It's Jimmy. Without saying a word he opens a door to his left. 'The meeting's in here.'

I follow him in and see a round table surrounded by chairs, all made of wood. I touch the table top and instantly know its heritage. It comes from a tree more than a thousand years old. Oak. English. 'What happened last night?'

'There was an – *incident*.'

A lump rises in my throat. 'Was anyone hurt?'

As I ask this question Shaun and Mr Carter walk through the door. Straightaway I feel the tension in Shaun. Though his thoughts are a scrambled mess, his distress is clear. Distress for Ethan!

'Shaun, what's wrong? What's happened?'

He looks across to where I'm holding the high back of a chair. 'There was an explosion.' He swallows deep in his throat, flicking a nervous glance to no one in particular.

Inside, my chest feels as if it has been enclosed in a straitjacket ten sizes too small. 'How is he, Shaun? Is Isabel with him?'

He leans heavily on the table top with open palms and groans, his eyes weary and troubled. 'Isabel has been with him for hours. I'm told that we'll know his condition soon.'

Matt walks in looking a complete mess, his clothes dishevelled, hair askew, as if he has spent the last few hours trying to pull it out. But it's his eyes that give away his grief.

Shaun practically jumps at him. 'Tell us what you know.'

But Matt has nothing to give. He drops into the nearest chair. 'Arkarian sent me away hours ago. He wanted me to rest and put me in a quiet room. I haven't seen him since.'

I look at each of them, anger brewing inside. 'Someone has to know something! Where is Arkarian? He will tell us!'

Hands suddenly grip mine. They're Jimmy's. But as soon as he touches me he springs back with a jerk. 'Whoa, girl. Look what you're doing!'

I glance down at the chair. Beneath my fingers the timber has partially disintegrated. A smell of burning wood fills the room.

Everyone stares at me and I feel like a freak. I throw my hands behind my back. Out of sight they settle into a calmer state of energy.

Silence follows that nobody feels inclined to break. Feeling the intensity leave my hands, I carefully pull out an undamaged chair, sit in it, and wait.

At last Arkarian materialises. Before anyone gets to ask their first question, it's clear that someone else is coming. It's Isabel. Her form takes shape more slowly beside Arkarian, as if she is weary beyond belief. The instant she stabilises, Arkarian supports her with his arm.

Isabel looks exhausted. This is definitely not a good sign.

Shaun and Matt jump to their feet. Isabel touches her brother's arm gently. He holds out a chair for her and she collapses into it. Arkarian holds up his hand for everyone to be quiet. But this is too hard. I need to know if Ethan is all right, and I need to know now!

Arkarian hears my thundering thoughts and glances at me. He catches sight of the disintegrated chair and frowns. My thoughts scream out to him to forget the chair. Just tell us how Ethan is!

Hell, I'm making such a fool of myself. But I can't seem to help it.

At last Arkarian announces, 'Everyone, Ethan is OK.'

The room fills with the sounds of sighs and murmurs.

The relief is palpable.

'He's just getting his thoughts together and will be here soon.'

Such relief washes through me that I can't help a flood of tears from springing to my eyes. Ethan suddenly begins to materialise before us. I quickly turn away. I don't want him, or anyone here, to see my tears. In the background I hear the others greeting him. I wish I could be with them. I just want to let Ethan know how glad I am he's all right. But what would he do if I embraced him like the others, only with tears clinging to my lashes!

Eventually everyone begins to quieten and at last I get my emotions under control. I turn around and, because my legs feel like liquid, sit down quickly. Ethan glances at me and I say, 'Welcome back.'

He nods an acknowledgement, then notices the damaged chair beside me. 'What happened? That chair looks worse than I did a couple of hours ago.'

'Oh, that?' I reply before anyone else gets in. I hold up my flashing hands for a second. 'Unexpected burst of energy. I'm still getting used to them.'

Ethan accepts my explanation, then briefly closes his eyes.

When he opens them, the chair is repaired, as good as new.

It has everyone around the table clapping and cheering. Prior to the enhancing of our powers, Ethan's skill with animated objects was entirely manipulative, like in the way he first caught Isabel's attention by making a pen spin. The other day he moved that space rock right off Mr Carter's legs when the rescue workers' machinery couldn't. It seems that now he can reconstruct objects.

Among the cheering Mr Carter's voice calls out, 'What on earth were you doing holding a stack of dynamite in your hands?'

Ethan glances back at him. 'But I wasn't.'

'Huh?'

Arkarian breaks the silence. 'If Ethan had been holding the bomb when it went off, he wouldn't be here right now.'

Mr Carter doesn't let the story end there. 'Tell us what happened, Ethan.'

'What does it matter?' Matt interrupts in a sharp tone meant to discourage further conversation.

Mr Carter doesn't take the hint. 'Of course it matters. Tell us, Arkarian. It sounds like a fascinating story.'

'*No!*'

Mr Carter freezes and Matt softens his tone, 'Look, thanks to Isabel, Ethan is fine now. That's all anyone needs to know.'

In an attempt to ease the awkwardness in the room Arkarian distracts everyone by starting the meeting. 'Firstly I want to thank everyone for coming, especially after the trying circumstances of last night.'

As he speaks I remember what I promised Neriah last night, just as I was getting into the car. 'Ah, there's something I need to tell you.' Arkarian glances across at me, and the eyes of all the others follow. 'I invited Neriah.'

'To this meeting?' Arkarian asks through a surge of murmurs.

'I went over to her house last night.'

'But Rochelle,' Mr Carter says smugly. 'Who do you think you are, making such important decisions on everyone else's behalf?'

Arkarian flicks him a glance accompanied by a wince.

'What Marcus means, is what makes you believe Neriah is ready to join us?'

'She's stronger than you all think.'

Mr Carter scoffs at this. 'I would know, Rochelle. I'm with her at school every day. I'm monitoring her progress.'

'And you treat her as if she's made of glass. It's a mistake. Sure, she's cautious. Look at how she was raised – private tutors, guards watching her every movement. Now that she's in a normal school, it's natural that she would be shy. She's just not used to being around so many people. She's quiet, not weak.'

'Just how much does she know?' Matt asks.

'She knows that her Initiation will … *complete* us.'

My words are followed by silence, where everyone looks around at each other.

'The uniting of the Named,' Arkarian whispers.

Heads begin to nod.

'There's something else.'

'Go on,' Arkarian says.

'She has concerns.'

His face forms into a deep frown. 'Then we shall listen. When will she be here?'

'She's coming now.'

Arkarian uses his wings and disappears before our eyes. He's going to meet her on the outside. He doesn't do this often; it's too dangerous for him to be seen circulating in our world. But he's back in only a few minutes, opening the door. And Neriah walks in.

Shaun is first to get up and greet her. He kisses the air on either side of her face. 'You have grown into a beautiful young woman, the image of your mother. How is she these days?'

'She is well, thank you.'

'I'm glad we have this opportunity to meet at last. I have many things I would like to talk to you about.'

Neriah looks at Shaun astutely, her deep brown eyes narrow in contemplation. 'I know you were the one who disfigured my father's face. Please do not worry about the past. You were just the catalyst for what had to be.'

'You are as kind as your mother.'

Shaun sits down as Jimmy exchanges places with him and gives Neriah a welcoming hug. The rest of us know her, having seen her at school for the past few weeks. Arkarian produces a chair for Neriah and she sits next to Shaun on the other side of the table. She glances at me and smiles, letting me know how grateful she is to be here.

Arkarian takes control of the meeting again. He looks around the circle at each of us. 'So, now we are nine. And,' he adds, 'the news from Athens is that King Richard is completely healed and can take his place at the Tribunal circle. At last Veridian has its own king.'

Ethan's face lights up. 'Yes!' He punches the air with his fist.

Well, he should be excited. He was the one who saved King Richard's life in the past and shifted him through time physically.

Matt is also excited, but for different reasons. He breathes a strange sigh of relief. 'At last! Then you don't need me any more.'

Everyone knows where Matt's coming from, but he's wrong, and everyone knows that too. Arkarian explains, 'Matt, King Richard will rule from afar. He is Veridian's representative on the Tribunal – our governing body. According to the Prophecy, you will lead the Named –

101

the nine of us here in this room – into battle.'

Matt thumps the table and turns his face to the wall.

Arkarian gets back to the meeting, explaining his reason for calling us together. 'Yesterday, Rochelle and Matt and I travelled to the underworld to find the key to the treasury of weapons.'

Among the murmurs, Mr Carter's is the loudest. 'Excellent! Did you find it?'

Arkarian groans beneath his breath. 'Unfortunately, we were too late.'

'Are you saying Lathenia has it now?' Shaun queries.

'We think she has it secured in a vault in her palace.'

'And the plan is?' Jimmy asks. 'You know I'm good with locks and things.'

Arkarian smiles at Jimmy. 'Yes I do, Jimmy. And yes, there is a plan. Some of us will be going to Lathenia's palace on Mount Olympus, but we don't stand a chance of being successful until ...' He pauses, and the tension in the room catapults. He glances across to Matt. 'Until Matt comes into his powers.'

'Oh great!' Matt exclaims. 'Well, we all know that could be for ever!'

'Matt,' Arkarian says softly. 'How do you think you were able to cradle that explosive pack of dynamite against your chest, curling your body around it like a plasticine ball, and walk away with only a few scratches?'

Matt stares up at Arkarian with wonder in his eyes.

'You have power, Matt. And your new mentor will show you how to unleash and control it. You leave tomorrow.'

Everyone starts murmuring.

Isabel, still looking exhausted, asks first, 'Can I go with him?'

Arkarian rests his hand on her shoulder and stares at her with such tenderness, such adoration, no one in the room could possibly be unaware of his great love for her. 'The only thing you'll be doing tomorrow is resting.' He turns to address the rest of us. 'This is a journey Matt has to make alone. And when he returns, we will go to Lathenia's palace and bring back the key, and at last the Guard will have the balance of power back in our hands.'

Arkarian looks to Neriah and asks if she would like to address the meeting. Glancing around the table with a nervous little smile, she gets to her feet. 'At home last night there was a breach in security.'

'What happened?' Arkarian asks, sitting down.

'It happened when Rochelle came over.'

Mr Carter interrupts at the sound of my name. 'Well, doesn't that explain it then?'

'Marcus!' Arkarian attempts to shut him up.

I go on to explain, 'I was walking through the grounds when I heard someone's thoughts nearby, but when I searched for the source, I saw something that resembled an animal. It threw me because I was expecting a person.'

'So what do you think it was?' Arkarian asks.

'It could have been a dog. Its eyes glowed a silver colour.'

'Was there anything else that stood out about this creature? Something unusual perhaps?' Arkarian prods further.

'When it realised I could see it, it ran off across the yard.'

Jimmy calls out, 'When it ran across the yard did it still resemble a dog? Or did it gather itself and leap? Or maybe hop like a rabbit?'

I think about this for a moment, remembering those eerie glowing eyes and how the head turned, followed swiftly by the rest of it. 'All I remember was that it was sleek, graceful and fast.'

Arkarian says to Neriah, 'I'll organise a thorough check of the grounds, and step up security, doubling your mother's guard. But Neriah, you must be careful too. Your mother's life isn't the only one in danger.'

'My father doesn't want me dead, Arkarian. But he does want to murder my mother. He is driven by revenge, and my mother is high on his list.'

I think Neriah's confidence in her own safety is naïve. 'But Neriah, Marduke tried to kill Isabel, and she didn't do anything to him.'

'She was part of his plan to exact revenge on Shaun. He uses people as if they are merely instruments at his call.'

Her accurate assessment of Marduke's character raises a comment that I can't help airing. 'You seem to know a lot about someone you haven't seen since you were a toddler.'

She glances down at her fingers resting lightly on the table top and her face starts turning red.

Mr Carter jumps to her defence. 'What's that supposed to mean?'

'Nothing,' I reply quickly. 'It's just, I know Marduke. He's manipulative. He can ... *persuade* you into doing almost anything.'

My comment raises a few eyebrows, but it's Arkarian who understands where I'm going with this. 'When was the last time you saw your father, Neriah?'

She seems to hesitate, but her answer is decisive. 'Not

104

since the morning he lost half his face.'

Nothing more is said and after an awkward silence Arkarian gets to the whole point of this meeting. He stands and everyone's eyes follow him. 'When Matt, Rochelle and I went to the underworld, we saw something ...' He pauses, gathering his thoughts. 'We saw Marduke commanding an army of the living dead.'

'What!' Mr Carter calls out. 'That's abominable!'

'Tell us what you saw,' Shaun says.

Arkarian holds his hands up to quiet everyone down. 'You've heard us speak of the wren – creatures that are part human, part animal and part bird. For those of you who haven't seen one, they are easily identifiable by their red eyes and awkward-looking wings.'

Murmurs erupt, but quickly die down again as Arkarian continues. 'There are other creatures there too. In fact, there are thousands, and they are all dead, according to human lore. More than likely Marduke will send out a division of scouts first. They may be wren, they may not. I want everyone to be on the lookout. If you see anything suspicious you should let each other know and let me know quickly.'

Jimmy asks, 'What does this all mean, Arkarian?'

'It means Marduke is planning to invade the earth with creatures that we can't kill with ordinary weapons.'

'Then how do we fight them?'

'Not with guns or ordinary swords.'

'There must be something we can use!' Mr Carter sounds panicked.

'The wren fear water.'

'How do you know this?'

'While locked away in his debriefing, Dillon has been a great informant. He was one of Lathenia's highest-ranking soldiers and his knowledge at this level has been exceptional. He has not hesitated to share it with us. His debriefing is almost over. He will be joining you all soon as a member of the Guard.'

This is incredible news. Dillon has only been away for a short time. Around the table the others mutter and whisper among themselves.

'Is this wise?' Mr Carter is first to make his opinion known.

Arkarian waits until the room falls quiet. 'It is not for us to make that judgement. From what I have been told, Dillon's knowledge and experience will make him a valuable member. He has worked closely with the wren of the underworld, and has told us how they can be destroyed.'

'Through water?' Shaun queries.

'Their wings are cumbersome and quite useless. Under water they become clogged and heavy. They panic, and while submerged their own fear kills them.'

'Well, that's a start. Is there any other way to kill these wren?'

Arkarian glances at Matt. Matt feels his stare and turns his head away. 'We need the weapons in the treasury.'

'For heaven's sake!' Mr Carter exclaims. 'We don't have the blasted key! And we have to wait until Matt comes back from his journey to whereverland before we can even go looking for it! Do we have the time to spare, Arkarian?'

'Probably not, Marcus. But whatever time we have, it will have to do.'

Chapter Nine

Matt

Isabel sleeps for eighteen hours without stirring. I don't want to wake her, but it's time for me to leave. Arkarian is waiting for me in his chambers. I shake her gently.

'Isabel.'

She wakes with a start and grips the top of her quilt. 'Is it Ethan?'

'He's fine.'

As her mind starts to focus, it dawns on her what I'm doing in her room. She pulls herself into a sitting position and runs a hand over her dishevelled hair. 'Are you going now?'

I nod and we sit side by side on the bed.

'Do you know how long you're going to be away?'

'No, but Arkarian says that where I'm going time is measured differently and that the people who live there take no notice of it. So I could be away for months or for just a few days. I've told Mum, since school is out for the rest of the week, I'm going up north to visit some friends and get away from this cold.'

She nods, but can't help keeping her concern from showing. She bites down on her lower lip and when she looks at me, there are questions in her eyes.

I wish she would tell me what's troubling her. I get the feeling it has to do with something that happened in the underworld. I don't want to leave her like this.

'Ever since we came back from the underworld there's been a strange vibe between us, like we're hiding something from each other. But, Isabel, I don't have any secrets. Not from you.'

She takes a deep breath. 'Then you really don't know?'

What is she talking about? 'Know what?'

'You're the oldest. You should remember stuff from our childhood better than me.'

'Are you talking about Dad walking out? I remember that day.'

'Not just that day, Matt. What about conversations you had with him? How far do your memories go back?'

'I do have some odd memories of my childhood that don't make much sense.'

'Tell me what you remember. Tell me everything.'

I glance away for a second at the movie poster on her bedroom wall. How much should I tell her? Some of my earliest recollections are too strange to say out loud. I decide to be honest; I'm tired of being confused. Who knows, maybe Isabel will know what I'm talking about. 'My earliest memory is of the moment I was conceived.'

Maybe not. She looks at me as if I'm pulling her leg.

'If you want me to stop …'

She reaches out and touches my arm. 'No. Keep going.'

'OK. It was as if I had been conceived with all-seeing eyes and fully developed emotions. I can even remember the thud of my heart's first beat.'

'I'm not sure why, but I do believe you, Matt. It's just a strange concept. Tell me what you remember about … our father.'

My elbows slide to my knees and I glance away to the floor. How do I explain these feelings of guilt I have inside? And a strong suspicion that the reason our father walked out of our lives was my fault. 'I remember that he loved you – *adored* you. And that he didn't love me.'

Her hand on my arm tightens its grip. 'Remember when we were in the underworld, and we had to pass through that mountain of ice?'

'Yeah, that was the most unbelievable experience.'

'Well it wasn't for me. It was horrible.'

At the time I had no idea. 'Tell me about it.'

'He came to me there. He told me things.'

A dread settles deep in my gut. 'What did he say?'

'He told me that … you weren't his son.'

The words shock. But there's a truth in them that I can feel. 'I should have known.'

'Why do you say that?'

'Didn't you ever wonder why he used the strap on me so much, and never once touched you?'

A helpless look fills her eyes. Of course, what could she have done? And if he had wanted to lay into her, I wouldn't have let him! At least I would have tried not to. He was strong with that strap in his hands. 'He held me at a distance and I felt it.'

'I was too young to understand. He was just my dad, and I loved him.'

We're quiet for a moment, contemplative. 'So who is my father?' I ask, not really expecting an answer.

She sits up straighter and her eyes suddenly fill with tears. 'I think you're about to find out.'

I get up and start pacing the room. 'Are you serious? Has Arkarian said something to you?'

'No. Not really.'

A couple of those tears she's fighting back start to trickle over. I can't stand to see them. I hate seeing her so worked up and worried. 'What is it, Isabel? Why are you crying? I'm going to be all right, you know. I have every intention of coming back!'

She forces a smile to her face. 'I'm scared this journey is going to change you. You're going to find out things about yourself, your heritage, that are going to draw you away from me, from your family.'

'Never!'

'You may not be able to help it.'

A tap sounds at the door and Jimmy's voice follows. 'You'll have to hurry, Matt. It's nearly time.'

I turn back to my sister. Suddenly my own vision blurs and I drag her into my arms. 'Whatever I discover about myself, I will *always* be your brother. We share blood, Isabel. The blood of our mother. Nothing and nobody can ever take that away from us. OK?'

She nods, but doesn't answer.

Chapter Ten

Rochelle

Ethan starts training Neriah, and, as Arkarian organised, I have to accompany them on every session. It's a good idea. Of all of us, I probably understand Marduke the most. The downside is I have to watch Ethan and Neriah interacting. They look good together. Very good. So far, he's mostly going through the motions, seeing where her talents lie, and part of the training is nurturing her paranormal skills. She hasn't gone on a mission yet, so there's that to prepare her for as well.

But it doesn't take long for Ethan to discover that one of Neriah's powers lies in her artistic talents. Her paintings are more than they seem. I've seen some of them at school. They're really special. Whether it's just a charcoal sketch, or a painting in oil or some other medium, she makes everything seem so real.

Right now she's giving Ethan an example. I wander close enough to hear what she's saying. 'It doesn't matter what I use – a brush, a wand or a stick,' she says. 'Watch this …' She picks up an oval-shaped pebble and starts scratching away at a rock. Ethan peers down to get a closer look. When their heads come up, Ethan looks astonished. There's a trickling stream between us that is

111

starting to ice over. I leap over it to get a closer look.

Ethan sees me and calls out, 'Look at this.'

Neriah giggles, then takes the pebble and makes the outline of a small creature resembling a mouse. As soon as she's finished, the drawing comes to life in the form of a real live mouse. It runs towards me.

'Wow! Is it an illusion?' I lift my feet out of the way, but it breaks up, completely disappearing.

'I don't know,' she says, lifting her shoulders. 'So far the animation only lasts a few seconds.'

'Her powers are still developing,' Ethan explains. 'Arkarian thinks that one day Neriah will be able to open a portal through time with just the few whisks of a paintbrush.'

'That's impressive.' And I really am impressed. She will be a valuable asset to the Guard if she is able to do this. At the moment Lathenia controls the opening of the portals.

'We should keep moving,' Ethan suddenly says.

We decided this morning not to stay in one spot for too long. So far we've moved three times. I point to a field on the other side of the lake, but Ethan shakes his head. 'I used to train there with Isabel.' He's about to explain how Marduke appeared there one night to pass them a message and nearly scared the life out of them. Instead, he holds on to the thought, not wanting to distress Neriah. He glances at me, realising I've read his mind again. His eyes narrow, revealing anger and disgust.

'Look ...' Feeling drawn to defend myself, I attempt to explain. 'I don't do it on purpose. And you should learn to stop projecting your thoughts so loudly. I'm not the only Truthseer, you know. At least your thoughts are safe with me.'

112

'Are they?'

Of all of their distrust, Ethan's is the hardest to take. 'Darn right they are!'

Neriah keeps looking between the two of us, but her thoughts are locked securely behind a screen – something Ethan should try harder to accomplish.

I look away before he sees how much his lack of faith affects me. The thing is, if these guys don't trust me, what hope do I have to trust myself? Maybe Marduke was right. Maybe evil never dies, and once in your blood, stays there for ever, lying dormant until something comes along to trigger it. Is that how it is with my father? He's still in jail today for the crimes committed against my stepmother. Marduke saw evil in me. He sensed it. And look at the things I've done, the people I've hurt. Can anyone really change?

I walk off and leap back over the stream and down the hill. It's not till I get to the bottom that I realise Ethan is right behind me.

'Rochelle, stop.'

'What do you want?'

'I do trust you.'

For a moment I can only stare, and he adds, 'I've always trusted you, even when the Tribunal suspected you were Marduke's spy but we didn't know for sure. I stuck up for you.'

'You did?'

'Yeah, and I didn't even know why at the time. It was just my instinct. And well, it's been right before.'

He starts to back away, looking, if anything, embarrassed, and maybe even a little annoyed at himself for giving me this admission. He flicks a look up the hill to where Neriah is standing. We're not to let her out of our sight, so Ethan is taking a risk in more ways than one to tell me this.

'I just wanted you to know that.' He briskly turns and goes back up the hill.

I follow at a short distance, keeping an eye on the landscape for anything suspicious. It's quiet. Almost too quiet. Something doesn't feel right. I could do with Mr Carter's extrasensory hearing right now, which sparks a thought, and I decide to try it. Pulling off the gloves Arkarian gave me this morning, I put my hands to the ground. Instantly an image of the earth's crust forms in my head – fossil-rich rocks of limestone over a layer of clay. I try to push past these images and 'feel' for other things. Suddenly the ground starts to thunder beneath my hands and I'm swamped with a visual image of horses. Many horses. Wild and free and running at full pelt along the valley floor. I look up and see that Ethan and Neriah have drifted almost to the top of the hill. If they don't change direction they're going to run straight into the brumbies!

'Ethan, stop!'

He hears me and turns to look. I wave my arms towards the wooded area to the right. The horses will not run into the woods when there are wide open spaces to choose from. 'Run into the woods! Quickly!'

But the horses are too fast. The thunder of their pounding hooves can now be heard clearly.

Neriah screams as the large herd of powerful beasts crests the top of the hill, only metres from where they're standing. Instinctively she throws her hands into the air. It all happens so fast. One second the horses are galloping at incredible speeds, the next they're kicking their front legs up and pawing the air. It's an amazing sight. I run as fast as I can, my heart pounding with the thought of what can only be a terrible tragedy unfolding above me. But when I get to the top, the scene is hardly tragic. I stop and stare. The horses are calm and placid – playfully vying for Neriah's attention.

She croons to each of them, nuzzling their faces with her own. They come up to her one at a time, gently nudging each other to be the first in line.

Ethan is staring too. These are, after all, wild horses, running free all their lives. No one would even attempt to catch one, let alone tame it. 'You have a definite connection with animals,' he says.

'Wow,' I can't help exclaim for the second time today. 'What else can you do?'

She shrugs her slender shoulders. 'I don't know. But the other day, since the enhancing of our powers, all sorts of things have been happening to me.'

After a few more minutes of patting and stroking the horses, we move off down the valley. The brush with the horses makes us hungry, and Ethan breaks out some sandwiches. Neriah takes one, then Ethan holds the lunch box up towards me.

I didn't even think of bringing anything to eat and now I'm hungry. But I'm not going to take his lunch from him. 'Oh no, that's all right. I'll get something later.'

'Don't be an idiot. I knew we'd be all day. I packed this for you.'

I take a closer look and see two sandwiches still left in the box. I take one, my face feeling hotter by the second. I wonder if it's possible to make a bigger fool of myself than I'm doing today? Somehow I doubt it.

After lunch Ethan runs Neriah through some technical exercises to see how skilled she is in these arts. I watch from a short distance, splitting my concentration between the area immediately around us, and the grassy fields on the outer perimeter. Neriah's having trouble with some basic martial arts. Ethan is behind her now, one arm around her waist, the other her throat. I know this move. She's supposed to drop at her centre and pull Ethan's elbow downward, making sure to place her chin in the way of the choke. I've done it a thousand times, but until you do it the first time, it seems impossible.

She has a go but they both end up sliding to the floor. They burst out laughing, while helping each other to their feet. The sight of them getting along so well, and having fun doing it, starts to grate on my nerves for no other reason than I wish it were me. I decide to go for a walk. The fresh air should knock some sense into my head. It would be a good idea to check the area out, anyway.

When Neriah sees me walking off she calls out, waving me over. I hesitate, because I really don't want to feel their beaming happiness up close.

'Rochelle!' she calls out loudly. 'Come and show me how it's done.'

I can't believe what she's asking! She looks at Ethan. 'A demonstration would be a big help. What do you think?'

At first he doesn't say a word, but just looks at me. Finally he gives in to Neriah's whim and shrugs his shoulders. 'Sure.'

Slowly I make my way over, wishing instead that I was buried deep in a cave somewhere on the other side of the world.

With slow steps Ethan moves in close behind me. And then his arm comes around my waist. He presses in at

116

my back and I feel his chest inhale deeply as his other arm closes around my throat. For a moment everything is still and I become conscious of the fact that if I turn my head just slightly to the right, my eyes will meet his. The pressure to do so becomes intense and for a second I can't resist. Slowly, I turn.

But he's not looking at me. He's looking straight across at Neriah and smiling.

If it's possible to die from embarrassment, then I should be flat on the ground right now with no breath in my lungs. Instead of dying, I decide to do the next best thing. Manoeuvring my chin into position to break the stranglehold, I drop downwards, pulling Ethan's elbow along with me. Turning my hips now I keep pulling Ethan's elbow away from him. He loses his balance and hits the ground hard.

Neriah laughs and can't seem to stop, doubling over.

Ethan looks up at me from the ground, shaking his head. But there's a grin there, so at least there's no hard feelings and I can walk away with my pride intact.

Just as I go to walk away I hear a noise and spin quickly to my left, flicking a knife from my boot.

Ethan is up beside me in a flash. 'What is it?'

'Footsteps.'

I hear them again, and this time Ethan does too. He lunges for Neriah, shoving her behind us. Her expression changes quickly from one of fun to fear. Her big brown eyes grow even rounder.

'Stay quiet,' he says softly and propels a knife from his boot to his palm.

A crackling of twigs has the nerves at my neck rippling. The footsteps are getting closer and now there's the shadow of a man coming towards us.

Surprising me, Ethan puts his knife away.

'What are you doing?'

He starts walking over to the man, and then I see why. It's our friend, Dillon. Arkarian said he would be joining us soon.

Ethan and Dillon grab each other's arms. 'Hey, it's good to see you,' Ethan says. 'You weren't away long.'

Exactly. Dillon and I have both defected from the Order now, but where my debriefing took almost a year, Dillon has only been gone a few weeks. I remember the months of doubt I went through and I wonder how in control Dillon can be after such a short time. Loyalties are difficult to break. But who am I to judge? Dillon doesn't have evil in his blood. His parents were drunks and they fought a lot, but they weren't murderers, like my father.

Arkarian and Lady Arabella must be confident of Dillon's successful transition to have put him through the program so quickly. And they are the two people I trust the most in the world.

Chapter Eleven

Matt

Arkarian transports us both to the Citadel, to the room with the high coloured ceiling crafted in eight panels. He points to the centre of the octagonal shape marked out on the floor. 'I'm going to propel you into another world.'

A feeling of déjà vu passes through me. I've been here before. 'Be careful, Arkarian. I don't want to end up in that dark place all by myself.'

He gives me a reassuring look. 'Don't worry, Matt. If I propelled you into the underworld by mistake, I would come straight after you.' He laughs. 'My life wouldn't be worth living if I lost you.'

'If it's Isabel you're thinking about, I wouldn't worry too much. I'm sure she would forgive you for losing her brother!'

Arkarian's eyes drop and he mumbles, 'I wasn't thinking of Isabel, actually.' He looks up. 'You don't understand yet just how important you are.'

His words are unsettling. I decide to change the subject. 'Will you be able to see me wandering around in this world?'

He shakes his head. 'No. The outer worlds are closed

to our viewing. But I will be informed of your safe arrival.'

'By the man who is going to be my mentor?'

'Yes.'

'Isabel thinks this man is my father.'

Arkarian peers at me with a considering look. 'You're asking your questions to the wrong person. Just a little more patience, Matt, and I'm sure that at least some of your greatest mysteries will be explained.'

He moves back. 'Wait!' I call out with one more concern. He reads my thoughts, and his eyes soften instantly, but for my own benefit I need to hear his assurance out loud. 'Will you do what you can to protect Isabel?'

'Of course. I will use all that is within my power.'

'I don't want her to get hurt.'

'I would never do anything to hurt Isabel.'

We're silent for a moment. Arkarian can tell there's more I need to say. I stare over his shoulder while I get my thoughts together. 'Look, I know the two of you are close. But, well, you both have the gift of agelessness. There is plenty of time before you should feel the need to deepen your relationship.'

Arkarian pauses before he answers. 'Don't you think that's Isabel's decision?'

'Of course, but … she will love you with all that she is, and that gives you power over her.'

'Only because you are her brother, Matt, will I allow that insult to pass.'

The ceiling panels begin to spin, so, with no other option, I put my trust in Arkarian's hands. A burst of brilliant light spills over me from above and the spinning turns into a frenzy of colour and motion. Suddenly I'm catapulted into a dizzying wind. It lasts for a moment longer than I'm comfortable bearing, then I find myself falling. I hit solid ground and start to roll, down and further down, tumbling head over heels.

At last I stop, but my head is still spinning. I open my eyes and try to focus. There is thick foliage in my face. As I lift my head my eyes are drawn to the sky.

'Oh, wow.'

I stare at this strange sight without blinking. There are two suns! One orange, one blue. How can this be? And while it's obviously daytime, the sky is alive with moving colour – shimmering lights of reds, blues, yellow and indigo. What would it look like at night?

Dragging my eyes away I take a look at my surroundings. There seems to be no one around for as far as the eye can see. In the vast distance, there's a mountain range, while closer sprawls a deep green valley with a stream rushing through it. Beneath me, and for kilometres around, are fields covered with wild flowers in a variety of colours. I lift my hand and crushed beneath it find a flower with twelve different-coloured petals. While staring at this amazing phenomenon, the flower springs back into shape again.

'Unbelievable,' I whisper.

A voice from behind me has me jumping out of my skin. 'There you are! I thought I'd gone and lost you!'

I stagger to my feet, spinning around. There's a man in strange baggy clothes running down the hill towards me. His hair is brown and long and flowing freely down his back.

'Matt,' he says, holding out his hand. 'My name is Janah. I have been sent to welcome you and be your guide.' He holds his arms out wide and looks up and around. 'What do you think of this realm so far?'

'It's beautiful. You have two suns!'

'Actually we have seven, but the others haven't risen yet. There's one for every level. Up here we get them all.'

Janah sees me frown and leans his head to the side. 'It's all right, Matt. You're not expected to understand. There are many facets of this realm that will prove beyond your comprehension. Like this, for example.' He grips my hand again, but this time his hand goes partially through mine.

It surprises me. 'Hey!'

'Everything here is real and solid in form, if that is what we desire, but there is a freedom in our bodies and especially our minds. You'll see what I mean in a minute, when we start our journey.'

'OK. I don't know how I would find my way without you.' I wave my arm around the magnificent countryside. 'This place looks endless. Are you the only one who lives here?'

He laughs, but there is no condescension in his eyes, only a reflection of his obvious inner contentment. 'Many people live here. In fact, a couple of friends of yours only recently arrived. I believe you knew them as John Wren and Sera.'

'Really? Will I see them?'

'Not this visit. But rest assured, Sera is very happy.'

'And John Wren? Is he happy too?'

'John is on a different level.'

'What does that mean? Is that good or bad?'

'Here, there is no bad. Remember I told you there are seven levels to this realm?' He waits for me to acknowledge. 'Well, John is on the first. When he's ready he'll move to the next level and so forth. Probably in a few thousand years from now.'

I can't help frowning again. Janah shakes his head. 'Don't try to understand, Matt. That's not why you're here. Dartemis is waiting for you in his palace.'

'Who is this Dartemis?'

'All will be explained in due course,' Janah replies.

'Is this palace we're going to far away?' I ask.

He taps the side of his head lightly. 'What's that mortal measurement for distance again?'

'Kilometres.'

'Ah yes. You are ninety billion kilometres from your destination.'

For a second I'm completely speechless. 'Are you serious?'

'Absolutely.'

My thoughts grow confused. I glance up towards the hill I just rolled down. If I were to run up there as fast as my legs can move, would there be a chance Arkarian could take me back? I start to move away.

'Janah, I'm afraid I can't stay. To cover ninety billion kilometres would take more than my lifetime – a thousand of my lifetimes!'

He touches my arm and I feel peace flow through my body. 'But not in this world, Matt. Trust me.'

I guess I don't have any choice.

His touch on my arm turns into a solid grip. 'Come with me, Matt.'

'Where are you taking –?' I don't finish the question as I realise Janah's feet are no longer touching the ground. He has lifted – literally – off the surface of this world.

Janah's body tilts further in the direction he is tugging my arm – an effortless motion, as if his limbs are now made of a malleable substance and not bone. 'We should leave now. You're expected for dinner.'

'Janah, wait.'

His feet come back down to touch the soft grass.

'I'm not … like you. I don't live here. The rules of this world don't apply to me.'

He simply smiles. 'Did your Trainer not teach you how to clear your mind and find your central focus?'

'Well, he tried.'

'Do it now, Matt.'

I close my eyes and try to appear to be doing what he says. The truth is that every time I tried with Ethan, I never completely succeeded. I knew it frustrated him no end, and so sometimes I *pretended* to achieve this ultimate moment of inner peace and stillness of mind. I draw on the calmness emanating from Janah's touch.

To my surprise I feel myself lifting. I open my eyes to check. I'm hovering just above the ground!

Janah looks on with amusement. 'Well, it's not much, but it will do.' He moves his hand to my elbow and with a gentle upward thrust, my body tilts sideways.

And then we're moving. Beneath me the grassy fields begin to skim past. We remain close to each other, our bodies almost horizontal to the surface, and for a while I can see the landscape below. We lift higher and pass over many mountains and valleys, so many that I lose count. A city comes into view on the horizon, with lots of people in and about it. The buildings are multilevelled, and appear as if they are part of the landscape, woven among the trees, with golden bridges that float from one collection of buildings to another. There's an abundance of creeks and waterfalls everywhere. And then a third sun crests the horizon – this one purple. The shimmering colours in the sky shift and change again with purples and pinks added to the streaming mix.

Soon we're travelling at such speed that below and above me become a coloured blur. There's a lightness in my body that is difficult to explain in earthly terms. I still feel solid and real, but it's as if inside I am nothing but air.

Eventually we start to slow. The time draws nearer to meeting the one person who can give me the answers to the mystery of my birth. As we slow right down, an unsettling sensation hits my stomach. What if these answers are life-changing? Is Isabel right to have fears about this journey? Is her fear generated from love, or has she seen something in one of her visions?

We stop and all questions fly from my head. It's enough to cope with just taking in the sight that stretches out before me. There's a building, an incredible palace, made up of what must be at least a thousand rooms. It's mostly white, with gold and silver turrets, arches, columns, shimmering crystal windows and an array of gold-framed doors. But it's not even this splendour that has me stunned and staring in awe. It's *where* this palace is sitting. Though 'sitting' isn't the right word. It can only be described as *hovering*. Hovering, that is, at the very end (or is it the beginning?) of the universe.

I take a breath and try to slow my racing thoughts. But it doesn't help. I shuffle my feet, just checking the ground is solid beneath me. Over where the palace is hovering there is no ground at all. Nothing. It's like this incredible building is floating off the edge of the universe. Around it there is no sky, no suns, no stars. Maybe even no air.

'I've never seen anything like it.'

'It's incredible, isn't it?'

125

'Who would live out there? Will you tell me now who this man is?'

'You already know his name is Dartemis. He is an Immortal. One in a set of triplets born to the ill-fated Gods Athenia and Artemis.'

'Then he is Lorian's brother.'

'And Lathenia is their sister. But she thinks Dartemis is dead, slain by Lorian many millennia past. And so that she does not detect his presence, Dartemis lives out there.'

'Outside the universe.'

'Yes. Now come. Look.' Janah points up ahead to where a man dressed in a white suit is standing at the palace doors. 'He is ready for you. As I understand it, he's very excited.'

'To meet *me*?'

'Yes. Don't you know, Matt?'

'Know what?'

Janah explains, 'You are the culmination of his entire life's work.'

That's what Arkarian hinted at. That this Immortal has lived his whole life waiting for me to turn up. But why? Why me? The earlier spinning in my head is back again. This is all too much to take in. The air grows thin around me. I breathe in as much of it as I can. It has no effect. Everything keeps spinning, swirling away and then back again. Janah must notice my distress; I hear him call out something. I think it's my name. And then I am cradled in someone's strong arms and I feel myself moving.

I wake inside the palace, lying on a couch with a damp cloth across my forehead.

'He's stirring, my lord,' Janah's voice says through the

fog in my brain.

'Let him rest now, Janah. Leave us.'

'Yes, my lord.' Janah takes the cloth from my face and leaves the room.

I look up and straight into the eyes of the Immortal. I have only seen Lorian once, at my sister's recent trial, and the likeness between the two brothers is distinct. They are both taller than any human, with unusually long fingers and the same luminescent skin and eyes that could have been shaped from a precious stone. But where Lorian's eyes are violet in colour, and I'm told Lathenia's are silver, the pair looking at me now are yellow. Yellow-gold.

'Are you my father?'

He laughs, and the sound is hearty and strong. 'You like to get right to the point, don't you, Matthew?'

Actually, it just seemed to pop out. But now I've gone and asked it, I do want to hear the answer.

He laughs again, a little more subdued this time. He must be reading my thoughts. I wonder if he's a Truthseer?

'Yes,' he says.

'Yes?' Now I'm confused. Was he answering 'yes' to my thoughts or to the question I asked out loud?

'Both,' he replies. 'And now that the formalities are over, we can begin your training. That's what you're here for. And we can't waste any more time, Matthew. My sister is in a hurry to conquer all that she can, all that doesn't belong to her. She is upsetting the balance of life. The result will be catastrophic for all creatures that roam the earth, and it is up to you to ensure this doesn't happen.'

'But, this all sounds ... horrific.'

'It is horrific. What you have on the earth is precious. It cannot be found in any other realm. And believe me, Matthew, there are many, many realms. Some are light, some are dark, some are grey, where the lost and disenchanted wander. And then there are those that no one would want to see. You have been to the underworld. It was once a beautiful realm. Now it is one of darkness, where the most horrid creatures of the universe live deep within its bowels. But the earth ...' He leans forward, his gold eyes piercing mine, making me feel as if I am being swallowed whole. 'The earth is the last of the living.'

I look around the room for a moment, trying to absorb what he's saying, when a pair of lions appear at an open doorway, one male with an incredible golden mane, the other female. Instinct has me bringing my feet up underneath me on the couch. They stroll in as if they're well used to moving around the place. When they get to Dartemis the male gives a low, almost mournful roar. Dartemis urges it to come even closer, then strokes it behind its ear, crooning comforting words.

'I would never forget you,' he whispers, his head bent right down to the massive lion's face. The lioness nudges her partner out of the way and sticks her muzzle in Dartemis's hand, seeking attention. Dartemis grabs both sides of the lioness's head and gives it a shake. 'I missed you too,' he says. 'But I'm busy, and you will have to wait for my attention. Now off you go and find Janah. He'll give you something to eat.'

The big cats leave, and I try to drag my jaw off the floor, and my thoughts back to what we were talking about. Dartemis does it for me.

'Here, in this realm, we have the ultimate contentment

of our hearts. But you can't reside here until you have first lived a mortal life. And because the earth is the only place left where that is possible, if Lathenia is successful, the last remaining realm to provide balance to the universe will be destroyed. The dead will walk among the living and the goal of attaining true peace will never eventuate.' His arms swing out towards the shimmering sky and sweeping lands of breathtaking beauty. 'Eventually all this will also be threatened.'

His explanation leaves me speechless. How can this happen? How can this be happening to *me*? It seems like only yesterday the most serious thing I had to think about was my next assignment, and when it was due.

'It's a lot to take in. And Matthew, you have a lot of doubts. Unfortunately, I can't rid you of those. But I will draw out the powers that are already within you. It should help you to believe. But like all humans, it will be up to you to use them of your own free will. I will guide you, Matthew, but that is as far as I will go.'

From somewhere deep inside, my voice finally returns, 'Sir –'

'Wait. Since you are uncomfortable with the term *Father*, call me by my name, Dartemis.'

'All right – *Dartemis*. I need to tell you something.'

'For your benefit you may say it with words.'

'I think you have made a mistake.'

A smile appears on his face, and I think he is playing with me. 'Tell me my mistake.'

'I'm not the one for this job. In fact, I don't even think I'm your son. You see,' I go on quickly before he stops me, 'I come from a small town in Australia called Angel Falls. I have a regular mother and everything. And well, there are a lot of people down there who have exactly

129

the kind of "special" talents you think I have. Arkarian, for instance. I think he could be the one you really want.' I take a deep breath. 'What I'm trying to tell you is that I'm not the leader type. I'm no hero. I don't have the skills you think I have. Believe me, I've tried to find this inner source of power, or whatever it is, but really, it's not happening. You see, it's just not there. So,' I get up and look around for a door, preferably in the opposite direction to the way the lions went, 'if you don't mind, I'll just be going now. I don't suppose there's a shortcut out of this place?'

Dartemis suddenly disappears, reappearing directly in front of me, his chest in my face. I lift my eyes, tilting my head right back to see into his eyes. He is staring at me with his mouth slightly open and a frown between his brows. A deep frown. Suddenly his head shakes from left to right and back again repeatedly, as if he can't believe what he's hearing. Finally he speaks, but his words are not directed to me exactly, more of a general grumble.

'There is more work to be done here than I first thought. So much more.'

Chapter Twelve

Rochelle

School opens again on Friday. Friday! For heaven's sake, what would one more day have cost them? Apparently the scientists have all that they need. They moved in quickly and carted all the space debris back to government labs. After some minor repairs, all but one building has checked out all right. So training Neriah today will have to be done after school.

Mr Carter takes us for history and is inundated with a barrage of questions over his apparent 'miracle' escape. He handles them well, laughing off most of the class's questions while answering just enough to satisfy their curiosity.

While Mr Carter fends off the questions, Dillon lets me know he wants to come to Neriah's training session this afternoon. He's sitting directly behind me and keeps shoving his thoughts into my head. It feels like he's sticking a hot poker into my brain. Dillon isn't a Truthseer, but he obviously knows I am, and his forcefulness is really starting to bug me.

Over the last few days Lady Arabella has found time to help me control the power in my hands, enough so that now I don't feel like a danger to all and everybody. It's all got to do with my emotions and adrenaline and stuff like that. The gloves Arkarian made me were her design, constructed from impenetrable fabric she produced herself. They're great because they look just like skin. And Arkarian is helping me learn to control the onslaught of thoughts that have been driving me crazy since the enhancing of our powers. But even so, Dillon manages to break through all my barriers, and it's driving me crazy!

As soon as class ends we file outside and I turn on him. 'What the hell are you doing?'

He shrugs and gives a boyish grin that some girls might think is cute. I don't. My head is sore.

'You gotta help me, Roh. You're my ticket to Neriah. She'll listen to you. Tell her what a great guy I am.'

I would scream if it didn't attract unwanted attention. I should tell him that if he needs a third party to explain what a 'great guy' he is, maybe the girl isn't interested enough to notice for herself.

We start walking to our next class, and, great, Dillon's got the same one. He follows me all the way to the science lab. At the door I turn and face him. 'First of all, I don't do anybody's dirty work for them. You want Neriah, you make that happen yourself. And secondly, my name's Rochelle, pronounced Ro-shell, and not any other form or variation. Got that?'

By the time the final buzzer sounds for the day, I'm ready to pull my hair out. Dillon comes running over. 'Roh, I need you!'

I stare at him as hard as I can. He hasn't even the courtesy to remember that I don't like my name shortened. And I thought I made it clear I'm not going to plead his case for him with Neriah. He's ignoring that too. Does he find it impossible to hear anything except his own thoughts?

I walk out of B Block and look around for Neriah and Ethan. I see them at last, walking across the courtyard together. They look like a couple, and the sight makes me feel as if my ribs have shrunk. Neriah spots me and gives a wave. Beside me Dillon sighs and moans like a love-sick puppy.

'I'm beggin' you, Roh. Tell me where you're training today.'

I need to get him off my case, and then I think of a way that just might do it. 'All right. We're training inside Arkarian's chambers.'

It works. He says, 'No way!'

'Yeah, in one of his training rooms.'

'But his chambers are off limits to me.'

'Really?' I try to disguise my sense of relief, smothering it in a tone of astonishment, even though I already know this. Arkarian told me so only this morning.

'Yeah, I haven't been given clearance at that high a level yet. It won't be long, but …' He peers at me sideways. 'You have clearance, don't you?'

'So?'

'So you can smuggle me in.'

I can't help but laugh at this.

He takes offence immediately. 'What's so funny?'

I try to calm down. 'You can't get anything past Arkarian. It's like he has eyes everywhere and can see everything. And he controls the door. No one gets in without his permission. Your idea is ludicrous. And you shouldn't be thinking of doing things like that, especially if you want everyone to trust you.'

'Hey, I can be trusted. You want to take an issue with that?'

133

'Of course not! I was just giving you some advice.'

'I don't need your advice. Just help me get to Neriah. What do you say, Roh? Will you do it for me? For old times' sake?'

This last part has my blood simmering. What does he think? That because we both used to work for the Order of Chaos, we owe each other something? My loyalty is not to the Goddess any more, and certainly not to Dillon! Fortunately I'm saved from having to answer, as Neriah and Ethan make it over.

'Are you coming training with us again, Dillon?' Neriah casually asks.

Maybe she *is* interested in him. I glance sideways, wondering what it is about Dillon that might arouse a girl's interest. Probably his vivid green eyes. They're his best feature for sure. Suddenly he smiles. Yeah, there's that too, I guess.

Ethan glances at me with a frown. His thoughts let me know he thinks I'm the one who invited Dillon to come along. I open my mouth to explain, but shut it quickly when Neriah says, 'We're going to the field on the western side of the falls.'

Oh, just great. Thanks, Neriah.

Dillon's eyes shift sideways to mine. 'But I thought …' He doesn't finish. Instead, he looks at me as if I just put a knife in his back. 'Really? That's interesting.' He turns his attention back to Neriah. 'Of course I'll be there.'

'Actually,' Ethan suddenly says, 'we've had a change of plans.'

'But …' Neriah starts, then quickly stops. 'Of course, that's right.'

'We're training inside Arkarian's chambers today.'

Relief floods through me. I try not to make it so

134

obvious. But at least now I won't look like a conniving liar, just trying to throw Dillon off the track. Lady Arabella obviously trusts Dillon; that should be enough for me too.

Dillon acts all hurt and innocent. In some warped way it's kind of cute. His playful tone makes Neriah laugh. Eventually he remembers his bus is about to leave and takes off. I start to breathe easy for the first time all day.

'Your car's here,' Ethan says, and we walk Neriah to the car park.

'Meet you there in half an hour,' she says as she climbs into the back seat of the black Mercedes and greets her dogs.

When her car drives off I mumble softly, 'Thanks for that.'

Ethan keeps his eyes on the Mercedes as it leaves the school grounds. 'For what?'

For a moment I forget that Dillon and Ethan are friends – have been since kindergarten or maybe even before. I shrug my shoulders. 'Dillon can be distracting. I don't want him watching you guys train. I'd rather he wasn't there.'

His eyes shift to mine, his frown intense. 'I thought you liked him hanging around. Isn't that why you invite him to come with us so much?'

I can't believe what he's saying! 'I've never invited him. OK?'

'OK, but …'

'But what?' I ask when he pauses.

'I've seen you two walking around the school, hanging together between classes and during lunch. You look,' his eyes flick away for a second, 'like you're enjoying his company.'

135

His words leave me speechless. Firstly, he couldn't be more wrong. 'We have a few classes together, that's all.' I would really like to pick up Ethan's thoughts right now, but I don't dare, and, well, he's not projecting them. He's screening them as hard as he can.

He runs a hand through the top of his hair suddenly and starts to move off. 'We better go. Neriah is so keen, there's no way she'll be even one minute late. We don't want her hanging around waiting for us alone.'

I doubt that would happen. Her chauffeur William is a trained guard. He's hardly likely to leave her alone on an isolated mountainside deep in the national park. But I follow Ethan anyway, and try to put his strangeness out of my mind.

We leave the school grounds through the back gates, quickly making our way up to where Arkarian's chambers are hidden.

We're quiet as we wade through snow gums and other eucalyptus trees that predominate this part of the forest. It grows darker as we head into thicker growth.

A sudden movement to my right catches my attention. I stop for a second to listen.

'What is it?' Ethan asks, coming up beside me.

'I don't know.' I point to where a narrow creek runs down an embankment. 'I heard something over there.'

As we peer in the direction of the trickling water, a similar sound from behind us has us both spinning around. 'There, look!' I point to a four-legged creature slinking away through the trees ahead. 'I think that's the same animal I saw in Neriah's yard.'

'Let's check it out,' Ethan says, and we take off after it.

We run through the forest, yanking vines and bushes out of the way, leaping over fallen logs and being careful not to trip on the moist leaves, moss and mulch lying around.

'Up there!' Ethan leaps over a fallen tree. 'It's a dog – a Great Dane.'

We run further and further into the forest, but the dog stays ahead of us the whole time. We get to the top of a rise and finally stop, panting with exertion, only to find the dog peering at us from over its golden shoulder. Its eyes give me the creeps. It's as if it is using them to communicate with us. Or … to laugh at us.

And then I understand what it's doing – luring us deeper into the forest, just keeping ahead enough to entice us further.

'Oh, hell,' Ethan says beside me. 'I've seen that dog before. It's one of Lathenia's hounds.'

'It distracted us.'

We look at each other and his thought clashes with mine. 'Neriah!'

We run back the way we came as if our feet are on fire, clawing at the forest growth that gets in our way, leaping over fallen logs, tree stumps and meandering creeks. Neriah's in trouble; I feel it in every one of my bones.

Finally we break free of the forest and head straight up the mountain. We get to the secret door of Arkarian's chambers. He forms before us, looking very worried.

'Good, you're here.'

'Where's Neriah?' Ethan asks.

'Still at home. There's trouble there. They need our help. Ethan, you and I will use our wings. Rochelle, you make your way over as fast as you can. Jimmy, Dillon and Isabel are on their way now. Are you both clear?'

'Wait,' Ethan says. 'I'm not going to use my wings.'

'But, Ethan, it's the quickest way. You're not still having trouble using them?'

'No. But we saw one of Lathenia's hounds in the forest. I'm not going to leave Rochelle alone with that thing lurking around.'

'I don't need you to protect me!' I tell him, then add, 'I know a shortcut that won't take me long.'

'Where is this shortcut?'

'It's the old fire trail that runs around Devil's Ridge. It links up to the western side of Neriah's place.'

'Yeah,' he says sarcastically. 'I know the one. It runs straight through the thickest part of the forest.' Ethan makes it sound as if this shortcut only proves his point.

Arkarian glances from me, back to Ethan, but remains quiet.

I try to put an end to this ridiculous discussion. 'We're wasting time arguing, when you and Arkarian could be there already.'

'I'm not leaving you,' Ethan says stubbornly. And for a second I let myself think he's doing this because, well … maybe he does have …

Then he says, 'That hound was trying to lead us into the forest, whether to distract us from coming here, or because Lathenia has something else planned, I can't say. But I do know that since you defected, Lathenia would love to see you dead. And so would Marduke! They would probably torture you first.' His shoulders lift in an offhand manner. 'If you go off on your own, you become easy pickings. The Guard doesn't need to lose any of its members right now. The situation is critical as it is.'

'You're right, Ethan,' Arkarian says. 'You two follow as quickly as you can. Now be careful.'

With these instructions Arkarian uses his wings and

disappears. Ethan and I are left alone. I shrug off my confused emotions and start moving towards the forest. Ethan catches up and we quicken our pace. We're both relatively fit – it's part of the job. So at this rate, we should be there in only a short time. So far at least there's no sign of that Great Dane that Ethan says is one of Lathenia's hounds. While I was one of the Goddess's soldiers, I worked solely for Marduke and rarely saw Lathenia. All the same I have heard of her seven hounds. I thought they were in an eternal sleep. The story that circulated among her soldiers was that there was once a litter of nine pups that belonged to Lathenia's younger brother, Dartemis. They were devoted to him. Then one day he was murdered and the two eldest pups disappeared off the face of the earth, or wherever the immortals lived in those days, while Lathenia raised the remaining seven.

With this story still going round in my head I miss the first sign of trouble. But Ethan, just slightly ahead of me, doesn't. He stops and throws an arm in the air. I close in quietly behind him.

'What is it?'

He doesn't get a chance to answer. Suddenly, from among the tops of the trees, a dozen large birds swoop down towards us, shrieking wildly. They have a ghostly look and give me the creeps. Especially their eyes. They don't resemble normal birds' eyes at all, but rather, human ones, including the ridge of their brows, giving their faces a strange human resemblance.

Ethan grabs my arm. 'I know these birds. Take cover!'

We find a fallen log, but the cover is paltry. Ethan starts to close his eyes, probably to create an illusion, but the birds are on us too quickly. They have sharp beaks, so sharp they pierce through my black wool coat without any trouble.

'Oh no, you don't!' I scream at several of them that are trying to get at my eyes. Keeping my head down, I yank off my gloves and grab one by the throat. My hands practically sizzle with the energy generating in them. The bird shrieks and falls to the ground. It looks dead, but I can't be sure.

Ethan glances at me, his head nodding. 'Nice work. Try to keep them off me for a few seconds, will you. That's all I need.'

While Ethan sinks to the ground I whack one bird after another as they fly down and try to attack us. It's hard work because my hit only stuns them for a few seconds and then they get back up again. Only the one that had my hand around its throat hasn't moved.

'Are they invincible?' I ask.

'Remember what Arkarian said – they're already dead and can't be killed by human hands.'

My eyes drift to the motionless one with the scald marks around its throat. I guess my hands aren't 'normal' any more. But if Ethan is right, how on earth are we going to get away from them? One suddenly latches its claws around the back of my coat collar and starts digging its beak into the exposed skin at the back of my neck. The jerk is painful; the bite goes deep. Warm sticky liquid oozes down my back.

'Hurry, Ethan. I can't hold them off much longer!'

The sound of more wild shrieking fills the air. Another dozen birds fly down from the trees. Now there are so many there's no way we can get through this. Ethan starts to get up.

'No, stay down,' I tell him. 'There are more.'

But he gets up anyway, and that's when I realise the second lot of birds are Ethan's invention. They start attacking their own kind.

Satisfied that his illusion is working, Ethan pulls on my arm. 'Let's go!'

We take off at a run and soon the sound of the shrieking birds recedes into the distance.

'How long will your illusion last?'

'Long enough if we move fast.'

But I'm not sure how long I can keep this pace up. I think that bird at the back of my neck earlier hit deeply. My back is soaked with blood now, and I'm feeling weaker by the second. If only I could stop the blood pouring out so quickly. But my heart is pumping hard and that's definitely not helping.

We run and keep running until at last we see the high brick walls of Neriah's fortress. I fall against the wall and try to catch my breath. Ethan notices. 'Are you all right? You're white as a ghost.'

'I'm fine. Just keep going. They need you in there.'

'They need you too. Are you sure you're all right?'

'Yeah, go. I'll catch up. I just need to get my breath back.'

He looks reluctant and I wave him away. But he doesn't move. And suddenly someone is coming. My eyes are starting to glass over and it's difficult to make out exactly who it is. Now she's up close, and her arms come around me, dragging me to the ground.

'Where is she hurt?' Isabel yells at the top of her voice. 'Where, Ethan? Tell me!'

'I … I don't know. I didn't know she was hurt.'

'My neck,' I whisper.

Isabel pulls back my collar. 'Oh … look at that!'

'What is it?' Ethan comes over. 'How bad is she?'

'Quiet, Ethan. Let me work.'

For the next few minutes there is nothing but silence and a strange sense of a probing invasion into my body. But the probing has a subtle, gentle feel. Very quickly I start to feel stronger and my eyes focus again. I see Ethan staring at me in a state of shock, but there was no way he could have known I was in trouble. I'm not in the habit of crying out with pain. I never have been.

Isabel starts to help me up. 'How does that feel?'

Amazingly, I feel absolutely normal again. 'Thank you.'

She smiles. 'We'd better hurry. Arkarian, Dillon and Jimmy are trying to keep the house safe, but it's nothing short of a living hell in there.'

Chapter Thirteen

Matt

I've been here for seven days and seven nights and the only thing I've been practising is meditation.

'You have to reach a place within your soul,' Dartemis explains – *again* – while sitting on an opposite sofa. 'And you can only achieve this when you are completely still, completely empty, and the route to getting there has been effortless.'

I can't help shaking my head. 'I've tried. It's hopeless.'

'I could take you to this level, Matthew, and we can begin your training, but because you won't have reached this point through your own means, you will have learned nothing. Now close your eyes.'

I do what he says, but really, I can't see how this is going to work – the learning, I mean, the reason I'm here. If I can't relax, close my mind to all the thoughts going around up there, then what's the point?

'Close your eyes, Matthew.'

And that's another thing. Why does he call me Matthew? I can't remember anyone else ever calling me by my full name.

'Because Matthew is what I named you.'

My eyes fly open. 'Were you at my birth?'

He doesn't answer at first. 'The details of your conception and ultimate birth are complicated. And in your present … mind-state of self-doubt, you would not understand, or believe, and I would be wasting important learning time.'

'But I have a right to know!'

He leans forward, elbows on his knees, his wide, oval-shaped eyes narrow and contemplative. 'It became necessary to create an immortal. My brother's earlier attempt had failed and it was decided I would try, even though it would mean leaving here for a brief flicker of time. I took the form of a human male and walked the realm of earth as a free man. It was not long before I met your mother. We were drawn to each other as if we were magnets. When she was with child I had to leave. It was not an easy decision, but the risks of remaining on the earth were too high. Lathenia had started to sense another immortal's presence. In fear that she would discover my existence, I had to remove all traces of our relationship from your mother's memory. The only thing I made sure she recalled was your name.'

I can't believe what he's saying. 'You used her!'

'I chose her. I loved her. And she loved me. Never doubt that, Matthew.'

I stare at him and he says in a softer tone, 'One day she will live here with me.'

'But she can't do that.' She would have to be dead, the thought comes unspoken. 'My mother is … in love with this man that lives with us.'

He smiles, and his whole face changes, illuminating from within. It's a secret smile, one that says he's unwilling to share any more secrets with me. Of course he's reading my thoughts as I think them. He sighs dramatically, as if

144

relenting against his will, then says, 'The Protector.'

'What did you say?'

'Jimmy is the protector of my family on earth.'

'Oh yeah? Well what about the man who came before Jimmy? Isabel's father. Was he one of your protectors too?'

'No. Now close your eyes, Matthew.'

'Wait! I have more questions.'

His eyes flutter closed for a second, as if he is only just hanging on to his patience. 'Go on.'

'If you are my father, then how come I don't look like you? Your skin is kind of see-through, and your eyes are … well, different. And you're really tall. I mean, so much taller than a normal person.'

His face breaks into a grin. 'You have fortunately taken after your mother's side,' he says, then adds, 'And who says you have stopped growing yet?'

The very thought makes me a little sick inside. 'No offence, Dartemis, but I don't ever want to grow as tall as you.'

'*Ever* is a long time,' he answers cryptically. 'We'll see.'

'You make it sound as if I'm going to live for a long time.'

His eyebrows lift. 'You are immortal. Doesn't that explain everything?'

'No. I don't understand. When I cut my hand, I bleed.'

'Yes, but your body repairs itself. The more severe your injury, the quicker the healing takes place.'

I nod, recalling my recent experience with a few sticks of dynamite. 'OK, so I'm going to live for a long time.' Well, so are Isabel and Arkarian. It won't be too bad.

'Isabel and Arkarian will live a mere fraction of your lifetime.'

'Well, I'm going to be lonely then, aren't I?'

His head tilts in a gentle, caring way. 'What sort of father do you think I am?'

Now he has my full attention. 'What are you talking about?'

'Before you leave here, I am going to give you a gift. A very special gift that you must give to one person.'

'That's a hell of a responsibility! How do I know I'll pick the right person?'

His eyes glow like fire. He stands up, and though he says nothing, I feel his anger shoot through every cell of my body. He continues to stare at me as I try to work out why he's suddenly so irate. Does he think I know nothing about responsibility? I've been responsible for my sister since her father ran out of our lives. And I've looked after my mother as well, until Jimmy came along!

We stare at each other for a long time, but I'll be damned if I'm going to be the first to look away.

After a while his head nods and his body relaxes. 'You will know, Matthew. You will know her by looking into her mind.' He sits again and adds, 'And when you give her this gift from me, remember not to mention my name. Now close your eyes. We have so much yet to cover.'

I take a deep breath and try to do what he says, but there are so many thoughts circulating in my head right now it proves impossible to relax. Dartemis sighs under his breath, but his tone is more soothing than angry.

'I will show you how to create magic,' he says. 'Of course, the magic I speak of is simply an extension of your powers. You will use it as a tool and sometimes a weapon. You need to learn magic, Matthew, for you cannot undo what you do not understand. During your time here I will show you many things.'

His voice has a warm timbre to it now that is easy to listen to.

'You will learn to command the elements.'

What is he saying?

'You will learn to move the winds and the waters of the earth, to create and extinguish fire, to mould mountains and valleys and rivers. And you will learn how to commune with the animals, and take the shape of any that you desire.'

Am I hearing him right?

'But these things of nature, Matthew, you will not do with magic spells and potions. You will do them with just a single thought from your soul. One thought.'

One thought?

'You will become invisible whenever you need to, and you will be able to create invisibility for others in your company.'

His words are difficult to absorb, yet they have a strange hypnotic effect. At last my heart rate starts to slow and my breathing comes in gentle effortless puffs. Eventually I give in to the incredible lethargy overcoming every one of my muscles.

It's as if Dartemis is speaking to me now from a vast distance. His words float across this ever-increasing void softly and slowly. He talks about life and the strength my powers have over the living.

For a long time I am unaware of my surroundings, of who or what I am, what I am doing, if I am hungry, tired or cold, whether it is night or day, or even if I am still breathing. I feel nothing except a sense that I'm floating and that my body is weightless, my mind empty. Time passes that could be minutes or hours or days.

Eventually I become aware of a disturbance below. A voice penetrates. A man's, but not Dartemis's.

'Sorry to disturb you, my lord.' Slowly I recognise the voice as that belonging to Janah. He sounds worried and my consciousness grows. 'But the news is grave.'

The sense that I'm floating starts to dissipate.

'Slowly, Matthew,' Dartemis warns.

But I'm new at this sort of thing. I open my eyes to see that it isn't a *sense* of flotation I'm experiencing. I really am floating! Almost to the ceiling.

But not any more!

I start to drop, and quickly hit the floor with a hard thump.

Dartemis winces, then turns his attention to Janah. 'What news?'

'Your sister has entered the middle realm and destroyed the white bridge.'

I scramble off the floor and rush over to where the two are standing. 'What does this mean?'

Dartemis glances at me with a frown between his brows. 'It means that the lost souls will never reach their true destiny. Tell me more, Janah.'

'My lord, Lathenia has opened a rift, forging a tunnel between the realms. Where the white bridge once stood, there is now a joining of the middle realm with the underworld.'

Dartemis whispers almost to himself. 'So now my sister controls the souls of the lost as well as the damned.' He glances down at me. 'Matthew, until I am satisfied, you will train day and night now. Do you understand?'

There's no mistaking the seriousness of his tone. A

148

shiver darts through me and I nod.

'Good, let us begin. Janah, leave us.'

'But my lord …' he starts, then hesitates. 'I have more news.'

The frown returns and Dartemis groans as if resigning himself. 'Tell me.'

'Marduke is attacking the fortress.'

'What fortress?' I ask, feeling nauseous all of a sudden, and not knowing whether it's from my recent floating experience or Janah's news.

He says, 'Neriah's fortress. It's where she lives with her mother under the protection of the Guard.'

'*What?*' I call out.

Dartemis rests his hand on my shoulder. I look up into his luminescent face. His golden eyes shimmer the colour of fire once more.

'Matthew,' he says. 'We must hurry.'

Chapter Fourteen

Rochelle

As the three of us stand at the gate to Neriah's fortress an unsteady opening forms in the protective barrier, closing behind us with that familiar sucking sound. My heart is pumping hard at the prospect of danger, yet not knowing what to expect. I have only seen this yard at night. It was creepy then and it's even creepier now, full of flickering shadows.

A sudden cracking sound from above draws my eyes to the dome, and then I understand the reason for this strange and eerie twilight. 'Look at that.'

'What the hell …?' Ethan takes in the scene overhead too.

The protective barrier is covered with hundreds of birds – the same kind that attacked Ethan and me in the forest. They outline the entire dome, making it visible. The birds are pecking away at the barrier with their sharp beaks, thumping it with their bodies. Others tear at it with their claws.

'They're almost through,' Isabel says.

Another cracking sound, then another further away. Squawking and shrieking sounds grow louder. Goose bumps break out over my skin. 'How long will the barrier last?'

Isabel starts to move. 'Arkarian thinks it won't be long. We have to get into the house, 'cause once the barrier is down, Marduke will be able to get in.'

Marduke? And the birds? *Hell!*

That eerie crackling sound, like the breaking of dozens of egg shells, quickly becomes one continuous roll.

'Run!' Ethan yells.

We take off, running as fast as we can towards the shelter of Neriah's house up ahead. But the path is long. Birds, a few at first, then dozens at a time, come pouring through the widening breach. And then the barrier gives away completely. It shatters and starts raining down over the top of us.

'The barrier's made of crystal!' Ethan screams out, then has an idea. 'Throw us your coat, Rochelle.'

I'm not sure what he wants to do with it, but I shrug it off anyway. He throws it horizontally over the three of our heads. It offers us some protection from the shattering crystal. But the coat is no barrier to the birds. They come pouring down, fighting each other to get to us.

Arkarian and Dillon appear by our side and start yanking the birds off our backs and heads and beating them with their bare hands. As well, Neriah's dogs, in their snow leopard form, come bounding down the driveway. They're quite magnificent to watch, graceful with the hint of incredible power. They leap high, and the birds they attack drop straight to the ground and remain motionless.

We make it to the front doors where Neriah and her mother beat back the birds trying to get in around us. At last the doors close and the snow leopards change back into dogs. But the squawking outside continues. The birds bang their bodies and wings against the walls, windows and rooftop. The noise is deafening. Aysher and Silos claw at the door, but Neriah orders them back and immediately they sit calmly by her side.

Arkarian looks around and spots one of the house guards. 'Any word from Jimmy?'

The guard replies, 'He's just about done.'

Almost simultaneously the entire outside surface of the house, including the walls, windows and rooftop, begin to buzz and glow softly. The birds screech and fly off as if burned, then return again, only to screech with such ear-piercing ferocity we all have to cover our ears. They lift off the house at last and settle in the branches of the trees in the yard.

Jimmy comes running into the room and heads straight for a window. They've been boarded up, but through a crack he can see where the birds have settled. He turns to us with a grin. 'It's working.'

Arkarian thumps his back. 'For the moment we have a reprieve.' He turns to Ethan and me. 'Good to see you made it here all right. No trouble with Lathenia's hound?'

Ethan shakes his head, then motions out the window. 'But we had trouble with those birds.'

'Were either of you hurt?'

Ethan's eyes shift sideways to me, but he stays quiet. I try hard not to pick up any more of his thoughts. I don't want to know what's in his head. He may not be adept at screening his thoughts all the time, but he sure knows when I'm reading them. It only makes him hate me more. And now that I have control over my Truthseeing powers again, I can safely stay out of his head for good.

Arkarian is still waiting for an answer.

'We're fine.'

'Good, now we have to act fast to get Neriah and Aneliese to safety.'

'So what's the plan?' Ethan asks.

'I can shift Neriah to the Citadel,' Arkarian explains, then turns to Neriah. 'You will be safe there until we decide where it will be best for you to live. But ...' He pauses, glancing at Neriah's mother for a moment. 'I can't take you, Aneliese. Only those with the powers of the Guard can endure the pressure of such a timeless zone.'

Aneliese touches her daughter's arm. 'You have to go, Neriah.'

Neriah turns to her mother with a wild look in her eyes. 'I'm not going to leave you! And besides, I want to stay. I want to help.'

'Your training's only just begun,' Arkarian reminds her. 'Your powers are still limited.'

'I'm fit and capable, Arkarian. And I can help in other ways too. I'm not going to let Marduke harm my mother!'

Arkarian says softly, 'I'm not doubting your ability, Neriah. But sometimes you have to give your trust over to others. It's what we do in the Guard all the time. And I'm asking you to do that now. You do trust me, don't you?'

'Of course! I know you would do anything in your power to protect us both, but if the situation becomes desperate ...'

She bites down on her lower lip as if she is trying to stop the rest of her words from rolling out of her mouth. I try to read her thoughts – nothing. But it's obvious she

153

has some sort of plan.

'Marduke would do you harm too, Neriah,' Arkarian makes sure she understands.

'I don't think he would.'

'What makes you so sure?'

'I'm his daughter, and he loves me!'

Everyone goes still at Neriah's display of emotion. Aneliese grabs her arm, knowing, like the rest of us, there's more going on in Neriah's life than she is telling us.

Arkarian says, 'You told us you haven't seen Marduke since his fight with Shaun.'

Looking reluctant to explain, she finally says, 'Sometimes he speaks to me.'

Aneliese's eyes grow wide and she shakes her head.

Before the questions come, Neriah quickly adds, 'But only in my dreams. He has spoken to me in my dreams.'

'Neriah, I know Marduke,' I try to explain. 'I know how he works.'

Dillon interrupts, 'Yeah, so do I! He's a madman who will stop at nothing to satisfy his appetite for revenge.'

Dillon's words seem to only prove her point. 'Exactly! He wants to take his revenge out on Mum. He will kill her!'

'Look, Neriah –' I start to explain, but Dillon interrupts me again.

This time Arkarian puts a staying hand to the front of Dillon's chest. 'Go ahead, Rochelle.'

'I worked very closely with Marduke. He can be very persuasive. I succumbed to his power of persuasion many times. He convinced me that I belonged to the Order because of my heritage, that it was my destiny, and that my soul belonged to the Goddess. When I looked at him I saw my own father. Sometimes I even saw my father's face, smiling at me in a way that I always longed for. And when Marduke praised me, it was as if my own father did.'

Except for the occasional squawk of a bird outside, I become aware of complete silence and everyone's eyes on me. I hate to open myself to their scrutiny like this, but Neriah has something dangerous planned, and I must try to stop her.

'You have to see that when Marduke comes into your dreams, he's trying to manipulate your emotions, just like he did with me. He is the Goddess's servant, the Master of her troops, and, until his fateful journey to the middle realm, her lover as well. Whatever she commands him, he won't hesitate to do it. Believe me, his loyalty to Lathenia will come before his love for you.'

Dillon scoffs loudly. 'Love! That creature wouldn't know what the word means.'

But Dillon doesn't know Marduke as I do. His loyalties and his passions run deep. He gives his all to everything he does, whether in servitude or in love. And he expects the same in return. He feels his losses deeply, and over his long lifetime he has lost plenty. 'I think he knows love only too well.'

There must be something in the way I say these words that creates a sudden tension in the room. Nobody seems to know where to look.

But our thoughts are suddenly interrupted by a loud explosion. It rocks the house, shaking the walls around us. Jimmy throws Arkarian a bag. Arkarian opens it and pulls out black masks. He throws us one each. 'Put these on to protect your identities.' They cover our entire heads, bar our eyes and mouths.

'Ethan and Rochelle, take Neriah and Aneliese into the tunnels,' Arkarian orders. 'Aneliese will lead you to the one that will take you to my chambers.' He turns to the others. 'Everyone else, come with me. We have to stall Marduke long enough for Neriah and Aneliese to reach safety.'

With Aneliese and the dogs in front, we run down a narrow flight of stairs, through a doorway, then descend another stairwell. Down this far, it's completely dark. Aneliese fumbles for a torch from a shelf to her right. Down the bottom is a door bolted with an iron bar and lock. Aneliese yanks a chain from her neck. There are several keys on it. She takes one and opens the lock. Ethan lifts the bar and the door creaks open.

The tunnel is made entirely of sandstone and bricks. Aysher and Silos leap off ahead like scouts, but stay within sight. Overhead we hear the sounds of rumbling thunder. It must be Marduke. It sounds as if a battle has started. It grows louder by the second. I hope they can hold him off long enough for us to get Neriah and Aneliese to safety. And I hope this tunnel isn't too long. I'll be glad when we get out into some fresh air and can take these masks off.

We run and keep running, the dogs leading the way. Then at last we slam to a stop. The tunnel has split into three.

We take a few deep breaths.

'Where do they end up?' Ethan asks as we stare down the three separate paths.

Aneliese explains, 'The left tunnel goes all the way to the northern entrance of the forest.'

'But that's …' I have a quick think.

'A long way,' Ethan finishes. 'What about the middle one?'

Aneliese shakes her head. 'It ends at a point almost dead centre at the bottom of the lake.'

The thought makes me frown. What would be the point of a tunnel that ends under a lake?

Aneliese must see the confusion on my face. She explains, 'It links up with an entrance to the underground city. But this tunnel is of no use to us. The entrance was sealed many years ago.'

'What about this one?' Ethan points to the tunnel on the right.

'That's the one we want. It will take us to Arkarian's chambers.' She rattles the keys in her hands. 'One of these will let us in.'

As we peer into the tunnel that leads to Arkarian's chambers an explosion rocks the walls. Dust surrounds us, making us cough. We glance at each other nervously. What's going on up there? We should be far enough from the house now not to hear the battle taking place. I get a sudden sickening sense in my stomach. Marduke is a formidable enemy. Coming face-to-face with him is something I'm dreading more than anything else in the world. But now I understand why Arkarian sent me and Ethan down here. It's our lives that are most threatened. Me for being Marduke's personal spy and turning traitor on him. And Ethan for putting the knife in his throat just over a year ago that resulted in his altered appearance.

'Let's go,' Ethan says.

But just as we start, another explosion hits, this one very close. The force of it catapults us backwards. The tunnels fill with dust and debris, so much that it becomes difficult to see and breathe, especially with dust clinging to the masks. Aysher and Silos clamber all over us, tugging and pulling on our clothes, getting us up.

As the dust begins to settle, one thing becomes clear – we won't be able to use the tunnel that leads to Arkarian's chambers. It no longer exists. It's completely blocked by a wall of shattered bricks and earth.

'Great,' I call out, trying to wave stubborn dust out of my face and find some clear air to breathe. 'What now?'

Aneliese looks uncertain, her soft brown eyes growing huge. 'I don't know. But we can't go back to the house.'

'Let's take the tunnel to the forest,' I suggest. 'We can eventually find our way to Arkarian's chambers, and at least we'll be out of this death trap.'

Without arguing, the others follow my lead. After a while, loud thumping sounds come at us from behind. We throw our backs up against the wall and stay silent while the thumping sounds draw closer. Suddenly Dillon runs past. He sees us and pulls to a stop.

'There you are!' He pinpoints Neriah, goes right up to her with a dreamlike expression in his eyes, and touches her arm. 'I was so worried about you.'

It's a sweet thing to say, but it takes Neriah by surprise. She's obviously unaware of his growing infatuation. She moves her arm away gently.

'What's happening to our house?' Aneliese asks. 'Is everyone all right up there?'

Dillon doesn't even hear her; his eyes – his whole attention – are focused solely on Neriah.

'Dillon?' I remind him. 'What's going on?'

'Marduke and some of his soldiers are destroying the house, one room at a time, looking for Aneliese.'

Neriah grabs her mother's arm. 'He won't stop until he finds you! Now is his chance.'

'We're going to make sure he doesn't come near either

of you,' Ethan says.

Dillon adds, 'Arkarian wants you to get to his chambers as fast as you can.'

'That tunnel's gone,' Ethan explains.

'So where does this tunnel lead?'

'Outside,' I explain.

'Did you pick it?'

I nod.

Dillon frowns, but ultimately agrees. 'OK. Let's go then.'

A rushing, flapping sound starts up in the distance, quickly followed by a shriek and squawk. All five of us look at each other with concern. The rushing sounds and shrieking grow louder and Ethan gets us going again. 'Let's get out of here!'

We take off, running as fast as we can, but the flapping of wings and wild shrieking close in on us with every step. I glance backwards and see a few of Marduke's birds catching up fast.

Ethan shoves me in front of him. 'Don't look back!'

We run and run, only just staying ahead of the birds. Eventually we come to a dead end. With nowhere to go, the three birds catch up and start attacking us with their vicious beaks and claws. The dogs change into snow leopards and help keep them back, but the birds are persistant.

At least one thing goes our way when Aneliese calls out, 'This is it!' She yanks on a trap door in the ceiling. 'This is the exit.' She reaches up to put one of her keys into the lock, but her hands are unsteady and she drops them.

The birds close in again and the set of keys is trampled under foot in the chaos. The flooring here is more dirt than bricks and the keys soon disappear. Hands everywhere try to search for them, making the task more difficult.

'Everybody stop!' I call out. 'I'll find them!'

I skim my hands across the surface of the floor. My gloves are still in my coat pocket somewhere back in the house, and so my mind zooms straight down through layers of rich black soil, sandstone and granite. I lift my focus and 'see' two-hundred-year-old bricks covered with a fine layer of trampled dirt.

'Here.' I hold up the chain with the keys dangling from it. Aneliese searches for my hand among the turmoil, but I pull it back before she connects and gets burnt. 'I can do it,' I explain, and start fitting one key after another in the lock.

Then the hatch is open and light floods in from the surface, blinding us momentarily. The birds are first to fly out. We follow quickly.

'Oh no!' Ethan mutters under his breath at the sight that greets us.

It's Marduke. Waiting patiently. Smugly. He has half a dozen soldiers with him, also masked, all dressed in black, with only their eyes showing. They have formed a circle around the exit, armed with knives, swords, spikes and other martial arts weapons.

'We're in trouble,' I mutter.

'Big trouble,' Ethan mutters back.

'Good work, Roh,' Dillon whispers sarcastically.

'Don't say her name!' Ethan hisses. He flicks a knife from his boot to his hand, then offers it to Dillon. 'Do you need this?'

Dillon shakes his head and pulls a whip chain out from his jacket pocket with one hand, a knife with his other.

'Well, look at what we have here,' Marduke says in his rough, sarcastic voice. 'Quite a collection, I would say.'

Marduke's eye drifts to Aneliese and glows bright red. She stares back and for an unguarded moment I hear her thoughts. She's recalling what Marduke looked like the last time she saw him and how much he has changed. She notices his face is still half missing, with one empty eye socket and jagged scars running down the length of his disfigured mouth. But now there is more of a beastly look in the encroaching growth of hair upon his brow.

Marduke's glare shifts to Neriah. And it is while he looks at his daughter that his chest expands and his glowing red eye swells. No mask will protect her identity from him.

Neriah tugs a dagger out from her belt and Aneliese does the same. I would too, as I always keep a knife in my boot, but lately my hands have become more dangerous than any weapon.

Marduke notices the flickering electric currents, and his one eyebrow lifts as he peers straight at my eyes. 'I knew there was more power in you. What we could do with those hands together – you and I.'

The very thought sickens me and a sarcastic reply quickly forms. But Ethan is quicker to react. 'You would have to kill me first.'

I stare at him but he doesn't look my way.

'That would be my pleasure,' Marduke replies, touching the sword at his waist. 'But since it is not the traitor I have come for today, I will let your tempting offer pass.'

Neriah says in an amazingly calm voice, 'We have an agreement in which you gave me your word.'

Aysher and Silos growl, their leopard teeth bared at Marduke.

161

Dillon pulls on her arm. 'What are you talking about?'

Neriah slides her arm out of Dillon's grasp. 'Leave me. I know what I'm doing.'

'Don't make the mistake,' I quickly explain, 'of believing Marduke honours agreements.'

Marduke laughs. 'But it is *you* who deceived me. Where do your loyalties lie? Does anyone here know?'

I try to ignore him. 'Hold on to Neriah,' I whisper to Dillon. 'She thinks she can trust him because he's her father, but she's wrong.'

Dillon agrees and takes a firm grip of Neriah's arm.

She pushes away from him and he tries to grab her again. Neriah looks around at us all frantically. 'You don't understand. If I do this, I can prevent your bloodshed as well as my mother's.'

Ethan hisses, 'Let us do our job. That's what we're here for. To protect the two of you from this madman.'

Marduke shrugs and looks amused. 'Are you going to protect Neriah in the same way you protected your sister?'

If I had the power to project objects I would take the knife right out of Ethan's hand and hurl it into Marduke's throat myself. But I know this beast, I know what he's trying to do.

'And what about how you protected Isabel?' he adds. 'As I recall, she took a walk into the middle realm because of your so-called *protection*.'

'Don't listen to him. He's just trying to rile you so you'll lose concentration.'

Ethan's eyes drop and slide in my direction, giving me the slightest nod. He understands, but it's also clear that Marduke's words have found their mark.

Marduke sees it too, and laughs. And with the

slightest motion of his head, he signals to his soldiers. They move in to attack, and the fighting begins.

Dillon and Ethan try to keep Neriah and Aneliese in their sights at all times, but it becomes difficult against the barrage bearing down on them. Dillon is strong, his kicks powerful, while his technique with the whip chain can't be flawed. He sends two soldiers flying, but they soon return for more.

Ethan wounds one of Marduke's soldiers in the shoulder, then finds himself on the ground as another comes at him from behind with a spinning baton. Meanwhile he uses his power to animate objects to deflect a series of throwing stars back at the soldier who cast them. A soldier comes at me with a shimmering dagger. While I'm reluctant to reveal just how powerful my hands are, I really don't have a choice. I let him run as close as I dare, then slice away his clothing from shoulder to chest with my knife. Focusing all my energy into my exposed hands, I lunge at him. My hands flicker brilliant colours. The soldier screams and falls to the ground whimpering.

Marduke notices. 'You have come far. Your talents are wasted here.'

I ignore him as best I can and hope that no one else is taking any notice. I couldn't stand it if they thought Marduke actually tempted me.

While we struggle against Marduke's soldiers, it's Aysher and Silos that gain the most ground. After making sure Neriah is coping with the soldier she's dealing with, they begin a powerful attack. One soldier struggles out from beneath Aysher, and, scared for his life, runs into the forest. The leopards then turn their attention to Marduke. They look threatening, and it's clear their aim is to take Marduke down where he stands. If any of us could do it, it would be them. With teeth bared they leap in his direction. Marduke sees them and throws his hands out. From his fingers a beam of green light shoots out towards them. Neriah screams and Dillon has to hold her back as the leopards take the brunt of Marduke's power and are hurled into the air. They hit the ground behind us, stunned.

We fight the remaining soldiers and, as Aysher and Silos start to come round, Marduke's amusement turns into annoyance.

Neriah whispers, 'We're winning! Everything is going to be all right after all.'

I don't want to kill her enthusiasm, but knowing Marduke, the fight's not over until his last soldier is annihilated and he has used every trick in his book.

My fears soon become a reality as Marduke reveals his irritation at his soldiers' incompetence. He raises his hands into the air again, and this time the green power that erupts from his fingers creates a wave of sizzling energy. It flickers and swells like a tidal wave, then whips around us with the speed of lightning, enclosing us in a dome-like prison.

Those of Marduke's soldiers that are still able, get up and stand beside him, looking relieved and somewhat smug, while Marduke maintains the pulsing dome of power with his outstretched hands.

Ethan and Dillon try to break free of our prison, but when they touch the light, it flings them back with the force of an electric shock.

'Any ideas?' Dillon mutters.

'He's going to release this field to get Neriah and Aneliese out. That will be our chance.' Heads nod at my hushed comment, and keeping Neriah and Aneliese behind us, Dillon, Ethan and I form a triangle around them. Aysher and Silos maintain their snow leopard shape and fall in among us.

Marduke tilts his head towards one of his soldiers. 'When I release the field, grab the woman. It's time Aneliese paid for stealing my child.'

Neriah hears this and screams out, 'No! You promised! Take me!'

Marduke gives a signal and two soldiers move towards the pulsing dome. Meanwhile Marduke keeps his eyes intent on Aneliese. Neriah sees this and starts to panic. She looks desperately at her mother, fear making her think only with her heart.

In a flash of understanding, I get what's going on. Marduke is being his conniving, manipulating self. It's his plan, and he's been hatching it for a long time, speaking with Neriah through her dreams, establishing a rapport. The worst part is Neriah has started to trust him. Marduke doesn't really want Aneliese. His plan is to get Neriah. And Neriah is falling right into his trap.

She breaks out from behind, shoving past me towards the green light vibrating and shimmering around us.

'No, Neriah!' I lunge and grab her arms, but as soon as my hands touch her skin, she screams and drops to the ground. I've burnt her, and instinctively I let her go.

In that same second she stumbles forward, so determined to get to Marduke that she crawls on her hands and knees through the opening in the dome. Just before she reaches Marduke, she turns back. 'Tell them not to come for me.'

Aneliese goes after her, but the opening in the dome closes, its green energy shimmering stronger than ever. Ethan grabs her, yanking her away just in time. Aysher and Silos growl fiercely, their eyes growing wild at the thought of their mistress on the other side with the enemy. Ethan tries to calm them, but they snap their heads left and right, warning us to stay away. Then they leap. My heart skitters at the thought of what will happen when the pulsing energy goes through them.

'No, don't!' I call out, wanting to go after them myself, but Arkarian's warning that I could kill an animal with my bare hands comes back to haunt me.

The leopards keep moving through the shimmering green field. They whimper helplessly as the power thunders through their bodies, their fur standing on end. But still they keep propelling themselves through it. And just as it seems that they're going to make it to the other side, their bodies start to break up, until there's nothing left but green shimmering air.

Suddenly the circle of energy disappears with a sizzle. We stumble out, searching, but all that is left are the outlines of Neriah, Marduke and his soldiers, as their bodies disappear.

Chapter Fifteen

Matt

When I return to the Citadel, Arkarian is there to meet me, his usually clear eyes strained and dark.

'I've called an urgent meeting in my chambers,' he says.

'Let's go, then.'

'First, I want to tell you what happened.'

'I've heard about Neriah,' I explain, saving time.

We appear in one of Arkarian's many side rooms. The others are already there. Some are seated in chairs that form a circle, much like the Tribunal circle, others are standing around talking. Dillon is here too. A new addition to our group. I wonder who approved his clearance into Arkarian's chambers? Probably Lady Arabella. She has been working with him the most. So now, though we are without Neriah, we're still nine.

'Matt!' Isabel sees me first. She starts to run over, then hesitates.

She's obviously concerned about recent events, just like everyone else in this room, but there's more in her eyes right now. A troubled, almost timid look. Something I'm not used to seeing in her. I know what the problem is: she thinks my journey to see Dartemis has changed me. Has it? I can't really say. I feel the same, only I know things now that I wish I didn't. Some things I've learned to do, I still can't believe. But my new powers are untried, and so much depends on my having perfected them. I hold my hands outward and try to joke.

'What? No greeting? I've been away for six whole months! Haven't you missed your brother?'

She grins and walks over. I can't stand that look of hesitation still lingering in her eyes; instinctively I pull her into my arms. She lays her head on my chest and squeezes me tightly. Holding on for a moment longer, she looks up. 'Actually, you've only been away seven days.' She pulls back and whacks my shoulder playfully. 'That's hardly worth a hug.'

For the next few minutes I'm greeted by the others, but the seriousness of this meeting soon has us all looking for a seat. Arkarian purposefully sits to my right, then nods at me. He wants me to run the meeting. Is he kidding? He sends me his thoughts. Between Truthseers, conversations can be held without speaking. He thinks I'm ready. Ready to start playing my role according to the Prophecy. I wish I had his confidence. I take a deep breath and it comes out like a sigh of resignation. In a way I guess that's how I feel. I may have developed my powers, Truthseeing being one of them, but I'm going to need a lot of practice before I feel confident using them.

Everyone is looking around uncomfortably. Arkarian's thoughts push me one step further. *It's time, Matt. Believe in yourself and take control. Show everyone in this room that you are our leader.*

I look around and wonder if I'm worthy to lead these people. Half of them are older than me. One is my teacher! There's Ethan's father, for heaven's sake!

Small steps. Arkarian's thought hits me, and I wonder what would be the first one. It helps take my mind off my inhibitions. It feels good to focus on something else, and suddenly I feel as if some space has freed up in my head. My eyes skim around the stone walls and earthen flooring. 'Is this room safe?'

Arkarian replies, 'All the rooms in my chambers are safe.'

'Can we be overheard by … *anyone*?'

'I can't guarantee that.'

I look around the room, surveying it for cracks and fault lines. 'I want everyone to keep their heads lowered until I tell you it's all right to look up.'

Without question, they do what I say. Using my new skills I flood the room with a blue light. But the light thickens like a dense fog and makes Dillon and Mr Carter cough. I blow gently into its centre, the idea being to create a clear inner sanctum in which we can talk and not be overheard. To my relief, it works.

'You can look up now.'

They look around, taking note of the way the mist appears to cling to the ceiling, walls and flooring around our feet.

'The room is protected,' Arkarian says softly. 'Nice work.'

'Thanks, but …' I stop myself. What is the use of letting everyone know how insecure I feel? If I'm going to have a chance at securing their belief in me, then I will have to at least *look* as if I believe in myself. Across from me I notice Dillon fidgeting. He can't stop tapping his feet, rubbing his hands through his hair, or cracking his knuckles. 'Before we start, do you have something to say, Dillon?'

'Yes!' He practically jumps off his seat. 'Have you heard? Marduke has Neriah!'

'I have heard, and we will get her back.'

'Whatever the plan, I want to go!'

I hold my hand up. 'Tell me what happened first.'

He scoffs loudly and points to Rochelle. 'She led us into a trap and then she let Neriah go!'

Rochelle gets to her feet and gasps. 'That's a lie!'

From beside her, Shaun coaxes Rochelle to sit down.

Dillon continues, 'She had Neriah in her hands, but let her go, straight into Marduke's arms!'

Rochelle raises a hand to her forehead as if the action will stop her brain from falling out.

'These are serious accusations, Dillon.'

'I'm telling the truth. Ask Ethan. He was there.'

'Let's hear from Rochelle first.'

She looks at me, her usual deep green eyes red and surrounded by dark circles. She holds her hands out in front and is unable to disguise a tremor. She stares at them as if they are alien parts and not her own flesh and blood. In the eighteen months that we were together, I never saw her this distressed. 'It was my hands that burnt her. As for the tunnel, I thought it was the right choice.'

Beside me, Arkarian says, 'You have your gloves on now. Where were they at the time?'

'In my coat pocket,' she says, 'back at the house. I didn't have my coat with me when we went through the tunnel. I went back and got them later.'

'How are your lessons going with Lady Arabella?' he asks.

Before she answers, Dillon jumps up, his whole body shaking with rage. 'You've had lessons to control them and you still burnt her?' He answers his own question with another accusation. 'I don't think so! You're still working for Marduke, aren't you?'

Ethan is up in a flash. 'Shut up, Dillon! No one has the right to accuse anyone in this room, do you hear? Rochelle is not on trial here!' He turns to face me. 'I saw what happened, and yeah, Rochelle let Neriah go. But it wasn't on purpose. Neriah screamed when Rochelle's hands touched her. Rochelle let go by instinct. And the tunnel was the only logical choice after the one to Arkarian's chambers was destroyed.'

In the silence Rochelle says softly, 'Things got really intense. I lost control.'

Dillon replies, 'Yeah, and we lost Neriah.'

'Then we will just have to get her back,' I try to reassure everyone. 'Now there'll be no more accusations made in this room.'

Dillon sits restlessly. 'All right, but you have to take me with you on the rescue mission.' His eyes shift to my right. 'Arkarian, make him take me.'

Silently, everyone waits for Arkarian to reply. His eyes flick briefly to me, but his words flow around the room addressing everyone. 'Matt makes all the decisions from now on.'

'Yeah?' Dillon asks, surprised. 'Well, whatever, I just want us to get Neriah back. OK?'

I try to ignore Dillon's persistence, though his passion for Neriah is harder to overlook. It will cloud his judgement, which could put any rescue mission in jeopardy. Yet … his passion makes him fearless, and that would be a strength, especially considering where we have to go.

In the silence Rochelle says, 'Neriah thinks that as long as she is with Marduke, her mother is safe and

171

there will be no bloodshed. She told me to tell you …'

She stops and I prod, 'Go on.'

She swallows deep in her throat. 'She said, "Tell them not to come."'

Dillon jumps up, ready to explode.

'Sit down, Dillon! Your protest has already been noted.' I turn to Rochelle. 'Do you think she is safe with Marduke?'

She doesn't even hesitate. 'No way!'

'Do you think we should rescue her?'

'Absolutely. And as soon as possible.'

From beside her, Shaun throws me the question, 'Do you know where Neriah has been taken?'

'She's being held prisoner in Lathenia's palace on Mount Olympus.'

'Oh, hell!' Dillon exclaims, then sends Rochelle another hate-filled look. 'Good work, Roh. Now how do you propose we rescue her from that hell-hole?'

Dillon's reactions are too intense. If he keeps this up, he will definitely be a liability to take along.

He gets up again and starts pacing the open area before him, his arms sweeping in a wide circle. 'You people don't understand. Getting into Lathenia's palace is next to impossible!'

'You sound as if you've been there.'

He finally stands still and looks to me. 'Yeah, well, I have. Believe me, it's a frozen fortress from hell.'

What is Dillon saying? 'A little more detail might help us understand your distress.'

'It has these high outer walls, made from impenetrable stone, marble and crystal. The whole place has a tight security system. Around-the-clock guards man the balustrades, with three in every watchtower on every corner. They have these weapons – crossbows. The darts are tipped with poison that kills in seconds. And if you somehow manage to get past the outer walls, there are Lathenia's hounds to contend with – seven of them. They're kept hungry and trained to attack anyone or anything that penetrates the inner walls. Oh, have I mentioned the witchcraft?'

This raises murmurs from around the circle.

'The whole place is booby trapped with magic spells and evil enchantments.'

'Thank you, Dillon. You can sit down now. I think we get the picture,' I say.

As he sits, I realise, even with his unstable emotions right now, I have no choice but to take him along. His knowledge of Neriah's prison is too valuable. Unless … I glance at Rochelle.

'What do you know of this palace, Rochelle?'

Her shoulders lift slightly. 'Nothing, really. I've never been there.'

'No, you wouldn't have,' Dillon says with spite. 'You were Marduke's *personal* assistant. He wouldn't want to share you with Lathenia.'

This comment sets emotions flaring all around the room. And while Ethan is first to jump up and condemn him for it, Dillon faces angry reactions from just about everyone else as well. Surprisingly, it's Mr Carter who makes his opinion known the loudest. 'That's enough, Dillon! You go too far!'

'What are you sticking up for *her* for? Everyone knows you don't trust her.'

'Trust is something that is earned. You should remember that.'

I hold up my hands to try to bring some order back

173

into the room. 'There are other things we have to talk about before we … before I decide who goes where. The first is the location of the missing key.'

Arkarian suggests, 'Why not search for it once we're inside Lathenia's palace?'

Heads nod in agreement.

'Because the key will not be found there.'

Questions come flying at me. When they quiet down I explain, 'It appears that Lathenia was not the one who took the key from the ruins of the temple.'

'It must have been the traitor,' Jimmy says. 'But who would have that power? It's a feat in itself to get in and out of that underworld.'

Arkarian asks softly by my side, 'Do you know where the key can be found?'

Silence. They wait. I remind myself not to mention Dartemis's name or to even project it in thought. 'I have been told to search for it in Athens.'

'The *palace* in Athens?' Jimmy asks in disbelief. 'But everyone we trust is there.'

Shaun adds, 'Whoever it is, the traitor has to be some-one who has the powers and clearance to access high-security areas as well as other realms.'

'Do you know who exactly is under suspicion?'

'Names were never mentioned,' I explain.

Isabel reaches across Ethan to touch my arm. 'We can't do this on our own. Is there anyone at the palace we can trust?'

I nod to reassure her. 'Our own King, Richard. He will help us.'

Everyone murmurs agreement.

When everyone quiets down, Arkarian asks, 'So what do we do now?'

I take a deep breath and hope that my decisions will be the right ones. 'Ethan, Isabel and Rochelle will go to the palace in Athens to bring back the key, and, hopefully, uncover the traitor. But, if identifying this traitor puts your own lives in danger, keep the name of this person secret and return to me.'

'If Lorian doesn't know the key is in his own palace, what chance do we have of finding it?' Ethan asks.

'Very little, but you are all resourceful, and Rochelle's hands will be invaluable.' I glance at her to make sure she understands, then realise I have things to say to her that are better not said out loud in case they're misconstrued. And so, using my new-found Truthseeing skills, I project my thoughts solely to her. *Don't think of your hands as evil weapons but as tools.*

My thoughts startle her and her eyes widen, but she remains silent. I go on quickly before the others become uncomfortable and possibly resentful at our silent communication. *There is a vast power that can yet be developed in them. Work on it, and don't be afraid. Just be careful.*

I turn to the others, quickly drawing their attention. 'Arkarian and Dillon, you will come with me to Lathenia's palace to rescue Neriah.'

Dillon has a typical reaction, practically jumping out of his skin. 'Yes!'

Jimmy looks across to me. 'Matt, I'm not sure if you're aware of my talents –'

'I've been briefed.'

'Then you must see that I could be of great service to you in that palace.'

Jimmy's words bring a silent groan to my throat, which I try to swallow down. While the two of us have never got along, and I've been resentful of his presence in my home, Dartemis holds Jimmy in the highest regard. That will have to be enough for me.

'Right now your talents are more needed here at home,' I say. And to all of them I explain, 'Lathenia has gained control of the middle realm. She has increased her army to include the souls of the lost. As you know, creatures of the dark world are already appearing on the earth. We have to do all we can to keep them from making human contact.' I look back at Jimmy to make sure he understands the mission I am assigning him. 'There is a real threat to Veridian. If the ancient city is infiltrated, the situation could be devastating for us. Jimmy, go down there and fortify it. Find a way to protect it, should the worst happen. Bring me a plan. There is more to the city than what you see when you walk along its corridors and paths.'

'I'll do my best.'

'What do you want me to do?' Shaun asks.

'With Arkarian gone, you have to watch the sphere. Lathenia is planning something huge, something that will have a devastating effect on the present and the future. Watch for signs of a portal opening. When it happens, we will have to get a team in there quickly.'

There is only one person left.

'And me?' Mr Carter asks.

'Marcus, you're needed in the Citadel. With six of us travelling through time, your co-ordinating skills are going to be essential. You're going to have to be more accurate than you've ever been before.'

Chapter Sixteen

Rochelle

Mr Carter drops us directly in the middle of that now familiar golden courtyard within the palace walls in Athens. It's night and the evening air is warm. Behind us, birds are singing, a melody of sharp clear notes. I spin around to see what breed could make such a pure, yet mournful sound. Even though their voices are the sweetest I've ever heard, it does nothing to prepare me for the actual sight of them. Beautiful beyond words, they take my breath away.

Isabel comes up beside me. Her eyes also become glued to the pair of lovebirds sitting side-by-side on a perch made of wood from an olive tree. 'Have you ever seen anything so exquisite?'

'Never,' I mutter back.

Ethan comes over. 'What are you looking at?' Then he sees them. 'Whoa! Are they real?'

'They sound real enough,' Isabel replies as the pair pick up another melancholy tune.

An urge comes over me to lay my hands on the cage. I get the feeling that if I did, I would be able to 'feel' their souls. The urge becomes so overwhelming that I can't resist it, and start to peel back my gloves.

A whooshing sound from directly behind makes me jump, and my heart starts beating hard. It's Lady Arabella. I tug my gloves back down. She comes and stands beside us, glancing into the cage.

'I see you've found my birds.'

'They're yours?' Isabel asks. 'I didn't know you had birds, my lady.'

'I found these just recently,' she says. 'Or I should say, they found me. Aren't they beautiful creatures?'

All three of us nod, while Isabel asks, 'Are their feathers made of real gold?'

'It would appear so.'

'And their eyes?' I ask. 'Are they real diamonds?'

'Pink diamonds, the rarest in the universe.'

Lady Arabella is hardly able to contain her own enthusiasm for her new-found pets. 'I have to confine them for their own protection. When they came to me they were severely injured and unable to fly.'

Isabel gasps. 'Who would do that to such beautiful creatures?'

Lady Arabella stares at her birds with wonder in her eyes. 'Who knows, my dear?'

'Would you like me to try to heal them, my lady?' Isabel offers.

Lady Arabella shoots her a surprised look, then says in a soft, yet firm tone, 'Your offer is generous, but the birds are healing well enough in my care. They trust me.'

Ethan remains quiet, studying the birds now with a slight frown.

Lady Arabella notices. 'Don't you like them, Ethan?'

'They're amazing, my lady. It's just, I've never seen anything like them before.' And before he shuts off his thoughts, wayward ones come bursting out. *At least not*

178

in this world! So where have you been wandering?

I step on his foot. His head jerks in my direction. He realises that I've heard him, and if *I* have, then it's possible Lady Arabella did too. She looks at Ethan for a long moment, her ice-tipped eyelashes fluttering uneasily. Finally she smiles. Relief washes through me. This mission is going to be tricky. We really have to watch every one of our thoughts. We've only been here a minute or so and already Ethan is having trouble accomplishing this.

Suddenly Lord Penbarin appears. 'There you are!' At first I think he means Lady Arabella, but I soon realise he means the three of us. 'Lorian requests your presence. Now. In his private chambers.'

A cold sweep of fear starts at my head and slithers through my entire nervous system. But Matt did warn us. There's not much that goes on here – or anywhere – that Lorian doesn't see or know about. Our task – to search for the key and uncover the traitor – will be almost impossible to accomplish. But we're here, and we're going to at least try. Anything we uncover could help.

As Lord Penbarin leads the way down one spacious corridor after another I pull Ethan back a little. 'It might be a good idea if you stayed outside of Lorian's chambers.'

He gives me a hard stare. 'Why?' And then he gets it, and as always gets mad at me. 'You're reading my thoughts again! Can't you stay out of my head?'

'I don't do it on purpose,' I try to defend myself.

'Don't you have any control over your own powers?'

I hiss at him, 'Of course I do! But you're projecting your thoughts as hard as if you're throwing tennis balls at my head!'

'Don't give me ideas!'

'I shouldn't have to. You know, Ethan, it's dangerous.'

'Maybe I just can't help it,' he says in a softer tone.

I try to keep my voice low too. 'Don't you see, that's my point.'

Lord Penbarin glances around briefly, but thankfully decides to ignore our discussion. But Isabel wants to know what's going on. And even though I haven't heard any of Isabel's thoughts lately, I decide to check all the same.

'How good are you at screening your thoughts these days?'

She gives a sniggering laugh. 'You learn very quickly to master that particular skill when you start going out with a Truthseer.' She looks candidly at Ethan and adds in a whisper, 'Maybe you should try it.'

I feel my face heat up at her suggestion. There aren't too many of us Truthseers around. Arkarian is one, Marduke another. Matt is one too now, and all the Tribunal members.

We arrive at a set of magnificently carved doors, etched in gold and silver. Lord Penbarin turns the handle and lets one open inwards. 'Lorian wants to see all three of you. And you had better have a good reason for being here unannounced and uninvited.'

Well, that resolves the issue of whether Ethan should stay outside or not. One after the other, we go in.

The room turns out to be several rooms on different levels, separated by marble archways and alabaster rails. The walls are mostly white but the lamps burning in brackets here and there give them a golden glow. There are dark drapes hanging from a number of windows.

Some are closed tight while others are pulled back by braided ropes with hanging tassels. The furniture is elegant in its sparseness. A table made entirely from white stone sits in the centre of the first room surrounded by high-back matching chairs. There's also a deeply-cushioned lounge suite, again in white.

I start to wonder where Lorian is, when I see him making his way towards us. He is tall, and he's wearing a white floor-length tunic with silver trim around the neck and sleeves, which makes him appear taller still. He is incredibly striking. Arkarian introduced me to him once during my debriefing, but then he was wearing a cloak, his face practically hidden. Today, Lorian's hair flows around his shoulders, long and silver, while his pale, luminescent skin glows softly around deep violet eyes.

Tilting his hand, three high stools appear, topped with red velvet cushions. I'm not sure about Ethan and Isabel, but I'm grateful for their appearance. My legs feel like mush all of a sudden.

Lorian remains standing, and up close like this I find it too difficult to look at his face. There's a cold and angry aura about him. Isabel slides a concerned look my way. I carefully go over some of the reasons we came up with for our presence here.

'Tell me why Matt's first meeting as leader was shrouded within a protective screen,' says Lorian.

At first the three of us remain speechless. We're not expecting this question. I urge Ethan to keep control of his thoughts. The silence stretches uncomfortably and the three of us start to squirm under the Immortal's intense violet inspection.

Eventually I speak. 'It was Matt's idea.'

Isabel gives me a warning stare, probably wondering

where I'm going with this.

I try to keep my explanation casual. 'He was just trying out one of his new powers.'

Lorian focuses his stare directly on me and I feel him probe right into my brain. Suddenly I have to close my eyes and concentrate on the simple act of bringing air into my lungs. I start to tremble and my head goes all fuzzy and light. From a distance I hear Ethan call out. 'My lord, she's one of the Named now.'

The light-headedness starts to clear but I'm left feeling disoriented as if I'm falling. I hit the ground with a thump and Isabel and Ethan help me back on to my stool.

'What happened?'

'It's all right. It's over,' Ethan says.

When I look up I see Lorian's glow abating. 'You have not been Initiated.'

'No, my lord.'

'What is the reason for the delay?'

Ethan explains. 'Arkarian has been very busy. I'm sure he'll get to it as soon as he returns.'

Lorian is still not satisfied. And for a moment I lose concentration. My head is still reeling from the connection with Lorian's only moments ago, and my thoughts come tumbling out. *Because I am not trusted!*

Oh, great! My head starts throbbing and feels so heavy I have to lift my hand to my forehead to keep it from dropping off. The throbbing quickly becomes unbearable. On top of this, a thrust of warm energy starts sifting through my head. I look up to see Lorian standing close in front of me, his hand hovering in the air. I feel compelled to close my eyes. I do so and almost instantly the gentle surge pulses through my entire body. It's over in a second and Lorian steps back. I look up and notice everything is clear again, the headache gone. In its place is a contented feeling of warmth, and, stranger still, a sense of belonging.

'You will be Initiated tomorrow at dawn.' And to Ethan, Lorian says, 'In Arkarian's absence, will you stand in for him and present Rochelle to the Tribunal, so that she will receive their gifts and grow in the acceptance of her elders?'

'Of course, my lord.'

'Then it is settled. Now tell me what you are doing here.'

Ethan says, 'We're here to update our King on the situation in Veridian. So much has happened, as I'm sure you are aware.' And then he adds, 'Personally, my lord, I'm looking forward to meeting King Richard again.'

Lorian's head dips and his eyes flutter closed for a second. 'In that you should, Ethan. Lord Penbarin awaits outside. He will show you to the North Wing, where you will find your King. Make yourselves comfortable while you are here. Tonight the palace is yours to wander around at your leisure.'

Outside Lorian's chambers, Lord Penbarin eyes us carefully. But things couldn't have gone better. We have Lorian's permission to look around! I try not to think about what's going to happen tomorrow at dawn. A concerned look must appear on my face, as Isabel touches my arm.

'Don't worry about the Initiation. I remember mine. I was so nervous my knees were like jelly. But it was all right. And you already know Lady Arabella pretty well –'

'And you know me,' Lord Penbarin adds with a glint of humour in his eyes. He looks at me for a lengthy moment, a finger falling across his full red lips. 'Hmm, what gift shall I endow you with? Any suggestions, Ethan?'

Lord Penbarin is having some fun with us. Isabel laughs. But Ethan takes him seriously. 'Why do you ask me, my lord?'

Lord Penbarin smiles, looking from Ethan to me, and back to Ethan again. Turning away he mutters, 'I thought that was rather obvious.'

The matter is thankfully dropped and a few minutes later we're standing outside another set of high double doors. Before we even get a chance to knock they're opened by King Richard himself. While not exactly tall, his long robe gives him that appearance. He looks well, and is certainly cheerful enough. He greets Lord Penbarin with a grin, welcoming us inside. When he sees Ethan, he embraces him with a hearty hug.

'At last we meet again!'

'How are you, sire?'

King Richard laughs, throwing his head back. 'Excellent, my good man.' He waves his hands around, showing us his luxurious surroundings. 'Much better than that filthy prison you rescued me from.'

Ethan can't get the grin off his face either. They're like two old friends meeting after years of separation.

King Richard drags Isabel into his embrace next. 'My dear Lady Madeline –'

'It's Isabel, sire,' she reminds him, and not the name she used when she had last seen him in the past. I remember it, I was there. I put poison in her glass.

'Of course!' King Richard exclaims. 'I must say, undisguised, you look lovelier than ever.' The King turns to me, instantly picking up that I'm a Truthseer. He becomes a little guarded. It's a natural response. No one likes their personal thoughts on display. 'And who have we here?'

Lord Penbarin introduces me. 'This is Rochelle Thallimar, to be Initiated at dawn. She is one of your Named.'

King Richard nods deeply. 'Welcome, my dear.' He takes my hands, and even though they are gloved, he feels their power. His eyes linger on mine for a minute, assessingly, but he doesn't say anything. I'm swamped with an uneasy feeling, but he soon lets go of my hands and the feeling evaporates as if it never existed.

Lord Penbarin excuses himself, and the second we're alone, King Richard's demeanour does a full about-face. The eyes aren't laughing any more. He has picked up on the underlying gravity of our visit.

'Can I order some food for you, or do you want to get straight to the point?'

Ethan says, 'We need your help, sire.'

Without hesitation he replies, 'Then you shall have it. Tell me, what can I do?'

'Well, you could show us around.'

'The palace?'

'Yes, sire. All of it.'

'That could take all night.'

'Then we had better begin.'

Trusting us implicitly, King Richard begins our tour. And without anyone noticing, I slip off my gloves, shoving them into my pocket for fast retrieval if needed. We go through many rooms, including the suites of the lords and ladies that live here, including their servants' quarters. Only King Richard could pull this off so smoothly. He is obviously a seasoned diplomat and well liked by all.

And while in all these rooms, Isabel and Ethan distract whoever is in there with conversation so that I can do my work – inconspicuously touching the walls, floors, furniture, anything that might harbour a secret panel, doorway or cavity. I only have to lay my hand on the wall in one place, to feel – to *see* – what lies within or behind it.

Dawn approaches as we finish searching the palace, and still nothing is found. We end up in the courtyard, looking around. Lady Arabella is here, cleaning out the bird cage, emptying the tray of food, sweeping the floor of droppings and refreshing their water supply. It strikes me as strange that she should be doing this menial job herself. Of course I don't say anything. Maybe she loves her birds so much, she doesn't trust anyone but herself to look after them.

As I think these thoughts I pull my gloves out of my pocket and start putting them on. Lady Arabella notices and goes quietly still.

'What are you doing without your gloves on? How long have they been off?'

Her voice is harsher than I've heard it before, and this takes me by surprise. She notices and quickly softens it. 'I don't mean to alarm you, my dear, but I thought I taught you to keep those gloves on at all times.'

I try to think of an explanation quickly. 'They're a little tight, my lady. Occasionally I like to stretch my fingers.'

She mulls over this explanation for a minute. 'I'll talk to Arkarian to see what he can do. For now, you will have to put up with them. You'd better hurry.' She points to the approaching dawn. 'You still have to change.'

Isabel grabs my arm with excitement. 'Come on, let's

186

see what tunic they've picked out for you.'

'What are you talking about?'

She explains, 'White is for a novice apprentice. I had a white tunic at my Initiation, but was lucky 'cause they gave me a blue sash. This gave me status above the usual novice Initiate.'

We get to our allocated chambers to find a deep purple tunic laid out on the bed, with a golden sash beside it. Isabel gasps at the sight, running her hand down the velvet fabric.

'Oh, wow.' She calls to Ethan, 'Look at this! What does it mean?'

Even though I agree it's a beautiful garment, I don't know why Isabel is making such a fuss. Ethan comes over and takes the sash in his hands and lets it run through his fingers a few times. 'The gold sash is the Guard's highest honour.' He glances at me, and his thoughts catapult into my head, wondering what I've done to deserve it.

Isabel too looks perplexed, but her inner thoughts are under control. 'What about the purple tunic?'

Ethan backs off a little. Turning away, he works hard at screening his thoughts. He knows, but doesn't want to say.

'What is it?' Isabel asks.

He glances at me with a frown between his brows. It gives me an eerie feeling that something is terribly wrong.

'How would I know?' he says. 'You'd have to ask Arkarian.'

Isabel picks up the strange vibe coming from him and drops the subject. But their reactions only make me want to know more. They start moving around as if the

187

conversation never came up. I drag on Ethan's arm.

'Hold on. Tell me what you know.'

'Nothing!' he snaps, his eyes flicking away.

'Tell me, Ethan, or I'll probe your thoughts until I dig out the information along with half of your brain.'

A flash of annoyance comes into his eyes. Then he says, 'Look, all I know is that purple stands for loyalty.'

There's more, I can tell. 'Go on.'

Reluctantly he adds, 'A loyalty so strong that the wearer is likely to … give their life for the cause.'

'The colour of martyrdom,' I mumble mostly to myself. Is that what Lorian picked up in me when he probed my brain last night? Come to think of it, that line in the Prophecy that's supposed to relate to me talks about victory and death. How does it go? *Take heed, two last warriors shall cause grief as much as good, from the midst of suspicion one shall come forth, the other seeded of evil, yet one shall be victorious while the other victorious in death.*

A loud knock on the door and Lord Penbarin lets us know the time has arrived. Ethan leaves the room and I change into the tunic, trying to put that disconcerting idea of death out of my mind. Isabel helps me adjust the sash, then the matching cloak, pulling the hood right over the top of my head.

'Look,' she says. 'Don't worry about what Ethan said. That stuff about martyrdom, he could be wrong. He often is.'

A smile tries to form, and I relax a little, but only a little. The prospect of dying for whatever cause is hard to shake from my thoughts.

'Ethan thought he was my soul-mate once,' Isabel goes on. 'When all the time it was Arkarian.'

'Yeah? So how do you know who your soul-mate is?'

She shrugs. 'All I know is that Arkarian said we all meet our soul-mates at least once in our lives. It's up to us to recognise each other, or else miss out on true love.'

What a melancholy idea. But even this thought takes second place when we open the door and find Ethan arguing with Lord Penbarin.

'But who picked it out?' Ethan demands to know.

'That's something I can't –'

They notice us and stop in mid-sentence. Lord Penbarin bows his head in recognition, while Ethan simply stares at me with his mouth hanging open. 'You look amazing.'

'Here, here,' Lord Penbarin mumbles. 'Now that you're ready, my dear, I'll let the Tribunal know.' He turns, gives Ethan a hard stare, then hurries off, taking Isabel with him.

'Arkarian will be sorry he missed this,' Ethan says.

I want to bring up the reason for his argument with Lord Penbarin, but my nerves are feeling the pressure of the coming Initiation. I decide I'd rather not know. Ethan's words make the Initiation sound like a momentous event and my hands begin to shake. I double-check that my gloves are on, then slip my hands into two side slits in the long cloak.

A few minutes later we arrive at the Tribunal Chambers, and Ethan takes a deep breath. 'Are you ready?'

'No way,' I reply honestly. 'I'm not prepared. I don't know what to expect. I've got a sick feeling of dread inside. And I think I'm going to throw up.'

He tries to reassure me. 'You'll be fine. They're going to welcome you in there.'

'I'm a traitor, Ethan. I was a member of the Order and

I turned on my own kind.'

A look of outrage fills his face, his eyes widening, the blue turning cold and hard. 'The Order is not your kind! It never was, OK?'

'Of course it wasn't! I didn't mean that.' He watches me quietly. 'It's just, there's a stigma attached to what I did and I can't get rid of it. I see it in people's eyes. Everyone here knows my history. And because of that fact, they don't trust me.'

'It's just your nervousness, Rochelle. You're imagining it.'

'I'm a Truthseer, Ethan.'

He glances away to the ceiling for a moment. 'Arkarian trusts you. And, well, I've already told you I do too.'

His words are comforting. He has no idea how much. I watch his face as his eyes turn from the ceiling towards me. They lock with mine, and for the world I can't look away. Something passes between us, something I can't name, but is as real as my hand or my heart.

Behind us the doors swing open, making us aware that we're not alone any more. Ethan puts his hand under my elbow and I follow his lead as he takes me to the centre of the room.

'My lords and ladies,' he announces, then turns to bow directly to our own King Richard, sitting to the right of Lord Penbarin, 'and kings and queens, allow me to introduce the eighth Initiate of the Named. Her name is Rochelle Thallimar.'

A round of applause follows. There are others in the room. Isabel is one, and a collection of strange faces sitting on stalls to one side. A stool appears behind me and I sit on it, as Ethan walks from the circle to go and sit beside Isabel. He grips her hand as if he's suddenly become nervous. I try not to think why; I have enough of my own nerves to contend with.

Lorian stands and everyone's eyes zoom to him. He raises his hands towards me, then motions them to the surrounding circle of ten.

'In a moment all the good lords and ladies will honour you with a special gift, welcoming you to the Guard. Before they do so, I am going to bestow *my* gift upon you.'

Murmurs ripple around the room. Apparently this is not the normal procedure. Lorian quietens everyone with one stern look. When all is still and silent, he comes over to me and raises his hands over my head.

'Rochelle Thallimar, do you swear fealty to the Guard and its cause?'

'Yes, my lord.'

'My gift to you is the entwining of your powers of Truthseeing and touch, so that from this moment on you will not only be able to hear the thoughts of others, but, through your hands, know their *loyalties* as well.'

The murmurs grow louder and Ethan runs back into the circle. 'My lord! A word, please.'

Lorian's hands lower and he sighs as if half expecting Ethan's reaction, yet dreading it at the same time. 'You may speak.'

'The gift is very generous but … also dangerous.'

'Perhaps, but we are all in danger now, Ethan. A skill such as this –'

'– is a death sentence.'

Lorian remains silent. Ethan continues. 'We all know there is a traitor among us. With this gift you are empowering Rochelle with the ability to identify him or her. If the traitor is in this room, Rochelle will be killed before she leaves this palace, and you know it. My lord –'

191

'Ah, but if the traitor is identified in this room, right now at this gathering –'

'This is preposterous!' Lord Penbarin and Lord Samartyne call out together. Queen Brystianne is next, gliding off her seat, followed by Lord Alexandon, looking just as outraged.

King Richard comes right into the circle. 'My lord, is it correct to assume you suspect one of the Tribunal members to be this traitor?'

'I wish it were not so,' Lorian replies in a weary tone.

As I think about what Lorian wants me to do, I see his point. The traitor has to be found, and if Lorian can do this through me, then I don't see how I – or anyone – can say no.

'There is one serious flaw to your plan, my lord.'

All heads turn to the back of the circle. Sir Syford steps off his stool and comes towards me. 'Should Ms Thallimar name one of us, it will be one traitor's word against another.'

The murmuring starts again. Ethan spins around, staring hard at the Tribunal members agreeing the loudest. I shake my head at Isabel, and she tugs Ethan back into his seat.

But no one is as outraged as Lorian. His eyes turn from a deep purple to darkest blue, while his skin takes on a stunning golden glow. He raises his hands and everyone takes a deep breath. It's as if everything in the room suddenly shrinks, including the air. Lorian holds his hands up a moment longer, heightening the tension.

'Has not one of you read the Prophecy?' He quotes, *'Suspicion will cause disharmony!'*

'I will do it.' I say the words softly, but in the silence they're heard clearly around the room. 'I know the risks, and I do this willingly.'

'Rochelle!' Ethan calls out. 'You don't know what you're saying.'

I turn my head to speak directly to him. Everyone is listening, but that can't be helped. 'I have to.'

'Why, for heaven's sake?'

'You heard them, they don't trust me. This is an opportunity for me to earn that trust. If I can reveal the traitor, how much better off will the Guard be? Everyone will see that I'm not aligned with the Goddess or Marduke any more.'

'But it's too risky.'

'I'm used to risk.' I turn and look at Lorian, and for the first time find it possible to meet his gaze. His eyes seem to pour through me and the feeling is welcoming. He brings his hands over my head, not touching, but so close that my hair stirs. 'Close your eyes.'

For a second I feel a moment of doubt, but quickly shove it aside. This is the right thing. Marduke was wrong about me.

A light pours down from Lorian's hands, forming a golden glow. I take a deep breath, exhaling slowly to settle my nerves. As I do this I feel the air around me rise to a higher temperature. I breathe in this strange warm air. It soaks into my skin through thirsty pores.

When it's over I open my eyes to find Lorian staring straight at me. 'The gift is complete.'

Ethan sighs, a deflated and troubled sound. I have a flash of misgiving. Well, there's nothing I can do about it now.

Lorian explains what's going to happen, 'The lords and ladies will each bestow you with a gift. After they have done this, they will kneel before you –'

Murmurs of discontent make Lorian momentarily pause and look up. When he takes up the explanation again he addresses the Circle in a commanding voice. 'And then Rochelle will lay her hand on the top of your head. You will remain still until Rochelle indicates otherwise.'

It's so quiet now I would be able to hear a pin drop down the hall.

'Who will be first?' Lorian's voice vibrates throughout the entire chambers.

King Richard stands. 'I will.' He looks reluctant. Where is his jovial manner now? 'Firstly, my dear, a warm welcome to the Kingdom of Veridian.' King Richard lifts both hands and rests them over my head. 'My gift to you is the ability to see the truth … in oneself.' After a quiet moment, he kneels before me and his eyes drift to mine. 'It is your turn now. Don't be afraid.'

My hands are shaking. I take off my gloves, inhale deeply and lift one hand to hover over the top of King Richard's forehead. I have a sudden fear of burning him.

'Go ahead,' Lorian calls out.

I lower my hand and close my eyes. Instantly I see a glowing light. It's as if this light is coming from King Richard's centre. It swells like a flame for a second before forming a funnel at its core. I focus into this core and find myself suddenly swamped with a sense of faith, gratitude and trust that I know is true.

I lift my hand and King Richard withdraws, returning to his seat.

The others follow. Lady Devine, with her long, blood-red hair, kneels before me with hands clasped tightly together, while Lord Alexandon's thumping footfalls let everyone know his displeasure. Lord Meridian, the smallest of the Tribunal members, wears a look of outrage. Queen Brystianne is next, with tightly-pursed lips, while Sir Syford's stride is filled with arrogance and disgust. One by one they bestow their gifts on me, but if I were asked what these gifts were, I swear I couldn't answer.

It takes an age but finally we are down to the last two – Lady Arabella and Lord Penbarin. As if she doesn't realise she is next, Lady Arabella sits unmoving.

Lord Penbarin tilts his head in her direction. 'After you, my lady.'

She sends him a hard stare. Lorian notices. 'Arabella, do you hesitate?'

She gets up, straightening her shoulders sharply. 'Not at all, my lord. But I do protest.'

'Noted,' he replies. 'Along with everyone else's.'

From beneath her floor-length gown, blue satin slippers can be seen as Lady Arabella walks right around me, stopping only when she is directly at my back. She raises her hand to my head, where she lets it hover close but not quite touching.

'My gift is that of *control*,' she says, emphasising this last word. I don't understand her sharp tone, though it's obvious she's referring to the power in my hands, flickering away on my lap. I get a sense of her gaze going straight over me and my eyes follow. Ahead, Lorian is staring back. It's as if the two of them are the only ones in the room – in the universe! The connection is so strong, so overpowering, that it throws my thoughts into confusion. What's going on? Do they have feelings for each other? I don't think so. I mean, Lorian chooses to be neither male nor female, everyone knows that.

Finally she comes around and kneels before me, her

head bowed. I close my eyes, lift my hand to her forehead, and try to focus on what I'm supposed to be doing. Finally I see the familiar flame burning inside. It surges quickly into a raging fire, swirling and hissing and edged bright red. I focus on the flame, looking for the funnel to form, but it keeps moulding and changing shape. I get a sense of something unidentifiable, definitely not the clarity I received from most of the others. Doubts begin to form in my head, when suddenly the flame holds still and forms into the shape of a burning heart.

With a sigh of relief I withdraw my hand, releasing her. It is only love I see. A powerful and deep love, but one that also burns with remorse and sadness.

Lady Arabella returns to her seat. I glance at Lorian and notice his eyes following Lady Arabella. They linger on her for long moments after she has settled in her chair. Only when his attention returns to me does Lord Penbarin give a loud groan and come over.

'Many welcomes, my dear, from the House of Samartyne. I have given this gift much thought. It is not the one I originally intended.' He straightens, lifting his hands over the top of me. 'I endow you with the gift of forgiveness.' Then he adds, 'Forgiveness of all who misjudge you.'

Taking care with his gown, Lord Penbarin kneels before me. My touch instantly reveals a flame burning clear, pure and true. Releasing him, he takes his seat and everyone starts murmuring. Lorian hushes them with just a look.

'What have you found?'

'I found many things, my lord, but nothing that would condemn any member of this Tribunal.'

The murmurs turn into relieved mutterings. Lorian

raises a hand, knowing I haven't finished yet. The room falls silent.

'I did find loyalty, my lord. An abundance of it.'

'What else?'

'Concern, gratitude, fear … and love, my lord.'

Lorian looks contemplative for a moment. 'Love and hate are two sides of a coin. How can you be sure that what you saw was true?'

I recall the intense emotion that swept through me along with the sense of overwhelming love that Lady Arabella projected. And I recall the love I felt that passed from Lorian to her, whether he's aware of it or not. 'The love I felt was true, my lord. I am sure of it.'

A relieved murmer ripples around the room. The Tribunal are off the hook. Not one of them is the traitor, as Lorian feared.

Suddenly Lorian stands and I think at last this ordeal is over. But Lorian's skin has started to glow again, his eyes sparkling like glittering jewels. To me he says, 'You are mistaken.'

There is loud protest. Lorian raises a hand and a sweep of cold chilling air fills the room. I rub my arms through the cloak to warm them.

'Either your gift is not yet developed sufficiently, or you have been tricked. Somehow I sense the latter.'

Lord Penbarin shakes his head. 'Do you have proof, my lord? Is that why you are so sure the traitor is one of us?'

From within his cloak, Lorian pulls out a crystal that sits neatly on the inside of his palm, a pyramid shape within a base of an octagon. As it glistens and shimmers under the lights, gasps and murmurs fly around the room; and I realise I am staring at the key – the same key we were sent to find!

'This is the proof!' he bellows, the chamber becoming chillier with every angry breath. 'Yes, look at it carefully. It is the key to the treasury of weapons.'

And then he does the most unbelievable thing. He comes over and holds it out in front of me. 'Are you wearing your gloves, Rochelle?'

Quickly I put them on, making sure not one scrap of skin is left exposed. 'Ah … yes, my lord.'

He nods. 'Then take this key and deliver it to one who will keep it safe.'

Sir Syford calls out from behind me, 'My lord, where did you find it?'

'When Rochelle, Ethan and Isabel came to see me last night, I discovered that they were sent here to look for the key. At first I was aghast and outraged at the very idea of such treachery in my own palace. But then I went looking for it. As you can see I found it – hidden in a safe box in a secret chamber buried in the courtyard garden.'

Lorian's eyebrows lift as he surveys the Circle. 'Under our very own feet, but undetectable. A clever place – accessible by all, yet untraceable to any. But one of you put it there. And before you start laying suspicion on your soldiers or staff members, only the rank of a Tribunal member or higher would have the power to prepare the impermeable box I found it in!'

Lorian lowers the key into my hands. My eyes become glued to its shimmering facets. From above me Lorian's voice continues to chill the air. 'And because my plan to reveal the traitor this day has failed, I must protect the innocent child before me, for as her powers grow, she will find herself immersed in more danger.'

He lowers his gaze to me, while both of his hands hover on either side of my head. In a loud voice that forms an echo in the chamber, Lorian announces:

'Whosoever shall harm this child and cause her death, shall they themself turn to stone and die before the sun sets.'

Oh, hell! The Immortal has just laid a curse on the person who takes it into their head to kill me!

Ethan runs into the circle, his arms open wide. 'My lord …!'

Lorian sees him coming and groans under his breath. 'I have protected her, Ethan. What have you to complain about now?'

Ethan takes a deep breath. 'Who is to stop the real murderer from hiring an assassin?'

Ethan's right. My life is still in danger. Lorian gives an odd, almost regretful, acknowledging nod.

'It is the best I can do.'

Chapter Seventeen

Matt

They have the key. Dartemis told me I would know when it was close. And I feel it now. I'm standing with Dillon and Arkarian in one of the rooms leading off Arkarian's main chamber. We're going through our last-minute preparations before our journey to an area around the top of Mount Olympus. Lathenia's palace is at the place where Mount Olympus stands today, but in a time that belongs to the ancient world of legends. She has created a virtual realm of her own.

'Do you really think Mr Carter can pull this off?', Dillon asks as we contemplate this strange phenomenon.

'It will be difficult. And because of the protective enchantments surrounding the palace, he will have to place us and pick us up outside the palace walls.'

Arkarian mulls over Dillon's doubts. 'Why don't you tell us how *you* travelled to Lathenia's palace?'

Dillon shrugs lightly. 'The Mistress always kept me close by her side, and I just went along for the ride. She gave me my wings years ago; I guess that helped. But somehow I think Lathenia's magician, Keziah, had a lot to do with the transportation.'

I try to reassure them both. 'Marcus can handle this

chore.'

'You have a lot of faith in that man,' Dillon says. 'He's only human, you know. I've seen him make mistakes before.'

'Those who are above us will guide his hand,' I say.

Dillon remains unconvinced and still curious. 'Oh yeah? Like who?'

Like the angels, the thought comes, but I keep it between myself and Arkarian. *Also known as the survivors, they fled to earth when their world was overtaken by the dark and became the underworld. After their first settlement here was destroyed, they established the ancient city of Veridian, saving their superior technology, which still pulses silently and secretly behind its decaying walls. And while their race lived on for thousands of years, it was those first survivors who were rewarded with the honour of overlooking the earth and its growing inhabitants. It is their mortal bodies, preserved in human form, that we borrow when we travel through the labyrinths of the Citadel and into the past.*

Arkarian barely glances at me when he adds his own thoughts, agreeing it's a good idea to keep this conversation between ourselves. Gently he reminds me that Dillon is waiting for an answer. I try to recall what he asked, but in the end don't have to reply. A strong hand knocks heavily and hurriedly at the door.

Arkarian opens it. Shaun is standing there heaving as if recovering from a marathon run. 'Quick, Arkarian. Something is happening to the sphere. It's going crazy!'

We follow Shaun to the octagonal chamber that houses the sphere. The sight of it used to unsettle me, but now that I understand where it comes from, where all of Arkarian's machinery comes from, it doesn't affect me so much. The sphere is spinning wildly, creating a continuous humming blur.

Dillon remains unimpressed. He has only one thought. 'We haven't got time for this! What about Neriah?'

Arkarian puts his hand on Dillon's shoulder. 'You're right, Dillon. And the speed at which the sphere is spinning means it could do so for a while yet. Shaun, stay here and keep watching it. When it stops, and the time period is revealed, look for anything suspicious, anything that will give us a clue to what Lathenia has planned. If we're lucky we should be back before it stops spinning.'

With wide and worried eyes Shaun nods, pulling a stool beneath him.

I tilt my head towards the sphere. 'Any idea where it's headed?'

Arkarian's eyes darken, revealing his grave concern. 'Only that Lathenia is going deep into the past. Very deep. We'll need to get back as quickly as we can, Matt.'

'Then what are we waiting for?' Dillon calls out.

Arkarian shifts us to the Citadel, to the room with the high panelled ceiling and floor marked in an octagonal shape. Standing within this shape he produces and hands us each a long silver cloak. 'Put these on.'

Dillon takes his but can't stop looking up and around. 'What are we doing in this part of the Citadel? This isn't the labyrinth. Don't tell me we're using our own bodies?'

'Where we're going is out of ordinary time –'

'Yeah I know, but … if she sees us. If she sees *me*!'

'She won't see any of us,' I try to reassure Dillon.

'You have no idea what you're talking about. I've been to Lathenia's palace. There's no way she won't see us.'

'Trust me.'

Dillon glances at Arkarian. He trusts him more. Arkarian nods deeply, and finally Dillon grows silent. As the three of us stand within the octagon shape, wrapped in our cloaks, Dillon can't help one last comment. 'Let's just hope Mr Carter doesn't place us *too* far away from the palace walls.'

Silently I agree. Without another thought or sound, the three of us begin to dematerialise. Within seconds we are re-forming on unsteady ground. I stumble forward blindly. It's night and a blustering wind throws sleet in our faces.

'Is everyone all right?' Arkarian's voice struggles through the gale.

I turn around, tugging the hood of my cloak over my head, and see them both doing the same. 'Where are we?'

Dillon looks around, still adjusting to the darkness. 'Good question.'

'Does anything look familiar?' Arkarian asks Dillon.

His head shakes as he peers into the miserable weather. 'We should probably stick to a northerly direction.'

Arkarian shares a look with me. A concerned one. We don't have much time to waste searching unknown landscapes.

We move off, the sleet in our faces reducing visibility to almost nothing.

'I told you it was a big ask,' Dillon mutters.

An hour later, cold and weary, we come to a rocky hill. Suddenly Dillon gets excited. 'I know this place.'

At last! We follow, clambering over boulders on all fours to the top of a hill. And there, sprawled below in the darkness, stands a palace that looks like something out of a fairy tale – a dark fairy tale. Most of it is obscured by a swirling mist. But lights glow from the turrets and along the battlement walls.

Arkarian squints into the darkness. 'I have never seen crossbows quite like that before. They look more like pistols.'

'They're the weapons I was telling you about,' says Dillon. 'The ones with poison darts that cause instant death. They're accurate with those things for up to three hundred metres. The needle-like bolts don't even have to penetrate to kill. Just pierce the skin. Isabel's healing would be useless, even if she were here or we could get back to her quickly enough. I hope these cloaks are protective, otherwise we'll soon be three dead men.'

'Thanks for that, Dillon.'

'Look, Matt, it's all right for you to say all I have to do is trust, but I have to ask – how are we going to do this thing without getting killed first?'

Making sure we're still out of sight of the watchtowers, I explain the essence of my plan. 'When I know exactly where they're keeping Neriah, I'm going to place a shroud of invisibility over each of us.'

'You're going to make us invisible?' Dillon checks, and looks hopeful for a moment. 'It's a good idea, but won't the hounds still smell us?'

Arkarian lets me know in his thoughts that Dillon has a point.

Dillon adds, 'And don't forget the protective barrier around the palace. That's magic, you know.'

'Getting inside won't be a problem. Once I know which room they're keeping Neriah in, I'm going to disable the enchanted barrier long enough so we can use our wings to materialise directly into her room.'

'You can do that?'

'Yes.'

'OK. But once we have her, how do we get her out? Neriah doesn't have her wings yet, does she?'

'I'll make her invisible too, and we … walk.'

'Yeah, right!'

'It will work, Dillon.'

'There's one thing you're forgetting.'

'What's that?' Arkarian asks.

'We can't use our wings if we can't visualise where we're going. And we don't know which room they're holding her in.'

Lightly I lay my hand on Dillon's arm. My plan depends entirely on his memory. 'Didn't you say you've been inside this palace before?'

He nods and I explain, 'I want you to remember it for me, room by room, passageway after passageway. Recall the images. I will use them to enter the palace with my mind and find Neriah. When I do, I'll tell you which room she is being held in. You know the palace, so you'll be able to use your wings to get there. As for Arkarian, we're both Truthseers, so I can share a visual image with him that will show him the way.'

At last Dillon begins to believe this rescue might just work. He grins at me, looking eager to begin. 'I get it. All right then. Let's see …' He closes his eyes, and I do the same. 'The front gates are made of iron, twelve metres high. Can you see them?'

Dillon's memory is clear; he has no need to describe anything verbally, but if he's more comfortable doing it this way, then that's OK.

'The gates are massive,' I tell him. 'How do they open?'

'The locking mechanism is operated by the Gatekeeper.'

'Show him to me.' The image of an armed soldier appears. He operates a series of handles in a set pattern. I watch carefully. The gates open, and along with Dillon's mind, I move through them.

'The outer courtyard is open with no shelter,' Dillon explains. 'See the cobbled path to your right? Watch. It will lead you to the inner courtyard doors.'

As the doors swing open, a dark and empty cobbled area appears. This could be an advantage when we try to leave. But then Dillon informs me, 'This is where the hounds prowl.'

Dillon is proving to be a great source of knowledge.

'Look to your right,' he says. 'There's a tunnel. It's made entirely of thick curved glass. You can see through it to the outside yard, but everything is blurred.' The tunnel appears. 'The palace doors are at the end of this tunnel. They're brass with gold adornments in the shapes of lions' heads. They stretch six metres high and are arched at the top.'

I see them and zoom up close.

'Behind them is the great hall. It's a huge, open space. There's not much furniture, just a couple of long tables and stools. At the end a fire will be burning. It will be completely encased in glass. Lathenia has a thing about fire.'

I know this. I've been told, but I keep my thoughts to myself. 'Keep going.'

Dillon continues to visualise and describe the palace interior, from the great hall to its adjoining corridors, to a huge library, studies, bedrooms, kitchens, drawing rooms and so on. As he does so, I search for signs of Neriah.

She seems to be nowhere.

'Would there be dungeons downstairs?' Arkarian suggests.

'Of course there are,' Dillon replies. 'But ... Marduke wouldn't put his own daughter down there, would he? There are things down there that shouldn't be in this world. Any world!'

I'm reluctant to visualise Neriah in this scenario, but the dungeon needs to be checked. After a moment's silence, Dillon takes a deep breath as if mentally preparing himself for the worst.

'That corridor you saw at the far end of the great hall, the one with the padlocked door, is the one you must go down. See the stairs? They're long and deep and dark, but just keep going. At the bottom turn left. There's a tunnel made of brick. It's moist and slippery, but there should be a lamp on the wall. More stairs. Take them and go right down to the second locked gate.'

The corridors are narrow and made of bricks. It's dark here, just as Dillon says, but lights from burning candles flicker eerily across the cobbled floor. Once through the second gate I see rooms on either side. I step lightly on the moist cobbled path between cells and try not to gag. The stench is unbearable, but more than that, there's a sense of such evil it is almost incomprehensible.

Dillon falls quiet as I go on to explore the dungeon cells. What I see shocks me and I balk at the sight. Someone – *something* – is in that first cell, but it's definitely not Neriah. It's not even human. It paces restlessly backwards and forwards, restricted by the size of the cell, and makes loud grunting noises. My mind zooms into the cell beside it, where another creature lurks. It grows restless and throws itself against a wall. The entire chamber reverberates, and moisture drips from the ceiling. Another thump, this one nearer to me. I take a closer look and see that the tip of an animal's horn has pierced the ancient brickwork. I doubt even Lathenia would put Neriah in this microcosm of hell, but to be sure, I project my mind into all six cells before withdrawing.

I open my eyes to find Dillon and Arkarian staring at me with questions in their eyes. My whole body shakes as I try to shrug off the lingering sensations from the dungeon.

'Nothing.'

'Then where is she?' Dillon groans.

'Think,' Arkarian tells him. 'Is there any room, any space within the palace walls that you have forgotten to show Matt?'

Roughly, he pushes his hood back. 'There is one other possibility. But no ...'

'Tell us,' Arkarian says softly.

He heaves a deep breath. 'It's a tower, but not a tower.'

'Where is it?' I try to form an image quickly. We've been here so long already, and we're still on the outside.

'Somewhere in the southern end of the inner courtyard.'

No image forms. 'That's not very clear, Dillon,' I say.

He rubs fingers over his temples, frustrated. 'I've never seen it, so I can't really help you. If Neriah is in there, then we're lost.'

'Tell me all you know about this tower.'

'Like I said, it's not exactly a –'

'Tell me anyway.'

'The Mistress calls it her cage.'

'It's a *cage*?' Arkarian asks, sharing a concerned look with me.

'It hangs in the air about a hundred metres up, suspended by magic, or so I've been told.'

Arkarian's frown deepens as he looks at Dillon. 'You know the palace as if you've lived here a lifetime, so how can you have never seen this …"cage"?'

'Every time I looked, it was covered in that grey mist that hangs around here all the time.'

'Hmm,' Arkarian mutters. 'The perfect prison cell. One that you can't see.'

'Maybe …' My thoughts spill over into words. 'But I seriously doubt its perfection.'

'What are you thinking?'

'That nothing hangs suspended in midair, magic or not. I think the magic is in the concealment of its entrance and exit.'

An idea hits me, a way that I can see this 'cage' for myself. I start to move away, then remember the others.

'Stay here. I have an idea. I'm going to check out this cage for myself. But if I'm not back in twenty minutes, I want you to go back to the Citadel and wait for me there. It's not safe here on these boulders. Sooner or later the hounds will catch your scent. I don't know exactly how long my invisibility screen will last, so I won't create it until we're ready. And Arkarian, you will need to check on the sphere before long.'

'Hey,' Dillon argues. 'I'm not leaving here for one second without Neriah.'

Trusting my instincts, I ignore Dillon's demand, sensing that his passion could put us all in danger. I direct my thoughts to Arkarian. *If you leave without him he may try to rescue Neriah on his own.*

I move off into the darkness. When I'm out of sight I try to work one of the powers I learned when I was with

Dartemis. It's the one that shocked me the most, not just the first time I used it, either, but every time since. I close my eyes and find my inner focus. Without trying too hard, I centre my entire being on one thought. *One thought!* And then it flows from me. *Eagle.*

With a smoothness I'm still getting used to, my arms change into massive wings while my legs and the rest of my body re-form into the shape of a bird. Even though I've done this many times now, I'm still surprised by the sensation of almost complete weightlessness and buoyancy of my chest and lungs. Using my wings, I propel myself up and take flight into the dark, snow-driven wind in the form of a golden eagle.

I soar high above the palace, making sure to rise above the enchantment that protects it. There's a lot of swirling mist below, but the view from my eagle eyes is remarkable. The palace yards are large and open spaces. I spot Lathenia's hounds prowling restlessly. One howls, and soon the others follow. They sense something. We are going to have to be very careful.

I soar down and fly as close as I can without being detected, looking for signs of the 'cage'. I almost complete a full circle of the yards before I spot it, shrouded in mist. When I'm close enough I focus on removing the enchantment directly above the cage.

From here I see how it got its name. It hangs in the shape of a dome, seemingly in midair, the mesh so fine it would contain the smallest bird. But it's not a bird that occupies it at the moment. Neriah is there, sitting with her arms wrapped tightly around her knees, shivering on the glass brick base.

I take a close look at the fine silver mesh that surrounds the cage. No way will my eagle form get through that, nor will it pass through the enchantment surrounding the cage itself. Quickly I work at first identifying, then unbinding the enchantment that keeps Neriah's cage a secure prison. I then transform into a moth. The adjustment is strange at first. Everything seems oversized. My wings flutter madly and very fast, but they do the job, only scraping the mesh once or twice on the way through.

Inside I re-form into my human shape again.

Neriah jumps back at the sight of my changing form and scrambles away across the floor.

'Neriah,' I whisper. 'It's Matt.'

She turns her head and sees that it's me.

'Speak softly,' I warn. 'We're a long way up, but we don't want our voices to carry to the hounds.'

'Is it really you, Matt? How did you get here?' She waves a hand in the air. 'No, don't answer that. You were that eagle staring into the cage a moment ago.'

She gets up and approaches me, her steps tentative. 'Do you have news of my mother?'

I quickly reassure her. 'She's well and is being looked after. You don't have to worry about her.'

'Are you just saying that so I will return with you?'

'I'm not lying, Neriah. Your mother is back on the island where you were raised. It's the safest place for her right now. So you don't have to stay here any more. I swear this is the truth.'

She nods, believing me. Then asks, 'Aysher and Silos? Are they all right too?'

For a moment I don't know who she's talking about, but a mental image of her dogs sweeps into my head. Unconsciously my eyes flutter closed as I gather my thoughts together to give her the news. She catches on that something is wrong.

'Tell me, Matt. Hurry! I can't stand being apart from them. I feel as if both my arms have been ripped from my body. Tell me they're all right. Please.'

'I'm sorry, Neriah. They're gone.'

'Gone? How? What do you mean?'

'When Marduke drew you out of our world, the dogs went through too – but I'm told they disappeared the moment they made it to the other side. They haven't been seen since.'

With a soft cry of pain Neriah turns her back on me and grips the mesh with her fingers until they turn bone-white. I lay my hand on her shoulder. She straightens her back and sniffs away her tears. 'I'm all right.' A moment later she turns and looks up at me. 'I didn't want you to come here.'

'With your mother safe, there's no reason for you to stay.'

She glances around the fine mesh surrounding us. 'Not all of us can turn into moths small enough to escape this prison.'

'No, but there is another way to get you out. I have Arkarian and Dillon waiting on the hill outside the palace walls to help me. I have to return to them now to show them the way to this tower, and then all three of us will use our wings to get in here. Then I'm going to create an invisibility screen. For it to conceal us entirely, we have to be careful not to utter a single sound. But first, I have to ask, who put you up here? I know Marduke is a monster, but … he's also your father.'

'At first he prepared a beautiful room for me and we spent hours and hours together. I felt as if I was getting to really know him.'

'So what happened?'

'While Lathenia was watching, I came into one of my powers. It surprised her and she locked me in here so that I couldn't escape.'

'And Marduke agreed to this?' I wave my hand around at her harsh cold surroundings.

'They argued all night. At one stage I thought I heard him ... *plead*,' she whispers and falls silent.

I don't push for more information. It's obviously painful for her to continue. And besides, time is passing too quickly. Arkarian will wait twenty minutes and not a second more.

'I have to go now, but I will be back soon.' I produce a protective silver cloak the same as my own. 'Here.' I hold it out to her, but just as she reaches for it, I shake it out, deciding to place it around her shoulders myself. As I do so, I feel her warm breath flutter across my throat. It unsettles me and when I go to secure the cord beneath her neck, I fumble, my fingers feeling suddenly more like twenty than ten, and twice the size.

She brings her hands up to secure the cords herself, but her fingers brush against mine and the next thing I know our hands are clasped together. I look into her face; she looks up into mine.

'Matt,' she whispers. 'Do you know me yet?'

It's a strange thing to say. I have no idea how to answer her question. Instead, I stare, mesmerised, at her angelic upturned face. Her mouth, so rich and red, draws me towards it and I lean down. Now I am so close that the heat from her body entwines with the heat from mine. It would be so easy to go that one more step.

What am I doing?

But it's there in her eyes, uninhibited acceptance of

who I am, who she is, what we could be together.

As I stare into her eyes I feel myself falling. It's a good feeling, as if the fall is something I should be doing. I get the sense that at the bottom of this drop there is only freedom. A kind of freedom that I have never felt before. I step closer and the need to become one with her is compelling. Urgent. I think about doing it – right here on this cold crystal floor.

Her hand comes up to the side of my face. Her touch is soft and warm, but it is this very touch that brings me back to reality. Love will make me weak. So before I make a huge mistake I jerk my head away. 'Don't do that.'

A look of sorrow fills her face and I turn from her.

She says, 'What's wrong, Matt?'

There is only one way to make sure I don't become attached to this girl. 'I'm not interested. OK?'

Her eyes flicker briefly as if in shock.

Just to make sure she understands, in the moment before I change into the shape of the moth again, I add, 'I never will be.'

In a flutter of powdery-soft wings I fly out of the cage, quickly turning into the eagle; and without glancing back, lift high above the palace yards and head for the safety of the boulders.

Arkarian and Dillon are glad to see me. Dillon jumps in first. 'Did you find her?'

I nod, but before I explain anything, Arkarian fills me in. 'The hounds have become restless, which has alerted the guards. We have to hurry, Matt.'

Quickly I explain where the cage is, and moments later the three of us materialise inside it. Neriah acknowledges our presence without making a sound.

Dillon embraces her. She returns it stiffly while staring over his shoulder at me. Dillon senses something and pulls back. He sees her looking at me and his eyes narrow. But everyone knows not to speak, not a word, and wherever his thoughts have taken him, he keeps them to himself.

Silently Arkarian and I start searching for the exit to the cage. Neriah shakes her head. She doesn't think there is one. But there has to be – all we have to do is find it.

Arkarian does so quickly. With one thought I will the trapdoor in the cage's glass base to open. It springs up, revealing a shimmering crystal stairwell, descending in a spiral all the way to the ground.

Dillon urges Neriah down first. I grab her arm to stop her. I haven't created the invisibility screen yet. Arkarian understands and motions with his hands for everyone to stand still. Closing my eyes I bring stillness to my mind, then, with one thought, make us all invisible. It works. I can't see the others, but I'm conscious of them beside me. And of course, when I reach out, their touch is real enough.

We start descending the steps. It takes us a long time – there are just so many. It's very tempting to use our wings and get the hell out of here, but Neriah doesn't have this skill, and if we run into trouble, we'll need all our powers to protect each other.

We make it to the bottom and find ourselves facing a thick glass door. Through it everything is blurred. From my recollections of the position of the cage, the outside of this door should be shrouded in grey mist, and hope-fully not under strict surveillance. Carefully I turn the handle. The door opens and I peer outside. No one is looking in this direction. Only two hounds are prowling the yard nearby. I hope this invisibility screen lasts longer than any of my previous attempts.

One by one we file out of the tower and make our way across the paved courtyard, and, as agreed, Dillon takes the lead. We almost make it to a second set of glass doors, when two hounds appear at the edge of the court-yard, looking strangely confused. They sniff the air and walk slowly around us in an arc. They sense something, but our invisible presence has their reasoning powers in a spin.

Keep walking, I will the others. But the hounds are clever; they start sniffing the invisible footprints we're leaving behind. One suddenly lifts its head and howls. It's a sign. The turrets come alive and beams of light start criss-crossing over us.

'Halt! Who goes there?'

Other voices call out, 'Show yourselves or we'll shoot!'

At least they still can't see us. And that means neither can these hounds, no matter how clever they are. We keep walking, quickly, crossing the last few metres to the shadows of a deep alcove.

When we're out of sight of the searchlights, Dillon finds a door and opens it very slowly. We pass through and away from the sniffing hounds. Once inside Dillon touches my arm. He's making sure I'm following. It's in this moment I see him as Lady Arabella must, and my confidence in him strengthens.

Suddenly he has us all pull to a stop. And then I understand why. There are voices nearby. I soon realise the voices are coming from the corridor we need to pass through to get to the great hall. Standing still, we wait, huddling together in a doorway. It soon becomes appar-

216

ent who owns one of the voices. Lathenia. Arkarian grips my forearm and squeezes it tightly. He's identified the other voice and it has shaken him badly. Then I see Lathenia walking towards us, and beside her, a man with a jovial laugh. There is an intimacy between the two, as if they are very close. The man is wearing a long red robe. I see his face and the sight makes me lose concentration. For a moment the invisibility screen weakens. Quickly I work at restoring it.

As they pass in front of us Arkarian's grip on my arm tightens. He's in shock. We both are. We are watching our long-awaited King walk arm-in-arm with our greatest enemy. Richard turns his head, and for a moment it's as if he is staring straight at me. But he can't see me, and soon his eyes return to give Lathenia his full attention.

For now, Matt, we keep this to ourselves. I hear Arkarian's thoughts thunder into my head.

As soon as the door closes behind the pair, Dillon gets us moving. Arkarian and I can't seem to drag our eyes away from the door that now conceals our King. The door to Lathenia's bedroom.

The inside of the palace is quiet, with only a few servants lingering, and so we make it without incident to the front brass doors and down the glass tunnel. Still reeling from seeing King Richard with Lathenia, it takes me a moment too long to realise what's about to happen. Dillon has his hand on the door handle, ready to turn it. But this door is completely exposed to the courtyard and the guards in the turrets. And while we are still invisible, an opening door is sure to attract attention.

Dillon's hand starts turning the handle, and both Arkarian and Neriah are between me and him. I can't call out and give away our position. *No!* My thoughts

217

push through to Arkarian. He reaches forward, but too late. The door swings open.

Almost instantly a guard in the watchtower notices. Searchlights shine directly in our faces. But we're not far from the outer courtyard walls. As long as the invisibility screen lasts, all we have to do is make a run for it, and stay ahead of the hounds.

But the hounds are too quick. They chase after us, and though they still look a little confused, they run straight in our direction. While running I keep my eyes on them. I soon notice their eyes growing more focused. Saliva gathers as they pull back their gums and snarl. The invisibility screen is disintegrating! Darts slice the air around us. There's no point in maintaining silence now.

'Run hard!' I call out, while the hounds come bounding after us, and darts from above become more accurate.

As the invisibility screen completely disappears, I grab Neriah's hand and put it in Dillon's. 'Take her and run for the gates. I will protect you from here and make sure the gates open. Keep the coats wrapped tightly around you to protect you from the darts. When you get to the hill, call Marcus. Remember, because of the protective enchantments surrounding the palace, you can't call him until you are outside the palace walls. Don't wait for us. You got that?' He nods and grips Neriah's hand hard. She looks at me for a moment, reluctant to leave. 'Go!'

They turn and run.

'I'll deal with the hounds,' Arkarian volunteers.

But the first two hounds are fast, and before Arkarian harnesses his power over them, they leap over the top of us, and just keep going.

'They're going for Neriah!' Arkarian hisses.

By the time we spin around the hounds have already attacked. Dillon quickly pushes away the one on top of him, but the one over Neriah takes a vicious swipe at her throat.

Between the two of us we manage to get the hound off her and Arkarian uses his powers to contain all seven that have gathered. But his grip is tentative. They stand back, but only just, snarling and ready to attack again.

Dillon tries to help Neriah up. 'Quick! She's bleeding from the throat. Look what it's done!'

She's hurt, but there's nothing I can do here in this courtyard with darts showering down on us from the turrets, and footsteps coming quickly. Any moment we will be surrounded by guards and Neriah will have no chance of escape.

'Dillon, Arkarian, use your wings and get out of here!'

Dillon shakes his head. Neriah is weakening fast in his arms. 'No way. You just want her for yourself. You want to be the hero.'

I grab his shoulders from behind, lifting him, and hiss into his ear, 'Do you hear that sound?' I point to the cobbled path. 'They're soldiers' footsteps and they're coming fast. Do you want to get caught in Lathenia's palace? Tell me, Dillon, what do you think she would do to you, her once trusted soldier? We've both seen her dungeon. You don't want to go there.'

His eyes flick briefly to Neriah. 'OK. I'll go.'

Arkarian hisses over my shoulder. 'Don't make me leave you.'

'You said that from now on I give the orders. I'm ordering you to go.'

He glances away briefly, then nods, clearly uncomfortable with my decision. But thankfully the two of them

219

disappear. At least they will return home safely. I lean down to help Neriah to her feet. A dart whips between us, so close that Neriah's hair lifts with the wind.

I yank her hood back over her head. 'Keep the cloak around you tight.'

'Use your wings,' she mutters weakly.

I grab her hand and thrust it over the top of her wound. 'Keep it there and hold it tight against your wound.'

'Matt, please go!'

With Arkarian gone, the hounds grow restless. *Retreat!* I force the thought at them. They whimper and cower, dropping their heads to the ground.

The pounding footsteps arrive in the form of a dozen guards. They lift their crossbows and aim them directly at the two of us, poison darts ready to fire. Marduke is one of them, and when he sees Neriah, her neck and shoulders soaked with blood, colour draining from her face as fast as the blood that oozes between her fingers, he snarls and grunts an unpleasant sound.

'Give her to me!'

At the sound of Marduke's harsh voice, the hounds regain their courage. Like the guards they look to their Master for direction.

'Hold your fire!'

'She needs a healer, and quickly,' I tell him.

'We have a healer here.'

'And then what? Are you going to let Lathenia keep her imprisoned in that bird cage again? It's freezing up there. How long do you think she will last?'

His one good eye glows and swells, his half-mouth draws into a straight line.

A light flashes from a balcony on the inner courtyard

wall and Lathenia appears – alone. 'Is there a problem, my pet?'

Marduke heaves, a loathsome sound, then turns slightly. 'None that I can't handle, Mistress.'

Neriah almost passes out, and Marduke makes to run to her. I help her steady herself, and she opens her eyes. 'Father ...'

Marduke seems to hesitate, whether on purpose or not I may never know. But it's the one moment I need to work some magic of my own. Thinking quickly I peer into the freezing, sleet-filled air.

'Watch him!' I hear Lathenia call out.

Too late, Goddess. Even the guards don't stand a chance. With one thought I change the sleet into fire. Suddenly the air is thick and alive and impossible to breathe. The hounds whimper and run for cover from the burning air. The guards are thrown into confusion.

'The air is on fire!'

'What magic is this?'

'Run!'

From the balcony Lathenia screams, and the wail is heard far into the surrounding valleys. Fire is her one fear; she will do anything to avoid it. And in all the chaos I lift Neriah into my arms and run for the front gates. Operating the series of handles with my mind, the gates unlock and swing open. Then we are out and I am calling Mr Carter's name.

As we begin to shift back to the Citadel, I take one last look at the palace. Guards are running around trying to put fires out everywhere. Many are on fire themselves. The watchtowers, mostly made of timber, are ablaze. Lathenia is nowhere to be seen. Nor is her new lover, King Richard. Only Marduke is standing still. He hasn't moved. He's still in the same spot, buried deep within his protective cloak, staring with one fiercely glowing eye. But there is a difference. Drool is seeping from his snout-like mouth and nostrils, and his yellow teeth are bared.

In this moment I understand that here is a creature that has lost too much.

The look on his face will stay with me for a long time. It is the look of madness.

Chapter Eighteen

Rochelle

The sphere is still spinning. And while Arkarian watches it, growing more distressed as each hour passes, the rest of us have to go on with our normal lives, whatever that is these days. That's why I'm sitting on the bus this Monday morning going to school. In a way I'm glad for this 'normal' part of my life. So much is happening lately in my other worldly life, it's almost a relief to have something ordinary to do. And since returning from Athens, everyone knows about my new power that tests loyalty and the curse Lorian has set in motion. A curse, for heaven's sake! He may as well have marked my forehead with a hot iron brand; I couldn't feel any more isolated.

At least our mission to Athens was successful. The key is now in Matt's hands.

The bus pulls up to the school front gates, and even before getting off, I see them – Matt, Ethan and Isabel in a little group. By the time I get off the bus and through the security guards, Neriah is with them too. She looks paler than usual, but then, I've heard what happened to her.

At least Neriah is someone I can relate to – both our fathers are monsters. Mine is in prison where he belongs, so at least *I* don't have to see mine any more – he's the one locked in a cage.

At the foot of the stairs Dillon approaches me. 'Hey,' he says. 'Heard about the curse. Good one,' he laughs. 'That should make you popular around here.'

What's up with him this morning? He's even more cynical than usual. For a second I get the urge to reach out and touch him without my gloves on, but of course I wouldn't do that. 'What's with you?'

His eyes glue themselves on Neriah. 'Huh? Did you say something?'

My own eyes follow and see Neriah talking to Matt, and if Matt's body language is anything to go by, something's happened between these two for sure. I can *feel* the tension from here! Matt's wound up like a spring, and trying to look everywhere except at Neriah, especially into her eyes. Beside me Dillon can't stop staring. Of course he's noticed too. Who wouldn't? Except Dillon's eyes have turned into narrow pinpoints of envy.

Neriah lays her hand on Matt's arm to get him to look at her, and beside me, Dillon turns greener than a frog covered in moss. He starts to take off, and there's no need to read his thoughts to know where he's heading, or what's on his mind.

I try to get him to come back. 'Hey, wait!'

He keeps going. This can only be trouble.

I call out again, 'Dillon, stop!'

He doesn't stop, but stomps right up to Matt. 'What do you think you're doing?'

Matt looks surprised, his eyes shifting sideways as if he's wondering if it's him Dillon is talking to, or someone beside him. 'I'm not doing anything. What's wrong, Dillon?'

'What's wrong? *What's wrong?* I can see what's happening here. While I was away, you moved in on Neriah!'

Neriah's mouth opens wide. 'Dillon, I think you've got the wrong idea. Let's go somewhere quiet and talk.'

He stares at her, and while I can't see his face from this direction, it makes Neriah step backwards. 'This is between me and Matt,' he says between gritted teeth.

Isabel and Ethan lift their heads to listen. Some other kids nearby look at them too.

Neriah starts to say something in protest, but Matt lifts his hand to stop her getting any closer. 'Look, Dillon, I haven't made a move on Neriah.'

Dillon scoffs loudly. 'Yeah, right! Just look at her, she's lovesick for you!'

Both of them turn and look at Neriah. Her skin turns from pale pink to bright red. She goes to speak but words don't form.

Matt tries to get Dillon to calm down. 'I'm telling you I didn't do anything behind your back. You have to believe me.'

Dillon sees red. 'Well, I don't believe you. I've got eyes of my own, and they don't lie.' He shoves Matt, who flies backwards and lands on his butt, his back thrust up against the seat Ethan and Isabel are sitting on. They scramble out of the way.

It's a big hit, way too hard for what looked like an easy shove. I remember that one of Dillon's powers is strength.

Matt gets up, red in the face. 'Now listen here, Neriah isn't your property. She isn't anyone's. She makes her own decisions.'

'That's right! And she was deciding on me until you turned up and stole her from me!' This time Dillon shoulder-charges Matt straight in the gut.

Matt falls backward again and looks winded.

'Get up!' Dillon calls out. 'Come on. Get up and face me. Or are you scared?'

Matt gets up, and, to his credit, lifts his hands in a peaceful gesture. Dillon ignores it completely; instead, punches Matt square in the jaw. Matt goes flying, crashing into bags and dragging a bench metres backwards.

'Dillon!' Isabel screams, while Ethan's thoughts come pounding into my head. He too is aware of Dillon's infatuation with Neriah. Seems like everyone knows. But Matt's done nothing wrong, and Ethan can't believe what Dillon's doing, out here in public.

He goes over and grabs Dillon from behind. 'Cool it, OK?'

Dillon jerks his shoulders and Ethan drops off like a fly.

As Matt gets up, Neriah tries to calm Dillon down. 'You've made your point, Dillon. We'll settle this now, without fighting. Come with me and we'll talk.'

But Dillon is out of control. He waves Neriah to the side, intent on squaring off with Matt again, but the power throbbing through him is way too strong. She runs into his arm and falls backwards, hitting the ground. Matt sees red.

By now a small crowd has formed around them, everyone jeering them on. The security guards keep glancing over, but seem reluctant to leave their posts at the gate. Matt comes over with his fists drawn. He lands a punch to the underside of Dillon's chin. And now it's Dillon who goes flying, crashing into Ethan, knocking him over again. The crowd starts cheering and hooting.

I look around for Mr Carter. Someone has to stop this

before it gets any more out of hand. Knowing one of his powers is incredible hearing, I call his name. If he's anywhere on school grounds, he should come.

Nothing.

'Come on, Mr Carter, where are you?' If he doesn't come soon and break this up, it's going to be too late, if it's not already. The fighting grows more intense as they continue swapping blows. The security guards have finally decided the fight is getting serious enough for them to intervene. They start shoving kids aside to get to the two at the centre.

But the teacher on duty, the vice-principal Mr Trevale, reaches them first. 'Hey! You boys stop this now!'

He gets in between them, holding them apart with a hand on each of their heaving chests. They stand and stare at each other until Dillon makes a move, but Mr Trevale screams at him, 'That's enough!'

Mr Carter finally turns up at a run, and when he sees that it's Dillon and Matt fighting, his eyes nearly fall out of his head. 'What's going on here?'

Mr Trevale looks from Dillon to Matt, making sure the situation is stable and he's not about to get his head punched in. 'I have no idea, Mr Carter, but I'm going to find out. You two boys get to my office now!'

Matt exchanges a quick look with Mr Carter, who gives an almost imperceptible nod.

'If you like, Bob, I know these two boys, I can look after this.'

Mr Trevale thinks about this and I hear his thoughts clearly. He's got a lot of work on his desk and he has to teach a class in a few minutes that will keep him tied up for most of the morning.

The buzzer sounds and everyone groans. Mr Trevale

227

gives them all a sharp look. 'You heard the bell. Now get going to your classes, all of you.'

Mr Carter tries again. 'I don't have a class right now. I can get to the bottom of this.'

Mr Trevale finally relents. 'Detention goes without saying, Marcus.' He gives Dillon and Matt a strong look. 'Perhaps even a suspension might be in order. We'll discuss it this afternoon. You boys are both seniors. You should know better!'

At last everyone moves off to their respective classes. Mr Carter shakes his head, disgusted. He would be. 'You two go straight to my office. We're going to have a little private conversation.'

Dillon starts to move off, his head hanging as if he can't believe what he just did. I go back to where I dropped my bag, intending to go to class, but just as I pull it on to my back I hear Matt talking to Mr Carter. 'I want Rochelle to come too.'

Mr Carter glares at him for a moment, clearly not understanding why.

'It's important or I wouldn't ask,' Matt continues.

Mr Carter calls me over. 'Matt wants you to come to my office too.'

'What for?'

Matt says softly, 'I want you to test Dillon's loyalty.'

'*What?* Are you serious? Why?'

'You saw what happened. Dillon initiated that fight with no thought of the consequences. The Tribunal will wonder if he started the fight on purpose to reveal my identity, or the identity of us all. Testing his loyalty will be one way to put everyone's mind at rest, and quickly.'

I can't believe this is happening! Damn Dillon and his temper! 'Matt, don't make me do this.'

228

'I don't see why you've got a problem with it. You did it to all the members of the Tribunal. That couldn't have been easy.'

'It wasn't, but … Dillon's one of us. It feels wrong. He's going to hate me.'

Like everyone else!

This wayward thought hangs between us, and for a moment I'm confused as to whose head it came out of – mine or Matt's.

Mr Carter urges us to hurry. 'We're better off having this conversation in the privacy of my office.'

Without taking his eyes off me, Matt's eyebrows lift, pressuring me to agree.

'All right, I'll do it. But it has to be now, with only Mr Carter as a witness. I don't want to humiliate Dillon in front of the others. OK?'

Matt checks with Mr Carter. 'That's fine. I'm not expecting the other teachers back for another hour or so. All the same, we'd better hurry.'

Mr Carter's office is a small room with three desks crammed into it and stacks of books lying around. The walls are lined with overflowing bookcases and filing cabinets in haphazard fashion. Dillon is already there, stretched out in Mr Carter's reclining desk chair.

'What took you's so long?' He sees me and sits up. 'What's *she* doing here?' He gets it in a second. 'Oh no, she's not touching *me* without a glove on. You can't do this. I want to see Arkarian.'

Mr Carter sits in another chair, dragging it over to his desk so that his face and Dillon's are less than one cen-timetre apart. 'Do you have anything to hide, Dillon?'

'Nothing!'

'Thanks to your little display out there, what do you

think everyone's going to think? For starters, the strength you exhibited would have to look suspicious. The Tribunal are going to be furious. They may even demand a trial. The very least they'll demand is for Rochelle to test your loyalty. So you have the choice: do it here in front of me and Matt, or in the Circle with Lorian and all the Tribunal members watching.'

Dillon groans, but it's a sign of resignation that everybody understands. Mr Carter pushes his chair back and pulls down the blind. Matt nods at me to go ahead. I make my way around a briefcase, its contents half spilled out on the floor alongside a garbage bin, and stand directly behind Dillon. For some reason I don't want to be looking at his face when I do this. I feel as if I'm betraying him, and it's a feeling that doesn't sit right. I tug off one of my gloves with my teeth. Sparks sizzle and bright electric charges form a zigzag pattern from my wrist down every one of my fingers.

Dillon hears it, probably even feels it, and jerks his head away. 'What the hell!'

Mr Carter gives a low whistle.

Matt frowns. 'Your power is surging. Does it hurt?'

I shrug, trying to make light of my hands, even though they're starting to keep me awake at night with pain. 'They're just a little stronger since Lorian enhanced my Truthseeing skills.'

A noise in the foyer has Mr Carter glancing at his watch. 'We really shouldn't be doing this here. We're going to have to hurry and keep our voices down.'

Dillon tentatively shifts his head back. 'You burn my hair and you'll pay –'

'Shut up, Dillon,' Matt says.

When everyone is silent I close my eyes and focus my

breathing – steady, slow, in and out. When I feel ready, I place my hand on top of Dillon's head, my fingers resting lightly on his forehead. A vision of a wildly burning flame reveals itself. It surprises me and I jerk backwards, clasping my hands together.

'*What?*' Dillon says in quick defence.

The others look at me with questions in their eyes. I shake my head. 'Nothing. It's just the vision is stronger this time and I wasn't ready. Lorian thought this might happen.'

Finding my focus, I try again. This time the flame flares wildly and I centre my attention into it, searching for the cause of this intensity. An image of the core soon develops and I see that Dillon's anger is a result of feeling cheated. Cheated by Matt. He believes Matt manipulated Neriah into falling in love with him when Dillon was away becoming a member of the Guard. There's pain and doubt there too, that Neriah might prefer Matt over him, but deeper there's the pain of his childhood, the loneliness of being with parents who thought only of themselves. But this is not what I'm looking for. I wade through all this hostility to the very depth of the flame. Finally I see it.

I open my eyes and lift my hand off Dillon's head. He pushes his chair away and spins around to face me. Now all three of them are staring at me, waiting for my verdict. I open my mouth to explain, when suddenly the door opens. Quickly I throw my hand behind my back and struggle to put my glove back on.

It's Mr Trevale, looking hurried. 'Just thought I'd pop in and see if everything's all right.' He spots me and a frown creases his brow. 'What are you doing here, Rochelle?'

231

Lost for words, I look to Mr Carter. He says, 'Well, Bob, it turns out that … ah … Rochelle is involved in this dispute.'

'What do you mean, Marcus? How seriously?'

'Well …' Now it seems Mr Carter is lost for words.

Mr Trevale decides to put his own spin on the situation. He looks at both Matt and Dillon. 'Were you two boys fighting over the attentions of a girl?'

Well, technically they were, except the girl isn't me. They both grunt and nod a kind of acknowledgement.

Mr Trevale makes a scoffing sound. 'I should have known. Seventeen year olds and their hormones!' He starts backing out of the door. 'Well, I'll see all three of you in detention this afternoon, shall I?'

As soon as the door closes I spin on Mr Carter. 'That's not fair, sir! He's got no right making me stay back for detention!'

Mr Carter groans and lifts his shoulders. 'What do you want to do, Rochelle? Go and argue with the Vice Principal? Draw more attention to yourself and Matt and Dillon?'

I fold my arms across my chest to try and calm down, then mutter under my breath, 'You could have said something.'

We fall silent. Of course Mr Carter's right. I'm not going to make a fuss over one afternoon's detention, but it's still unfair.

Mr Carter brings me back to the real reason I'm here. 'Rochelle, before we were interrupted, you were about to say –?'

I wave my hand in the air. 'Dillon's loyalties are true to the Guard.'

'I could've told you that,' Dillon mutters.

Mr Carter double-checks. 'Are you positive? No doubts?'

'He's clean, so to speak. He has no doubts about his decision to become a Guard.'

Matt's head nods and a smile eases the serious look he's been sporting lately. 'Now, about Neriah –'

Dillon's whole body tenses. 'You knew how I felt about her before I went into that safe room.'

Matt's head swings to the side for a moment. 'I'm only going to say this one more time: Dillon, I'm not interested in Neriah.'

'It doesn't look that way to me.'

Matt pins Dillon with a sharp look eye-to-eye. 'I'm not looking for a relationship.'

'Well, I think she's hung up on you,' Dillon mutters.

'Honestly, Dillon, I wouldn't know. I have no control over what Neriah thinks or feels. But I've made myself clear to her. OK?'

'How good is your word, Matt?'

'How long have we been friends?'

Dillon's head bobs up and down, looking pleased. 'Then promise me you won't go after her.'

Matt stares off into space as he contemplates the challenge Dillon throws him. Mr Carter says softly, 'Be careful what you promise, Matt.'

But it doesn't take Matt long to make a decision. 'Dillon, you have my promise. I won't make a move on Neriah.'

Dillon jumps out of his seat and whacks Matt on his back. 'You're a real mate. D'you know that?'

Dillon is happy. Well, why wouldn't he be? The way is clear for him to go after Neriah knowing there's going to be no competition from Matt. But Matt's promise leaves me with an uneasy feeling inside. If there's one thing I know, Matt doesn't make promises easily, nor does he take them lightly. But I reckon this one is going to be the greatest challenge he's ever taken on.

Dillon can hardly keep still. 'Can we go now, Mr Carter?'

Mr Carter starts to wave us away, when suddenly he calls out, 'Wait! Be quiet, all of you.' He closes his eyes and keeps them that way for a few moments, making my spine prickle. Mr Carter's not a Truthseer, but obviously he has some sort of communication system worked out with Arkarian.

Finally Mr Carter opens his eyes. 'There's a mission on tonight.'

'The sphere?' Matt asks. 'Has it stopped spinning?'

'Yes.'

The prickles on my spine are now fully-blown shivers. 'What year did it stop at?'

Mr Carter looks up, his eyes wide, round and glazed. 'Nine thousand, five hundred and ninety-six, *BC*.'

'*What?*' Dillon hisses.

Matt frowns deeply. 'That doesn't make any sense. That's prehistoric. What city could this be?'

Mr Carter's tone is filled with awe. 'It could only be Atlantis.'

234

Chapter Nineteen

Matt

I need to see Arkarian, and quickly. But first I have to finish detention. Detention! Forty whole minutes of 'silent contemplation', as Mr Trevale puts it, while he sits at the front marking homework sheets. For the first half I put myself into a trance. Since spending time with Dartemis, I've learned just how relaxing and replenishing deep meditation can be. Dillon could sure do with it. He hasn't been able to stop fidgeting since we got here – jerking his arms or tapping his feet. He's drumming his fingers on his desktop right now.

Sitting in front of him, Rochelle spins around. 'Do you have to do that? It's driving me insane!'

'But Roh, this is such a waste of time.'

'We all know that, Dillon, but you don't have to make it a torture session.'

I feel a moment of sympathy for Rochelle. She's stuck here because of me, because I used her power to check Dillon's loyalty. I used her even while she made it clear how uncomfortable it made her feel, and now she's being punished unjustly. *Sorry!* The single thought propels from my head to hers.

For a long moment there's no reaction, and I wonder if

she's heard me. Slowly she turns. She doesn't say anything, or propel any thoughts back, but the look in her eyes tells me that my one spontaneous thought has made an impact. Her eyes are glistening. She quickly looks away.

Mr Trevale gives a dramatic moan from the front of the room and makes a scene out of glancing at his watch. 'That's it, then. You can go.'

Relieved, we start to get up, scraping chairs and gathering our bags, but he doesn't dismiss us without a final warning. 'Don't let me catch this behaviour from you boys again. Now get going. I'm sure you have a lot more enjoyable things to get up to than school detention.'

We can't get out fast enough, but once we're out of earshot Dillon just has to ask, 'Do either of you guys know where Ethan's training Neriah today?' He glances at his watch. 'D'you think I've missed it?'

Rochelle's head shakes.

'They're in Arkarian's chambers,' I tell him. 'But it's a closed session. No visitors. And since they're protected in there, even Rochelle's not needed any more.'

'Right then,' he mumbles, but there's obviously more he wants to know. 'So now where does she live? I mean, since her home was destroyed.'

He's not going to like this, but there's no other way to put it really. 'She's staying with … Isabel.'

'Yeah?' And then it hits him. 'But that means she's staying with you!'

'Yeah, well, Arkarian thinks it's the best place for her right now.'

'With you? Oh that's convenient!'

'Jimmy's there too, in case of trouble.'

'You couldn't have it any better, could you?'

My temper snaps and I grab his shirt front, dragging him forward so that my face is right into his. 'I made you a promise. That's all you have to remember.'

Rochelle puts her hands between us, shoving us apart. 'Quit it! Do you want to get us into trouble again?'

We pull apart and she starts backing away. 'I'm out of here.'

She takes off through the front gates almost at a run. Mr Trevale comes out of the office, making a beeline for the car park. He sees us and frowns. 'Everything all right, boys?'

It's enough to get us moving – in different directions. Dillon catches up with Rochelle, while I head straight for the back gates. I need to see Arkarian, and I'm late enough as it is. I walk through the deserted school grounds wondering why I got so worked up today. I lost control this morning, and well, I almost lost control again a few moments ago. What's going on with me? It doesn't take long to figure it out – no wonder Lorian thought the only way he could be a fair and impartial ruler was to rid himself of male and female emotions. Well, there's no way I'll go that far! All the same, I see his point. The heart is a strange thing. It's also a significant weakness.

The secret door to Arkarian's chambers disappears the second I've passed through it. There's a sense of urgency inside; I feel it as I walk through the corridor.

'Good, you're here,' Arkarian says when he sees me. 'Come and look at this.'

Up close the sphere is an amazing sight. It reveals an ancient city with unusual buildings made of white stone and trimmed in red and gold. They're mostly tall, with round pillars at the front. Nearly all of the buildings are

237

many storeys high. Arkarian spins the sphere, and I see the city on a broader scale. The streets, cobbled and decorated with colourful glass and crystal chandeliers, shimmer under a brilliant sun. And right down the middle, the city is split by a canal of rippling ocean water. This canal is obviously used for both trade and sport, by the looks of the ships and canoes dotted along it. There are people everywhere, dressed in long tunics and strange turban-like hats. Arkarian spins the sphere again and the magnification centres on one incredible building – taller than all the others but with those white marble pillars out the front.

Arkarian explains, 'That's the temple you have to find. Locked inside an underground vault is a sphere much like this one, except small enough to fit in your hand.' Arkarian makes sure I'm looking at him before he goes on. 'Protect it. The sphere must go down with the city, all the way to the bottom of the ocean. Do you understand, Matt?'

'What's so important about this sphere?'

'It works much like this one here in my chambers, except where this one searches and finds the past, the Atlantean sphere finds the future.'

His explanation leaves me speechless for a moment. 'So what you're saying is …?'

'This sphere was the last sophisticated piece of technology the Atlanteans invented before the cataclysm of earthquakes and tsunamis saw the island destroyed. They only used it once, in its testing stage, so we know it works. Now Lathenia wants it.'

'Sorry for not quite getting this, but what good would it do Lathenia to be able to go into the future, if the future hasn't happened yet?'

'The battle for final control of the realms is looming. It's closer than ...' He pauses and his serious look kicks off a series of shivers down my spine. 'Closer than we want to acknowledge. And with this tool, Lathenia will not only be able to see the future, but possibly have access to it.'

'So she could view the battle, see how it's going to be played out, then structure her own defences to surprise us when the actual battle begins. She could change the outcome. Arkarian, she could change everything.'

'There's more that you have to know, Matt. More reason that the sphere has to sink with the island. I'm not sure how much you already know, or how much you've been told, so I'm going to explain it anyway.'

'Go on, Arkarian.'

'The Atlanteans were an advanced society. Too advanced for the earth in its time, and even still today. The technology that they created hasn't all been invented yet.'

'And that's why this machinery hidden in the ancient city has to stay that way?'

'That's right. It's not time to reveal it. The world – the earth – isn't ready. It would upset the natural balance. No one nation can have access to this sort of power. Not yet. Not for a long time. And of course, the Atlantean sphere is the most powerful piece of technology they invented. It was lost when Atlantis sank.'

'All right. But how will we be able to protect this sphere?'

Arkarian moves his hand over his own sphere and it spins, revealing the same beautiful city he showed me a moment ago, except this one is in turmoil. Thick ash and smoke almost obscure my view. Beneath this deadly cloud, people are running frantically, some pulling carts with belongings falling from them. Animals, including elephants, trample over those who can't get out of the way fast enough. A loud reverberating sound shakes the land and people scream and clutch each other. Some pray openly, while others push past them in their haste to exit the city. Most people appear to be heading for a distant mountain range.

'The last three days have been chaotic, but today, the day the portal has opened, is the day Atlantis will sink. Look over there.' Arkarian points to a rising part of the landscape that reveals an erupting volcano, lava spewing a torrent of fire from its mouth. 'You will have to get to the temple and make sure the sphere goes down with the city, then get out before you too are sucked into the ocean. Remember, all you have to do is call my name. I will be monitoring your progress the whole time. I will hear you the second you call. From what I have ascertained, the Order is sending two soldiers on this mission. One is Lathenia herself.'

'Great.'

'The other is unknown. We think it's a girl who is highly skilled. This soldier, whoever she is, is proving untraceable. So I suggest you take two allies with you.'

I try to think who would be best, but I'm still new at making these decisions. 'Which two would you take?'

'Considering the seriousness of this mission, and the fact that you will be going to an advanced society in the midst of utter chaos, the ideal team would consist of yourself with one male and one female, both Truthseers, both with wings. Two of you to handle Lathenia and her soldier, one to secure the sphere.'

Silently I go over everyone that I know and their

powers. Ethan has his wings, but isn't a Truthseer. Mr Carter doesn't have either. Jimmy and Shaun have their wings, but aren't Truthseers. As for the girls, Neriah's still coming into her powers and I don't even know what they are. She wouldn't be ready. And neither Isabel nor Rochelle has wings. 'If I can't take you along, Arkarian, then I have nobody that fits the criteria.'

'While Ethan isn't a Truthseer, he does have his wings and his illusionary powers could be a great advantage in Atlantis.'

'OK, then Ethan will come. And the girl?'

Footsteps behind me have me spinning around.

'Well, I don't have my wings yet, but I am a Truthseer.'

It's Rochelle. Arkarian must have asked her here, knowing she should be part of the team.

Another set of footsteps and Ethan comes into the room. 'Hey, so where are we going?'

'Atlantis,' I tell him. 'On the last day of its existence.'

Chapter Twenty

Rochelle

We land in a room in the Citadel, one after each other. Matt is first, while Ethan arrives a moment after me. I take a look around and as always wonder at the meaning of the room the Citadel chooses for us. This one is dark, heavy with shadows, the air thick and moist.

'Look at that,' Ethan says.

I spin around to see movement on the wall. It's a vine of some sort, and it's growing rapidly, spreading its tentacles up and across the ceiling. In seconds the growth is so thick vines start dropping around us.

'This room is creepy,' Ethan says.

Matt agrees. 'Let's get out of here and get our identities.'

We follow Matt up a disappearing staircase and find ourselves in a room with more limited clothing than we normally find in a wardrobe room. I end up clothed in yellow pants and matching long tunic over the top, both made from fine silk. Around my waist is a gold sash like the one I wore at my Initiation. My hair is still black, but way longer. A plait drops down my back almost to my calves. I glance in one of the many mirrors provided and see my face looks different too, more heart-shaped than usual.

Matt and Ethan are in similar pants and tunic sets, though theirs are both white. Matt now has short hair with a red tinge, while Ethan's is dark and thick. And even though we're all disguised, our eyes, of course, remain the same. Ethan looks at me and can't seem to look away. Matt notices and shakes his head.

His bad attitude irritates me. 'Just because our relationship ended in pain doesn't mean every relationship will,' I tell him. 'How many times do you want me to apologise for what I did to you?'

Matt opens his mouth, but I don't let him say whatever he's about to. 'Look, who knows what's going to happen? Or how long any of us have to live?'

He looks at me now with a puzzled expression. 'What are you talking about?'

And, without meaning to, my doubts come flowing out. 'Oh come on, we've all read the Prophecy.'

'So …? I don't get it.'

'Take heed, two last warriors shall cause grief as much as good …' I start to recite.

Ethan takes it up. *'From the midst of suspicion one shall come forth, the other seeded of evil.'*

'Yeah …?' Matt asks.

'Yet one shall be victorious while the other victorious in death,' I finish.

'And you think this last part refers to you?'

'At my Initiation I was given a tunic to wear.' I tug on the sash at my waist. 'A purple one with a gold sash like this.'

'You're not making any sense, Rochelle.'

Ethan explains, 'Purple is the colour of self-sacrifice.'

For the first time in a long time Matt looks at me

243

without scorn or anger. 'You're not going to die, Rochelle. Don't even think it.'

But his words are only words, and hardly comforting. 'How do you know? Can you see the future?'

He hesitates and his jaw slides left then right. 'Of course I can't, but then, neither can the Tribunal. Lorian wouldn't even have that power.'

A fleeting moment of calm sweeps through me. Not wanting Ethan to hear my next words to Matt, I speak to him through my thoughts only. *Ethan isn't interested in me, so you don't have to worry about my corrupting him or breaking his heart, but, if there were some chance that he … that we could at least be good friends, please don't wreck it for me.*

A door opens, letting us know we've stayed here long enough. Matt doesn't answer. I take this to mean he's at least thinking about my request.

We go out the doorway and straight up a disappearing staircase, followed by another and another. High into the upper levels we finally arrive. An opening in the opposite wall forms immediately. We go over and all three of us linger at the sight that reveals itself below. It's a long drop, right into the midst of utter chaos. Thunder is rumbling through the panicked streets, while buildings collapse with breathtaking force all over the place. Animals and people alike run screaming, attempting to make it to the distant hills. Hills that are hard to see from here as they are covered in a layer of thick cloud and ash. A building suddenly collapses right below us – mortar and bricks and slabs of marble scatter in every direction before sinking slowly into a gaping hole that has opened in the earth. And more alarmingly, this hole quickly fills with bubbling ocean water. Another explosion and the other half of the street disappears into the sea. A zebra caught at the edge tries helplessly to clamber out.

Above my head I feel Matt and Ethan exchange glances. I look up at them and they share their concern with me through their staring, almost vacant eyes. Matt is the first to pull himself together. 'Arkarian is going to deliver us as close to the temple as possible, so we won't have to walk those streets down there for very long.'

Ethan nods. 'He'll keep a close eye on us.'

'We've only to call his name –'

'No point in prolonging this and making ourselves more nervous. We know how this works. Let's just jump. But stay close. We don't want to end up at different ends of the city.'

On three we jump … and land on a set of stone steps that is shaking and breaking apart beneath us.

'Run!' Matt calls out. 'This way.'

The steps lead to the temple that houses the sphere we're after. Helping each other not to fall, we start to climb.

'Watch out!' Ethan suddenly yells out.

One of the huge marble pillars up ahead is breaking up. We charge to the top of the stairs as boulders smash left, right and all around us, finally dismantling into myriad smaller chunks.

'We have to get inside,' Matt calls out.

But an explosion out front shakes the earth along with the entire remains of the temple, sending my heart into a galloping skitter. A cloud of gaseous fire starts billowing up the temple steps. Without even a second to think, we scramble on all fours into the interior as fast as we can. The fireball smashes into the remaining front pillars, its flames cresting and surging towards us like liquid fingers of gold.

Matt gets up first. 'Quick – this way.'

We run after him. At least he knows the way. Arkarian briefed us all in his chambers earlier, but right now, among this rubble, everything looks different. We do know we have to go down several levels. We follow Matt, but it soon becomes hard to breathe as the corridors fill with ash and smoke and pockets of gas. My eyes start to burn.

'Follow me!' Matt runs off ahead and round a corner.

Another explosion and the walls on either side shake and start to break up. One crashes downwards. Ethan and I run hard, escaping just in time as the thick marble sheet shatters behind us, creating an even thicker cloud of dust.

'Down here!' Matt's voice trails up a set of descending stairs.

At the bottom of these stairs we're confronted by a sealed door. Matt runs his hands over it, looking for an entry.

'Great,' Ethan says, his eyes shifting to me. He's thinking of my hands, and if they will be able to locate this secret lock. They will. We might be housed in different bodies, but our souls transport with us. That means our eyes and, of course, our powers too.

I yank off my gloves. 'Here, get out of the way.'

Both Matt and Ethan stand back, and I lay my hands on the door. It's made of a metal I can't identify. It's as if this metal doesn't exist on the earth. These people must have brought it with them. It has qualities similar to copper and brass, but it's stronger than both of these combined. The door itself is a good thirty centimetres thick.

I move my hands and almost instantly find a weakness. 'Here.'

I move back and Matt stands before the lock and closes his eyes. I hear his thought – one word, *Open*. A soft click and the door slides away soundlessly.

The room is like a prison cell. There are no windows and the walls are made of the same strange metal that makes up the door. The floor is marble. In the centre of the room stands the only piece of furniture – a glass cabinet on a slab of white rock. A light shines directly into the glass, revealing a golden sphere not much bigger than the size of a man's hand.

Up close we see the sphere hovering in midair and gently spinning. 'Wow,' I can't help saying, wondering at how it is possible to defy gravity like this.

Suddenly the vault door bangs shut. An eerie feeling consumes me, but is soon replaced by real fear, as Lathenia makes herself known. And just as Arkarian said, she's here with another woman, a girl about my own age. While Lathenia never bothers with a disguise, I can only assume the girl's identity is well concealed. She's wearing a tunic like ours, but black. A scarf is coiled around her head with only a slit to reveal her eyes. She could be anyone, even someone that I know at school. But I don't try to work out who she is. There is really no point, and Arkarian warned me not to risk exposing my identity.

'I didn't think it would take you long to get here,' Lathenia says sarcastically. 'How is it that while I control the opening of the portals, you always manage to arrive a fraction before me?'

'That's simple,' Ethan says. 'We're better than you.'

Her silver eyes flare. 'Really? We shall see just how well you do this time.'

While she holds conversation, she manoeuvres herself around us, and I get what she's doing – searching our identities, giving herself enough time to figure out who we are. Her next words confirm my suspicions.

'Ah now, let me see. Who do we have here today?'

I keep my eyes averted, focusing instead on the sphere. But the immortal is quick to notice my nervous manner. She comes over and tilts up my chin with her long fingers. I jerk my head away, but a glimpse is all she needs. She hisses air sharply through her teeth.

'Marduke's been looking for you. He misses you terribly. You really shouldn't have run away like that. There are some things you just don't do if you enjoy living, my dear. You will come back with me to where you belong.'

Matt moves to stand between us. 'She doesn't belong to you. And neither does this sphere.' He's trying to shift the focus off me.

Her eyes shift to the sphere and without appearing to think twice, she shoves her hand into the cabinet, smashing the glass. But just as she attempts to grab the sphere, it starts spinning madly and flies out through the opening, away from her reach.

Her silver eyes flash blue as she realises where the sphere has gone. Ethan, using his power to animate objects, has the sphere safely in his hands.

'Give me that sphere!' Lathenia's command is thick with menace.

Using his thoughts Matt tells me to get back. I take a tentative step, but it attracts Lathenia's attention. She flashes her eyes at me. It's the only warning I get. Streaks of iridescent blues and green propel from her fingers. Like laser beams they burst across the room, smashing into my body. Like a ragdoll, I'm flung against the wall and pinned there.

'Give me the sphere or I will burn Rochelle Thallimar from the inside out!' And to me she says, 'Now that I control the middle realm, dying will put your soul exactly where I want it – in an eternity of torture.'

With a calm I've never seen in Matt before, he says, 'I wouldn't do that if I were you.'

'Explain yourself.'

'Lorian has placed a curse on the person who should take it into their head to kill Rochelle.'

'A curse?'

'Whosoever shall harm this child and cause her death, shall they themself turn to stone and die before the sun sets.'

Lathenia's eyes shimmer deeper blue. 'Why would my brother choose to protect a traitor?'

I try to squirm and jump down, anything to escape Lathenia's hold, but each time I move, pain seers through me.

'She's not a traitor to the Guard,' Ethan says.

Lathenia stares at him, her eyes narrowing as she tries to work out who he might be. 'How can you be so sure?'

'I know her,' he says, with the most amazing conviction in his voice. Unbidden, tears spring to my eyes. I shake them off.

'Really?' Lathenia's word drips sarcasm. 'I don't think you do. Can you tell me where she was only *last* night?'

I see it instantly. Doubt. It flickers like a living flame and passes in an exchange of looks between Matt and Ethan.

'Ah,' she says, as if she knows she has already won. 'Need proof?'

'Don't listen to her!' I scream out.

'You lie,' Ethan says to Lathenia. 'You have no proof.'

'Don't I? Look here ...'

Suddenly her eyes shift sharply to her left. An image forms in the air, so real, it's as if the scene is happening right here in the room with us. I'm in this image, along with Marduke. He's talking over me, leaning down as he often did in a manner that could easily be misconstrued as gentleness. I recall the scene well. It was the moment I confronted him with the knowledge that I suspected he was the one who murdered Ethan's ten-year-old sister. Here, he is trying to convince me it was not him. He is using all his persuasive powers, right down to a gentle touch to the side of my face. In the next second I will shove his hand away and a vicious confrontation will follow, but Lathenia doesn't show this part.

Matt and Ethan look as if they are both struck dumb.

I try to object, to explain, but Lathenia projects another burst of high-voltage energy through me.

Just as I feel as if I'm about to lose consciousness, Lathenia withdraws her attack. I drop to the ground coughing and catching my breath.

And while Ethan and Matt's thoughts are distracted, the girl accompanying Lathenia suddenly moves. Spinning like a whirlwind and reaching an amazing height, she leaps across the room. Surprising Ethan, she kicks him in his kidneys, knocking him forward. Spinning again, too fast for the human eye, she appears nothing more than a momentary blur. Stopping suddenly she lands another kick to Ethan's head, then another to his gut. On the third kick he drops the sphere. It rolls across the floor.

'Quickly!' Lathenia calls out, stretching her own fingers out for it.

At last my strength starts returning. I reach for the

sphere too, but my legs are still weak and I can't get up. The girl dives for it. We can't let either of them get their hands on it. If this should happen, they will disappear, leaving this time period instantly. And the sphere will then be Lathenia's.

But Matt has a plan. As the room is shaken by a thunderous tremor, he closes his eyes for a fraction longer than a normal blink. The sphere lifts away from Lathenia and her soldier's searching fingers. It hovers in the air for a moment before flinging into his own safe hands.

In a flash the girl leaps on Matt, but he shoves her aside easily. She rolls across the floor and hits the opposite wall, looking stunned.

As Ethan straightens up, Matt throws him the sphere. 'Protect this while I deal with Lathenia.'

I get to my feet and Matt asks, 'Do you think you can deal with the girl?'

'I'm fine now. I can do it.'

A moment later she leaps on Ethan. She's so fast her movements are almost indecipherable. They roll across the floor together, the sphere trapped between them. I decide to run over with the intention of using my hands on her, but she's quicker than even my thoughts. She gets up and stares at me with large oval eyes, ready to spring into action. My best chance is to let her come to me. In a flash she spins. It happens quickly. One second she's across the room, the next she's right in my face. I grab her arms and rip the sleeves off them. Then I release as much energy as I can into her unprotected flesh. She screams and clambers off me fast.

Meanwhile Lathenia is stretching her hands out to Matt. She's going to use the energy that flows from her fingers. But an even louder explosion directly overhead makes us all stop and stare. Suddenly a crack appears in one of the bright red walls. It grows larger as the whole room shifts downwards with a jerk.

'It's sinking!' the girl calls out as the rest of us struggle to keep upright.

Lathenia forgets Matt and shifts her attention to Ethan. He's the one with the sphere. He's the one she wants now. To her soldier she hisses, 'When the water surges, swim to the surface as fast as you can and wait for me there.'

Lathenia's words of water make my skin erupt in shivers. Another reverberating explosion overhead plunges the room into darkness and we start to sink as the marble flooring breaks into two halves. Ocean water floods in. Within seconds the room is half full, and then all my nightmares come at once as the surrounding walls break apart and an entire wall of water floods the chamber. The pressure is intense, and great chunks of metal and marble swirl around us.

The girl starts to swim, kicking herself up towards the surface. Below me, Lathenia has grabbed Ethan and is dragging him deeper and deeper towards the ocean base. She can out-breathe any mortal for sure. She's going to hold Ethan underwater until he drowns, then take the sphere, swim to the surface and return to her own time.

Matt dives down, following them, but Lathenia is fast. I can't believe this is happening. No way can Ethan's lungs hold out much longer, let alone get to the surface from the depths she has taken him already. And still she continues to drag him deeper. With my own lungs nearly bursting I dive after them. Matt sends his thoughts to me. *No! Go back. Get to the surface.*

I have to help!

252

He turns for just a moment. *Trust me! Now go and get ready to resuscitate.*

I stop and tread water. Resuscitate? He should have brought Isabel here instead of me! I watch Matt swim away, and even though visibility is next to nothing down this far, I can just make out his body changing shape. I peer into the darkness, trying to see what's happening. For a second I think I see a shark. A shark! It disappears into the murky depths in fluid movements. With my lungs on the verge of exploding I start kicking my way to the surface.

I break through and suck in huge gulps of putrid, ash-filled air. The sky is completely obscured. Only a few pieces of rubble protrude from what is now virtually complete ocean. Lathenia's soldier is sitting on one such miniature island. I decide to swim for another, further away.

Dragging myself from the water, I collapse on what is more or less a pile of large boulders, one of the last remains of what was once a beautiful city. I search the water, knowing that as each second passes, the worse it will be for Ethan.

Bubbles breaking the water are the first sign of movement from below. But it's Lathenia's head that crests the first waves. This must mean she has won. She spots her soldier and waves a weary-looking arm to her. But the arm is covered in blood, and my heart lurches at the sight. Whose blood could it be?

Matt and Ethan are still nowhere in sight.

Lathenia disappears from the water, reappearing on the small island where her soldier scrambles to assist her. The Goddess is bleeding badly from several wounds. She looks as if she's been in a fight with a … shark!

Suddenly both Lathenia and her soldier disappear. And for a long moment there is nothing but the sound of waves thrashing across the lower edges of the boulders. Time seems to stretch into eternity as I wait, constantly peering across the grey waves for signs of life, growing more agitated with every passing moment.

At last I see something. Bubbles have re-formed. But it's only a dolphin. The dolphin swims right up towards my island of boulders, as if it has something to tell me. That's when I see Ethan, sprawled unconscious along the dolphin's back. The dolphin changes and turns into Matt!

I help Matt drag Ethan ashore, rolling him over fast, checking his airways. They appear clear and I start resuscitating as I was taught last year at school. Minutes pass. I start to panic.

Matt drags himself over. 'I'll work his chest.'

Between the two of us, at last Ethan coughs. Quickly I roll him over again and he brings up a lot of water. Eventually he sits up, and the three of us stare at the destruction around us, exhausted. No one is inclined to break the silence.

It occurs to me that I didn't see Lathenia with the sphere, yet neither does it appear that Matt or Ethan has it.

'It's gone,' Matt says. 'It's at the bottom of the ocean.'

For a few more moments none of us says anything.

Eventually Matt calls Arkarian's name.

Chapter Twenty-one

Matt

'My father is in a rage.'

Arkarian's words surprise me. The two of us are sitting on stools in his central chamber. Behind us, the sphere is thankfully quiet. I've come up here to talk about Atlantis and to get some answers to questions this last eventful mission inspired. Now all thoughts of Atlantis disappear. The last time Lorian was in a rage, he rained fire over the earth and surged power into all of the Named.

'What's got Lorian all fired up this time?'

'There's a growing sense of disquiet among the Tribunal. He feels it, and it unsettles him.'

'Well, that's understandable. The traitor is one of them, and they're nervous.'

Arkarian shrugs lightly. 'There's no real proof, Matt.'

I scoff at this, my own doubts surfacing, and I can't help being sarcastic. 'Oh, come on! Didn't Lorian find the key buried in the courtyard? In a box that could only have been forged by someone with Tribunal powers?'

Arkarian's head lifts and his eyes meet mine. 'That might be true, but there are others with these powers.'

Since rescuing Neriah from Lathenia's palace I've come to my own conclusions about who the traitor is. And while Arkarian is right here beside me, apparently his thoughts don't follow the same line. I try to work out where he's heading. 'Don't tell me you think your own father has a hand in this?'

He doesn't hesitate. 'No, that's not what I mean.'

'Ah, so you think the Tribunal are being framed? By who? Marduke?'

He shrugs again and stares at his feet. 'I just don't want to believe the traitor is one of the Tribunal. Over the centuries I've grown close to each of them –'

'You've only known King Richard for a little over a year,' I remind him.

'And I have come to know him very well in that time, Matt.'

'Don't be naïve, Arkarian. You and I both know who this traitor is.' Using my thoughts I remind him of the image that stunned us both in Lathenia's palace not so long ago. An image of King Richard walking arm-in-arm with the enemy herself.

In a serene voice that is Arkarian's trademark, he says, 'Veridian has waited centuries for this King. I can't believe he is a traitor.'

So calm! So loyal! Can't he see what's right in front of him? 'The things we wish for can be as elusive as a dream, and just as far from reality.'

'But, Matt, without hope, where are we?'

I shrug, and he says, 'The worlds are so full of mystery that to shut ourselves off from hope, from dreaming, from believing in things that we cannot see, is to live a life without colour.'

'So how do you explain King Richard's presence in Lathenia's palace?'

'My father knew about our rescue attempt. Perhaps he

sent Richard to distract the Goddess and make our task easier.'

'If that were true, our good King Richard takes his job very seriously! Wasn't it the *bedroom* they disappeared into?'

Arkarian has no answer. 'All I know, Matt, is that we should keep this information to ourselves for the time being.'

'Why? If King Richard is the traitor, he should be revealed. And quickly.'

'If we accuse him and we're wrong, the real traitor will remain free, and we will have destroyed our King.'

Reluctantly I agree. For now at least. 'All right. But Dillon and Neriah were there. They saw him too.'

'Don't worry, I'll brief them. Just make sure you keep the key safe from … everyone. Right now we don't know who we can trust.'

'The key is safe, Arkarian. At least it is as long as the ancient city remains impregnable.'

'Jimmy is doing what he can, but he's only human.'

With these sombre thoughts we fall silent.

Arkarian speaks first. 'The issue of the traitor is not the only thing distressing my father.'

Again, he surprises me. 'What then?'

'In these difficult times he feels that all who are to be Initiated should be Initiated by now, but there are still two left.'

'Neriah?' I ask.

'Yes, Neriah and Dillon.'

The thought occurs that *I* haven't been Initiated yet either. Arkarian replies without my having to voice these thoughts out loud. 'Matt, there is nothing the Lords and Ladies of the Tribunal can give you, for you have been trained by one who is higher. Your time in *his* realm was your Initiation. Nobody questions your right to be a Guardian of Time, nor your role according to the Prophecy.'

Arkarian's explanation is a lot to take in. These people don't even know me. How can they trust me so unconditionally? I try to shift the focus of our discussion. 'Will Neriah and Dillon be Initiated together?'

Arkarian takes his time answering. 'Neriah's Initiation will be held in a closed chamber. Other than Lorian and the Tribunal members, the only guests will be me … and you.'

'Is this unusual?'

He nods. 'An Initiation is something of great joy, to be shared.'

'Then why is Neriah's ceremony going to be closed?'

'Neriah is … a special girl.'

'Well, sure, I get that. But you're not answering my question.'

'It doesn't matter … for now.'

I would pressure him into being more specific, but I'm not sure I want to hear what he's got to say. 'So when do we leave?'

'Tonight. When you get home, brief Neriah on the details. Dillon will be here in a few minutes and I'll speak with him.'

I leave before Dillon arrives. It's not that I'm trying to avoid him, it's just that there's been so much happening, I could do with a few quiet moments to myself.

The chill air outside helps to revive me from the semi-daze I've been in since experiencing the destruction of Atlantis. I shrug inside my jacket and embrace the early evening air.

On the walk down the mountain it grows dark. And while I'm not hungry, haven't had the stomach for food since last night's mission, the tempting scent of Mum's cooking wafts towards me, making my stomach growl. Lights are on in nearly every room in the house. Isabel is upstairs in her room, which she now shares with Neriah. The girls are talking. I can hear their voices, deep in conversation. Mum calls them for dinner. I see their silhouettes make for the door.

Ever since discovering that Isabel's father is not my father, that in fact, my father is someone from … well, another world, so to speak, I've felt on the outside loop of my own family. Isabel once worried that I would be different after returning from my training. She was wrong, and yet she was right too. I'm the same person, the same flesh and blood, with the same fears and doubts and inexperience, but the things I can do now mark me as different. It makes me reluctant to use my powers in front of the others. Especially the power of changing shape.

Jimmy comes out carrying a heavy plastic bag. He sees me and stops. 'Your mother's been worried about you. I told her you wouldn't be far away. Hold on till I dump this garbage and we'll go in together.'

Jimmy is hardly my favourite person, but since my time with Dartemis, I can at least tolerate him now – his presence I mean, here in this house. He runs back from the garbage bin and holds the door open for me.

I step inside at the same time Isabel and Neriah make it to the bottom step. Isabel stares at me with narrowed eyes. 'Are you OK? You look like crap.'

Jimmy comes in behind me. 'Cold's all he is, luv. Needs some of your mother's good cooking.'

While Jimmy and Isabel exchange a few more words, my eyes drift to Neriah. As usual when I see her, my chest constricts as if someone is holding a steel belt around my ribs, tightening it notch by notch. My breathing difficulties confirm I made the right decision about her.

For a second our eyes meet. What I see in hers nearly knocks me over. So much hurt, confusion, anger – a potent mix. 'Neriah …?'

Her head shakes negatively, and without saying a word, she turns and heads straight into the kitchen.

Halfway through an awkward dinner I excuse myself and go out the back for some fresh air. I sit on the bottom step of the porch, inhaling the cold night air, until I hear Mum and Jimmy rummaging around in the kitchen. Dinner is over and they're starting to wash up. I decide to go inside when the back door creaks open. I look up and see Neriah. I freeze at the sight she makes. Her eyes reach across the icy distance between us. I become overwhelmed by a need to hold her.

'I just wanted to say I heard about your promise to Dillon. A promise! Matt, that's so … final.'

Now I understand her earlier look and the awkward conversation at dinner. 'Let me explain –'

'I don't think you can, Matt. When Dillon first told me about it, I was really mad. I mean, I just couldn't understand. You see, I thought you felt what I felt and that all you needed was time.' Her head shakes. 'But now I get why you don't want to have anything to do with me.'

'What are you saying?'

'You've still got feelings for Rochelle.'

'*What?*'

She holds her hand out to stop me from getting any

260

closer. 'Listen, I didn't come out here to lecture you. It's entirely your choice who you want to be with.'

'You've got it wrong. I don't want to be with Rochelle. I'm uncomfortable just being in the same room as her.'

'Exactly. Why are you uncomfortable when Rochelle's around? It's been a year since you found out the truth. Why can't you let her go and move on?'

For a moment I go blank. 'Hell, I don't know!'

'Your pain is making you blind and scared, and so you're running for cover. But like I was trying to say when I came out here, I understand. And, well, I also wanted to say, however long it takes for you to heal, I'll be waiting for you.'

With these words she spins around and runs into the house.

Inside me there's an overwhelming urge to run after her, to grab her and hold her as tightly as I can. But I fight this urge with everything I have. It would be wrong to let her think there could ever be anything between us. I have to tell her about tonight's visit to Athens. She needs to be briefed, prepared for what's about to happen. But right now is not a good time. I think I'll leave it up to Isabel.

Chapter Twenty-two

Matt

This night just keeps getting weirder by the second. I put my thoughts of Neriah to the side for now, take a shower and go to bed. The sooner I fall asleep and get these Initiations over with, the better.

But sleep doesn't come. I toss and turn, then finally use my meditation training to settle my nerves. My breathing starts to slow and my body calms. As I do this, an image forms. But it's an image that doesn't belong to me and shouldn't be in my head. It takes a moment to realise what's happening. Isabel is having a dream. And I'm seeing it. The dream goes on and on. Vivid pictures flicker so fast it's like having an electric train storming through my brain. I wonder what it must be like for her. And then I understand what it is I'm experiencing – it's not a dream, it's one of Isabel's visions.

I get up and go into her room. She's thrashing around on the bed, gripping her head with both hands. Neriah is by her side in the dark, her large eyes looking frantic with worry.

'She'll be all right,' I explain and sit on Isabel's other side. 'It will pass in a moment.' *Hopefully!* I add silently. While I've seen my sister have visions before, several of them, in fact, I don't remember them looking this painful.

If all the powers of the Named have magnified, what must Isabel's visions be like now? I try to calm her by putting my hand on her shoulder. She goes rigid, sits up straight and starts digging her fingers into my arm. '*Matt!*'

'I'm here.' I try to keep my voice calm. The flickering images in my own head have ceased. I hope this means Isabel's vision is over now too. 'It's all right.'

'I saw … I saw …' She gulps deeply, her eyes looking wild.

I push her hair back from her face. 'Take your time. Get your breath back.'

Her head shakes. 'But you don't understand.'

'No, I don't, but if you calm down you can tell me.'

She takes a deep breath, acknowledges Neriah's presence, then starts to explain. 'There was so much. Fragments. Disjointed. Strange creatures. Some creatures I remember seeing in the underworld, but there were others too – grey and shadowy.' She shudders.

'What were these creatures doing?' I ask.

'The ones with wings were flying over the school. There were so many, they cast a shadow as if it were late afternoon.' She looks into my eyes. 'Matt, they were armed with chemicals – drugs from Marduke's garden, and they were releasing them over the whole of Angel Falls!'

'Do you know when this will happen, Isabel?'

She sighs and grabs both sides of her head. 'Soon, I think.'

'All right. I'm going to Athens tonight. I'll let the Tribunal know about your vision. There's nothing else you can do, so try and get some rest.'

Neriah adds softly, 'I'll stay right here beside you until you fall asleep.'

No! There's something else! Isabel's thoughts come thundering into my head as she skims a brief look at Neriah. Whatever else she's seen, she doesn't want Neriah to know. I turn her face towards me and urge her with my eyes to go on.

I saw Rochelle, she lets me know.

Only three words, but she says them with such intensity, I brace myself.

I tried to heal her, but the arrow went straight through her heart!

Stop! Don't tell me any more! my own thoughts scream back. But she's not a Truthseer and doesn't hear me.

The arrow tip was poison.

I take a deep breath and ask the same question I asked only a moment ago. 'Did you get a sense of when?'

'After the Citadel falls.'

I stare at her as if she were made of glass and I can see right through to her soul. 'What did you say?'

Suddenly Arkarian's voice is in my head. *Is Isabel all right?*

He's felt the vision too and is worried about Isabel. I let him know she's fine, just shaken. He tells me the Tribunal are waiting for Neriah and me to arrive, and that we should hurry. *I'll send Jimmy in to look after Isabel*, he adds.

A moment later a sleepy Jimmy comes running in and takes control. 'What's going on?'

'Isabel had a vision,' I explain.

'All right, I'll debrief her.' He looks at Neriah and me. 'Shouldn't you two be sleeping?'

Reluctantly I nod, then take Neriah out of the room with me. She won't get to sleep in there now, that's for sure. We're supposed to be in a state of deep relaxation for the transition to the Citadel to take place, but how do we reach that now, knowing what we've just heard? What *I* just heard? *After the Citadel falls!* Did Isabel really say that? What else did she see?

I open the door to my room and Neriah walks in and looks around.

I go over to the stiff chair at my desk and flop into it. 'You take the bed.'

She looks between the bed and chair. 'That chair is impossible to sleep in. Why don't you come and lay beside me, Matt. I promise I won't make a move on you.'

It's dark, but I think she's joking. I sense her smile more than see it. But it's not *her* making a move that worries me right now. I would love nothing better than to curl up in the comfort of her arms and wipe away the disastrous images of Isabel's vision. 'Thanks, but I've learned to meditate standing up if I have to. The chair will be fine.'

She lays on the bed and curls her knees towards her chest. She looks cold, and the urge to warm her over-whelms me and makes me tremble. I take the three steps between us and lift the quilt over her. She snuggles beneath it and I force myself to turn away to the chair. Closing my eyes, I finally slow down and get the sense of immediate transportation. Suddenly I'm falling. I brace myself and land in a room in the Citadel.

Arkarian is there to meet me, a worried expression on his face. 'Is she all right?'

He means Isabel. 'Yes,' I assure him. 'Jimmy's with her. He's going to go over her vision with her and try to put

265

some sense to it. Some sort of time frame would be useful.'

Neriah starts to form, her body taking solid shape.

Arkarian greets her warmly, then explains, 'We've been waiting so long, I sent Dillon on ahead. It's not good to linger in this place. Time means so many things here and takes so many forms.' He leads us to a wardrobe room where we all end up dressed in long tunics with matching cloaks. Mine and Arkarian's outfits are both silver, while Neriah's is white, broken by a sash of woven golden thread.

When we arrive, Sir Syford and Queen Brystianne are waiting for us in the courtyard. 'You're late,' Sir Syford says. 'But never mind, it can't be helped. Isabel's vision has already been recorded. It's very troubling.'

Queen Brystianne takes Neriah by the elbow. 'But that's not why *you* are here, my dear. This is a special occasion and you're very welcome. I have an exciting gift to bestow on you, and I cannot wait.'

'Well, hold on to yourself, my lady,' Sir Syford says. 'Dillon is first up. Everyone is prepared and waiting already.'

Arkarian nods and we follow Sir Syford and Queen Brystianne through several cool corridors. At last we arrive, and Dillon, tapping his foot on the marble flooring, waits for us wearing royal blue. 'Finally! They're impatient in there. Lord Penbarin's come out twice already.'

Arkarian takes his elbow and leads him away for some last-minute instruction. The doors swing open and Sir Syford and Queen Brystianne take their places in the Circle with the rest of the Tribunal members.

I start to lead Neriah over to the viewing seats to the

side, but as I do so, I glance across at King Richard and something happens. Our eyes meet and hold. Suddenly all my doubts about him re-emerge. A flash of anger rushes through me that proves hard to contain. Here is the man that is supposed to be King of Veridian, plucked from history to fulfil a prophecy written before all of us were born. So much rests in this man's hands, but just how loyal are they?

Arkarian appears in the doorway with Dillon by his side. He picks up my thoughts and hurtles a warning into my brain. *Shut off your thoughts!*

Quickly I move on, but as I pass Lorian I see him staring at me with a frown.

Arkarian leads Dillon to the centre of the Circle, quickly and purposefully getting everyone's attention. 'Father, my Lords and Ladies, allow me to introduce to you our newest Initiate. His name is Dillon Sinclair, and while his presence here is a surprise, it is a welcome one.' Everyone applauds, and in the hubbub I release a deep sigh.

Dillon sits on a stool looking nervous but excited. Arkarian takes a place beside me and Neriah. He doesn't say or think a word of what just passed between me and King Richard, but his stiff body language is speaking volumes. Finally his head turns to me and shakes slightly. He's telling me to forget the incident. Let it go. At least for now.

From the centre of the Circle, Lorian asks Dillon to swear his fealty to the Guard and Dillon does so with enthusiasm. And by the glances exchanged, everyone finds his manner amusing and refreshing.

One by one the Tribunal members bestow their gifts. Lady Devine gives Dillon the gift of wisdom. Lord

Meridian, the ability to see truth through falsity. Queen Brystianne offers humility, while Sir Syford gives strength, then adds, 'But since we already know of Dillon's superior physical strength, my gift is the strengthening of his spirit.'

Around the Circle the Tribunal members nod and murmur their appreciation. It's a good gift, as are all that Dillon has received so far. Lady Arabella is next. She glides over and lays one of her delicate, blue-veined hands on Dillon's head. 'My gift to you is fulfilment in matters pertaining to the heart. This gift will give you the ability to decipher when love is reciprocated … or left wanting.'

This time the Circle erupts in nervous chatter and the tension in the room hits the ceiling. Lady Arabella glances around, silencing everyone with her ice-cold look. Finally she focuses back on Dillon. 'All of today's gifts will take time to nurture and grow. You need to work on them as if you were an Apprentice learning his craft for the first time. Make sure you do that, Dillon.'

When Lord Penbarin walks over he glances at Lady Arabella with his bushy eyebrows raised halfway up his forehead. She sits and at last he turns his attention to Dillon. 'Vision,' he says simply. 'My gift is the drawing out of your second power, which appears reluctant to reveal itself. Of course, you haven't had the opportunity of a mentor, at least not one from within the Guard. I'm assuming this is the reason your second power is still dormant.'

'My lord,' Dillon asks, 'what does this mean?'

Lord Penbarin's hands lift in an unknowing gesture. 'It's *your* power, Dillon. Whatever it proves to be, nurture it and you may be surprised.'

Finally King Richard approaches. I make sure to keep any thoughts of traitors completely under control. 'My gift to you is the ability to share your knowledge so that one day you will become a Trainer.'

Dillon's face breaks into a surprised grin. He looks up at King Richard and nods a thank you.

When King Richard returns to his seat, all eyes turn to Lorian. And for a long moment the Immortal sits still with his head downcast. Nothing can be heard in the room except our breathing. At last Lorian stands and goes over to place his hands over the top of Dillon's head. 'What you did in choosing the Guard over the Order took courage most in this room would not have in a thousand years.'

I can't help feel that if he means to keep his Tribunal loyal, mocking them isn't the way to do it. Arkarian coughs beside me and I realise I failed to screen this particular string of thought. What the hell am I doing today? First the slip with letting King Richard know I have an issue with him, and now this! Slowly I become aware that all the Tribunal members have picked up my thoughts too. Lorian's head turns in my direction. His eyes bore into mine, asking how dare I sit there and judge him? But I can't and won't apologise. Even though I didn't mean for my thoughts to be heard, I still meant them.

Maintaining eye contact for what feels like an eternity of unpleasantness, Lorian is first to look away. Beside me Arkarian gives a distinct sigh of relief.

His attention back to Dillon, Lorian says, 'And while you are not Named by birth, you have earned the right to stand beside them as one. And so that you will feel their equal, my gift to you is the magnification of your power of strength, and your developing second power.'

Light descends from Lorian's hands to cover Dillon from head to foot. I feel the force of Lorian's power from here as clearly as if it were surging through my own body; and I wonder how Dillon is holding up.

When it is over, the light recedes into Lorian's open palms and Dillon tips backwards, the stool tumbling out from beneath him. Arkarian dashes over and helps him up, while the room erupts with clapping and cheering.

Lorian steps back and says, 'Go now, Dillon, for a sumptuous dinner awaits in your honour. And after Neriah's Initiation, the rest of us will join you both in a night of festivity and celebrating.'

As the cheering slowly recedes, everyone except those specially requested to stay, leave the room. When the last has gone, Lord Alexandon and Arkarian lock the chamber doors. Beside me, Neriah starts to shake. I take her hand between both of mine to try to calm her. 'You're going to be wonderful. They love you already. I can feel it.'

She smiles at me and lowers her head. Arkarian calls her over and she slides her hand out from between mine to take her seat in the centre of the Circle. And as Arkarian begins his introduction, I rub my hands together. My fingers are tingling.

The cheer is loud and expected. I wasn't lying when I told Neriah the Tribunal members love her already. The atmosphere in the room is overwhelmingly warm and full of adoration.

Lorian joins her at the centre. 'Do you, Neriah Gabriel, swear your fealty to the Guard and all its members?'

'Yes, my lord.'

270

He steps back and motions for Lord Penbarin to be the first to bestow his gifts. He goes and stands before her. 'Welcome, my dear. From the House of Samartyne I offer you the gifts of fortitude and mercy.' Lady Arabella is next. Her gift is that of seeing the truth through all forms of concealment and trickery. Sir Syford bestows Neriah with the ability to know when evil is present. When it is Queen Brystianne's turn she circles Neriah first, her flowing cream gown making a dramatic show.

'My gift to you is the enhancing of your affinity with animals, so that you will be able to communicate with them, and they will be able to communicate with you.'

This gift is as special as Queen Brystianne earlier boasted. Along with the others, I can't help but applaud. Neriah is overwhelmed with gratitude. She looks up to thank Queen Brystianne and her face is full of joy.

The remaining gifts are almost as exciting; clearly Neriah is a favourite among them. King Richard is last, and his is a physical gift. He hands Neriah a brush, a fine and delicate paintbrush that fits neatly in the palm of her hand. 'With this brush you will be able to paint passageways into other worlds. It will take time to perfect the skill, and one day you won't need the brush to accomplish this same task. It is a great responsibility, Neriah. You must use this power wisely. Practise with the brush but do not fret if you should lose it. It will work for no other hand, and the power I speak of is already within you.'

He sits and I think about his gift. It has the potential to be powerful beyond words. And I have to wonder, who is this girl – daughter of a traitor – who has won the hearts of all these honourable people?

Lorian stands and approaches Neriah with his gift.

Lifting his hands to hover over her head he says in simple words, 'I give you the gift of Truthseeing.'

Murmurs ripple around the room, but the consensus is that while the gift is generous, it is also befitting. As Lorian's gift is bestowed on her, and Neriah becomes a Truthseer, the Tribunal members and Arkarian start to applaud.

When it is over, Neriah goes to stand, but Lorian waves her down. 'There is one more of us here today who has a gift to pass to this girl.'

The Tribunal members start murmuring to each other, and heads bob up and down.

Lorian glances at me. 'Matt, will you come into the Circle?'

Though phrased in the form of a question, Lorian's 'request' is more of a command. I do as he says. 'Yes, my lord?'

'Do you have a gift to pass to this girl?'

His question takes me completely by surprise. Sure I have a gift for someone. It's my father's assurance that I will not live an eternity on my own. I remember his instructions well. I'm to nurture this gift until I find the right one. I would know her, he told me, by looking into her mind. I look down at Neriah now. 'Is *she* the one?'

Lorian smiles, and for a moment he almost resembles his brother.

'But …?' *If this is so, why can't I see it?*

'We have been wondering,' he says beside me, still looking amused.

Neriah glances around the room looking uncomfortable. She starts to get up.

'Sit down, Neriah,' Lorian commands, then looks at me and waits.

272

I go to take another look, but Neriah has suddenly become more interested in the subtle patterns of the tiled flooring. I take a deep breath to try and calm my racing thoughts, then with the tip of my finger under Neriah's chin, I lift her head. Our eyes meet, hold, and the truth suddenly hits me. Neriah is the one person I am destined to share my life with – *for ever!* She will one day become a member of the Tribunal. Everyone in this room knows it – that's why so many of her gifts were about judgement and mercy and such. It's also why the Tribunal members hold her in such high regard.

And then I remember my promise to Dillon. Mr Carter's warning suddenly comes flinging back at me: 'Be careful what you promise'.

'Oh no!'

Neriah's head jerks at my words, and I realise I've spoken them out loud. She squirms and looks uncomfortable.

In front of all these people I'm at a loss to explain.

'Matt, are you ready?' Lorian asks beside me. 'It's time to do this.'

I nod, half in a daze, and Lorian goes back to his stool.

Taking a deep calming breath, I lift my hand to rest against her forehead, just as Dartemis showed me. And with all the skill and power that my father taught me, I draw on the gift I have been minding on his behalf. 'Neriah Gabriel, I give you the gift of … *Immortality.*'

The instant the word is spoken the room begins to shake. Some of the Tribunal members gasp, others reach out and hold hands. Lorian tries to calm them. And as he does so, a golden light emits from my hand against Neriah's forehead. It pushes into her and her skin takes on a golden glow from the inside. It works its way through her body from her forehead, through her arms, chest, torso and legs, right down to her toes. You can even see it through her white tunic. Suddenly she shudders with the force. But it is soon over, and while her skin still glows, it does so softly now.

She glances at her hands, turning them over.

'It will pass. Your skin will return to normal by morning.'

Lorian comes over and motions for Neriah to stand. When she does, it is on slightly unsteady legs. Lorian declares we should now go and join Dillon in a sumptuous feast. The room erupts in cheering, and many of the Tribunal members come over to congratulate Neriah.

The doors are unlocked and soon everyone finds their way to a dining room laid out with tables of food and drink. Dillon comes over and comments on Neriah's gently glowing skin. Neriah is quick to explain it away, and I notice she doesn't tell him she is now a Truthseer. She probably needs time to adjust.

For most of the evening Neriah makes sure to never be alone with me. If she sees me coming, she quickly finds someone to talk to and immerses herself in conversation. Most of the time Dillon is never far from her side. He keeps his eye on her even when Lorian goes over to talk to him.

The room – in fact the whole palace – becomes stifling and I go outside. In the courtyard I find a pair of amazing golden birds locked in a cage. They see me and come right up to the wire and start singing. It is the most melancholy, mournful sound I have ever heard. I get the sense that they're trying to tell me something. I use my power to listen in their language, but their thoughts are blocked to me. Their singing grows faster. Their pitch rises. They start pushing against the fine mesh, flapping and scraping their wings.

Lady Arabella appears beside me, and the birds go silent.

'They seem disturbed,' I remark.

She starts fiddling with the trays at the bottom of the cage. 'With all the excitement today, I've forgotten to change their seed. They're just hungry, that's all.' She places the fresh seed inside their cage, but they don't touch it. 'There, there, my lovelies.'

'Where did you find them?'

'They found me,' she says.

'They don't belong in this world.'

She sighs. 'It must be why they sing so mournfully.'

'Why do you keep them locked in a cage?'

She gives me a wide-eyed look. 'For their protection. They're injured, and until they can fly again, they're in danger from wolves and other wild animals.'

'Ask Isabel to heal them. Then you can let them go.'

'She can heal creatures other than human?'

For some unknown reason I don't want to give her any more information about my sister. I try to think of something to switch the subject and run a hand over the fine craftsmanship of the cage. 'It's a work of art.'

'Yes. Jimmy is amazing, isn't he?'

'Jimmy built this?'

'I'm not sure if there's anything he can't do, or hasn't had a hand in making around here. He's very talented. And his timing is impeccable. Whether you need him or not, he always seems to be there, one step ahead of you.'

'Yes,' I murmur, unconsciously agreeing. Jimmy is the Protector. He has access to every high-security area, and he knows all the secret doors and passageways into and out of the city. In fact, they're his security systems that guard us all. But look what happened with Neriah's house – Marduke broke through its defences.

'Are you all right, Matt?' Lady Arabella asks.

But my thoughts are still with Jimmy. Arkarian trusts him with his life. *Dartemis* trusts him with the mother of his son! Do I have the right to doubt him? Am I just being paranoid? I recall Arkarian's warning to keep the key safe from *everyone* because we don't know who we can trust. Did he mean Jimmy too? Other than Arkarian, Jimmy is the only other person who knows where I've hidden the key. In fact, he's the one who helped me secure its hiding place.

From the corner of my eye I see Neriah running through a door at the far end of the courtyard. Lady Arabella notices too. 'Don't make the same mistakes Lorian has made.'

Not quite sure what she's talking about, I get the sense she believes I should follow Neriah and make amends. I think it's a good idea, and so I put thoughts of the traitor out of my mind for now. Anyway, I can't go suspecting people just because their skills give them access to high-security areas! And while I've had my issues with Jimmy, he's never given me any reason not to trust him.

The troubled birds appear to have quietened down now, so with one last look I pull away from the cage. My hands have dust on them and I brush them down the sides of my cloak. 'The cage is dusty. I thought it was new.'

Lady Arabella looks at me with a vacant stare. 'Dust? Oh, yes, it blows in on the night wind. I'll clean it right away.' And then she adds, pointing to the gate Neriah disappeared through, 'You'd better hurry. It's easy to lose sight of someone in the dark around these hills.'

I take off and soon find myself searching the hills outside the palace walls. I spot Neriah running past some scrub and bush. I follow and find her sitting on a grass-covered mound overlooking ancient Athens in the moonlight.

She sees me and gets up, looking around for a place to run.

'Don't go!'

She pauses and I catch up.

She says, 'What do you want?'

'To talk. To clear up our misunderstanding.'

'OK, that's simple. I'm sorry you have to spend the rest of your life with me.'

I stare at her in awe. Her skin is still glowing, but even without this, she is still the most beautiful creature I have ever seen. 'You knew our lives were destined to be entwined from the moment we first met.'

She thinks about this for a moment, then bursts into laughter. 'Of course.'

The sound of her laughter ripples through me. 'I could listen to your voice all of my life.'

She laughs again and twirls around and around. The moonlight appears to dance around her. I grab her arms and hold her still. 'Stop, you're making me dizzy.'

Breathlessly she whispers, 'But you are making me so happy.'

'I didn't think I could feel like this again. I didn't want to.'

'And now?'

'Now, looking at you, I know it's right.'

She smiles. 'Remember when you rescued me from Lathenia's palace, where she had me locked in an enchanted cage?'

'Yes.' I wonder where she's going with this.

'And I told you she locked me in the cage because I had come into one of my powers and she feared that I might escape?'

'Yes.' Now I'm really confused.

Neriah pulls away and starts to dance and swirl around. Before I realise what's happening, her long slender shape changes form. Her arms become fluttering wings, while her legs shorten and keep shifting until she transforms into the shape of a dove! She hovers in the air directly in front of me, and in my head I hear her say: *Come with me!*

My heart races at the thought. I will the shape of a dove and together we soar into the sky, and I feel freer than I've ever felt before.

We fly over Athens, enjoying the sight of this ancient city, but more so the company of each other. Time passes and it is easy to forget the dinner in the palace that continues without us. She understands my concerns and we fly back to the hill, changing into our human shapes as soon as our feet touch the ground. We find ourselves standing so close together, that our bodies touch from shoulder to knee. Without any effort we wrap our arms around each other. As if it is the most natural thing in all the worlds, my mouth finds hers and we kiss. We kiss for a long time, and all that is around us ceases to exist.

A rustling, snapping sound jolts me back to the reality of where I am and what my responsibilities are.

'What is it?' Neriah whispers against my chest.

My arms tighten around her, instinctively feeling the need to protect. Something, or someone is out there. The sound is too much like a twig being purposefully snapped in two. 'It's nothing,' I try to reassure.

'Is someone watching?' she asks again.

I don't voice my suspicions out loud and I screen them as hard as I can. 'Come on. We'd better get back before we're missed.'

But I suspect we have already been missed.

Chapter Twenty-three

Matt

The trip to Athens has an unsettling effect. When Arkarian shifts me back into my bed, I wake with a jolt, and glance at the digital clock on my bedside chest. It reads past two a.m. I roll over and try to get back to sleep, but thoughts of the promise I made Dillon go round and round in my head. This is a promise I can't keep any more. I have to talk to Dillon the first chance I get.

For no explainable reason I suddenly get a feeling that something isn't right inside the house. I close my eyes for a moment, searching for the cause. I wonder if this feeling is because of Neriah and what just passed between us. We returned at the same time. She should be sleeping next door in Isabel's bedroom.

I decide to check on Mum first. Even though she's with Jimmy all the time now, and his job is to protect her with his life, there are still many dangers. Except for her, everyone that lives in this house is a member of the Guard. This is a threat to her safety.

But Mum is sleeping soundly while Jimmy snores away alongside her. It's then, as I turn from Mum's room to Isabel's, that this eerie sense hits me full on. And now I understand exactly where it's coming from and why. I yank Isabel's bedroom door open, startling Neriah into wakefulness.

'Matt? What's wrong?'

'Where is she?'

She rubs her eyes. 'Who?'

'Isabel!' To prove my point, I switch on the light beside Isabel's bed, then pull back the bed covers, to reveal two pillows placed down the centre of her mattress to form the shape of her sleeping body.

Neriah tiptoes over to take a look. She looks at me with a puzzled frown and lifts her hands. She doesn't know, but her thoughts tell me she's quickly figuring it out. Realising I'm in her head, she scrambles her thoughts and stares at me with as blank an expression as she can find.

Inside, my blood begins to simmer. Jimmy comes into the room. The second our eyes connect I know he knows. And this thought makes my blood boil to exploding point. 'You knew about this?'

He comes towards me with his hands stretched out. 'Now wait a minute, Matt.'

'You knew and still you let her go! Don't tell me you were in on her little deceitful plan. What sort of a Protector are you?'

'Keep your voice down, you'll wake your mother.'

As I prepare to use my wings, Jimmy grabs both of my arms. 'Don't go there, Matt. Arkarian would never hurt Isabel. The two of them have nothing to hide.'

I shrug off Jimmy's grasp and he flies backwards with the thrust. 'If that were true, then why do they meet in secret in the middle of the night?'

I don't wait for an answer. Instead, I use my wings, and in the next moment find myself standing in the dark outside the secret entrance to Arkarian's chamber. He has brought her here. I feel their presence inside, even through all this dirt and rock. *Open the door, Arkarian! Open it now!*

Nothing. Like a spider's web I project my mind through the corridors inside, searching. *I know you have my sister in there, Arkarian. If you have nothing to hide, then why do you bring her up here in secret?*

The entrance opens and a dark corridor reveals itself. Inside, the hallway is lit by only one or two softly burning candles. I storm up and down the flickering shadows trying door after door, but they're all locked. I stand still for a moment and try to slow my breathing. It will help me work out which room they're in.

At last Arkarian appears before a doorway to my left. He throws his hands into the air. 'I know you're mad, but before you see Isabel, you have to let me explain.'

Explain! 'What is there to explain? Is Isabel with you, or not?'

The door Arkarian is protecting opens and Isabel comes out, sliding her arms into the sleeves of her long black coat. She works her way around Arkarian to stand between us. 'Will you slow down a minute? Not that it's any of your business, but we were just trying to find a few moments to be together.'

'You can explain all you like at home.'

'Matt, you're overreacting.'

'I saw your bed, Isabel. You planned this. That's what I'm upset about. The secrecy.'

'Matt,' Arkarian says softly, 'if you calm down you'll realise the only reason we came here in secret was because of the reaction we expected from you.'

'Oh, really? How do I know you're not lying when you

just proved how deceitful you can be?' I stand near the doorway. 'Isabel, I want you to come home now.'

'You can't tell me what to do,' Isabel says through gritted teeth. 'Matt, I'm *sixteen*, and you're not my father!'

'Well he's not here, is he?'

A look comes into her eyes, a look of pain and hurt. Instantly I regret my words. But I'm only trying to make her see. It's because of me that her father left us so long ago. He knew I wasn't his child and while he tried to make it work with Mum, this fact kept grating on him. He took to alcohol. In the end he thought Isabel was better off without him. That's why *I* have to look after her. The day Isabel's father left, I promised him I would.

Isabel sighs and follows me outside. Behind us the secret door re-forms. A shiver runs through me as the biting cold hits my bare arms. I didn't bother putting on my coat, or even a jumper over my T-shirt. But thoughts of the weather disappear as Isabel turns to me with glistening eyes. 'How could you?'

'What?'

'How could you humiliate me like that?'

I've never seen her this mad before. I reach for her in an attempt to soothe her and make her understand where I'm coming from, but she pulls away. Her voice lifts to an ear-piercing pitch. 'No! Don't you come near me! Don't you ever talk to me again!'

She runs off, leaving me to stand in the icy night air staring after her. If I've lost her, right now I'm not sure that I can bear it. My head drops back and I stare up at the clear starry sky. It's not long before it begins to lighten. It's been one hell of a long day, and I've made a total mess of it from beginning to end.

The sound of someone breathing behind me makes

me jump. It's Arkarian, and the look in his eyes is cold and distant. 'I've just been informed that King Richard has called a meeting of all the Named at dawn. We'll meet in my chambers. Notify the others.'

He disappears as quickly and as quietly as he appeared. A sinking feeling takes a firm grip in my stomach. King Richard is coming. I wonder what he wants? Usually I would have Arkarian's support, but I have just completely alienated him. He earlier told me to trust him, but I failed to do that. I've really stuffed up, and I'm not sure I'm going to be able to fix any of it.

I only just get through informing the others when dawn chases away the remains of the night. I end up being the last one to arrive. Even Dillon is here, and while he's not strictly Named, at his Initiation Lorian made it clear he is to be considered one of us. They're all sitting around a wooden table in one of Arkarian's rooms. Shaun, Jimmy and Mr Carter are side-by-side. Isabel takes a seat next to Ethan. Dillon is beside Neriah, Rochelle on her other side. Arkarian stands by the door, closing it as I pass through. I catch his eye, but he glances away, his thoughts completely closed to me.

As I enter the room Jimmy looks up and breathes deeply. I've hurt him too, accusing him of not being a capable Protector. And I still have to talk to Dillon yet, who is staring dreamily at Neriah. As they realise I'm here, one by one they stop talking among themselves and look to me. I've never felt so isolated, so alone. It's as if they're all strangers suddenly. Neriah's eyes narrow and in her thoughts she asks me if I'm OK.

Before I answer, King Richard's form begins to take shape. He doesn't acknowledge anyone else in the room, just taps my shoulder with a firm finger. 'You and

284

I must talk. Now.'

He disappears and I'm left wondering where he's gone. I catch Arkarian's eye. He says softly, 'I'll come with you.'

It's a relief, but I can't read too much into the gesture. 'Where's he gone?'

He points to the ceiling. 'He will be up there somewhere.'

Using my wings, I follow Arkarian to the top of the ridge, and sure enough, King Richard is strolling beside the lake. We catch up with him and he acknowledges Arkarian with a tight yet welcoming nod. But it is to me he directs his question.

'Tell me, Matt, do you think I am the traitor?'

And for the first time since seeing him walking into Lathenia's bedroom I have doubts about my assumption. His eyes are so clear as they stare at me, so true, that I find it difficult to believe he would do such a thing. I explain why I have suspected him. 'We saw you in Lathenia's palace. The two of you were laughing together.'

He nods. 'We don't just sit around in a circle all day, you know, Matt. All the Tribunal members have their work to do.'

'Are you saying you were at Lathenia's palace to distract her?'

'Oh, I do a lot more than simply distract Her Highness,' he says, looking amused. 'I was raised a royal, and I'm very familiar with the indiscretions of the high born.'

And now I understand. 'You're Lorian's spy.'

He gives a little laugh. 'I rather see it as … protecting Veridian. I would do anything to ensure my subjects remain unharmed. I'm not the traitor, Matt. But apparently one of the Tribunal members is. Lorian seems sure of it. And I believe him. What you did in those chambers

285

was almost unforgivable. By throwing suspicion on me, you ran the risk of revealing my mission.'

I groan as understanding sinks in. 'I'm sorry, my lord.'

'Like I said, "almost unforgivable".'

He's being kind. My eyes catch Arkarian's; this time he doesn't look away, and I see pain and hurt darken them. *I've made a mess of everything,* my thoughts reach out to him. *I knew I wasn't ready for this.*

But it's King Richard who replies. 'Rubbish. You'll make a fine leader. I have much to do in Athens, and other places. I can't always be here, Matt. That's your job. Now there's something else I want to discuss with you. It's about Isabel's vision. Specifically, it's about Rochelle.'

'She saw her death,' Arkarian says in a hoarse whisper.

King Richard nods. 'I believe it would be a good idea to keep this information from her.' We remain silent and he continues with his thoughts. 'I also believe you should appoint a watch over her. Someone you can trust.'

'Like a bodyguard?' I ask.

'Exactly.'

It's a great idea and I start to think about who this person could be. The responsibility is enormous, to watch over and protect Rochelle's life. 'I will do it.'

But King Richard shakes his head. 'You will be too occupied with other matters. It has to be someone else.'

'It shouldn't be Ethan. He has … feelings for her. And knowing her possible fate would … affect him.'

I think about Dillon, but discard the thought quickly. He can be a little unstable with his emotions. I look across to Arkarian. 'Who do you think it should be?'

He stares back at me and I think he's not going to

answer. Then he says, 'It should be Isabel.'

This is someone I didn't think of. 'Why?'

'For starters, she already knows. She's seen with her own eyes how it might happen. She would be the first to recognise the scene when and if it should begin to unfold.'

Of course he's right.

'As well,' Arkarian continues, 'her defence skills are excellent, and ...' He pauses for a long moment. 'Ethan is her best friend. She cares for him deeply. She's aware that Ethan cares for Rochelle. She would do anything in her power not to let either of them down. She's also true to the Guard. She would take on her role as protector with the utmost loyalty. And while she will not be able to watch Rochelle twenty-four hours a day, Isabel will be effective. Lastly, Isabel is a healer. If the worst happened and Rochelle was harmed, Isabel would be right there.'

While I flounder, Arkarian's explanation is perfect.

'It's settled then,' King Richard says. 'And now, before we descend into that suffocating pit below, there is one more matter that needs attention.'

King Richard looks directly at me. 'Your burgeoning relationship with Neriah should remain a secret until you have spoken with Dillon.'

Across from me Arkarian's eyebrows lift.

'You know about us?' I ask.

King Richard's hands come up together linked at the thumbs. He moves them, making them flap like the wings of a bird. 'I saw you last night, flying over Athens together.'

'That was *you*? I thought ...' *it was Dillon.*

'It almost was Dillon. He went looking for Neriah, and when he couldn't find her, he started looking for you. I noticed because, Matt, I am always watching the backs of my people. I told him you were in the cellars looking at the wine collections down there and that Neriah had gone to test her new powers with Lady Arabella's birds in the courtyard, and that he wasn't to disturb her. That's when I came looking for you.'

He makes the flying motion with his hands again. 'The two of you will really have to be careful where you secretly meet, at least until Dillon comes to terms with your deception. Now, we should go back. I want to speak with the Named. We have to be able to trust each other. We are on the verge of a battle that has the potential to destroy humankind as it currently exists. We can't go to the battle field divided, or we will lose. We must ...'

As King Richard continues, Arkarian stares at me with a look of accusation, and I realise that the strength I have drawn from his friendship is no longer offered.

Chapter Twenty-four

Rochelle

I'm getting over my fear of dying. I mean, when I first read the Prophecy it shook me up, but really, the meaning of that particular line is hardly clear. Matt reckons nobody knows the future. That makes sense. And the Prophecy doesn't necessarily have to play out word for word. Depending on the balance of power, the Prophecy itself can change. It's probably changed right now and that line doesn't even exist any more.

I shouldn't worry myself by imagining things that will probably never happen. I also don't need to add to the tension in this room already.

Isabel won't look at Matt, even when he speaks to her. And Neriah has let me know she's a Truthseer now – a gift from the Immortal. She can hear Dillon's thoughts and she's starting to really worry.

I have to talk to him! she cries out in her thoughts. *I have to make sure he understands I'm not interested in him in the way he wants me to be.*

Good idea. The sooner the better. Look at him.

I know! I can't believe how much he's misread our friendship.

With this last thought lingering in her head, Neriah

glances at Matt, reminding him that he has to talk to Dillon soon too. Their eyes meet and hold, and the sudden connection nearly bowls me over. Whoa! What's happened between these two? No wonder Neriah is worried about Dillon. Just as well he's not a Truthseer, and hasn't the ability to pick up thoughts in the way Truthseers can. Arkarian sends me an interesting look. This time I pick up a sense of loss. What the hell is wrong with everyone this morning?

As for Ethan, it looks as if he's avoiding me. Don't tell me he believes those images Lathenia showed him in Atlantis?

After another long pep talk, King Richard calls the meeting to a close and we start to file out of the room. Everyone has somewhere they should have been five minutes ago. Jimmy goes down into the ancient city. Lately it's as if he lives there, fortifying it, whatever that involves. Mr Carter says he's late for a staff meeting and practically knocks Dillon over in his hurry to get out.

As Isabel gets up to leave, Arkarian hunkers down beside her. 'Can you stay? I have to talk to you.' His eyes flicker to me once as I pass, but, as usual, his thoughts are a total blank.

Outside the air is chilly with the threat of snow. I fold the sides of my coat over each other. As I do this, I see a figure darting away into the national park. It looks like Mr Carter, but it couldn't be him. He was in a hurry to get to a staff meeting.

A short distance down the mountain Isabel catches up with me. 'Hey, wait up.'

'I thought Arkarian wanted to talk to you.'

'Yeah, well, he did. It was just some little thing.'

Our conversation is broken by an awkward pause. I'm

not sure what she's doing here. We don't usually converse unless we have to, like on a mission or something. It's not that I don't like Isabel. She's about the most genuine person I know. When I was going out with her brother, there were lots of times she tried to befriend me. I was the one who pulled back. Guilt has a way of doing that – interfering in every facet of your life.

I try to think of something that might break the ice between us. 'You and Arkarian are very close these days.'

It's the wrong thing. She closes up suddenly, like her face is the page in a book she's just slammed shut. She sighs. 'We would be if we could find some time to be together and not have to feel guilty about it.'

I get it straightaway. Matt is being his overprotective self again. But this time I get the feeling he's crossed a line with her. He's gone too far. I shrug, trying to lighten the atmosphere. 'Well, what's the hurry? You have the rest of your lives to be together.'

She gives me a strange look, but I try not to analyse it too much. My head's still in a whirl after that last mission to Atlantis. There are just so many questions that have come out of it. Suddenly Matt materialises before us, blocking our path. He looks straight at his sister. 'Can we talk?'

She glances away into the forest that runs beside us. 'You have nothing to say that will change anything between us. From what Arkarian tells me, don't you think you should be talking to Dillon?'

Her words have me completely intrigued. Matt hears my thoughts and has the sensibility to appear uncomfortable. 'Yeah, I'm going to talk to him now.'

'Well, you'd better hurry.' I tilt my head in the direction of where Dillon is already halfway down the mountain trailing Neriah like one of her lost dogs. 'He's driving her crazy, you know.'

Matt's head shifts up, alarmed. The 'Dillon' situation is worse than he realises, but right now he has other issues which take priority. 'Isabel, you need to take a quick trip to Athens.'

'I don't think so. I'm needed here.'

Matt ignores her abrupt manner. 'Lady Arabella has these two incredible birds.'

'I've seen them.'

'They're injured, and I want you to heal them.'

'I already offered.'

Matt frowns, and Isabel explains impatiently, 'When you sent us off looking for the key!'

He glances off into the forest for a moment. 'That's strange,' he mutters. 'Arabella didn't say.'

I recall the scene well. 'Isabel volunteered to try and heal them, and Lady Arabella said that she would look after their recovery.'

'What's the problem, Matt? Do you suspect one of the *birds* is the traitor?' Isabel's tone is full of sarcasm.

Somehow he hangs on to his patience. 'I don't think they're really birds.'

'Oh? So what do you think they are?'

Matt's eyes shift to me, then lower to my gloved hands. I can tell the second the idea hits him. He wants me to put my hands on those birds. He thinks my hands will confirm his suspicions that the birds are not really birds at all. 'No way, Matt. The touch of my hands could kill an animal. You know that! Those birds look fragile enough as it is.'

A sudden gust of wind has us all looking to the north.

'What on earth is that?' Shaun's exclamation wafts over.

Everyone can't help but stare in the same direction. A strange mist appears at the top of the mountain and starts rolling down the valley towards us. But this mist, or whatever it is, is unlike any other I've seen in these parts. It's dark like a widow's veil.

While still staring at this eerie phenomenon, Shaun makes his way over to us. 'Should we take cover?' he asks, then glances at Isabel. 'Is this what you saw?'

I wonder what Shaun's talking about. Isabel bites down on her lower lip. She knows something, that's for sure. She looks uncomfortable suddenly. This is not like her at all. Finally she says, 'I think it is. I think it's the wind.'

'Did you say wind? But, Isabel, it's completely visible,' Shaun tries to clarify.

Isabel explains, 'It's in the wind that the dark will come.'

My mouth goes dry, but still I have to ask, 'Do you mean dark, as in underworld dark?'

Before she answers, this eerie wind reaches us. Surprised by its force we stumble a few steps down the mountain, grasping our coats and jackets. It passes, leaving a dark stain in the air around us. Neriah and Dillon come running back up the hill.

'What's going on?' Dillon asks. 'That wind was freaky. It reminded me of the underworld.' He pauses and looks at Matt. 'Well? What was it?'

Matt's hands come up, palms outward. 'I don't know. Isabel says –'

'What do you mean, you don't know? Arkarian would know.'

'Shut up, Dillon,' I can't help snapping. Lately it's as if Dillon has to take a shot at Matt for every little thing.

293

And it's wearing on my nerves.

The wind picks up, swishing through the trees. It's frightening to watch this wave of darkness traverse, uninvited, across the land, turning morning light into an inexplicable twilight.

An awkward silence settles around us, but our thoughts are soon distracted as the sky to the north darkens further. 'What's that now? Over there on the horizon?' Shaun asks.

At first it appears as a shadow in the sky, but as it starts swelling and stretching towards us, its great size becomes clearer.

Ethan comes out through the secret doorway and frowns, looking around. He notices something strange about the air, but can't quite put his finger on it. He feels the extra chill and shrugs into his jacket. He comes over and sees us all staring up at the northern sky. 'What are they? Some kind of bird?'

Isabel gasps. 'Oh no! They're the birds from my vision!'

'Not Marduke's birds?' Shaun asks. 'So soon?'

My thoughts linger on the word 'vision'. Apparently Isabel has had one. An informative one at that! At least now I understand where her wealth of information is coming from. 'What vision are you talking about, Isabel? What else was in it?'

Isabel doesn't answer, just glances awkwardly at her brother, then quickly away. I get the feeling everyone knows about this vision except for me.

'Are they the birds you saw carrying the poison?' Matt asks her.

I can't help frowning, feeling very much on the out-side. Why would they keep such important details from me? The answer is obvious: they still don't trust me. Well, what do they think, that I'll go running back to Marduke with the information of what *he's* going to be doing with his own birds?

Ethan notices how annoyed I've grown and attempts to explain. 'Marduke has a garden in the underworld, where he harvests thousands of flowers, black irises, all of them. The flowers are a type of drug.' And then he adds, 'But why am I telling *you* this? You should be telling us what's going on.'

'Marduke never took me to the underworld,' I explain, hurt by his words. 'He didn't include me in *every* facet of his life. So I'm sorry to disappoint you. I don't know anything about the drugs.'

I glance up at the sky again. It's clear now that the shadow is a mass of birds flying in formation. They keep coming and coming as if there is no end to them. Even though I'm freezing cold, my skin feels clammy all of a sudden.

'I think they're vultons,' Dillon says, squinting. 'Yeah, I know these birds. They have these pouches built into their stomachs like a kangaroo.'

'Can they be killed?' Shaun asks.

'They're already dead. If you tried, they would just keep coming back at you. You don't want to make them angry either. They've been trained to kill by Marduke.'

'If they're already dead, how are we going to stop them?' Ethan asks. 'Tell us everything you know about them, Dillon.'

'Well, they have sharp claws like an eagle, but they're not as smart. They'll be following strict instructions and once they've served their purpose they'll be programmed to return to base, wherever that is.'

I look at Isabel. 'In this vision that everyone seems to know about, did you see where these ... *vultons* are going to drop their poison?'

Looking guilty she murmurs, 'Over Angel Falls.'

'What a lovely thought!'

'It will poison the water supply and put anyone who comes in contact with the drug under a spell – a mind-numbing spell that will last for days or longer, depending on their saturation level. They won't know who they are, or what they're doing. Then ...'

'Then what?'

'Lathenia will get into their heads. She'll twist their minds. And when the drug wears off, she'll have a whole new army at her command.'

A *human* army? People's friends, families and colleagues. Oh, great! I glance at my watch. 'It's almost time for morning classes. The school grounds will be packed.'

Everyone looks to Matt. His eyes shift away to the side as if he would like to run off into the adjacent forest and hide for a while. He starts rubbing the side of his neck. What's going on with him? I've never seen him look so ... incapable of making a decision.

Neriah sends me a worrying thought, but I don't have any answers. She touches his arm. 'What if we can get the vultons to drop the poison somewhere much less inhabited?'

He nods, looking relieved. He should be. It's a good idea.

'If we can get them to change their course, do you think the vultons will go back to wherever they came from?' Neriah throws this question out for all of us to consider.

Dillon is first to answer. 'Marduke will be furious, but

296

yeah, I reckon it could work. But it won't be easy. Marduke will have a firm grip on their minds. Once the Master gets into your head his hold is next to impossible to get rid of.'

From my side vision I notice Ethan's eyes shift my way, then slowly drop. On the outside I ignore the insinuation, but on the inside his doubts of me, after all this time, hurt and make me angry. What will it take to prove myself to these people? I try to get a grip before anyone notices how unstuck I've become.

At last Matt has an idea, but his voice is filled with hesitation. 'I … I might have a plan. But well, um, I'll need some help.'

'Take me!'

You've got to give it to Dillon, he's always the first to volunteer.

'I've seen these birds before. I know how they work.'

Neriah looks straight at Dillon. 'Matt will need someone who can fly –'

'That's right. And I've got my wings.'

Matt says, 'I think Neriah means fly *literally*.'

Dillon stares back looking confused. 'What are you talking about? Maybe this leadership stuff is a bit too much for you to han—'

'You also need someone who can get into the birds' heads,' Neriah interrupts, drawing everyone's attention back to what we're supposed to be thinking about. 'Thanks to Queen Brystianne's gift, I can help you with that too.'

Matt looks relieved, and Neriah smiles at him. The smile would melt Dillon's heart, except she's not sending it to him. Dillon notices, and for the first time in his life has nothing to say.

A squawk draws our attention back to the sky. The birds are close but not yet overhead. Shaun touches Matt's shoulder. 'Whatever you two are going to do, you'd better hurry.'

They take a step away from the rest of us. It has us all looking at them expectantly. They don't let us down. Before our eyes, their bodies begin to change, limbs shortening and shifting. Within a few seconds they have both taken on the forms of hawks. They hover and flutter their impressive wings for a few moments. Everyone stares up at them in awe.

Isabel asks Ethan, 'Did you know they could do that?'

He shakes his head. She looks at me and raises an eyebrow. 'What about you?'

'I saw Matt turn into a shark once, and a dolphin, but he's never actually *told* me.'

Suddenly the larger bird, Matt, flutters its massive wings in a furious action. A feather from his chest drifts towards Isabel. She holds out her hand and it sails into her open palm. She looks up and the Matt-bird peers at her through his bird-eyes for a moment longer.

As the shadow of Marduke's vultons stretches halfway across the sky, the pair of hawks fly up to meet them. For a moment I feel a stab of such intense jealousy I wonder where it's coming from. And then I realise it's the sight of Matt and Neriah in their bird forms soaring into the atmosphere. How free they must feel with every graceful flap of their wings, the wind in their faces.

When I eventually drag my eyes from them, I notice that Dillon is mesmerised too. But his eyes remain focused on the smaller Neriah-bird. His thoughts let me know he wishes he was the one flying beside Neriah, sharing her skill, sharing her power. Poor Dillon. He's fallen in love with the wrong girl.

'They will have to work fast,' Isabel says. 'I can't imagine how hard it will be to get a flock like that to change direction.'

Neither can I. There are just so many of them.

'Matt will do it,' Shaun says.

A voice suddenly starts up in my head. It sounds distant at first, but the urgency is unmistakable. It's Arkarian. My hand lifts to shush the others. He's inside his chambers and his thoughts call out. *Where is Matt?*

Busy with a flock of Marduke's birds, I reply. *He could be gone for hours.*

Silence, and I can almost *feel* his disappointment and frustration. *Arkarian, what's wrong?*

Isabel and the others look at me, understanding something is going on.

Marduke is in Veridian! He has soldiers with him and is preparing to install his army of wren. Send everyone you can!

For a moment I am so stunned I can't talk. My mouth drops open but words don't form.

'What is it?' Isabel asks. 'What's wrong, Rochelle?' She grabs my shoulders and shakes me. 'Did something happen to Arkarian?'

The fear in her voice breaks through my shock. I assure her quickly. 'Arkarian is fine. He sent a message.'

'Well,' Dillon says. 'What is it?'

'The ancient city is being invaded by Marduke, his soldiers and an army of wren!'

Everybody starts running, straight back up to Arkarian's chambers. The secret door opens the instant we stand before it. Arkarian ushers us inside. 'We have to hurry. There is so much to do.'

Isabel makes him stand still. 'How bad is it?'

Arkarian turns on us all with dark and worried eyes. 'After all these years, Lathenia has finally located Veridian. And with the help of Marduke she has forged a tunnel below the city. They evaded discovery by constructing their tunnel so deep within the earth that neither sound nor vibration could be detected. And now twenty of Marduke's soldiers are through, guiding the wren in by their hundreds. They've started tearing the city apart already.'

Everyone goes silent. They're not used to seeing Arkarian look so agitated. Their thoughts grow frenzied. They come thundering into my head all at once. 'Everyone slow down!'

Isabel touches Arkarian's arm. 'Why are they tearing down the walls? What on earth are they looking for?'

'They're after the technology of the Atlanteans – the survivors of the underworld.'

Isabel asks, 'What are you talking about?'

He sighs. 'It's because of the Atlantean technology that the Guard can do the things we do. It's here in my chambers.' His hands sweep widely around him. Our eyes follow. 'It's the sphere and everything you see. Without it, we can't protect the earth from Lathenia. She figured out how to travel into the past and built the original Citadel. The technology of the surviving Atlanteans is what the Guard uses to stop her meddling there.'

Everyone has questions; Arkarian holds his hands up. 'We don't have time for long explanations.' But he can see we need more. 'When Atlantis started to fall, some of the inhabitants managed to escape and went in search of another uninhabited landform. After many years of searching they found Angel Falls and secured their machinery here. They established the ancient city and kept it secret. This technology must remain out of Lathenia's hands. She will use it to build a sphere to the future. We can't let this happen.'

'*What?*' Dillon exclaims. 'Can she do that? Build a sphere to the future?'

We all look to Arkarian for the answer. He says simply, 'Yes.'

Shaun moves forward. 'Arkarian, at this time, wouldn't it be advantageous to have the weapons from the treasury available to us, for how else are we going to deal with these creatures?'

Arkarian runs a hand roughly through his hair and it shimmers blue in the light. 'The reason I am ... agitated, is because the key to the treasury is down there.' He points to the door that leads to the shaft into the city.

'*What?* In the city with all those wren running around pulling it apart?' Dillon exclaims. 'So whose brilliant idea was it to put the key down there? I bet it was Matt's.'

Isabel gives him a sharp look, and Arkarian says, 'It was a good idea, Dillon. The city has been safe for the last eleven thousand years.'

'Yeah, well it's not now, is it?'

'Sadly, no.'

Ethan asks, 'Do you think Marduke knows the key is down there?'

'It's possible. It's as if his spies are everywhere these days.'

Except for Arkarian, everyone's eyes slide to me, then quickly move away. And now they look embarrassed. Well, they should be! I just caught them wearing their true thoughts of me on the outside. Not that I wasn't already aware of their suspicions. They just can't get past the fact that I used to work for Marduke. But trust is what the Guard is all about. Faith in what doesn't always make sense. This is exactly what King Richard was talking about. Didn't they take any of it in? Or is it just me they can't handle? They don't appear to have a problem trusting Dillon.

Arkarian touches my arm and a warm sense of calm fills me. I mentally thank him and he turns his attention back to the group. 'To retrieve the key, we need Matt.'

'But he's not here,' Dillon is quick to reply. 'He could be away for hours. Let me go, Arkarian. I'll bring this key back. Where is it exactly?'

Arkarian explains, 'Jimmy has constructed a secret panel in the floor of the vault at the centre of the maze.'

'Sounds easy enough.'

Dillon might think so, but nothing is ever as easy as it sounds.

Arkarian hears my thoughts and lets me know he agrees. 'Matt has performed an enchantment on the key. He has made it invisible. Only he can remove the enchantment, or see through its invisibility.'

'What?' Dillon exclaims.

'And remember, the key is deadly to touch.'

'Oh that's just great, isn't it? So how are we supposed to retrieve this *invisible* key?'

'I can touch it,' I say into the silence that follows Dillon's sombre comment. I wave my hands in the air. 'As long as I have these gloves on.'

Arkarian turns to me with a gold box in his hand. 'Once it is safe in this box, anyone can hold it. But you still can't go, Rochelle, because you don't have your wings.'

'So?'

'Without the weapons, the only way to destroy the wren is by drowning them. As soon as the key is lifted from its lock, a trigger will release the flood gates. You can't be at the bottom of the city when this happens.'

I think about what he's saying. 'So how long will it take to flood the city?'

'Exactly nine minutes.'

'I'm a fast runner, Arkarian. I can do it.'

'It's all uphill!' Ethan calls out.

I ignore him. Sometimes he almost sounds as if he cares. 'Just let me try.'

Arkarian peers at me, his head shaking. 'Not without your wings, Rochelle. You wouldn't make it.'

So maybe this is my destiny. Maybe the Prophecy can't be changed after all. And without Ethan in my life, what would be the point anyway? I don't want anyone else. I know this now. I can admit it. And if I go, won't that prove once and for all my heart is true to the Guard? All I have to do is extract the key from the secret panel in the floor of the vault and place it safely in this box and my job is done. As long as someone who has their wings comes with me, I can pass them the box and they can fly to safety.

'It's simple, Arkarian. I will go.'

'There has to be another way,' Ethan says.

Arkarian's eyes lower to where I'm clasping my hands together. 'Rochelle, take off your gloves.'

I carefully peel each of them off. As my hands are revealed, the others gasp and stare. Since Lorian increased their power the electric charges haven't stopped growing stronger. Sparks fly off in a colourful display. I give them a shake. It feels good to give them some air. But the shake sends sparks flying around the room. Shaun and Dillon have to duck and cover their faces as several sparks fly straight towards them.

Arkarian locks his gaze with me as he takes the gloves from my hand. 'Why didn't you say anything? The pain must be excruciating.'

Stupidly, his kind words, his compassionate look, brings tears to the backs of my eyes. I blink rapidly before the tears turn into a flood and embarrass the life out of me. 'They don't hurt much,' I try to convince him. 'Really.'

He doesn't believe me, and while he's controlling his thoughts, his eyes are saying a lot more. He tries to put the gloves on, but his fingers are too long. He hands them to Shaun, but they don't fit him either. Ethan takes them next, but Ethan's hands are broader than his father's. Dillon reaches for them. 'Here, they'll fit me!' He yanks them down hard, pushing between his fingers, but it's hopeless.

I take the gloves back. 'That settles it. I'm going.' I take the golden box from Arkarian's hands and slip it into my coat pocket.

'I'll come with you,' Arkarian says. 'You will climb as fast as you can. You're a good strong swimmer too, aren't you, Rochelle?'

I nod, but Ethan has other ideas. 'You're needed here, Arkarian.'

Shaun touches his son's shoulder firmly. 'Are you sure, son? You've only just mastered your wings. What if they fail you?'

Ethan brushes his father's hand away. 'They won't fail me.'

Isabel looks from Ethan to Arkarian and back again,

304

distressed. She obviously loves and fears for them both, but appears to have one serious concern for Ethan. She steps up to him. 'You *will* use your wings and come back. Won't you, Ethan?'

Ethan looks at me and I can't look away. And for a moment I am filled with a warmth that is fuelled from a fire that comes from deep inside his soul. 'I'll do what I can,' he says. 'But I'm not making any promises.'

Chapter Twenty-five

Matt

The birds are flying higher than I first estimate. The closer we get the larger they appear. Their heads are shaped like condors', their bellies like pelicans', but that's where all earthly resemblance stops. They have small, round eyes that sit out on a bony ridge. The eyes have no pupils, and are just orbs of shiny black.

We should change into the shape of the vultons, Neriah suggests.

Though I am reluctant to turn into the shape of a bird from another world, Neriah is probably right. It would be our best chance to communicate with them.

Taking her advice I change form and she follows. Suddenly we both start dropping. It takes a moment to adjust to the heavier bodies, and their unusual shape with the weighty pouches attached to our chests. As we regain height, I wonder what it would be like to fly with a full pouch. I'm grateful for my empty one.

What's wrong with you? Why is your pouch empty? These thoughts from one of the vultons blast into my head. *Why didn't you fill up as the Master directed? What a waste, to come all this way for nothing!*

Neriah's head turns slightly to indicate she hears the

vulton's thoughts too. Soon another bird speaks out. *How much further, Lydia? My wings grow weary with this heavy load.*

The first bird, with the very human name of Lydia, replies, *Well, Justin, if you had paid more attention to the Master during training you would know that we are nearly there!*

Justin! Another human name. While making my way through the underworld I met and became friends with a wren called John. His human name was the only memory he could recall from his past life.

But this last comment from Lydia is my cue. I project my thoughts in her direction. *You're wrong, Lydia. We're still a long way from our destination.*

Who is that? Identify yourself!

The Master sent me to make sure you stick to the right path. Which, by the way, you have strayed from. The Master will be furious that you have led everyone in the wrong direction.

Now that we know which one is the leader, Neriah and I fly in closer, one on either side.

What are you talking about? Lydia demands to know, her head shifting from me to Neriah. *I have followed the Master's co-ordinates to the exact degree. Look below. There is the lake, and over there is the school.*

Neriah sends me a sharp look and takes over. *But Lydia, the Master sent us because there was a late change in his plans. We have new co-ordinates that you must follow and direct your flock.*

Lydia goes silent. I sense her confusion. She was ready to argue with me, but Neriah's voice sounds so convincing.

Also sensing this doubt, Neriah keeps going. *It's not*

such a long way. *In fact, it is only a short distance to the north and then west.*

But we came from the north! What are you talking about?

Lydia's not the only one who's wondering what Neriah's talking about. And then Neriah explains. *The Master gained new information about a secret meeting of the Guard. It's being held right now in the depths of Angel Falls forestland. He wants you to drop your loads right over the top of where the Guard's elite soldiers are meeting at this very moment.*

I keep my thoughts quiet. Neriah is doing a fantastic job. She almost has Lydia eating out of her … claw.

Below us the school becomes clearer. We will have to get the vultons to alter their course soon or it will be too late. Once they have the school and township beneath them, nothing much we say is likely to stop them from releasing the drugs.

Lydia squawks. *I think you must be mistaken.*

I'm not mistaken. Neriah flies out in front. Taking her cue I fly out beside her. It's a risk, as we could end up isolating ourselves from the flock. They're getting tired, and the idea of following two strangers on a new course, when their original co-ordinates are almost beneath them, could prove too much to ask.

I think you lie, Lydia says, her head shifting left to right and back again. *Down there is our destination.* And to the pack she commands: *Prepare to drop!*

It is you that is mistaken! Neriah explains calmly, but with a firm tone. *The Master speaks through me. To the forest! he commands. It is his chance to annihilate the Guard's most powerful soldiers!*

Lydia is silent for a moment, her head tilting slightly

as if she can't believe what she's hearing. *How dare you claim the Master speaks through you! I am the Master's favourite. I am the one he prefers! I demand that you identify yourself. Tell me who you are now!*

Neriah gracefully tilts her wings and circles around so that now she is flying backwards. She inches forward until she is beak-to-beak with Lydia. *I will tell you who I am, and you will never question me again, for I am the Master's daughter!*

Lydia is stunned into silence. Neriah's statement rings with truth. It is the truth! And Lydia can see it in Neriah's black eyes. The vulton finds herself at a loss as to what to say. To defy her Master would be unthinkable. And yet, here is Marduke's daughter, the Master's very own blood. *To the forest, you say?*

Neriah sighs, relaxing slightly now that she has won. *Follow me and I will show you the way.*

Neriah circles back around, and gracefully tilts her body in a northerly direction. I do the same, keeping slightly behind her. Thankfully Lydia follows, and her command is quickly passed on to the rest of the thousand or so vultons.

We make the turn in a massive arc. The school remains in our sights the whole time. At last we start to cover fresh ground. The lake zooms into view, with the mountains making a spectacular backdrop. From this height it is an amazing sight. Neriah gently swings to the west and leads the flock towards the dense centre of the forest.

As we pass, people look up and stare in wonder. Some cower at the sight of such a large and intimidating flock, but mostly they simply stare. Never have they seen so many birds in formation together.

When the forest is at its thickest, Neriah searches the minds of all the animals below and tells them to leave quickly. Sharing a look with me first, she then tells Lydia we have reached our destination.

When they release their loads, it is a strangely beautiful sight. The poison resembles dust, and then I remember that it is made from thousands of crushed flower petals. The grey, ash-like dust drifts downwards towards the treetops, disappearing as soon as it hits the moist green foliage.

As the last of it lingers, caught in a breeze, some brushes against my claws. I flutter my feathers to rid myself of it quickly, but the feel of it against my leathery skin has a strange familiar feel. It nags at my consciousness. I've felt this touch before. Then I remember. It was in the palace courtyard in Athens. On the cage of the two golden birds! But what does this mean? Are the birds drugged?

Lady Arabella said the dust swept in on the night wind. But who is sending it?

I glance at Neriah, wondering if I should let her in on my suspicions. But she's distracted by the vultons. Lydia, especially, has her attention. This particular vulton looks drained suddenly, and strangely lost.

For a moment I feel as sorry for Lydia as Neriah does. On the bird's return to the underworld she will have Marduke to face. All those years spent nurturing that garden for this very purpose. He will be outraged. But how do you punish a creature that is already dead? I'm sure Marduke will find a way.

Neriah listens to my thoughts, and is upset by them. She knows that while the vultons planned to bring havoc and chaos to Angel Falls, they were simply creatures following instructions for someone they believed in, and for their cause.

Lydia flies around in a circle, squawking and disoriented. She's starting to panic. But a lot of time has passed since we left the others, and I have a growing sense something is terribly wrong.

We can't just leave them!

Neriah's right. We have to show them the way back from here. But the sense that my powers are needed grows stronger with every flap of my wings. *Something is wrong in Veridian!*

I know. I feel it too. Matt, you have to go. The vultons trust me. I'll lead them home and make sure they all get back through the rift.

The last thing I want is to leave Neriah in the sky with a thousand lost birds that come from another world. What if they realise we fooled them? What if they turn on her?

I'll be fine, she implores. *I'll join you soon.*

With no other choice, I change into the form of a hawk, and head back to Veridian.

Chapter Twenty-six

Rochelle

The wren are everywhere. Up close they're hideous, with round, red eyes that glow even in the dim light of the ancient city corridors. They resemble pigs, but have these funny, awkward-looking wings with human feet and longish human hands. It's these hands that are their most useful feature. They have weapons – axes, chisels and hammers, but they're using them to dismantle the walls. At first they don't seem to be interested in us and let us pass. They're too occupied with peeling away layers of ancient timbers, mud and bricks.

A great open chasm spreads out before us and we stop. Below is a drop so deep and dark it's impossible to estimate its depth. I've been here once before with Arkarian. The only way across is via an invisible bridge. It's here somewhere. And if I remember correctly, it shoots directly from the brick path we've been following.

Without giving too much attention to the butterflies in my stomach, I mentally double-check the width of the path, and step out on to the left side of the invisible bridge. My feet hit solid ground and I exhale a relieved sigh. Feeling more confident now, I run across to the other side.

Ethan follows. Once on the other side he stares at me. 'You didn't even hesitate.'

No need to tell him I was so nervous about that first step that my legs felt detached from my body.

'The first time Isabel crossed it I had to build a bridge for her.'

'This isn't my first time,' I explain. 'And by the way, I'm not Isabel.'

'No,' he says, looking straight at me. 'You certainly aren't.'

If only I could tell what he means by that! While staring back I try to read his thoughts. He blocks me perfectly. It's a surprise, because he's not usually that good. 'Do you mind?' he says with a smirk-like grin. 'From now on I'd appreciate it if you could keep out of my head.'

His playful tone makes me smile.

'Wow,' he mutters. 'I think that's the first time I've seen you smile.'

Such simple words, but they knock the wind out of my sails.

'You should do it more often,' he adds.

He takes off, leaving me standing and staring at his back, my thoughts in a complete whirl.

'Come on!' he calls.

I start to take off when something heavy drops on me, knocking me to the floor. I twist beneath it, jerking my back to try and dislodge the weight. Wings flutter down around me, attempting to keep me trapped. 'Ethan!' I manage to call out, but he's back already.

He drags the wren off me by its wings, then kicks it in the stomach. The wren goes down over the side of the chasm, but another comes running and kind of flying over the invisible bridge.

Ethan helps me up. 'Quickly, let's go!'

We run down a narrow brick path, but the chasing wren catch up fast. I flick a glance over my shoulder and see many more.

We take a wrong turn and end up in a dead-end passage. Five wren follow and I swear they look amused and even excited at the prospect of their potential kill. Drooling and grunting, they close in.

Ethan defends with his fists and feet, punching and kicking. I take off my gloves, shoving them quickly into my pocket. Sparks fly around the room and for a moment it takes the wren by surprise. 'Come on!' I taunt the closest one. He leaps at me, knocking me over with his bulk. But his neck is in my clear view. I put my hands around it, and without even having to squeeze hard, the wren goes limp with a high-pitched wail.

Within minutes all five wren are lying in a heap on top of each other, all with scalded and badly disfigured necks.

I slip my gloves on before I forget and accidentally touch Ethan. Now that my hands have grown more powerful, they're also more dangerous. I don't want to think about them. 'We should hurry.'

We take off, quickly finding our way again. We get to a point where we have a clear view over the lower levels of the city. The sight below makes us stop. We both lean on an iron railing and stare. There are masses of wren, all busily peeling away the walls of the city. Machinery like that found in Arkarian's chamber is exposed. Under the lights of the soldiers' torches, it shimmers silver and bright copper-red. Some of this technology has already been dismantled and is being loaded into carts, ready to take away. There are soldiers supervising, all wearing black and suitably masked. I wonder who they are, and if I know any of them in my normal world.

Ethan taps my shoulder. 'We're nearly at the maze. We'd better hurry. Those carts look ready to shift.'

We take off and in a few minutes find ourselves outside the maze. After a couple of wrong turns we make it to the centre. And suddenly I'm standing before the Prophecy, written across several walls. My eyes drift to the area where the line is written that refers to me. I wonder if it has changed. Ethan notices where my eyes are searching.

'Don't,' he says.

He's right. Do I really want to know? The only reason Arkarian showed me the Prophecy in the first place was because I insisted. I thought it would convince me that I really was Named, that it would alleviate my doubts.

Ethan's eyes bore into me. 'Are you coming?'

I nod and Ethan turns his attention back to the vault door. He asks it to open and it does, disappearing soundlessly. We step inside the room, relieved to find it empty. Without wasting any more time I go to work trying to locate the secret compartment hidden beneath the vault floor. Peeling off one glove, I lay my hand on the silver flooring near the centre. I find the cavity almost directly beneath my hand. Slipping my glove back on, I tug at the secret panel. And then the empty compartment is revealed, not much larger than the golden box in my pocket. But the compartment's not really empty. It contains the key that is temporarily invisible to the human eye.

'Is it there?' Ethan asks.

I pull the golden box out of my pocket and open it,

315

sitting it on the vault floor.

'Be careful,' Ethan warns. 'Make sure your gloves are on tight.'

'They're tight,' I assure him, and start to slide my hand into the box.

'Wait!'

I look up and he says, 'Check you don't have any holes in your gloves. You may have torn them in that fight with the wren earlier.'

'They're indestructible, Ethan. How else would I be able to touch the key?'

Finally satisfied, he goes quiet. I slide my hand into the compartment and feel the key beneath my fingers. It's a tight fit, but it doesn't take long to get my hand around it. I give the key a tug and it comes loose. For a moment there is nothing but silence, then a series of clicking sounds. Jimmy's security system has switched on. The trigger to the floodgates has been released. It's only a matter of minutes now before the entire city will flood and all the wren will be destroyed.

Ethan yells, 'Is it in the box yet?'

Carefully I drop the key into the box and close it. Making sure it locks tight, I hold the box out to Ethan. 'It's done.'

His mouth twitches, almost forming a smile. The first part of our mission is complete. All we have to do now is get the hell out of here. Something that is a lot easier for Ethan to do than for me. Somewhere nearby the lake is pouring in, but so far I'm still dry. If I hurry, maybe, just maybe, I can get out of here in one piece too.

Ethan secures the box inside his jumper. 'Now we run.'

But a shadow darkens the doorway. We're not alone

any more and our chance of a quick escape disappears. I know who it is even before looking at the monster. I can smell his evil scent anywhere, anytime, even in my sleep. Will I never be free of him?

Marduke lifts his hands into the air and roars, a victorious sound. And then I get it. He knew the key was hidden somewhere in the city, and he knew we would have to come for it. We've played right into his hands.

'Ethan, go!' I hiss at him.

But Ethan just stares at me. 'Not without you.'

I can't believe he's being this stubborn. 'What's wrong with you? Just go!'

'No.'

Marduke laughs. 'You think of honour at a time like this?'

'I have more honour in my little finger than you could have in a thousand lifetimes.'

'Perhaps. But honour will not save your life.' Marduke shifts his single eye to me. 'Nor hers. Now hand over the box.'

'You have to kill me first.'

Marduke hisses like a snake. Spittle flies from his snout. 'You have been the bane of my life! Killing you will be my greatest joy!'

I have never seen Marduke look so mad. So insane. 'Ethan, just go! Use your wings and take the key to safety!'

An eerie rushing sound distracts us all momentarily. Marduke tilts his head, his one eye shifting to the side as he listens and tries to decipher the meaning of the growing rumble. Of course Ethan and I know what it is – the water from the lake. And by the sound of it thundering along this lowest level, it's not far away at all.

And then it pours into the vault, hurling the three of us backwards against the walls. 'What's this?' Marduke bellows. 'The city is being flooded! My wren!'

He stares at the two of us as the first wave eventually settles and pools around our waists. His eye glows red and in a flash of strength he grabs me by the waist and secures both my hands within one of his behind my back. 'Give me the key or I will not let her go until it is too late!'

I catch Ethan's eye, imploring him to go before he drowns too. But Ethan has other ideas. 'You can't kill her, unless you want to die before the sun sets on this same day.'

Marduke's iron grip only tightens. I try to squirm out of my gloves, but his grip is too strong. 'I'm not a fool, boy. I know about the curse. But *I'm* not going to kill her. She was doomed the minute she walked into the city.' His eye shifts down to me. 'I always knew it was a wise decision not to give you your wings.'

Ethan rams Marduke in the shoulder. 'Let her go!'

It does nothing to shake him. And then another wave of water thunders through the passageways. On hearing it Marduke roars. It's a roar of anguish. Every fresh wave will destroy more of his wren. Their screams can already be heard.

Marduke hangs on to me tightly. Ethan tries again to dislodge him. Another wave hits and the vault completely floods. Marduke holds me down for a minute longer, totally submerged. Ethan swims around us and tries to loosen Marduke's grip with his own hands. But Marduke wants to make sure I don't have any chance of surviving. I go limp on purpose. Only when he is satisfied he has held me down long enough does he use his own wings and disappear.

At last I'm free. Ethan takes my hand, and together we swim our way out of the flooded vault.

It feels like for ever before we break the surface. Gasping, I push away one body after another of wren. Their screams are unnerving as they scramble and stumble over each other in a panic to get into the higher levels.

Ethan finds a stairwell and we stagger out of the water. But another surge is coming fast. Soaking wet, we run as quickly as our heavy clothes allow. I shrug off my coat in an attempt to lighten my load. The wave hits us and we try to ride it upwards, struggling to keep our heads out of the water. But the force of the surging wave is too strong. We end up thrown in all directions against walls and wren and even drowning soldiers. One soldier grabs on to Ethan. He's big and heavy and drags Ethan underwater as he tries to find solid footing. I reach out, grab the soldier's head by his hair, and smash my closed fist into his face. He lets go and Ethan resurfaces.

At last we stagger up another flight of stairs, but I don't know how long I can keep this pace going; we're still a long way from the top!

'You can do it!' Ethan encourages me. 'You *will* do it, do you hear me?'

But another wave soon hits, and this one sends us on a rollercoaster ride, up and down, into walls and quickly flooding passageways. When at last it passes we find ourselves in a dead-end corridor, the flood waters reaching almost to the top. We lift our heads to the ceiling and gasp for air. Ethan spins around, dragging on my arm.

'Quickly, we have to get out of here! This is a death trap!'

We attempt to make our way back when an explosion

sends us spinning and thrashing against the walls. And now the water is full of muck, while the remaining air is smoke-filled and dusty. But worse are the walls near the entrance. Weakened from being stripped of the machinery within, they collapse, blocking our exit.

We swim over and try to push our way out, shoving bricks aside. But after the first few it becomes obvious that the rest won't move. They're jammed tight! And then we hear the sound of another wave coming. In seconds this cavity will be completely flooded with no means to escape.

We lunge to the ceiling and grab our last mouthfuls of air. 'You have to use your wings, Ethan. You have no choice now.'

'There's always a choice,' he says. 'And I choose no.'

'Ethan, for god's sake! What about the key?'

'They'll find it,' he says softly.

It takes a moment for his meaning to become clear. 'No! You can't do this! Ethan, listen: don't throw your life away. What would be the point?'

The thunder increases to a deafening crescendo as a fateful wave surges towards us.

'I'm not leaving,' Ethan says. 'I won't let you die alone.'

I stare at him in disbelief. He can't be serious! But his eyes, the controlled calm I see there, tell me that he is.

Chapter Twenty-seven

Matt

By the time I get to Arkarian's chambers the sense of disaster is so prominent my hands are shaking. Arkarian appears before me, his clothes torn to shreds, bruises and red welts across the side of his face. I grab his shoulders. 'What's going on?'

'The wren are everywhere! They're tearing the walls apart!'

A creaking sound draws my eyes to the door that hides the shaft into the city. It opens suddenly and Isabel, Dillon and Shaun come stumbling out, all in as bad a shape as Arkarian. Shaun is holding his arm, blood oozing out from between his fingers.

'We can't go back down there!' Isabel practically screams as she peels away Shaun's fingers and starts healing him straightaway. 'The water is too high and filling up fast. The wren are dying by their hundreds.'

'The city has been flooded?' I ask in astonishment. This was always to be a last resort.

Arkarian's heaving starts to slow. 'It was the only way.'

'And the key?'

All eyes start looking around the room, searching. But it's not the key specifically they're looking for.

'Who's missing?'

'Jimmy's on his way out and I wasn't able to get word to Marcus, so he must still be at the school,' Arkarian says.

'Where are Ethan and Rochelle?'

Arkarian looks straight into my eyes. 'They went for the key.'

I don't wait for any more explanations. The situation is clear. I have to go in there and find them. But the city is vast. I'll have to locate them first. I close my eyes and search. It's dark, with only a few torches in the higher levels that are not underwater yet. I take my mind down the passageways, into empty annexes and corridors. But there are just so many! I try again, this time looking deeper into the flooded areas. Wren are floating everywhere. Some soldiers too. I project my mind down deeper. Where could they be? I come across a shattered wall, surrounded by murky water that looks as if it has only recently collapsed. It attracts my attention. I look around and find a small opening and project my mind through it. Then I see them, peeling away bricks from the other side, but getting nowhere fast and growing weaker with every brick they manage to work free.

'Hell!'

'What did you see?' Arkarian asks. 'Tell us!'

But I don't have time to explain. I can't wait one more second. I suck in a huge breath and disappear, re-forming directly outside the collapsed wall trapping Ethan and Rochelle inside. The water is cold around me, making me shiver. Quickly adjusting my body temperature, I control my thoughts and summon the power of strength to my hands. I go to work on the bricks, flinging them aside like ping-pong balls caught in a

322

wind. In seconds the passageway is clear, revealing a room that is dark and completely flooded. Adjusting to this darkness I see their forms. They're both still alive, but starting to drift off with their struggle to stay conscious. And we're so far down, there's no way they'll make it out of here without help.

They realise I'm beside them and turn and look. Their eyes have that wide, staring quality of only just hanging on. I spin around, releasing a few bubbles to ease the pressure growing in my own lungs. I have to do something fast! I start feeling the walls with my hands. My touch reveals only more bricks. What was it Arkarian told me about this place? It's full of passageways and secret compartments. Quickly I close my hands and punch both fists into the ceiling above. Fragments of rock and mud swirl in our faces. I punch again, and again. Rotted timber breaks away and at last a small cavity of air is revealed. It provides much-needed oxygen.

With just our faces above the water-line Ethan and Rochelle gasp and suck in huge gulps of stagnant, but life-giving air.

'That was close,' Ethan says between puffs.

'You have the key.' It's a statement. This close, I can feel it.

'Yeah, no thanks to Marduke. He knew the key was in the city. So what now?'

'Now you're going to use your wings and get out of here,' I tell him.

'But –'

'Go, Ethan! I'll make sure Rochelle gets out safely.'

He hesitates and looks as if he's going to argue with me.

'Go now!'

323

He nods and disappears.

Rochelle sighs and looks relieved. 'You can go now too.'

I just shake my head at her. We both know this little pocket of air is not going to last longer than the next surge of water, but what does she think, that I'm going to leave her here to die?

'In a second I'm going to turn around,' I explain. 'When I call out, I want you to take a big breath and get on my back. You got that?'

She peers at me with narrowed eyes and a deep frown, but her head is nodding.

A roaring sound warns us that another surge of water is coming quickly. 'OK, let's do this.'

She nods again. I turn around and focus. 'Now!'

She gulps and secures her arms around my shoulders. Quickly, as a surge of water thrashes through the opening I made earlier, I reshape my body into that of a dolphin and take off.

I swim fast, swishing around sinking debris and drowning wren. When we make it to the top of the city, I take my human form again and help Rochelle on to a dry platform. Ethan is waiting and guides us both into the shaft. As soon as the doors close and the shaft begins to shift us upwards, they collapse against the wall and slide down to the floor. Both are shivering.

'Blankets!' Isabel calls out as soon as she sees us.

Arkarian produces three, throwing one to me. I use it to dry my face. As I do, Jimmy comes running out of a side door. 'The city is completely flooded.'

The sight of Jimmy suddenly appearing triggers the question of how Marduke knew where the key was hidden. Other than Arkarian, Jimmy was the only other person aware of the secret compartment.

Arkarian hears my thoughts and grips my arm, tightly. 'What are you doing?'

I suspect Jimmy could be –

No! You're wrong!

But Arkarian, how can you be so sure? Jimmy is the one who handles the security. He was the only other person who knew where the key was.

It's not that simple. Maybe Marduke had Ethan and Rochelle watched from the moment they entered the city. He would then assume that if the key was hidden in the city they would lead him to it.

While Arkarian is right, I still can't shake these questions nagging at my brain. *But how did Marduke know it was possible to enter the city from beneath the lake?*

There was a tunnel from Neriah's house that led there. After the house was attacked, we blocked it, but Marduke may already have known where it led.

'What's going on?' Jimmy asks.

'I'm trying to figure out how Marduke got through your defences.'

He shrugs, looking bewildered. 'I wish I could tell you, Matt.'

'Maybe you can, but you don't want to.'

He peers at me closely. 'What are you saying?' He sighs defeatedly. 'Matt, tell me you don't suspect I'm the traitor. For pity's sake, you can't –'

And suddenly I recall the look of trust and adoration in my father's face at the mere mention of Jimmy's name, and I know I've made a mistake. 'No,' I try to assure him. 'I don't suspect anything about you.'

'But I see it in your eyes. Matt, I live in your house. I protect your mother and your sister. I even protect

Neriah now. You have to trust me.'

He's right. Jimmy is the *last* person I should be doubting. Where did I ever get the idea that he could be the traitor?

The room falls silent and Jimmy's eyes drift to Rochelle. He goes over to her and pulls on her arm. 'Rochelle, put your hand on me. Tell them I'm not the traitor. Come on, girl.'

But Rochelle is still huddled within her blanket on the floor and stares up at him with vacant eyes. 'Huh?'

Jimmy throws himself down on his knees in front of her. 'Give me your hand! I couldn't stand it if anyone suspected me. I couldn't stand it!'

I pull on Jimmy's shoulder. Dragging him up in one go I make him face me. 'I don't suspect you, Jimmy.' I run a hand through my hair as I try again to recall just how this ridiculous idea of Jimmy being a traitor came into my head in the first place. And then I recall Lady Arabella's words. *I'm not sure if there's anything he can't do, or hasn't had a hand in making around here. He's very talented. And his timing is impeccable. Whether you need him or not, he always seems to be there, one step ahead of you.'*

With the help of Arkarian's hand resting lightly on his back, Jimmy calms down. 'It's been a long day. Why don't you all go home,' Arkarian suggests.

Jimmy nods and releases a long sigh, then his eyes drift back to Ethan and Rochelle still huddled in their blankets on the floor. 'Are you two all right?'

Rochelle's head lifts and her eyes start to lose their vacant stare. 'Yeah, I think so. We almost ....' Her words drift off as she turns her head first to Ethan and then up to me. Slowly, she says, 'I didn't die.'

Heads nod and grin. There is such relief in her voice,

it's hard not to smile, and after the last awkward scene with Jimmy, Rochelle's words trigger a release of tension in the room.

Ethan reaches into his shirt, then holds up the golden box. The sight of it sets off a round of clapping and cheering.

But everyone's attention is soon drawn back to Rochelle. Her recent ordeal has started sinking in. 'I didn't die!' She staggers to her feet and looks around as if seeing everyone and everything in the room for the first time. She starts to move around, touching things, and the blanket drops to the floor. Water sprays off her hair as she twirls around. 'I didn't drown down there!'

No one is used to Rochelle showing so much emotion. It's a rare sight. Ethan gets up and stares at her, completely mesmerised. Rochelle keeps dancing around, oblivious. 'Look at me, I'm still alive!' She throws her head back and starts punching the air. 'Yes! I did it! I did it!' And then she adds, 'The Prophecy was wrong!'

Jimmy and Shaun force themselves to keep smiling. Dillon pats her back and Isabel gives her a hug. But what can any of us say? Apart from Ethan, and of course Rochelle, the rest of us in this room know the truth. Rochelle suddenly turns to me for some sort of confirmation. I have a hard time controlling my thoughts. I do not want her to hear them right now.

I reach out and pull her into my arms. 'You did good.'

She pulls back. 'Matt, you were right. You told me I wasn't going to die.'

She turns to Arkarian. His emotions are a mess. And even though he's an expert at keeping his thoughts screened, right now he's struggling, and the best he can do is to project them in a scrambled jumble. He holds her, and while her back is to the rest of us, he glances up at me. He doesn't have to say anything. As usual, Arkarian's eyes speak more than words. Whatever this was today, it wasn't what Isabel foresaw. The vision does not predict Rochelle's death by drowning.

Chapter Twenty-eight

Matt

Arkarian sends everyone on their way. Everyone except me. Isabel is the last to leave, and only after she gives Arkarian a long kiss. I glance away. I'm not going to bring the subject of their relationship up again. I know I have a tendency to overreact where Isabel is concerned. I have to accept that she's old enough to make her own decisions.

The secret door closes and for a long moment there is silence.

'I've spoken to Isabel,' Arkarian says. 'She's going to stick by Rochelle's side as much as possible.'

'Good.' Suddenly I feel weary and look for one of Arkarian's ancient stools. He produces two and I sit on one. 'Do you know if Neriah got back all right?'

He nods as he sits on the other stool, gripping the front with both hands. 'She's tired, but safe and well.' He continues to look at me, knowing there's something else on my mind.

'I have to go to Athens,' I explain. 'I know who the traitor is.'

He leans forward and looks at me with disbelief. 'And who is it this time, Matt? Last week it was our King.

Five minutes ago you thought it was Jimmy. You can't make accusations without proof. This is not a game we play.'

'Shift us to the palace in Athens right now and I'll show you all the proof you need.'

His eyes narrow as he peers at me. 'All right, but I can't stay long.'

'This won't take long. Believe me.'

One second I'm sitting on the stool in Arkarian's chambers, the next I'm stumbling to find my footing in the palace courtyard in Athens. Just as I do, a whooshing sound from behind has me spinning around. They know we're here already!

'Father.' Arkarian acknowledges Lorian's presence with a bowed head.

'My lord,' I say.

'Arkarian, Matt. What brings you here unannounced? I fear the news is grave.'

'There is a lot to tell you, Father, but first, Matt has some business to attend to.'

Arkarian's eyes slide to me, and suddenly I'm full of doubt. But the mournful sound of bitter-sweet singing starts up behind me and I get a surge of inner strength. I turn and walk towards the cage. The birds become frantic. They start singing wildly, melodies without rhythm, flapping their wings and throwing their chests up against the mesh. But they tire quickly, and I notice their golden feathers no longer glisten, while their diamond eyes look dull.

Lady Arabella appears and immediately starts making soothing sounds. She sees me and stops, her head turning in my direction. 'Matt, what's wrong?'

I point to the cage. 'This is what's wrong, my lady.

These birds, this cage, is proof that you are the traitor.'

She gasps, and a delicate hand sweeps up to her open mouth.

'Explain!' Lorian commands menacingly.

I take a deep breath. 'Release the birds and all will be explained.'

'But they're not ready!' Lady Arabella protests.

I run a finger along the top of the cage. Dust sweeps into the air and the birds fall silent.

Lady Arabella sighs. 'I've tried to get rid of it, Matt, but it flies in on the north wind through the night.'

I look around the spotlessly clean courtyard. 'Strange how the benches and paving remain clean, while this cage is constantly covered in dust.' I tug on a nearby olive branch, its deep green foliage smooth and clean. I scrape my hand along the top of the cage to make my point. 'This is the same dust the vultons tried to off-load over Angel Falls today. It was cultivated in Marduke's garden. It is poison. And the wind that blows in at night comes straight from the underworld.'

'Is this true?' Lorian demands Lady Arabella. 'Are you working with Marduke?'

'Of course I'm not working with Marduke! If this is poisonous dust, then I did not know it.'

Around us, others have started to gather. Lord Penbarin comes over. 'More evidence is needed, Matt. This is a serious accusation.'

'Earlier today I was on the verge of accusing Jimmy of being the traitor.'

Several of the gathered Tribunal members gasp at this notion. As they should. 'And then I remembered who put the suspicious thought into my head.' I turn to look at Lady Arabella.

331

'A notion is hardly proof, Matt,' Lord Penbarin argues.

Lorian agrees. 'What else have you?'

I look to the cage. 'Release the birds and I will show you.'

Lorian lifts a hand. 'Open it.'

'I would, my lord,' Lady Arabella says softly, 'but the birds are not well enough to fly yet.'

Lorian sighs, and the weary sound coming from this powerful immortal is unnerving. If he's rattled and exhausted by all that's happened lately, what hope do the rest of us have? 'We will settle this matter right now, my lady. Open the cage.'

'But, Lorian,' Lady Arabella pleads, holding her hands up to the cage. 'Look at them. They are so weak –'

'They are weak because they are too far from home,' I explain.

'They are weak because of their love.'

'What do you mean, Arabella?' Lord Penbarin asks.

'They are love-birds. They need to be together. They're stronger when they're together. That's how lovers survive, nurturing each other's needs ...'

The Tribunal members look around at one another uncomfortably. No one is quite sure what Lady Arabella is talking about.

'You will open the cage,' Lorian says. 'Or I will do it for you!'

With tears glistening in her eyes, Lady Arabella turns solemnly to the cage. 'Don't make me do this. The birds came to me with trust in their eyes. They knew that I was someone who could nurture them back to health. They knew that I would look after them.'

Lorian doesn't reply, but his look is enough of a command. Lady Arabella lifts a hand towards the front of the cage and an opening appears in the mesh. As the birds fly out, their wings open and stretch, and feathers fly off and shower over us as the birds continue to mould and change. Before they reach the ground, they completely transform into two stunning snow leopards.

'Aysher! Silos!' Arkarian calls out, and the snow leopards run to him, changing into their familiar dog-shapes at his feet.

The courtyard fills with stunned muttering and gasps of outrage. Lord Penbarin's gaze shifts from the dogs to Lady Arabella and back again repeatedly with disbelief. 'My lady, why?'

To her credit, Lady Arabella looks just as stunned as the others watching.

Lorian appears to grow taller all of a sudden and the courtyard goes silent as it fills with the icy rage pouring from him. Lady Arabella practically cowers before it. 'My lord, this is not what it seems. I didn't know. I swear, I didn't know the birds were the dogs we've all been searching for.'

'Save your excuses for the trial.' With a wave of his hand, two guards grip Lady Arabella from behind. 'Secure her in a cell from which she cannot escape.'

'My lord!' Lady Arabella screams. 'No! Don't do this to me! My lord, you can't doubt my loyalty. Remember, Rochelle has already tested me. I'm not the traitor. I swear!'

'When you were tested, Rochelle's powers were still developing. I believe you tricked her, disguising your disloyalty within a shroud of falsely-generated emotion.'

'No! I didn't do that. You have to believe me! I was only taking care of a pair of birds that came to me for help. They were so beautiful. So innocent and trusting. I

333

didn't question where they were from, I just wanted to keep them. Please, Lorian, don't lock me up. I couldn't stand it.'

No one says a word. Everyone is stunned.

'I'll never forgive you for this!' Lady Arabella's screams and pleading continue as the guards drag and half carry her into the palace and down into the lower levels. It's an eerie sound that will stay with me for ever. Finding the traitor brings no relief. Imprisoning Lady Arabella, someone we all love and trust, is nothing short of a tragedy.

Lorian puts a hand on my shoulder, and for a moment I'm swamped by an outpouring of his emotions and I can hardly breathe. He loves her. And her betrayal is breaking his heart.

Chapter Twenty-nine

Rochelle

Lady Arabella is being held in a prison cell in the palace in Athens accused of being the traitor! I can't believe it.

Dillon is walking beside me as we make our way towards our history class. 'Did you hear about Lady Arabella?' he whispers, sounding stunned too.

'Yeah. No wonder she didn't want Isabel going near her precious birds.'

'Apparently the poison kept the dogs locked in bird shapes so they couldn't communicate with anyone.' His head shakes.

We make it to class and find separate seats. It's the last day of school before the winter break. It's been a long semester with many strange things happening and the class is restless. Mr Carter walks in and announces that today's lesson will be a fun quiz. As the class cheers I look around. Ethan is in the row behind me. I quickly turn back. Since our underwater, near-death experience, we've hardly said a word to each other. And I don't want to bring the subject up. I still cringe at the memory of how excited I got when I realised I had actually lived through it. I can't believe I danced around those chambers singing! I feel my face heating up again. Ethan's sitting next to Chloe Campbell, his thoughts completely blocked to me. I should be pleased he's finally learned how to control them, but a part of me would really like to get into his head one more time.

I look across to the windows and out of the corner of my eyes I see his arm swing around the back of Chloe's chair. She giggles and spins him one of her most provocative smiles. Suddenly I wish I had Ethan's power of animating objects. I'd love nothing more right now than to pull that chair right out from under him!

Dillon notices where my attention is focused and sniggers. I send him a hate-filled smirk. Bored, he flicks a chunk of rubber across the room. Unconsciously he uses too much power. It whips past Mr Carter like a bullet, lodging firmly in the wall behind him. Mr Carter gives him a warning stare. Dillon lifts his shoulders, mouthing an apology while trying not to laugh. At least he's not thinking of Neriah right now. I've had enough of Dillon's obsession with her. She talked to him every day this past week about how she just wants to be friends, but it's as if he's gone completely deaf and only hears the words *he* wants to hear coming out of her mouth. Matt's been away for the past couple of days. This business with Lady Arabella has everyone in Athens in a spin. There's been endless meetings and documenting of evidence. But he's back this morning, so hopefully he'll get a chance to tell Dillon the truth. One thing is for sure, I don't want to be there when he does.

Mr Carter hands out the quiz. It's supposed to be fun, with a prize for the person who gets the most answers right. But his idea of 'fun' is a little warped. The questions are all cryptic. Maybe I'm just not with it today.

On his way back to his seat he stops at the window.

It's not an unusual thing to do, but there's something about Mr Carter's sudden stiff stance that sends a few goose bumps loose on my arms. His head tilts as if he's trying hard to pick up a sound.

Suddenly he turns and stares straight at me. It's a look I won't easily forget. His eyes are fixed and filled with fear. And while he's not a Truthseer, he knows I am. His thoughts come thundering into my head. *Close the door! Close all the windows! Get word to Matt and Neriah to do the same. They're coming, and they're coming fast.*

What is he talking about? Who are coming?

Now, Rochelle! Hurry!

I do what he says, projecting my thoughts with as much force as I can so that both Matt and Neriah get the message. It turns out Matt is nearby, but Neriah is down in one of the science labs and I'm not sure if my thoughts can reach that far. I tell Matt to make sure she gets the message.

What's going on? Matt sends his thought back.

As I help Mr Carter secure the room, I tell Matt I don't know. *Just do what he says, and make sure no one tries to get out.*

Ethan comes over and stands by the window. He doesn't say anything, but he's picked up that something is going on. So have other students in the classroom. Mr Carter puts his hands up to stop their questions, then quietly tells Ethan, 'Lock the door behind me and don't let anyone out. Don't open that door for anything. Do you understand?'

Ethan nods and Mr Carter takes off. I watch through the glass panels as he rushes from room to room. I see him pointing to the windows and then the doors. The teacher across the hall, Ms Burgess, simply stares at him.

337

He yells at her and she jumps. When he moves on to another room, she shrugs, but orders a couple of students to do exactly what he says.

Someone calls out, wanting to know what's going on.

'Who knows?' Ethan says with a light shrug. 'Carter's finally lost it.'

Dillon comes over to the window and several other students follow.

As we stare across the sporting fields on this dull winter's day, the waiting is almost too much to bear. But when the first sign occurs, it turns out to be right under our feet. The floor begins to vibrate. It sets the students off straightaway.

'It's an earthquake!' Bryce Wilson calls out and runs to the door. Finding it locked, panic quickly descends. 'Let us out of here!'

Ethan exchanges a look with me, then runs to the door. He pulls Bryce away and tries to calm him. 'It's OK. Stay calm and everything will be –'

Before Ethan finishes, the real source of the rumbling appears. Everyone runs to the windows, faces peering through the glass. At first the entire class is stunned, speechless.

Ethan peers over my shoulder. 'Here they come,' he mutters. Then, 'Everybody get away from the glass!'

A wave of thousands of black rats races across the sporting fields heading straight in our direction. Everybody screams. It doesn't take the rats long to reach the classrooms. Big and fat like hamsters, they darken the room as they make their way over the rooftop. Chloe and a couple of other girls are beside themselves, screaming and huddling together under a desk. But it's not just the girls that are freaked out. A couple of the guys look as if their eyes are going to fall out of their heads. As the rodents cross over the roof, the mass of students move to the other side of the room, tables and chairs crashing in the rush.

The sound of glass shattering down the hallway brings a stab of terror. I hope Mr Carter was able to get word to all the classes. But thinking of Mr Carter has me wondering if he found shelter for himself. A terrible sinking feeling kicks into my stomach and I whisper, 'Where are you, Mr Carter?'

'He'll be all right,' Ethan says, coming up beside me.

I can hardly hear him as the thunder the rats are making crossing the roof drowns out everything else, including the sound of screaming. Now the whole building is vibrating. I just hope the roof holds up under the weight. And then I see Mr Carter, running into the hallway just ahead of hundreds of rats. He manages to close the exit doors just before they reach him. Ethan holds on to the lock on our classroom door, ready to open it, but just as Mr Carter gets a few feet away, the rats on the ceiling find a way through some cracks and start pouring into the classroom. Mr Carter sees them and shakes his head.

'No,' he calls out, and starts backing away.

'But, sir, come back!'

Mr Carter turns and runs.

We watch in horror as the rats catch up with him. It all happens so fast. In seconds the rats are on Mr Carter's legs and crawling up his back. He falls on his face, and the rats cover him from head to foot.

Everyone is stunned and sickened, their faces pushed flat to the windows, fixed and staring.

Along with other students, I can't help calling out, 'We

have to do something!'

Ethan and Dillon stare at each other, and I hear their unconcealed thoughts bellowing into my head. To open this door would put the lives of all these students at risk.

'We can't leave him to die out there!'

Dillon smashes a chair, pulls off two legs and throws one to Ethan. But light starts to filter back into the classroom and it becomes clear that the rats are passing. Soon they are skittering down the other side of the building, heading for the lower classroom blocks. Ethan and Dillon burst out of the room, screaming and bellowing and thumping the rats off Mr Carter with their chair legs.

I get shoved to the side as Bryce and some other students run out after them. And soon all the classes in this block empty into the hallway, I finally get to Mr Carter. He's in a really bad way. Blood is oozing from just about every part of his body, his clothes in tatters from all the scratch and bite marks.

'Where's Isabel?' Ethan hisses to me.

I try to locate her thoughts, anything that will let me know which room she's in. But I get nothing. Come to think of it, I don't remember seeing her this morning at all. 'I don't think she came to school today.'

'I don't think she did either,' Ethan says, lifting Mr Carter into his arms. 'She's probably with –'

Ms Burgess shoves students out of her way to get to us. 'What happened to Marcus?'

Ethan pushes past her, ignoring her question.

'Ethan, what are you doing?' she cries out. 'The office will call an ambulance. Put him down.' He keeps walking. 'Young man, you bring Mr Carter back here!'

The further Ethan gets to the doors, the more distant

Ms Burgess's cries become. Once outside Ethan starts to run. Dillon offers to help, but Ethan just shakes his head. He's determined to take care of Mr Carter himself. But the effort becomes strenuous and he heaves. This time Dillon doesn't take no for an answer. He pulls Mr Carter out of Ethan's arms and takes off, straight up the hill towards Arkarian's chambers. With his superior strength, we get to the secret door in no time.

The opening appears and Isabel greets us on the other side. 'Quickly. In here.' She points to a door that Arkarian holds open. Dillon lays Mr Carter on a bed, and I notice its ruffled appearance. Arkarian pulls up the covering blanket, then shoots me an interesting look. I can't help but think how lucky Arkarian and Isabel are that Matt isn't here.

Dillon quickly returns my attention to the chaos at the school. 'I'm going back to see if I can help down there.'

It's a good idea. I should go too. I glance at Mr Carter; the bite marks are festering like acid burns. But there's nothing I can do here. It's up to Isabel now.

Chapter Thirty

Matt

The school is in chaos. The rats have caused plenty of damage, and a few students caught outside their class-rooms have been hurt. Badly. Where the rats have bitten, their flesh is puckering up like an acid burn. Their moaning fills the air. It's a relief to hear sirens in the distance drawing nearer. A whole string of them. But the most damage appears to be in the science labs. I make my way down there to where it is complete bedlam.

I wish I could find the others, but they don't appear to be anywhere. I could search them out with my mind, but I need a quiet moment to do that, and, well, that's just not going to happen here for a long time.

The plague has passed, but the rats are still out there, traversing the land, making their way to who knows where.

The science labs are a mess. A couple of students are still hysterical. That's when I spot Neriah, making her way from one to the other, trying to calm and reassure. The ambulances have arrived and those of us who are OK are asked to leave.

She sees me and runs straight into my arms. We go outside to the back of the building and I hold her close.

'Tell me what happened.'

She closes her eyes and shows me, projecting the images straight into my head. Mr Carter is running from one lab to the other, yelling for everyone to close their windows and lock their doors. But the rats are closing in. They're already hitting the front buildings. Many rats slide in before the students are able to close the last couple of openings. They seem to have one purpose, to search and find human flesh, as if in some crazy way it will help to make them mortal again. I see Neriah with her eyes open wide and staring, as the fear that grips the rest of the class grips her too. Screams rent the air, stools crash against desks. Students slam against each other as they try to get on top of desks and away from the rats. Some jump up and hang like monkeys off the ceiling beams. Mr Walker tries to calm the class, while flinging snarling rats off himself and the students near him.

Neriah draws herself to the side and closes her eyes. At first the room is still chaotic. She searches the minds of the rats, finding a way to communicate with them. To begin with nothing changes, but a few moments later the rats stop and lift their heads. It's an amazing sight. They make their way towards her as if hypnotised. She holds open a window and they file out. Thankfully, in the hysteria, nobody notices her gift.

'You did good,' I whisper over the top of her head.

She lifts her eyes to mine with a look I haven't seen in hers before – one of despair. 'Matt, I saw something.'

'What was it?'

'I saw into their minds.'

'The rats?'

She nods and gulps deeply.

'What did you see?'

343

'Disease,' she hisses. I tug back a wayward strand of her hair and she says, 'How do we fight this? Where do we begin?'

A shadow passes, but I pay it no attention. My thoughts are full of the mass of rats that bring disease to our world, and how we're going to deal with them. But the shadow has a voice, and it is filled with anger and accusation. 'How about beginning right here? Right here with me!'

For a moment we both freeze as Dillon starts to pace around us as if he is a wolf on the scent of his prey. 'So how long has this been going on?'

I put Neriah behind me. 'Dillon, let me explain.'

'Your hands around her, her hands around you. If you ask me, that says it all.'

'I wanted to tell you,' I try to explain, even though it's too late now. Why didn't I make the time earlier? I should have been upfront with him as soon as I realised my feelings for Neriah. If it comes down to it, there's no way I'll use my powers on him. That wouldn't be right.

Neriah steps around me. 'Dillon, I tried to tell you we could only be friends.'

'*Friends?* You think we can be friends now?' He walks up to my face. 'As for you, we've been friends nearly all our lives. Is this what friends do to each other? You knew I liked Neriah. You knew and you still moved in on her. You did it while I was locked up in that safe room being debriefed, and when I came out, you were too much of a coward to admit it!'

'It wasn't like that.'

'Now I get why the Tribunal members gave me all those gifts. They knew what you would do to me. Lady Arabella made a huge point about making sure I worked

344

on nurturing them.' He shakes his head. 'I should have listened. There were signs everywhere!'

'If you had taken notice of what we have been trying to tell you, you wouldn't be so upset right now,' Neriah says.

He hisses air through gritted teeth. 'I was thinking more along the lines that I would have worked out what was going on!' He turns to me. 'So what was that promise you made me? Were you mocking me, Matt?'

'No! I swear!'

He shoves me hard. My back hits the brick wall. The brick wall cracks.

Neriah tries to run between us.

No! Stay back! I warn her in my thoughts.

Dillon comes at me again and throws me to the ground. I get up and try to protect myself from his strength and power. He slams me into the wall again, smashing his fist into the side of my head. I shove him backwards, sliding away from the wall that's started tumbling down.

'Stop this, Dillon!' Neriah screams out as bricks fall around our feet.

Ignoring her, he comes at me again, grabbing my shoulders. I pull my hands up beneath his arms and try to break his hold. But his strength is incredible, and without using my powers, I haven't a hope. One more punch, and hopefully, he'll pull back and this stupid fight will be over.

But he doesn't pull back. He keeps coming and coming. I end up on all fours on the ground, bruised and beaten.

Neriah runs to me. *You have to use your powers!*

No! He'll finish soon.

Don't be an idiot! He's not going to finish until he kills you. Or at least beats you to a pulp.

She's right, but I won't use my powers on him. I stumble to my feet, wiping blood away from my face with my sleeve. 'Dillon, wait! Listen to me.'

'The time for listening is over!'

As he goes to ram me again, arms come around the back of him, holding him still. They're Shaun's. 'There is always time for listening.'

Dillon easily shrugs out of Shaun's hold. But it's enough to slow him, and he doesn't try to fight me again.

Shaun looks at the scene before him and shakes his head. 'I don't know what's going on here, but whatever the reason for this, it stops now.'

'What's happened?' I ask, slowly regaining my strength.

Shaun looks at each of us. 'The rift between worlds has been torn.'

'Oh, hell!' Dillon exclaims, punching a hole in the brick wall behind him. 'No way!'

The concern over Lathenia opening the rift was one of the many reasons I'd been called to Athens. The Tribunal strongly suspected this was Lathenia's next step.

'How large is the rift now?'

'Large enough so that all kinds of dark creatures can make their way into our world.'

'All creatures?' Dillon calls out. 'No way. She wouldn't open the rift for *all* the creatures that live there.'

'What happens now?' Neriah asks.

'*Now?*' Dillon mimics sarcastically. 'Now our *leader* takes control. Our *Master*, if that's what we can call this lying, spineless wimp! Let's see how you take control now.'

Shaun sends Dillon a harsh glare. 'Dillon, what's happened between you two must be put aside. It must! Do you understand?'

Dillon sucks air in through gritted teeth and continues to stare at me. But finally he backs down and gives Shaun a silent nod. 'OK. But there's stuff you don't understand. You don't know what dangerous creatures Lathenia has hidden in the underworld, locked beneath iron gates. And we're supposed to fight her with this weakling as our leader!'

Shaun attempts to ignore Dillon's sarcasm. He turns and looks at me. 'Matt, it's time. We need the weapons. The weapons that were made for the Named.'

Dillon shoots forward. 'There had better be one for me!'

Shaun's eyes slide to mine, then Rochelle comes round the corner, saving me from answering. 'What the hell is going on here?' She sees my bloody face. 'What happened to you?'

No one enlightens her, so I open my thoughts so she can understand the 'Dillon' situation quickly. She looks at Dillon and her mouth drops open. 'You did this?'

'He deserved it.'

She continues to stare at him and he says, 'Did you know about them too?'

She holds her hands up, fingers spread wide. 'Don't get mad at me, Dillon. But I'll be honest with you – I think you had to be blind not to notice that these two have something very strong between them. Maybe it's a guy thing. Matt couldn't see it at first, even though everyone else could. And when he did realise it, he'd already made that stupid promise to you. Not telling you was another mistake, but he didn't mean to hurt you on purpose.'

Her words are generous and maybe, just maybe, Dillon will listen to a third party. He shrugs and glances away, and Rochelle brings me her message. 'Lorian has released the chest of weapons that has been in his care. Arkarian has it. He wants us to meet on the ridge above the falls and for you to get the key.'

Shaun's head nods deeply. 'Let's go, then.'

'Where are the others?' I ask Rochelle.

'Ethan and Isabel are making their way to the ridge as we speak.'

'What about Mr Carter?' Dillon asks. 'Is he OK now?'

'What do you mean, Dillon? What happened to Marcus?' Shaun asks.

A woman walks around the side of the building. 'That's what I would like to know!'

It's Ms Burgess, and her words make Rochelle jump. 'Oh, Ms Burgess, I didn't see you there. Don't worry, Mr Carter's fine.'

'That's hardly likely, young lady, considering the condition he was in. I want a word with Ethan Roberts. Where is he? And where did he take Marcus?'

'I swear Mr Carter's fine. I … I saw him only a few minutes ago.'

Ms Burgess's face screws up in disbelief. She goes right up to Rochelle and swings a finger back and forward in her face. 'I'm telling you now that if Marcus Carter is not returned to this school in the next few minutes I'm going to call the police and heads will roll. Am I making myself clear, Ms Thallimar?'

'Emily, what's the fuss? I can hear you from clear across the other side of the oval.'

Finally something goes right. Mr Carter's appearance is timely. Ms Burgess gasps at the sight of him. 'Marcus, are you all right? Where did that boy take you?'

Mr Carter walks up to Ms Burgess and tugs on his jacket collar. 'I assure you, Emily, I'm perfectly well. This jacket is made of strong fabric. The darn rats couldn't penetrate it. Those rotten scoundrels gave me a fright, though. I'd gone and fainted. Ethan carried me away from the crowds, then ran and got some smelling salts and I washed the blood off.'

She frowns at him, and as she does so, he grins at her. She practically melts. I can't believe it! So Ms Burgess has a crush on our Mr Carter!

'I take it that classes have been cancelled for the rest of the day?' he asks, carrying on the conversation as if everything is normal.

'Oh yes,' Ms Burgess says as they walk towards the office together. 'Most of the parents have been contacted and have started picking their children up already. And buses have been organised to take the others home early. They've already started leaving. Can you believe what's been happening lately? This is the second time this term that school's been cancelled. What's going on, Marcus?'

'I don't know, Emily, but it would be a good idea to keep everyone indoors, just in case those rodents make a return appearance. I'll make an announcement right away.'

As soon as they're out of earshot, we start to move off, but my thoughts keep swinging back to Dillon and the look of intense fear in his eyes a few minutes earlier. It's there again now in his dazed look.

'Exactly what has Lathenia got locked beneath those iron gates you mentioned earlier, Dillon?'

He goes to speak, but no words come out of his mouth.

'You'd better tell us,' Shaun says.

He takes a deep breath. 'All right. But you saw them too, Matt.'

A shiver reverberates through me as I recall the brutish animals locked in Lathenia's dungeon.

Dillon explains, 'They walk on two legs like humans, they have two thick hands as well, and are just as tall as us. They have large heads with long curved horns coming out of them, and ... I don't know quite how to explain this, eyes that see right through you – black and glassy, like a window to a dark well of nothing. And down their backs are these pointed bones that stick out along the line of their spine. They're big and strong too. And yeah, did I mention the fact that they're attracted to the scent of living flesh?'

'I've seen these creatures impounded in Lathenia's dungeon. They're exactly as you describe. But I didn't see any in the underworld,' I say.

'No, you wouldn't have. She keeps them locked in a series of underground caverns and tunnels. They live there among their own kind, in their own filth, while Lathenia works out a way to control them.'

'How do you know all this?' Shaun asks.

Dillon turns to Shaun. 'She put me with them once. But she didn't contain my wings, and I escaped.'

Rochelle shudders. 'Dillon, what are these beasts called?'

'Demons,' he says. 'The darkest creatures in the universe.'

Chapter Thirty-one

Rochelle

By the time all ten of us are gathered on the ridge together it is noon. The area is checked, and with four Truthseers, Mr Carter's hearing and Neriah's two dogs, we should be safe from prying ears or unwanted visitors.

Arkarian sets the box down, then takes a place in the circle we have inadvertently formed. I stare at the treasury of weapons. It's a lot smaller than I imagined, the size of a bedside chest. It's made from some sort of metal that resembles gold or brass. It is ornately decorated with silver and jewels, and has the distinct pattern on the lid of the now familiar octagon shape.

Inside, I am a jumping bundle of nerves. I can't remember ever being this excited, not even as a child with a birthday present. Not that my birthdays were ever exciting events. A celebration was always an excuse for my father to get drunk. More often than not, my mother and I wouldn't mention them to him.

Matt takes the key and fits it neatly into the octagon shape. There is a click, then a creaking sound as the ancient mechanism is released. As he opens the lid I release a deep breath that I didn't realise I'd been holding. I'm not sure what to expect. Fireworks? Explosives?

A booming voice? But nothing unusual happens.

'While I was away I was shown the weapons inside this box and taught how to use them.' Matt lifts a longish object out of the box and goes and stands in front of Ethan. I'm on the other side of the circle, but it looks like a gold bow and arrow set.

As the bow and a single arrow are put in his hands, Ethan frowns. 'I'm not much of an archer. Maybe this would be better given to Isabel.'

Soft laughter floats around the circle. Matt says to us all, 'These weapons are made specifically to extend or enhance your natural powers. They may not be obvious at first, but as you learn to use your weapon and gain experience, you will understand.'

'So how does this bow and arrow set relate to me?' Ethan asks.

'It's an enhancement of your animation power and your affinity with the unreal. Here,' Matt says, taking the arrow and setting it in the bow. 'Use your mind to will this arrow to hit ...' He spins around and points to a distant spot somewhere between where Jimmy and I are standing, 'that tree over there with the broken branch hanging in mid air. Aim for the seed pod dangling at its end. But ...' He hesitates as he thinks, then points to a distant tree in the opposite direction. 'Shoot the arrow that way.'

'All right,' Ethan says. He takes aim to his left and lets the arrow go.

I don't see a thing; the arrow moves too fast. But I do hear a sharp whoosh as the arrow slices the air between Neriah and me, followed almost instantly by a popping sound and a flash as the seed pod explodes.

Everyone murmurs in amazement. Ethan grins,

looking pleased. 'Will it work every time?'

'Every time. From now on you will never be without an arrow and you will never miss your target.'

As Ethan examines his set, slipping the bow on to his shoulder, Matt moves on to Isabel. He puts a bar in her hand, and when I peer over for a closer look, I see the bar is more of a handle. Something one might find at the end of a sword.

She looks up at him. 'What is it?'

'It's a weapon of light. Its power generates from your own inner source. A person of darkness will find the weapon useless. In dark places it will extend your gift of sight.' He takes the handle into his own hand for a moment. A beam of light suddenly appears to the length of a sword. It shimmers brilliant white, so strong it almost burns my eyes. Matt lunges towards a nearby pile of boulders. The beam pierces through the centre of the top boulder with a sizzling sound. The boulder fills with light, holds its shape for a moment, then completely disappears.

Everyone stares in amazement.

'Now you try.'

Isabel feels the weight of the handle in her palm. 'How do I turn it on?'

'Relax your thoughts and don't try too hard. Let your inner light flow. It won't take you long to get the idea.'

Suddenly a beam of light generates and Isabel smiles. She lunges at a boulder and it shatters all over us. We're not prepared for the debris. Everyone ducks or scatters.

'Sorry!'

Matt just grins at her, then moves on to Mr Carter, handing him two metal bands with holes running through their centres. 'Slip these on your fingers.'

They fit Mr Carter's hands like fingerless gloves. 'Whoa!' he calls out, obviously impressed. As he bends and flexes his fingers, sharp metal darts punch out from the bands across every knuckle. They look lethal by anyone's standards.

Matt pats his shoulder and moves on to Shaun, giving him two beautifully-crafted swords with silver handles. One long, one short. 'To our master swordsman, two swords that have the power to kill with one strike.'

Shaun is impressed. He takes them both and feels them for balance. 'Excellent.'

As Matt moves around the circle, I can't help getting jittery. I wonder what sort of weapon has been made for me. What gifts of mine will be extended with these amazing tools? He gets to Jimmy and I'm almost jumping out of my skin with anticipation. For the first time in a lifetime I feel an overwhelming sense of belonging. This is what I am supposed to be doing. Standing side-by-side with these people, ready to do battle for the one rightful cause.

Matt puts a bag in Jimmy's hand.

'A bag of tricks?' Jimmy asks, feeling the contents within his palm. 'Or a bag of pebbles?'

Matt laughs. 'Something like that, except these "pebbles" have the power of a grenade, and your supply, though it fits neatly in your pocket, is a never-ending one. Not only are these explosives effective against the creatures of the dark, but they will bring down any barrier, no matter how it might be armed or locked.'

Jimmy grins, juggling the pouch in his hand, impressed by his weapon's light weight.

Next is Neriah. He takes her hand and, I swear, the entire circle can feel the power that flows between them with this sudden contact. It's as if when they are touching, they become an extension of each other. He pulls back and Neriah opens her hand. In her palm is something that can only be described as a fragment of lightning. It has everyone gasping and craning their necks to see. Even Aysher and Silos sit up and sniff.

'What can I do with this?' she asks as the lightning glistens and flashes in her palm.

Matt looks around. 'Point it at that shrub over there and use your thoughts to project its energy.'

She aims and points. Instantly a flash of lightning streaks from her hand, igniting the shrub and reducing it to ash within the space of one or two seconds. It has everyone staring in awe.

And now there are only three of us left. Me, Dillon and Arkarian. When Matt comes towards me I can't stop my hands from shooting straight out. They're trembling, but I don't care. He stands in front of me for a long moment, and when nothing happens, nothing is put into my hands, I look up.

'I don't have a weapon for you,' he says.

Suddenly the circle is dead silent. I take my trembling hands and slide them behind my back. 'I don't understand,' I manage to say.

'The reason I don't have a weapon for you is because you don't need one.'

I can't believe what he's saying. 'What do you mean?'

'The weapon that was originally made for you, I'm going to give to Dillon.'

'What?'

He tugs on my arms, bringing my hands around to the front. 'You have already proven that your hands can kill. You don't need a tool to help you. And because we are ten now, we are one weapon short.'

'So you're giving my weapon to Dillon!'

He nods. 'That's right.'

He starts to move on, turning back to the chest. I can't believe what's happening. Tears threaten. I blink fast and take a step backwards, ready to run. What am I doing here with these people? I shouldn't be a part of this ... this select, secret group. They don't want me. No matter how hard I try, they will never let me in.

Matt hears my uncontrollable thoughts tumbling out and turns, looking puzzled. I try to enlighten him. 'Don't I deserve a weapon?'

'Rochelle, it's not like that.'

I shake my head at him, at all of them, and start to back away. He comes after me and pulls on my hands. 'Listen to me: you're not being excluded. Your hands are your weapons. Look at them.' He yanks off my gloves; sparks fly in all directions. Everyone scatters or ducks out of the way. 'Here.' Matt puts a rock in my hand. It disintegrates into dust. He knew it would. My emotions are running high. Gasps and cries of astonishment flow around me. 'Stay. This is where you belong.'

Matt says 'stay', but my heart is screaming 'go'. I've never felt so humiliated. Arkarian comfortingly touches my shoulder. Silently I reach out and yank my gloves back from Matt's hands. When I have them on safely, and my freakish hands are out of sight, I return to my position in the circle and remain silent. I stare at my feet for a long time. I do not want to see what weapon Dillon has been given. I listen while Arkarian is given his, a whip of some sort. It has the ability to do anything with motion and matter, like igniting fires, moving masses of water, creating a dust storm, or simply destroying the creatures we're going to be coming up against. It's a good weapon for him. Of all of us here, he deserves the most powerful one.

The last weapon is Matt's. It turns out to be an axe. As he tucks it into the belt at his waist he explains how the axe – solid and strong and earthly – gives him balance.

At last it's over, and I finally get the courage to look up. Everything is blurry. I try hard to get rid of the few tears that doggedly remain. Ethan is staring across the circle at me. And while my eyes begin to clear, his remain fixed.

I'm not sure what to make of his expression. The word 'pity' comes to mind, but I push it aside. I couldn't stand it if Ethan pitied me. For a moment I'm swamped with the urge to reach out to him, see if I can hear his thoughts. Surprisingly they're open to me, but I don't do it. The feeling that I'm an intruder still lingers deeply inside.

But suddenly all thoughts are dismissed as King Richard materialises in front of us. A flash high in the sky overhead reveals the shape of part of a building. Something drops and hits the ground. Jimmy runs over and retrieves a couple of bricks. He holds them up for all to see.

King Richard explains, 'It's the Citadel. It's under attack. Bring your weapons, and hurry!'

Chapter Thirty-two

Matt

The Citadel may be under attack, but Ethan has decided to attack me. He thumps my shoulder, dragging me back from the others as they make their way to Arkarian's chambers. 'How could you do that to her?'

'I'm assuming you mean Rochelle?'

'Of course I mean Rochelle! Who else did you humiliate out there?'

'I didn't mean to humiliate anyone, and I know what I'm doing. It was the right thing.'

I go to pass but he holds his hand against my chest. 'It was a mistake.'

'I know her better than you, Ethan. Rochelle is strong.'

'You idiot! Don't you see how she always keeps her distance, never takes her gloves off, and hides behind that … that cynical persona she puts out?'

Arkarian hears and comes up beside us.

'Do you think I made a mistake by not giving Rochelle a weapon, Arkarian, even though she doesn't need it and we would have been one short?'

He takes his time answering. 'If a mistake was made, it was that you didn't speak to Rochelle in private first.'

Of course! Arkarian is right again, while I stumble and

make a mess of everything. 'I don't have the ability to be the leader of this group.'

Ethan groans while Arkarian says, 'Matt, we all make mistakes. That you do too just shows your human side.'

'But *you* never make a mistake!' I'm quick to tell him, easily convincing myself this is the right thing to do. '*You* should take my place. *You* should lead the Named. I would be proud to serve you.'

'Don't speak such thoughts.'

'I'm serious. I'm handing over my leadership to you.'

'Matt, think about what that would do to our morale. Take a look around – what do you see?'

I glance at the others, trudging up the mountain as if they are going to their death. Suddenly I understand. We are all reliant on each other. We all have our part to play, and mine is the leader of the Named. No matter what flaws I have, or uncertainties, this is who I am: son of an immortal, more powerful than all the Named combined. And while I'm far from perfect, with my inhibitions and doubts and inexperience, none of them is perfect either.

I stride up to the secret doorway and open it without Arkarian's help, because that's just one of the things I can do. Suddenly I'm tired of hiding my powers, hiding within myself. So before I step through, I turn and look at the others who have gathered before me.

'Know this, everyone!' I project my voice so that it rumbles across the mountain. 'We are about to go into battle to rescue the earth from the most foul evil that exists in this universe, and I am going to lead you. I apologise for my past weaknesses, but from this moment on, I will not be weak any more!' I raise my hands into the air and draw one thought to mind: *power*. I want them to feel it.

As the others follow me into the mountain I sense a difference in them. I don't pay it too much attention, nor try to analyse it – there's simply not enough time. Arkarian is the last to enter. Others make way for him as he passes them and comes to stand before me. 'Tell us what you want us to do.'

I lay my hand on his shoulder. 'Shift us all to the Citadel so that this battle can finally be resolved.'

Chapter Thirty-three

Rochelle

When we get to the Citadel Lord Penbarin is there to meet us. His soldiers are with him, guarding every entry point. They're armed with swords, knives and other martial arts weapons. They look a mess. There's been a battle here already. Lord Penbarin's clothes are dishevelled, his sword dripping blood. 'Marduke and another battalion of wren have infiltrated the lower levels, while the middle-world creatures are in the labyrinth.'

'How did they get in?' Matt asks.

Lord Penbarin's eyes drift to the high, eight-panelled ceiling. 'They took us by surprise. There were so many of them, they overwhelmed us. Lathenia is using the Citadel as a means to get her massive armies of the dead into our world. We can't let this happen. Those that are through already must be eradicated. The weapons from the treasury will help in this task.' He grips Matt's shoulders. 'Lorian is willing to destroy the Citadel if that's what it takes to stop any more creatures from getting through.'

'Destroy the Citadel!'

'We are bulging at the seams as it is. The pressure is already too much. And still she sends more. Lorian will destroy the workings, including all the transportation rooms and machinery to stop her. He is preparing a strategy right now with your King.'

'Let's hope it doesn't come to that, my lord.'

'Lathenia is bringing forth all manner of creature. But if she were to bring forth the worst the underworld has –'

'You mean the demons!' Dillon calls out.

Lord Penbarin winces at the sound of the very word. 'Yes, that's what I mean. The Citadel will be destroyed before this happens. The risk to the earth – to life itself – is too great.'

'OK, then,' Matt says. 'We'll split up and go where we're needed most.' He turns to look at Ethan, Shaun and Neriah. 'You three go to the central control rooms to help protect the high-tech machinery there.'

Lord Penbarin explains, 'Without this machinery transportation becomes impossible. Don't let them take it. We don't want the Order to be in a position to set it up somewhere else in the future. But it's not going to be easy. The control room has already been invaded.'

'Great,' Ethan says dryly.

Neriah squats between Aysher and Silos, patting them and smoothing down their coats. 'Looks like we've got our work cut out,' she says. The two dogs sit upright and stare straight into her eyes. 'Stay close beside me.'

Lord Penbarin nods in unconscious agreement. No one wants to see Neriah separated from her dogs again. 'Sir Syford and Queen Brystianne and their soldiers are trying to hold the control room, but they need your powers and your weapons too. Go quickly.'

Matt continues explaining where he thinks the rest of us should go. 'Dillon, I want you to come with me.'

'No way!' Dillon objects. 'I'm not pairing up with you. Forget it.'

Matt stares at him hard, and as he does so, his eyes change colour from his usual brown to shimmering gold for a second. The sight makes Dillon jerk backwards. 'We're going to defend this Citadel side-by-side. Do you understand me, Dillon?'

Dillon nods.

'Marcus, you stay here with Isabel and Rochelle. I want you three to help Lord Penbarin stop any further invasion.' He points to the eight-panelled ceiling, for the moment thankfully quiet.

A rumbling sound in the lower levels reminds us that we'd better hurry. Matt directs Arkarian and Jimmy to the labyrinth, inundated with creatures from the middle realm.

'You've seen these creatures before,' Matt says to Arkarian. 'You know how they work, but don't underestimate their power or their weaknesses.'

Jimmy asks, 'What are they exactly?'

'Some will be lost souls,' Arkarian explains. 'And now that the bridge is gone they will be wandering aimlessly. But there will be others that manifest from your exaggerated fears. From your nightmares.'

'Gee, thanks, Matt,' Jimmy jokes. 'I can't wait.'

'That's why I'm sending you two,' Matt says. 'Both of you have better control over your fears than the rest of us.'

Everyone takes off, but before Matt goes, he notices the knife I've drawn from my boot. 'What are you doing with that?'

'I'm getting ready. Any minute now we could be attacked. I want to be prepared.'

Matt looks at my hands. 'Take off your gloves.'

I shake my head. 'No.'

'Take them off, Rochelle.'

'But if I take my gloves off, I can't hold the knife.' This is an excuse. I don't want to take my gloves off because my hands are hideous.

'Your hands are your weapons, not that pathetic-looking knife. That will only get you killed.' He takes the knife from my fingers. He doesn't say anything else, but his look is so piercing, there's nothing else I can do, except to peel back my gloves and shove them in my pocket. Sparks shimmer and fly, hitting the walls far away and burning holes into them.

Lord Penbarin's eyebrows lift. 'When will the power stop surging?' he asks Matt.

Matt's mouth slides left, then right in an action of uncertainty. 'Each time I see them, they're stronger.'

My face heats up hotter than my hands for a moment. I wish they would stop looking at me! Even Mr Carter looks stunned.

Lord Penbarin asks, 'Has anyone been teaching you how to control them?'

'Lady Arabella was, my lord.'

'Hmm, we'll find you someone else. Are they painful?'

Lately they've been excruciating, but I keep these thoughts completely screened. 'No, my lord.'

'Hmm,' he mumbles.

Another explosion rocks the flooring from the lower levels, causing a large panel of glass to shatter behind us. We're all thrown by the impact as glass sprays everywhere.

When it's over, Matt calls out to see if everyone is all right.

Lord Penbarin picks himself up from the floor. 'Lord Alexandon is in trouble.'

Matt nods. 'I'm going. Come on, Dillon. We're needed in the lower levels.' As they take off, Matt turns to look at us. 'If you get into any trouble you can't handle just call me. I'll hear you, and I will come. OK?'

I nod and they disappear. Lord Penbarin's soldiers come back from checking out the shattered window. 'The wren are in the courtyard. Some have penetrated the internal stairwells, my lord,' says one.

And suddenly the eight-panelled ceiling starts to move overhead, picking up speed quickly. In seconds it's a blur of colour and motion.

Lord Penbarin glances at Mr Carter, Isabel and me. 'Prepare yourselves. They're coming.'

As he says this, doors to the side burst open and wren come charging in, snorting and flapping their wings. They're armed with axes, chains, swords and knives. I search for my own knife, but of course Matt has it. Oh, great!

Lord Penbarin and his soldiers move in to attack the wren, attempting to force them back down the stairwells before whatever other creatures arrive through the ceiling. And while they're excellent swordsmen, the wren, once slain, are quick to get up again. The Lord and his soldiers do not have the weaponry to eradicate them, only to slow them down.

Isabel glances at the weapon of light she is holding. Right now it's completely inactive. She looks at it as if wondering what to do.

'Use it as Matt showed you!' I yell.

My words move her into action. Tentatively at first she lunges as a wren goes to jump her. A long beam of shimmering light pierces its wing. Both of us are propelled backwards as the wren explodes with a burst of heat, scorching our faces.

We stumble to our feet and Isabel glances at me with an apology on her face.

'Don't worry about it. Try again.'

This time the beam is accurate, straight through the centre of the wren's chest. It shudders for a second, then completely disintegrates.

Mr Carter deals with several wren at the same time. Aiming his punches well, his weapon is direct, powerful and effective.

But there's no break from the onslaught. Just as the number of wren begin to diminish, the spinning panels accelerate into a humming blur and the chamber fills with incredible light, blinding everyone momentarily. The chamber quickly comes alive as creatures start falling from the ceiling. Hundreds of them pour down over us, screeching wildly. They're thin, like skeletons covered in nothing but grey skin. Their faces are gaunt, and the feel of them as they fall on us is wet and sticky. Luckily for me, as soon as they come in contact with my hands, they disintegrate with a high-pitched squeal.

It's pandemonium as Lord Penbarin and his soldiers struggle under the attack. I run over and start yanking the bony creatures off them, grabbing them by their throats.

Isabel helps one of the soldiers, while Mr Carter gets rid of one after another quickly with his deadly fists. But as more come flying down at us from the ceiling, it's obvious we're not going to be able to eliminate them all. We keep fighting, and when next I look around, Lord Penbarin is in real trouble. Mr Carter catches my eye and runs over to help him. But I can't get away as quickly. One creature has me from behind and appears to be trying to work its way through me. Eventually I get a grip on its long limbs and throw it over my shoulder. It clings there for a second before disintegrating, and its stickiness seeps into my clothes.

I run over to Lord Penbarin, where Mr Carter has managed to get all but one of these horrid creatures off him. There's a look of intense relief in Lord Penbarin's eyes as he sees his freedom is only moments away. But as I reach down to get my hands on the creature's neck, Mr Carter punches it. Our hands clash and hold for a long moment, skin against skin. I feel the sharp metal points of his weapon as they pierce my palms, while he gets the full brunt of my sizzling, electric hands.

And then, as if the contact has created too much energy between us, we're catapulted apart. Mr Carter looks at his burnt hands. For me, the connection with Mr Carter has an entirely different effect. Sure, my hands are bleeding from the metal that pierced them, but that's not the reason I'm sitting here, completely blown away. When my hands touched his I felt something. Something strong, and yet also familiar. A sensation that will never shift from my memory for as long as I live. I felt it a few weeks earlier when I went to Neriah's house and her hand brushed mine.

Mr Carter notices I haven't moved. He gets up and starts to walk around me with eyes staring and wide. 'Are you all right?' he asks me slowly.

Instantly I understand that he suspects I felt something in my touch. I have. And it has shaken me to my core. Mr Carter and Neriah are linked. And the link is strong and close, like blood. Yet, where Neriah's touch revealed her spirit is nothing but light, Mr Carter's touch revealed his spirit is all darkness. 'Yeah … um … I'm fine.'

'Why are you looking at me like that?'

'I … I was just worried that I might have hurt you.' And there it is again, that look he always has in his eyes for me – the look of reserved and underlying hatred. I have always posed a threat to him. Especially since Lorian increased the power of my hands to test loyalty. One touch would have revealed the truth.

'What's wrong, Rochelle?' His voice is teasing. I skim a look to Isabel and the others, but they are still under attack from these nameless creatures and remain oblivious to what's happening here. Even Lord Penbarin has moved off. 'You have the look of a rabbit. A rabbit with one leg caught in a snare who has just realised she's about to die.'

I get up and he moves with me. I back away towards Isabel, but he moves to block me. I try to distract him with conversation. 'Ethan was always right about you. He had a gut instinct you were bad.'

'What a pity no one took his suspicions seriously,' he mocks. 'They should have, you know. Instinct is one of Ethan's strongest gifts.'

'Why did you save the school?'

'Because, my dear, heroes are always the last to be suspected.'

'Lady Arabella isn't the traitor.'

His smile is slow. 'That little secret is going to remain for ever between you and me.'

For a moment we're silent as I take this in, and wonder what his plans are for me. 'You have Marduke's blood in your veins.'

'Hmm,' he murmurs, moving closer. 'Well I would,

wouldn't I? After all, he is my brother.'

His words are meant to shock, to make me freeze to the spot. It's then I realise he has manoeuvred me into the centre of the room. I look down at my feet and see that I am standing within the shape of the octagon. It's exactly where he wants me. I look up and call Matt in my thoughts. *Come quickly! I'm in over my head! Hurry, Matt! Hurry!* But even as I project these thoughts, I realise it's too late.

The panels overhead are spinning again and the light indicating imminent transportation is generating quickly. Mr Carter has manipulated the machinery. If anyone would know how, it would be him. He has been the co-ordinator in this Citadel for the last twenty years. He has access to every room, every level, every open portal, including transportation to other worlds.

'How long have you been working for the Order?'

'From the day I found out Marduke was my brother. The same day his face was sliced in half and he wanted to die. I looked after him. I helped him see that there could be life again for him. He wanted revenge and I helped him get it.'

'So why did you stay with the Guard?'

'I was much more useful that way. I had liberty to inside information and access to high-security areas.'

I look over his shoulder and catch Lord Penbarin's eye. He's heard my thoughts but is under attack again. Isabel looks up too, and there is a look of wonder in her eyes, but the light keeps brightening to an unbearable degree. 'You framed Lady Arabella.'

'That was easy. She was vulnerable. Her love for Lorian blinded her. She couldn't resist looking after those "birds".'

'You used the poison from Marduke's gardens to keep the dogs' identities disguised.'

He lifts one shoulder in a carefree manner. 'With my brother's help, I could get a hold on just about anything I wanted.'

'Even the key.'

He nods. 'Especially the key. Until Matt got his hands on it and hid it in the vault of the city.'

Suddenly the lights above surge and blind us both for a second. I try to make a run for it, but Mr Carter grabs me around the waist and throws me back. As I struggle to get to my feet again, the shifting sensation kicks in, and I am catapulted into another world.

Chapter Thirty-four

Matt

I have never been in this part of the Citadel before. It is a city in itself. It is also where the survivors live who watch over the earth. Should it be destroyed, what will happen to them? There are other consequences of this possible destruction. Would it mean the end of transportation as we know it?

The stairwell is deep. The lower we descend, the louder the rumblings of war. I hope the others are holding up all right. They have only just received their weapons, but are masters in their crafts, so they should be fine. This thought reminds me of Dillon. His weapon, originally created for Rochelle, will feel foreign in his hands.

I motion towards his wrists. 'Do you think you can handle those things?'

He looks down. 'Sure.' He yanks his arms out and the gold, pointed wristbands with their miniature crossbow heads are revealed. 'I mean, they feel strange, but in a good way. I've been trying to connect with them, like you said, with my thoughts.'

'They're very powerful weapons. Your will is their will.'

He stares at the delicate crossbow heads thoughtfully. 'I was wondering why you did that. You know, why you gave them to me. I was just surprised that you could trust me so much.'

'When you were with the Order, weren't you one of Lathenia's highest-ranked soldiers?'

'Yeah.'

'You're obviously trained to handle the responsibility that accompanies power and authority. Lathenia saw it in you. Arkarian believes in you. And so do I.'

'But you have to know how angry I am at you right now. How can you still trust me? Aren't you worried I'll take this pulsing rage and run back to Lathenia?'

'Is that what you want to do?'

He remains silent for a moment and a door to the side bursts open. A dozen strange-looking people come running into the stairwell, rushing straight past us.

'Did you see that?'

'They're the survivors,' I inform Dillon, who continues to stare at their strange appearance. And then I see what has them running so fast – hundreds of creatures are coming towards us. Most of these creatures are wren, but there are birds too, and others that hover like dogs on all fours. Those that have hands are armed with swords and daggers, hammers and axes.

Lord Alexandon and a dozen of his soldiers charge up the stairwell just in front of them. 'Back!' he calls out. 'There are just too many! We have to retreat and form a strategy.'

The first to reach us is a flock of birds with human faces and pointed beaks. Dillon lifts his hands. Darts that are more like luminous flecks of light shoot from his wrists. The six birds making their way up the stairwell explode. Unfortunately, they explode right over the top of us, and we end up bathed in their blood, shattered flesh and feathers.

Lord Alexandon and his soldiers nearby turn and stare at him.

'Oops!'

Wiping blood from my face with the back of my sleeve, I mutter back, 'Try thinking *total* elimination, flesh and blood included.'

'Got it,' he says, retracting his weapons.

By now the wren, birds and other four-legged creatures have pushed forward and are practically over the top of us.

'Run!' Lord Alexandon calls out.

'Wait!' I call back, instinctively sliding my hand to the axe at my waist. 'Get behind me, all of you.'

As they do so, I decide to leave my weapon in place and will one thought to mind – *wind*. The wind that generates is mighty. I thrust it towards the Order's army. The wren and other nameless creatures, including the birds, are caught in this force. I blow gently and the whirling creatures are thrust back into the interiors of the lower levels.

Dillon and the soldiers quickly bolt the doors.

'There's another exit,' Lord Alexandon explains, pointing to a corridor to our right. 'Lady Devine is having trouble holding it. I told her you would come as soon as you could. But be careful, Matt. Marduke is there.'

'Dillon, let's go.'

Halfway along the corridor, one of Lady Devine's soldiers meets us. 'My lady sends me. She says to hurry. She can't hold the dark forces back much longer.'

When we get there the doors are bursting. Lady

Devine comes running over. 'It's hopeless.'

'Are any of your people inside?' I ask.

'Not that I know of.'

'Good, now everyone get back.' As soldiers scatter up the stairwells and around the back of me, I bring another powerful thought to mind – storm. No. *Firestorm*.

The doors burst open and I thrust the storm straight into the attacking creatures. It spreads like a fireball, sweeping through the masses, expanding into the lower level corridors. Screams rent the air.

Dillon stands beside me, staring at the wave of fire as it continues to sweep through the corridors. He says calmly, 'That's impressive. Did you pick that up in "Immortal School"?'

He makes me laugh. But the laughter is short-lived, as a wave of heat comes flooding back in our direction.

Dillon feels it too. 'Uh-oh.'

Lady Devine comes up on my other side just in time for me to warn her. 'Get your people to cover. Up the stairwell, now!'

As she runs back I grab Dillon, throwing him down under me. The wave of fire bursts over the top of us. Some of Lady Devine's soldiers don't make it up quickly enough, including Lady Devine herself. Their screams of agony go right through me. When the flames pass, I help Dillon to his feet and turn to check on the injured. But Dillon grabs my arm, stopping me from moving. I look to see what has him so distraught and find him staring straight into the face of Marduke.

And now I understand why the flames returned. He stands in the doorway and raises his singed hands above his singed head and gives an almighty roar. Around him a wave of wren and other creatures surge, reinvigorated

374

by the sound of their Master's voice.

'Use your weapon on them.' I point to the wren. 'I'll deal with Marduke.'

Dillon takes aim at the mass of wren pushing out the doorways and heading for the stairwell, and this time when the darts hit, the creatures disappear without mess, without even a trace.

Marduke is impressed. A mocking look fills his one red and swollen eye. He wills a sword to his hand. 'How interesting. But let us fight as the mortals do.'

His aim is to detain me, so that his army can penetrate the upper levels and do their damage. They file out around us. Dillon chases after them, along with Lady Devine and her soldiers. Marduke lunges towards me, and I withdraw the axe from my belt. Marduke is a master in this physical craft, and, well, my skills are hardly expert. But my axe has the power to kill even this monster. All I need is one good thrust.

Come quickly! I'm in over my head! Hurry, Matt! Hurry!

Rochelle's thoughts thunder into my head, so loudly that for a moment I'm distracted and Marduke gets the better of me. He shoves my back up against a rail, quickly swinging his sword to the base of my throat. His breath is foul. In fact, his whole body reeks. I shove him hard and he flies backwards. I attempt to answer Rochelle, but now Marduke is in a rage. He attacks. It is all I can do to keep up. Sword strikes axe until my arm tires and for a moment I think he's going to thrust that sword into my ribs. I will my arm to strengthen, and luckily it does, enough for me to keep the battle going. But keeping it going is not enough. At the very least I have to disarm him so I can quickly go to Rochelle.

I call her with my thoughts, but there's no reply.

375

Nothing. It's as if she suddenly doesn't exist. Her silence, the empty sense I'm getting now, chills me. It's enough to send a surge of power to my arms. This time when we rally, it is frantic and fast. Marduke must be tiring; but he's not human any more, though what type of beast he has become is difficult to tell. He lunges, attempting to strike me in the chest. I slide my axe beneath his arm, stopping him. His sword flings loose from his hand and flies across the hallway. At last!

For a moment we both remain silent, gathering our breath and sizing one another up. His one eye shifts to where his sword landed. He wants it back. But this is my chance to get to Rochelle. She needs me, and I'm worried that I have already let her down. I have to go now!

Finishing off Marduke will have to wait.

Chapter Thirty-five

Rochelle

I fall hard into a world of complete and utter darkness. My hands, shimmering with their electric charges, offer the only light. But it's not enough. I spin around blindly, starting to panic, when a hand curves under each of my elbows. I feel the spikes and try to pull away, but Mr Carter's hold is firm. Suddenly I'm spinning and a heavy chain wraps tightly several times around my body, locking my arms by my side, and making my hands useless.

Mr Carter grunts and steps away. Then there is light. Mr Carter has a crystal in his free hand. It's enough to reveal the area around us. And now I see that the chains wrapped around my body are connected to the chain in his hand. I try to move my arms to make use of my hands, but the chains are too tight. He stares at me and for a moment I think I see regret. But the look is fleeting, and changes to one of cold annoyance.

'You know, if you kill me you will be giving yourself a death sentence.'

'I'm not going to kill you,' he smugly replies.

'So what are you going to do with me?'

He looks around at the darkness surrounding us and pulls on the chain. I jerk forward, stumbling. He yanks me up by my hair and pulls me harder. 'There are a series of underground tunnels that have only one way in – or out.'

I can't believe what he's saying. 'You're going to lock me in an underground tunnel? In this darkness? All alone?'

'Well, no. You won't be alone.'

The way he says this sends a chill straight through my heart, making my legs numb. But he doesn't elaborate, no matter how hard I try to get more information from him. We walk for what feels like hours and I grow weary, physically and mentally. I'm petrified of the dark. It reminds me too much of when I used to hide from my father.

He stops suddenly, and, lost in my thoughts, I nearly run into him. He shoves me backwards and I fall to the ground. I try to loosen the chains around me, but they're so tight I can't get any leverage.

It's then I notice the look on his face as he peers through an iron grate into the ground. 'What is it? What's wrong?'

His head turns in my direction. 'They're gone!'

I crane my neck to peer into the grate. There's a deep drop into a cavern that appears to be empty. At first I feel relief, but it quickly dawns on me that there are greater ramifications. 'What does this mean?'

Heaving with the effort, he drags the iron grate to the side. 'It means this is your lucky day.' He tugs on my chain, dragging me towards the gaping hole in the ground.

'No, wait! You can't do this. I'll die down there. And you will have caused it.'

'Your death won't be from my hands. I'm sure it won't be long before they return.'

'Before who returns?'

I don't think he's going to answer, and then he says, 'The demons.'

'*What?* You're locking me in a pit that belongs to demons?'

'If you're lucky you'll go insane before the first of them returns home.'

With these words he brings both his arms around me from behind. 'Keep still while I unlock your chains.'

It's a promising thought. As he does so, I prepare myself to escape. But Mr Carter has this all figured out. His arms stay locked around me like a vice, his weapons digging into my arms. When the lock clicks open, he shoves me towards the hole. But I can't let him get away with this. I have to do something to stop him returning to earth and somehow explaining my disappearance with some plausible excuse. The chain unravels from around me as I tumble through the hole into the cavern, but, before it disappears completely, I grab hold of it with both hands and pull on it hard.

Mr Carter, holding on to the other end, is taken by surprise. He screams out violently as he loses his balance and comes tumbling into the cavern behind me. He lands on his side and quickly staggers to his feet. 'What have you done?' He leaps into the air, but falls far short of the distance needed to get back up.

He charges right up to my face, lifting the chain threateningly as if he would like nothing better than to wrap the thing around my throat.

I can't help but look at him smugly. Killing me with his own hands is something he won't do, for this coward is scared to die. Well, let's see how well he faces death now!

Suddenly he peers sideways, his eyes so wide it's a wonder they don't fall out of their sockets.

'What is it? What can you hear?'

'Footsteps.'

'Demon steps?'

He keeps listening, then sighs, a frustrated and annoyed sound. 'Female steps.'

'Female demons?'

He doesn't answer, but a reassuring voice from above does. 'You're going to wish we were demons before we're finished with you, Mr Carter.'

It's Isabel, with Neriah and her two dogs beside her. Both girls have a light in their hand, and from here, with the rays shooting up and around their faces, they look like angels. My angels.

'I've never been so glad to see anyone!' I call out. 'How did you know to come here?'

'Neriah heard your thoughts from the control chambers, dropped everything, and came running. And before you start denying anything, Mr Carter, Neriah also heard enough of your thoughts to convict you at your trial. You were so distracted organising Rochelle's abduction, you forgot to screen them.'

Neriah takes up the explanation. 'Isabel saw the look on your face just before you disappeared.'

'Yeah, it was enough to tell me you were in trouble,' Isabel adds. 'Lord Penbarin helped us follow you. After that it was simple, really. Aysher and Silos picked up your scents and led us here.' Isabel peers down at Mr Carter. 'You have a lot of explaining to do, but you can save it for your trial.'

'The same trial that Lady Arabella will have no need to attend now, except to give evidence of your treachery,'

Neriah adds as she hurls down a long rope.

Mr Carter dives for the rope, but I knock him out of the way. He tries to ram me, but I threaten him with my sizzling hands. 'They're not contained by my side now. And they will kill you. I guarantee it. Now step back, Mr Carter. I'm going to be the first one out of this smelly hole you put us in.'

He peers over his shoulder nervously and I have to wonder if he's heard something else. I can't see anything, but the rest of the tunnel system is in darkness. Mr Carter's head jerks and his eyes go wide again. There *is* something in the tunnel, and by his sudden wild look, it's not something pleasant. 'Hurry!'

But I have to put my gloves on, or I'll just burn the rope and it will be useless to either of us.

'Quickly!' Mr Carter screams. 'Can't you hear it?'

And then I do. Thumping sounds, coming fast.

With one glove on I grab the rope and give it a tug. The girls above start hauling me up. About midway to the top the demon makes an appearance, heaving and grunting. It sees Mr Carter and starts to drool. Mr Carter looks at me, halfway to the surface, and realises he hasn't got a chance. I reach my hand down towards him, but I haven't got my glove on this hand yet, and the other hand is still hanging on to the rope.

The demon scrapes its foot along the ground, a clearly hostile motion. Neriah and Isabel haul me up the rest of the way quickly, yanking me over the edge. I spin around and the girls drop the rope again, urging Mr Carter to grab it. But now the demon is between him and the rope. With one hand, the demon reaches out and grabs the rope, tugging it loose from the girls' hands. They both scream as they try to hold on to it, but

381

the demon is too strong and they're forced to let go.

Mr Carter gives us a long, pitiful look, then turns around and runs.

Chapter Thirty-six

Matt

We meet in a safe room. King Richard is with Lorian. They show me a holographic blue-print of the Citadel. As we examine it, two guards approach. 'Get word to the command centre to maintain our position above Angel Falls, but bring us down low,' Lorian orders. The guards acknowledge the command and leave instantly.

Lorian turns and studies me as I continue to examine the holograph of the Citadel. 'Focus, Matt. I need you to memorise strategic points.' He knows I'm struggling to concentrate. But the girls have been gone so long!

Lord Penbarin arrives and I practically jump at him. 'Do you have news of the girls?'

Lord Penbarin tries to calm me. 'Don't worry, Matt. They can handle more than you realise.'

'But they're alone in the underworld!'

King Richard chuckles. 'There are three of them, along with two dogs. That's hardly alone. And two of them have been there before. Now calm down, Matt. We can't afford for you to go too.'

He's right. I take a deep breath, but can't shake the feeling that I've let Rochelle down. I heard her call ...

'And you came as soon as you could,' Lorian assures

me. 'We still have Marduke to deal with. Not to mention my sister.'

A soldier approaches. King Richard asks, 'What news do you bring us?'

'The ladies, Neriah, Isabel and Rochelle, have returned safely, and –'

'Where are they?' I can't help interrupting.

The girls walk in and I go and embrace them all. Dillon is with them, and his eyes too are full of relief. King Richard also greets them, looking relieved. 'What did you do with our traitor?'

'Mr Carter didn't make it out of the cavern, my lord,' Isabel explains, and I get the sense there's a lot more to this tale. 'The cavern of the demons.'

The soldier behind them clears his throat aggressively.

Lord Penbarin realises he hasn't finished delivering his news. 'What is it, Milon?'

'It's the demons, my lord. The first one is through.'

Lorian's head freezes, his large violet eyes rounding into huge orbs. 'Has my sister gone insane? Surely she doesn't want to rule an earth inundated with evil beyond her own?'

Nobody has the answers he's looking for. But then a thought occurs to me. 'My lord, is it possible that Lathenia has found a way to control these demons?'

'If so, then she is more powerful than I have given her credit for, and we are in a more desperate situation than we ever thought possible!' He glances at the holographic blue-print. 'I will need your help, Matt. Between the two of us, we will have the power to destroy the Citadel. It will be a sad and sorry day for the Guard to have failed so miserably. But there is no other option open to us.' He looks at Lord Penbarin and King Richard. 'Get all our people out, and do it quickly! The Citadel is about to fall, and everything and everyone within it will be destroyed.'

The Tribunal members exchange a concerned look with each other. 'How long do we have, my lord?' King Richard asks.

'Wait, and I will tell you.' Lorian looks directly into my eyes and I feel the tendrils from his brain searching mine, assessing my power. It's not long before he works out how long it is going to take to combine our powers to bring the Citadel down. 'Seven minutes,' he says.

King Richard exclaims, 'Only seven minutes!'

'Seven minutes too long!' Lorian snaps. 'Do you know how many demons my sister can push through the Citadel in that time?'

Probably hundreds, but the Tribunal members have something else worrying them. 'My lord,' Lord Penbarin says, 'Arkarian and Jimmy are in the labyrinths.'

'My son is a Truthseer. Warn him.'

Lord Penbarin rolls his head around his shoulders, looking uncomfortable. 'Yes, my lord, but we haven't had contact from him for some time now. It's possible that our thoughts can't penetrate the labyrinth walls.'

Rochelle steps forward, pushing down her gloves. 'Let me go and get them out.'

Isabel follows. 'I'm going too!'

Lorian glances at the two girls and a fragment of a smile plays around the corner of his mouth. Finally he nods. 'So be it, but take this.' He hands them a crystal. Make sure you are out before this timepiece shows zero.' He looks at Neriah, who has just opened her mouth to volunteer. 'You go back to the control chambers. Ethan is still there. Make sure he gets out and anyone else still lingering. And you two,' Lorian says to Dillon and Lord Penbarin, 'spread the word to all. No matter what, they must leave the Citadel now.'

When everyone leaves, Lorian sits down at the table to prepare himself to create the power needed to bring down this incredible structure, when suddenly he sighs.

'Nephew, it has been a long day and I am weary, but, knowing my sister, the day is far from over.'

Chapter Thirty-seven

Rochelle

The labyrinth is quiet. Strangely so. Where are the creatures from the middle world? Will they be real, or manifestations from our nightmares? If that is so, I wonder what form my nightmares will take. I have so many!

Isabel screams in my ear and jumps practically on top of me. It freaks me out and I scream along with her even though I don't know what the hell she's screaming about.

'There!' She points to the ground near our feet. 'The hairiest, ugliest, largest –'

I push her off me so I can breathe. This is so unlike her I just have to take a look. 'What are you talking about?'

'The spider! Are you blind? It's the size of a soccer ball!'

I look again, but there's still nothing there except a shadow. 'Calm down, Isabel. I think I know how we're going to get through this place in one piece.'

'Yeah?' she practically whimpers. 'Will you hurry up and tell me? This spider looks hungry.'

'OK, for starters, there's no spider. That part's in your imagination.' I swing my hand down and run it through the shadow.

'No way! Don't do that!'

'It's only as real as Ethan's illusions. Nothing more.'

'He can bring reality into his illusions, Rochelle.'

'And he can just as easily dispel the reality with his thoughts. That's what we have to do in here. Got it?'

She climbs down off my leg, closes her eyes and takes a deep breath. When she opens her eyes and looks down, a relieved smile breaks out on her face.

'Is it gone?' I check.

She nods, and now that the fear is also gone, her face starts turning from white to hot pink. A hand comes up to tug back her wayward hair. 'Don't tell anyone, OK? Especially Matt and Ethan. They'll never let me live it down.'

'As if I would give them ammunition to get all macho on us. Your secret is safe with me.'

'Good. We'd better hurry.' She glances at the crystal timepiece Lorian gave her. It has started counting down already. 'We've only got five minutes left.'

We take off at a run and hop on to the first set of moving stairwells that confronts us. On a higher level, we race from room to room. 'Arkarian! Jimmy!' Isabel calls, while I use my thoughts. But no one answers. We take another set of stairs that leads to a series of empty rooms. Doors open and close as we enter and exit. I get the feeling the Citadel is helping us search, as if it too is worried.

We walk out on to a platform. It quickly starts to disappear. Running down the stairs I start to wonder at the sheer size of this place. While most of it remains concealed to the eye, it is obviously a massive structure. As I understand, time isn't measured here, so we could get caught without realising how fast mortal time is passing.

That must be why Lorian gave us the timepiece.

'There has to be a quicker way than searching room to room.'

'Like what?' Isabel asks.

I start to peel off my gloves. 'Cover your face. I'm going to give my hands a try.'

As the sparks fly I lower my hand to the rail beside me. Images form of timber many thousands of years old – river redgum, preserved in the dark waters of a flood that swept away the bank from which it grew. I try to focus on the images of Arkarian and Jimmy. 'Help us locate Arkarian and Jimmy.'

'Anything?' Isabel asks, glancing at the timepiece. 'We've only got three minutes left, and we still have to get out of here ourselves!'

The stairwell changes direction. I take this as a good sign, and for a moment begin to relax. But beside me Isabel suddenly stiffens. 'What's that?'

I glance up at the shadow forming at the top of the stairwell. As we draw closer to the platform, the shadow takes the shape of a man. A cold shiver runs through me. There is a ghastly familiar feel to this person. My eyes drift to the arm hanging by his side. Gripped in his hard-working fingers is a black leather belt.

'Isabel, tell me what you see.'

Isabel shudders. 'Just a shadow, but it has a very evil feel. It's creeping me out.' Her head turns towards me. 'Why? What do you see?'

The stairwell takes us right up to the platform where the man is standing. Softly I reply, 'My father.'

'Is he dead?'

'No, he's in jail.'

'Then he's not real.'

'He looks real.'

'Yeah, so did my spider. Remember?'

We get to the platform and the very real image of my father snaps the belt against a railing, jerking me backwards. Isabel cowers – and she's seeing only the essence of my father's evil, while I'm getting the whole picture!

'Arkarian! Jimmy!' Isabel calls out, trying to pull me along the platform with her.

But my father has other ideas and grabs my other arm. 'Now, sweetheart, is that any way to greet your old man after all these years?'

'Don't touch me!' I scream and try to jerk my arm from his hold. But his grip only tightens.

Isabel calls Arkarian and Jimmy again and tries to pull me down the hallway behind her. 'He isn't really here. He's still in jail. Remember he's not real!'

'But, Isabel, his grip on my arm feels real enough.'

'Isabel is right.'

I look up and see Arkarian, his soft violet eyes round and worried. Jimmy comes running out from behind him. 'What's going on? What are you girls doing here? We've almost finished. Hey, where did that guy come from? I thought we cleared this floor.'

Arkarian shushes him with one look. 'Rochelle, remember you brought him here through your thoughts. You have the power to dispel him.'

Isabel glances at the timepiece. 'Hurry! Two minutes and this place is going to explode.'

'*What?*' Jimmy calls out.

Whack! The belt comes down over my shoulder. I scream out and crouch halfway to the ground.

'You can stop him once and for all,' Arkarian assures me, and the meaning of his words finally sinks in. Here is my opportunity to do what I should have done long ago, what my mother never could.

'One minute!' Isabel hisses beside me.

The shadow of my father's arm lifts, and I watch as the belt starts its downward thrust. But this time, instead of cowering, I reach up and grab the belt, tug it towards me, then grab my father's arm and grip him tightly. He screams as my hand burns through his skin. I feel him go slack, then break up and disappear before my eyes.

'Ten seconds!' Isabel calls out.

Jimmy and Arkarian grab both mine and Isabel's arms and pull. Together we leap on to a moving platform. Isabel looks at the timepiece. 'Now!'

As Isabel screams this one word, the entire room and everything in it begins to glow first white, then yellow, then flashes brilliant red. Arkarian, Jimmy and Isabel suddenly look as if they're nothing more than skeletons.

'Oh no!' Jimmy moans.

'Quickly!' Arkarian pulls us all in close to him.

But I'm afraid it's too late. Beneath us the stairwell disappears, and all four of us start to drop.

Chapter Thirty-eight

Matt

Brick by brick, glass, marble and crystal, the Citadel falls. The survivors have gone to my father. He will welcome them with open arms. Their job is done here. They have earned their rest. I glance around the ridge as bits of the Citadel drift down. Another explosion shimmers in the atmosphere as more pieces of the Citadel shower over the mountain.

I look around, searching faces. Some Tribunal members are missing, but we know that King Richard has gone to Athens to release Lady Arabella. How wrong I was to accuse her! Lorian says he too treated her unjustly. 'Something I intend on addressing the very next time we meet,' he earlier explained.

As for the other Tribunal members, Lady Devine and many of her soldiers have also gone to Athens to be treated in the healing rooms there. Around me, Queen Brystianne, Lord Samartyne and Lord Penbarin take stock of their remaining soldiers. Shaun and Dillon join them. Not counting Mr Carter, six of us are still unaccounted for. Where are Ethan and Neriah? The last word was that they had fled the control room with the other Tribunal members and soldiers. Apparently no one has seen them since.

Another explosion rents the air as the final part of the Citadel shatters. It's the labyrinth, the part of the Citadel that Lorian and I made sure would blow up last. But there's still no sign of my sister, or Rochelle, Arkarian or Jimmy, who were all in there at the time. There is nothing we can do except wait, and hope they managed to escape. But as every second passes, and the dust begins to settle as the last bricks fall from the sky, agitation starts hitting us all.

Shaun is the first to crack. 'There must be something we can do! Some way to locate them!'

I search for signs of their thoughts, propelling my mind into the remains both on the ground and in the atmosphere. Nothing.

Dillon frowns and runs towards a strange object dropping from the sky. 'What's this?' He catches the object and brings it back to us.

It's a black leather belt. He holds it up for us to identify.

Shaun shakes his head. 'I don't recognise it. I don't think it's Jimmy's or Arkarian's either.'

I take it in my hand and a powerful surge of Rochelle's thoughts sweeps into my brain, letting me know where they are. I start to run in a southerly direction.

'Where are you going?' Dillon calls out, hurrying to catch up.

'They're coming. And they're going to hit the ground hard.'

All four of them land in a very close circle. As they start to get up Rochelle pulls her hands away, quickly putting her gloves on.

'Are you all right?' I ask her.

She nods. 'I think so.'

Isabel is next. She crawls over to Arkarian, checking him for injuries. He assures her he's fine and she moves on to Jimmy. 'Anything broken?'

'My ankle.'

'Be still.' She lays her hand on his leg and goes to work healing him straightaway.

Lorian speaks to me through his thoughts. He lets me know he is on top of the ridge and that we should hurry and get there.

'Is everyone else all right?' Isabel checks with me.

'Unfortunately we're not all here yet,' Shaun says with a tremor in his voice.

Rochelle has questions, but picks up that I'm still communicating with Lorian. His thoughts are troubling, bringing a deep frown to my forehead and a worried stare I can't conceal. She touches my arm. 'What's going on?'

'Lathenia is waiting with her army on the ridge.'

'What?' Dillon calls out. 'But we just destroyed her army. What more has she got in store?'

With that sombre thought we make our way to the top of the ridge, where Lorian's outline stands like a yearning shadow in the afternoon sun. When we approach, he turns to face us. His eyes reflect burning rage. When he sees Arkarian, the look softens momentarily, but quickly hardens again. Inside, my heart starts beating a slow thudding rhythm. What awaits us up here? And then I understand Lorian's look. Ethan and Neriah have been captured! Lathenia must have got to them in the midst of all that turmoil when the Citadel was falling. Now they're her prisoners, locked inside golden cages sizzling with green flashes of electric currents and suspended high above the ground.

But Ethan and Neriah are not the only weapons Lathenia has brought to this final battle. Behind the cages, in staggered rows that stretch back as far as the eye can see, stands an army of demons. Restless demons, that grunt and snort and pound the earth with their feet. There are many hundreds of them, maybe even a thousand. There is one in particular at the front that catches my eye. This one is their leader. He will be the one to watch, the one I will have to deal with.

Beside me I hear the others gasp and moan. Lord Penbarin's head shakes in disbelief. Queen Brystianne clutches the cloth at her throat. Both Tribunal members are in shock.

Shaun can't take his eyes off his son. 'How did this happen?'

Rochelle tries to comfort him. 'We will get them back.'

Inside me a fire is building. I go to pass Lorian, but he stops me with an open palm against my chest. 'Stay calm. You are no good to either of them if you lose control. Remember now more than ever the skills your father taught you.'

'I will kill the Goddess, along with every one of her army!'

'I will kill her first,' he mouths softly. 'For she has cost me much this day. The taking of these two hostages will be her undoing. She has gone too far.'

Isabel comes up beside me, her eyes skimming from Ethan to Neriah and back again repeatedly. 'They've been beaten. Ethan has broken ribs and can hardly breathe. Neriah is hurt too, but her injuries are repairing themselves.'

I look across to Neriah and our eyes lock. I feel her pain go through me as she propels her thoughts. *The cages are electrified. Nothing can pass through them. It's Lathenia's plan to take us with her. You have to save Ethan first. You have known him all your life. His mother cannot lose another child, and … I will be with you no matter what world I am forced to live in.*

No! You listen to me –

Lorian turns and says, 'Watch your thoughts. My sister hears them. Look at her smile.'

He's right. Lathenia's smile is devious and even … exultant. She wants me to make a mistake, to let my emotions rule. And to her right, Marduke stands watching. Occasionally his eye travels to where his daughter hangs, and I have to ask myself: how can any father do this to his daughter? Then he snorts, and spittle flies out from a pig-like snout, and I have my answer.

My eyes shift to the demon beside him. In one hand he holds a chain, the other an axe. He stares at me, and while holding my gaze, he lifts both weapons into the air and grunts. His message is clear. I search deeply for a steadying breath.

Shaun touches my arm from behind, making me jump. 'Why doesn't my son use his wings and escape the cage?'

'Maybe he can't,' Dillon says. 'He looks in a bad way.'

Rochelle adds, 'He won't leave Neriah to die by herself.'

Her words are true. There were times when I thought Ethan's character unworthy. How wrong I was.

Isabel suddenly sighs. 'I've been able to heal them, so at least for the moment they are breathing easier. And look, Ethan is closing his eyes. Matt, I think he's up to something.'

I search his thoughts. They're busy. Very busy. I withdraw so as not to interfere with whatever he has planned. Without taking my eyes off Ethan, I turn slightly to those around me. 'Prepare your weapons. Wait for the signal. Jimmy, you aim for the back lines. Isabel, take yourself into the middle. Arkarian, you go where you're needed.'

Isabel nudges me. 'Wherever you put Rochelle, put me with her.'

'Why?' Rochelle hears and snaps.

I give my head the slightest shake, enough to convey to Isabel that I will have Rochelle covered and to let the matter drop.

'I just thought we worked well together,' she finishes lamely, not wanting to alarm Rochelle. She's been through enough in the past few hours – she doesn't need more to worry about.

Quickly I finish giving out my instructions. 'Shaun, you and Dillon destroy the front rows.'

'Remember,' Lorian reminds me, 'Lathenia is mine.'

And while I would love to deal with that immortal myself, there is so much passion in my uncle's voice, I don't dare argue.

'What about me?' Rochelle asks.

'You released me once from Marduke's bonds, now I want you to do the same for Ethan and Neriah. And when you have freed them, come to the front lines and work beside me.'

'Can I have my knife back?'

'Your knife won't cut through those electrified cages.'

'I want the knife to fight the demons.'

I stare at her for a moment. Are we really having this conversation again? 'Your knife will be useless against those creatures. You have to use your hands.'

She glances at the beasts and shivers. 'But that means

I'll have to get close. Matt, you don't know how brutal they are. Mr Carter was petrified of them.'

'I'll be fighting by your side. OK?'

Lorian lets me know something is happening. Right before our eyes Ethan and Neriah begin to fade. In seconds the two of them disappear.

'What's happening?' Lathenia calls out. She jabs a sword through Ethan's mesh repeatedly. Sparks fly and electricity sizzles. The whole cage vibrates with the impact. Lathenia does it again and again, this time lunging her sword into Neriah's cage. Again, nothing. 'Marduke! Where have they gone? Did you do something to release them?'

He argues his innocence and their momentary confusion is my cue. We have to act fast to take the advantage. Who knows how long Ethan's incredible illusion will last? I raise my hand, then let it drop. 'Now!'

Jimmy sends his grenades soaring into the back rows, creating chaos among them. Marduke orders the demons to attack. They grunt and growl and strike the earth with their feet. Then, armed with axes, swords and chains, they come charging at us.

I hope I haven't underestimated these beasts. They are completely unlike the wren, or any of the other creatures we've dealt with so far. Their odour alone is enough to knock us out.

Shaun battles two demons at the same time. King Richard suddenly appears along with Lady Arabella. I will have to apologise, but now is not the time. Lady Arabella looks around, searching for someone, and I point down the ridge. 'He is that way, my lady, covering the northern flank.' She nods and takes off, while King Richard withdraws his sword and helps Shaun out.

I end up face-to-face with the demon who proclaims himself leader. Using his chain with incredible skill, he strikes, flinging my axe into his own hand. I will the thought of power to my fingers and, in the same split second, project this power towards him. Blue light flickers across the small space between us. It knocks him backwards. On the ground he grunts, and while there is now a wide gaping hole in his stomach, he still manages to get up. Surprising me, he charges again, head-butting my chest and knocking me off guard for a moment. He pulls back and comes at me again, wielding the chain and my axe with incredible force. I grab his arm and we fight for domination of the axe. With his other hand, he wields the chain across my back. The pain of it slices through me, over and over. Now it is my turn to grunt. I attempt to grab his other arm, but he is clever and avoids my grasp. With his sheer weight alone, he shoves me on to my back. Sensing success, he puts his knee into my throat, choking off my air supply. I would use my power to shove him off me, but I'm having trouble just finding air to breathe. And now he is lifting my axe into the air, aiming it straight at my skull. Still gasping for air, I watch as it starts to lower.

Suddenly the demon screams and arches his back. And then his weight is being lifted off me as he is tossed, a whip curled around his middle. In his place Arkarian, with his shock of vivid blue hair, swims into focus. He lowers his hand to me and I grip it.

'How did that beast get the better of you?'

I shrug, retrieving my axe from the dead demon's clutches. 'He winded me.'

Arkarian finds my comment amusing. 'That easy, huh? Anyway, you were wasting your time with that demon;

you're needed elsewhere. Lathenia is in a rage and Lorian has his hands full dealing with her.'

'What about Ethan and Neriah?'

He points, and my eyes follow. Rochelle has brought Neriah's cage down, and, using her hands, is in the process of destroying the mesh. Neriah is visible again and almost free, but Rochelle's actions have drawn the attention of Marduke. She needs more time.

I close my eyes and find an inner focus. Overhead, black clouds gather at my command, bringing a fierce wind with them. Marduke looks into the wind and a bolt of lightning strikes him. But the lightning doesn't come from the sky. It comes from his own daughter's hand. He lets out a wailing moan, and as Neriah stands before him, he snorts and disappears.

I take a look around. The battlefield is a mass of dead demons. The weapons are effective, and I'm glad to see Neriah was able to conceal hers even while captured by Lathenia. I hope Ethan was able to do the same, but somehow I doubt it. His weapon would be harder to hide.

Several more demons attack, and for the next few minutes, Arkarian and I are busy fending them off. Suddenly Neriah is beside me and using her weapon as a new wave of demons attack. She smiles and my spirits soar.

A scream unlike any other I have heard today suddenly pierces the air. It has everyone and every creature stop and look to the immortals. They have reduced themselves to physical combat, each wielding a sword and a knife.

'So this is what it has come down to, sister. I should have finished you off when I had the opportunity to do so in the womb.'

Eyes blazing, Lathenia screeches and lunges with her sword. 'Aha! At last you admit to cheating me of my birthright.'

'No,' Lorian replies, lunging back. 'I didn't cheat you, for you were never meant to be born first.'

'What are you saying?'

'Dartemis was.'

'You lie! He was the youngest.'

'He was always the clever one. He let us squabble between ourselves.'

'Are you saying he didn't covet the throne, even though it was rightfully his?'

'He is a god of peace. He is content to let it come to him.'

'You say that as if he lives today.'

'One thing is for sure, sister, you will never know.' And with these words, Lorian disarms Lathenia. Her sword flies into the air, and as her eyes momentarily follow it, he thrusts his own sword deeply into her chest.

For a second she freezes, then her bulging eyes stare down at the sword lodged between her ribs. 'You would kill me?'

'I must. Death is the only solution.'

With a lingering look of disbelief, Lathenia's eyes close. Lorian sighs and looks away. It is a mistake. Lathenia's eyes fling open and she half rises. In her hand she still has the dagger. Using the last of her immortal strength, she sends it flying with unparalleled force in Lorian's direction.

Lorian turns at the sound. It is another mistake.

'Father!' Arkarian calls out.

The dagger hits, lodging deeply in Lorian's throat. His

hands close around it, but the look in his eyes reveals that he is already aware of his fate. He knows, that like his sister, he is about to die.

He drops to the ground. Lady Arabella, Arkarian and Isabel run over, but it is already too late. Brother and sister are dead.

Chapter Thirty-nine

Rochelle

The immortals are dead! I can't believe it! They actually killed each other! Everyone is stunned and walking around in a daze. Isabel is comforting Arkarian. Lady Arabella is hysterical and Lord Penbarin is trying to keep her calm. Then I hear Matt's voice.

'We'll build them a Temple. We'll use the bricks from the Citadel so it will remain concealed from human eyes, and just like the Citadel it will float high in the atmosphere. Lord Penbarin, Queen Brystianne, can you prepare their bodies for entombment?'

'Yes, my lord,' Lord Penbarin replies.

Yes, my lord! I repeat in my thoughts.

Queen Brystianne comes over, wiping tears from her eyes. 'We'll have to shift them to Athens first. It is fortunate we saved some of the equipment.'

'Take them now, and when this is done, we'll hold a service in their honour. With Lathenia gone, my father Dartemis will be free to return to this world if he chooses. For the first time in his long life he will be liberated from his heavenly prison. I will not suppose to know his mind.' He glances at Arkarian. 'If Dartemis decides to remain in his realm, Arkarian, will you speak at this service?'

Arkarian nods. Matt grips his shoulder, then addresses the rest of the crowd in a softer tone. 'Everyone who is able, let's clear the hill and make preparations for the Temple. And when the Temple is complete, and the immortals are laid to rest, we will form a battalion and hunt down the soulless creatures that have inundated the earth. We will deal with the diseases they bring and repair the rips between the worlds.' His hand lifts to indicate the air that we're breathing. 'And when all of nature is in balance again, this dark wind will blow itself out, and the earth will be at peace.'

Matt is taking control. Looking around I see that it's exactly what everyone needs. And of course the job would fall to him. He is, after all, son of an immortal, and an immortal himself.

While Lord Penbarin and Queen Brystianne prepare to take the bodies of Lorian and Lathenia to Athens, the others start clearing the land of debris from the fall of the Citadel, stockpiling any usable materials. Shaun and Jimmy take on the onerous task of clearing away the remains of the demons that have, hopefully, all been destroyed.

In the chaos, I forget to put my gloves back on. While helping collect debris, I inadvertently put my hand on Dillon's. He jerks back and yells, 'Hey, watch it! What are you doing? For crying out loud, Roh, where are your gloves?'

People from all around turn and look at me. I glance at Dillon's hand, ready to apologise, but there's no mark there, and I wonder if his reaction is because he fears what my hands are capable of more than any actual injury.

'You keep those hands away from me, do you hear?'

After all that I've been through today, Dillon's over-reaction explodes my temper.

I turn and look at the crowd. Are Dillon's thoughts a mirror of theirs? Do they still doubt me, even after uncovering the real traitor and fighting with them side-by-side? Are they afraid that I will turn on them and use my hands as weapons?

'Is this what you all think?' They glance around at each other and I am swamped with their thoughts of embarrassment. *Embarrassment!* A lump forms in my throat. I swallow hard to dispel it. Can't even one of them stand up for me against Dillon's insensitive words? 'Do you really think, given the opportunity, that I would purposefully hurt you? Is that why no one dares to come near me? Or do you just think of me as a freak?'

I yank my gloves out of my pocket and make a display of putting them on. 'There! I will never take them off again. I promise! Do you feel safer now?'

Ethan takes a step towards me; his eyes and thoughts overflow with compassion. I hold up my hand to stop him getting closer. 'Don't come near me. I don't want your pity, Ethan. I never wanted that.'

Suddenly I need to be alone. I need to be anywhere but here with these people. With these … *strangers*, because that's what they feel like right now.

I turn and run off into the nearby forest. Behind me I hear them argue about who is going to come after me. 'Forget it, Isabel!' Ethan calls out. I tune out quickly. I don't want to hear any more. I just want to be alone.

I'm a good runner and I run fast. Branches and vines get in my way, but I don't care. They scratch my arm and my face, but I just keep running. One twig lodges itself in my sleeve. I tug on it hard until it rips a hole in my shirt.

Finally I get to the edge of the ridge and stop. At my feet a sheer cliff descends for a hundred metres into the valley of Angel Falls. In the far distance I can even see the ocean. The sight is breathtaking. I inhale a few deep breaths of the crisp mountain air and try to calm down.

The swishing of leaves and branches, and the thumping of footfalls behind me, let me know Ethan is near. He comes to a quick stop when he gets to the cliff edge, then turns and sees me. I don't need to read his thoughts to know that he is relieved. His face forms a flickering smile. He stands and stares at me while he gathers his breath. Suddenly my nerves are jumping. What is he doing here? Why did he insist on following me? Then he comes over and doesn't stop until he is standing right in my space, so close that I feel his breath warm against my forehead. He takes my hands and brings them up between us. Then, slowly, he peels back one of my gloves.

Instinctively I jerk my hand away. 'What are you doing?'

He grips it again, holding it tighter this time. Without answering he peels the glove right off. Sparks fly up that he must feel against his face, but he doesn't flinch. He takes the glove and throws it over the cliff face.

'Ethan!'

But now he's doing the same to my other glove. I try to grab it off him before he throws it, but his reach is longer. Over the cliff it sails.

'Ethan, why? I can't go back without them. And what about school?'

He takes my flickering hands in his and turns them over. 'These are your hands. They're a part of you, so this is who you are. I know you wouldn't purposefully hurt anyone, and nobody who knows you would think so either. From this moment on – at least until school starts again – you don't wear the gloves. The more you don't wear them, the better you'll get at controlling the power in your hands.'

'But Dillon –'

'Dillon mouths off sometimes. He can be insensitive and thoughtless. That's just who he is. I'm not sticking up for him, but he reacted off the top of his head back there because you intimidate him. You intimidate most of us, you know.'

I scoff at this.

'You're talented and beautiful, and, well …' he takes a deep breath, 'with these hands you're very powerful. You can see into our souls.'

As I digest this, Ethan lifts my hands to either side of his face. The action is so touching, tears well at the backs of my eyes. I try to blink them away, but stubbornly they persist. I have to ask, 'Why are you doing this?'

'Because I care about you,' he says, then frowns. 'No.'

'No? You don't care?'

'What I meant to say was, I'm doing this because I love you.'

I can't believe what I'm hearing. 'What did you say?'

He smiles at me and I can't drag my eyes from his. He says, 'I have loved you since that first moment I saw you. I wanted you then, and when I thought you didn't want me, I turned my love into hate. It was the biggest mistake I ever made.'

'Ethan …'

Before I say another word his mouth comes down over mine and he kisses me. For a long moment there is nothing else in my world. And everything is as it should be. We kiss again and hold each other. For the first time in my life I am content.

A thought penetrates my head. It has a familiar feel. I turn towards the wooded area to the north, searching for the source.

Ethan picks up that something is wrong. 'What is it?'

'I heard something. Did anyone follow you?'

His arms come around me tighter. 'Not that I know of. I made it clear I wanted to be alone with you. Maybe we should go back now.'

He's right and I nod. Then I hear the thought again and I go still trying to place it. But it doesn't take long to realise who these thoughts belong to. I was, after all, his spy for long enough. It's Marduke, and he's in the nearby trees. Somewhere very close.

I squint, looking for Marduke's position, but he's concealed himself well. His thoughts hit me again and now I understand what he's doing here. He has hung on to his bitterness for so long that his hatred has manifested into the form of one person, the one person who has thwarted every attempt he's ever made to exact revenge. Ethan. It was Ethan who recalled his image in his dreams. It was Ethan who fought and killed him, resulting in his return from the middle world as a beast. It was Ethan's fault that he lost Lathenia to another man because he was no longer human. And it is Ethan that Marduke now intends on killing, once and for all.

My heart starts thundering in my chest. Marduke has Ethan's bow and arrow set! I hear his thoughts as he lines one up in his aim. I spin around, searching – which direction is it coming from?

'Rochelle, what is it?'

Swish! Oh no! It's heading straight for Ethan! Determined to stop this poisonous arrow from reaching its mark, I leap in front of it. It hits. I feel the arrow pass through my ribs and straight into my heart. The sky blurs and I stumble.

Ethan feels me fall and catches me before I hit the ground. 'Rochelle!'

He sees the arrow and his eyes grow huge in horror. *'Rochelle!'*

I reach up and touch his face. 'Safe. You're safe.'

His head shakes. Eyes glisten. Tears start to fall. I try to wipe them away but my arms have no strength and fall to the side. I'm dying, but it doesn't matter. The Guard will honour my sacrifice. And more importantly, Ethan's love is locked in my heart. One day we will be together again.

He screams, *'Nooooo!'*

Chapter Forty

Matt

I will never forget the look on Ethan's face as he runs out of the forest with Rochelle's body lying limp in his arms, a golden arrow protruding from her chest. And I will never forget the sound of his impassioned plea as he lays her at Isabel's feet.

'Hurry, Isabel! Heal her, quickly!'

Isabel and Arkarian get down on their knees. Isabel lays her hands on Rochelle's face, her neck, her chest. She exchanges a pained look with Arkarian, then lifts her tear-filled eyes to Ethan. 'There's nothing I can do.'

'Of course you can. For God's sake, Isabel, you heal everybody! Didn't you heal me when I had massive internal injuries?'

Arkarian gets up and reaches an arm out towards Ethan's shoulder. 'But, Ethan, you were still breathing. Rochelle is already dead.'

Ethan jerks his shoulder away from Arkarian's soothing touch. 'No! She was ... we were ...' Suddenly his eyes light up. 'We can get her back, Arkarian. You and I. We can do it. We did it for Isabel. Remember? We went to the middle world and rescued her soul.'

Isabel frowns and her thoughts let me know she's

wondering what Ethan is talking about. But now is not the time to ask, and she remains quiet.

Arkarian looks Ethan in the eyes, his head tilting gently to one side. 'Ethan, Rochelle died while in the present. Her soul isn't wandering the middle world. Rochelle's body is right here before us. She's not breathing. Her soul is on its way right now to her final destiny. There's nothing we can do.'

Gulping deep breaths, Ethan falls to the ground. In a moment of madness he grabs hold of the arrow with two hands and rips it screaming out of her chest. Everyone gasps and looks away.

'The poison arrow is gone!' he bellows, a look of insanity in his eyes. 'Now she can be healed!'

Shaun gets down beside him, laying a hand on Ethan's arm. 'Easy, son.'

But Ethan will have none of his father's soothing. He jerks roughly away. 'Don't touch me! Don't come near me unless you can bring her back!'

That's when the thought occurs to him. I hear it clearly reverberate into my head. He looks up at me, the request shimmering in the dark whirlpools his eyes have become. 'Can you do it?'

My head shakes a negative. 'No, I can't.'

He gets up. 'But you're immortal! You have powers above the rest of us.' He turns to Arkarian. 'Can he do it, Arkarian?' Before Arkarian answers he turns to the remaining Tribunal members. Sir Syford lifts his hands in an uncertain gesture and Ethan screams out, 'Someone tell me!'

Spinning around he grabs my shoulders. 'Matt, you have to try!'

'Ethan, it's impossible.'

411

'*Why?* What are immortals if they can't bring back the dead?'

'Our powers lie in the living. We can extend life, as Lorian did for Arkarian and Isabel. On rare occasions we can even give immortality, as my father did for Neriah, but death ... death is our destiny. It can't be changed.'

Isabel, with red eyes and tears streaming down her face, grips Ethan from behind. 'I failed you. I'm so sorry!'

Ethan pulls her around and holds her, burying his head in her shoulder. He stays like that for a long moment, drawing strength, then lifts his head and looks into her eyes. 'It's not your fault.' He looks at all of us. 'It's not anyone's fault.' Then his eyes stop at Neriah. 'Except ...'

Pulling away from Isabel, Ethan inhales deeply. His whole body trembles as he releases a shuddering breath. 'There's something I have to do.'

Neriah's grip on my arm tightens. Like everyone else here today, she knows exactly what Ethan is talking about.

Arkarian reminds him gently, 'But, Ethan, Marduke is going to die soon anyway.' He looks to the west, where the sun is already beginning to set. 'The curse has been activated.'

Ethan shakes his head. 'I don't care about the curse! I have to do this!' In one sweeping movement he collects the golden arrow and takes off.

Arkarian's eyes fly to mine, and I nod. This is not something we will let Ethan do alone. We chase after him, catching up quickly.

He hears us and turns. 'Don't even try to stop me.'

Silently we fall in on either side of him. Words are pointless right now. It will not be long anyway before we find Marduke; signs of his passage are everywhere. He is running like a wounded bull, thrashing into trees and shrubs in his path. I take a broken branch in my hand. 'He's already dying.'

Ethan glances at the distant sun, lowering quickly behind the ice-covered western ranges. 'Then we'd better hurry.'

We find him sitting on a boulder, leaning forward and gasping for breath. Ethan's bow is at his feet. He senses us and looks up. The light has gone from his eye and he looks shrunken.

'You have my daughter. She belongs to the light now. What have you done with my brother?'

'He is deep in the underworld, where he belongs,' Ethan says through gritted teeth.

'Will he escape?'

'No.'

'And the Goddess?'

'Killed by her brother.'

'What of Keziah?'

'He has disappeared, but without his mistress to sustain his long life, he will wither away and die.'

'Then I have nothing left. Do what you must. Revenge is something I respect.'

For a long moment Ethan simply stares. Before him is the monster of his nightmares: his sister's murderer, the beast who robbed him of his greatest love. How easy, how fulfilling would it be to take Marduke's life?

But the arrow in Ethan's hand slips from his fingers to the ground. 'No. Even revenge is too great an honour for you.'

As night falls and brings an end to this long day of darkness, Marduke inhales his last staggered breath and his body turns to stone.

Acknowledgements One

The *Guardians of Time* series was created with the help of many people. The following stand out for special recognition.

The first are my children. Amanda for being my sounding board and for those 'just perfect' ideas. Danielle for her wonderful critiques when the manuscripts were almost ready. And my son Chris for his male, much needed 17-year-old perspective, and for his technical advice with the weapons.

I also want to acknowledge my husband John for his unfailing support and encouragement and those endless calming cups of tea.

I especially want to thank my agent Geoffrey Radford for his dedication, persistence and determination to get things done.

And finally I want to thank all the staff at Bloomsbury Publishing who have worked on this series. Most importantly I want to thank my editor Ele Fountain for her meticulous editing of all three books, for her uncanny ability to know exactly what's going to work, and for her enthusiasm for the unfolding story.

Marianne Curley

Acknowledgements Two

In 2004, I battled a serious illness called myelofibrosis. This was potentially a fatal condition that caused my bone marrow to malfunction and turn into scar tissue. Unfortunately, in my case, I had the kind of myelofibrosis that was quite aggressive. The only cure was a stem cell bone marrow transplant, which included many blood transfusions of pac cells, plasma and platelets. The transplant was performed at the Westmead Hospital in Sydney, Australia, in May, 2004, and has been a complete success.

One of the reasons I am writing this Acknowledgement is to ask you to think about joining the International Bone Marrow Registry and to also think about becoming a regular blood donor. Without the generous donations of blood products that I received during my illness, I would not be here today to continue writing and being with the people I love. Since my illness, I have realized how important and worthy it is to be on the bone marrow registry and to be a regular blood donor. You would have the potential to save many people's lives, and one day the saved life might even be your own.

I would like to take this opportunity to thank the wonderful and dedicated bone marrow transplant team of doctors and staff at the Westmead Hospital. I would particularly like to mention and thank from the bottom of my heart Professor Ian Kerridge, a brilliant and compassionate doctor who, today, continues to monitor my health post-transplant.

With best wishes,
Marianne Curley

MARIANNE CURLEY

was born in Australia and lived on a property hugging the Hawkesbury River until a flood washed away the family home when she was five. Her family then moved to a farm on the outskirts of Sydney, and with no close neighbours Marianne soon discovered her love of books.

Today she lives on a mountain surrounded by rainforests, and though her children are all grown and have left home, they still inspire her writing and are the first to offer their invaluable critiques. Marianne is the author of The Guardians of Time trilogy and *Old Magic*, all of which have been translated into many languages.

www.mariannecurley.com